SANDWORMS OF
DUNE

THE DUNE SERIES

BY FRANK HERBERT

Dune
Dune Messiah
Children of Dune
God Emperor of Dune
Heretics of Dune
Chapterhouse: Dune

BY FRANK HERBERT, BRIAN HERBERT, AND KEVIN J. ANDERSON

The Road to Dune (includes the original short novel *Spice Planet*)

BY BRIAN HERBERT AND KEVIN J. ANDERSON

Dune: House Atreides
Dune: House Harkonnen
Dune: House Corrino

Dune: The Butlerian Jihad
Dune: The Machine Crusade
Dune: The Battle of Corrin

Hunters of Dune
Sandworms of Dune
Paul of Dune (forthcoming)

BY BRIAN HERBERT

Dreamer of Dune
(biography of Frank Herbert)

SANDWORMS OF DUNE

Brian Herbert

and

Kevin J. Anderson

Based on an outline by Frank Herbert

TOR®

A TOM DOHERTY ASSOCIATES BOOK

NEW YORK

SANDWORMS OF DUNE

Copyright © 2007 by Herbert Properties LLC

A Tor Book
Published by Tom Doherty Associates, LLC
175 Fifth Avenue
New York, NY 10010

www.tor.com

www.dunenovels.com

Tor® is a registered trademark of Tom Doherty Associates, LLC.

Library of Congress Cataloging-in-Publication Data
Herbert, Brian.
    Sandworms of Dune / Brian Herbert and Kevin J. Anderson.—1st ed.
        p.   cm.
    "A Tom Doherty Associates Book."
    ISBN-13: 978-0-7653-1293-8
    ISBN-10: 0-7653-1293-X
    1. Dune (Imaginary place)—Fiction.   2. Life on other planets—Fiction.   3. Robots—Fiction.   I. Anderson, Kevin J., 1962–   II. Title.
    PS3558.E617S26   2007
    813'.54—dc22

                                                                            2006102742

First Edition: August 2007

Printed in the United States of America

0 9 8 7 6 5 4 3 2 1

We can never overstate the appreciation we owe to the genius who created this incredible series. Once again, this book is for Frank Herbert, a man of wondrous and important ideas, who has been our mentor as we continue to write new stories in his fantastic Dune universe. Sandworms of Dune is the chronological grand finale that he envisioned, and we are pleased to finally bring it to his millions of loyal fans.

ACKNOWLEDGMENTS

As with all of our previous Dune novels, we have depended on the efforts of a great many people to make the manuscript as good as possible. We would like to thank Pat LoBrutto, Tom Doherty, and Paul Stevens at Tor Books; Carolyn Caughey at Hodder & Stoughton; Catherine Sidor, Louis Moesta, and Diane Jones at WordFire, Inc; Penny Merritt, Kim Herbert, and Byron Merritt at Herbert Properties LLC; and Mike Anderson at the dunenovels.com Web site, as well as Dr. Attila Torkos, who worked on fact-checking and consistency.

In addition, we have had many supporters of the new Dune novels, including John Silbersack, Robert Gottlieb, and Claire Roberts at Trident Media Group; Richard Rubinstein, Mike Messina, John Harrison, and Emily Austin-Bruns at New Amsterdam Entertainment; Ron Merritt, David Merritt, Julie Herbert, Robert Merritt, Margaux Herbert, and Theresa Shackelford at Herbert Properties LLC.

And as always, these books would not exist without the unending help and support from our wives, Janet Herbert and Rebecca Moesta Anderson.

Soon after the Honored Matres careened into the Old Empire, the Bene Gesserit Sisterhood learned to hate and fear them. The intruders used their terrible Obliterator weapons to destroy Bene Gesserit and Tleilaxu planets, Richese with its vast industries and weapon shops, even Rakis itself.

But in order to survive the even greater Enemy that pursued them, the Honored Matres desperately needed knowledge that only the Sisterhood possessed. To obtain it, they struck like angry vipers, lashing out with extreme violence.

After the Battle of Junction, the two opposing groups were forcibly united into a New Sisterhood, but the factions continued to wrestle for control and dominance. Such a waste of time, talent, and blood! The real threat came from outside, but we continued to fight the wrong enemy.

—MOTHER COMMANDER MURBELLA,
address to the New Sisterhood

Two people drift in a lifeboat on an uncharted sea. One says, "There! I see an island. Our best chance is to go ashore, build a shelter, and await rescue." The other says, "No, we must go farther out to sea and hope to find the shipping lanes. That is our best chance." Unable to agree, the two fight, the lifeboat capsizes, and they drown.

This is the nature of humanity. Even if only two people are left in the entire universe, they will come to represent opposing factions.
—*The Bene Gesserit Acolytes' Handbook*

In re-creating particular gholas, we reweave the fabric of history. Once more, Paul Muad'Dib walks among us, with his beloved Chani, his mother the Lady Jessica, and his son Leto II, the God Emperor of Dune. The presence of Suk doctor Wellington Yueh, whose treachery brought a great house to its knees, is at once disturbing and comforting. Also with us are the warrior-Mentat

Thufir Hawat, the Fremen Naib Stilgar, and the great planetologist Liet-Kynes. Consider the possibilities!

Such genius constitutes a formidable army. We will need that brilliance, because we face an opponent more terrible than we ever imagined.

—DUNCAN IDAHO,
Memories of More Than a Mentat

I have waited and planned and built my strength for fifteen thousand years. I have evolved. It is time.

—OMNIUS

SANDWORMS OF
DUNE

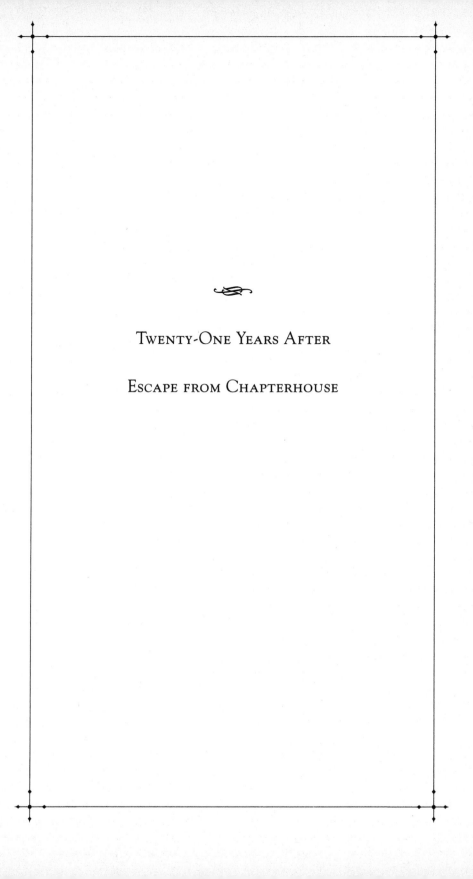

Twenty-One Years After

Escape from Chapterhouse

So many people I knew in the past are not yet reborn. I still miss them, even though I do not remember them. The axlotl tanks will soon remedy that.

—LADY JESSICA,
the ghola

A board the wandering no-ship *Ithaca,* Jessica witnessed the birth of her daughter, but only as an observer. Just fourteen years old, she and many others crowded the medical center, while two Bene Gesserit Suk doctors in the adjacent creche prepared to extract the tiny girl child from an axlotl tank.

"Alia," one of the female doctors murmured.

This was not truly Jessica's daughter, but a ghola grown from preserved cells. None of the young gholas on the no-ship were "themselves" yet. They had regained none of their memories, none of their pasts.

Something tried to surface at the back of her mind, and though she worried at it like a loose tooth, Jessica could not remember the first time Alia had been born. In the archives, she had read and reread the legendary accounts generated by Muad'Dib's biographers. But she couldn't *remember.*

All she had were images from her studies: *A dry and dusty sietch on Arrakis, surrounded by Fremen. Jessica and her son Paul had been on the run, taken in by the desert tribe. Duke Leto was dead, murdered by Harkonnens.*

Pregnant, Jessica had drunk the Water of Life, forever changing the fetus inside her. From the moment of her birth, the original Alia had been different from all other babies, filled with ancient wisdom and madness, able to tap into Other Memory without having gone through the Spice Agony. Abomination!

That had been another Alia. Another time and another way.

Now Jessica stood beside her ghola "son" Paul, who was chronologically a year older than she. Paul waited with his beloved Fremen mate Chani and the nine-year-old ghola of a boy who had in turn been *their* son, Leto II. In a prior shuffle of lives, this had been Jessica's family.

The Bene Gesserit order had resurrected these figures from history to help fight against the terrible Outside Enemy that hunted them. They had Thufir Hawat, the planetologist Liet-Kynes, the Fremen leader Stilgar, and even the notorious Dr. Yueh. Now, after almost a decade of hiatus in the ghola program, Alia had joined the group. Others would come soon; the three remaining axlotl tanks were already pregnant with new children: Gurney Halleck, Serena Butler, Xavier Harkonnen.

Duncan Idaho gave Jessica a quizzical look. Eternal Duncan, with all of his memories restored from all of his prior lives . . . She wondered what he thought of this new ghola baby, a bubble of the past rising up to the present. Long ago, the first ghola of Duncan had been Alia's consort. . . .

CONCEALING HIS AGE well, Duncan was a full-grown man with dark wiry hair. He looked exactly like the hero shown in so many archival records, from the time of Muad'Dib, through the God Emperor's thirty-five-century reign, to now, another fifteen centuries later.

Breathless and late, the old Rabbi bustled into the birthing chamber accompanied by twelve-year-old Wellington Yueh. Young Yueh's forehead did not bear the diamond tattoo of the famous Suk School. The bearded Rabbi seemed to think he could save the gangly young man from repeating the terrible crimes he had committed in his prior life.

At the moment the Rabbi looked angry, as he invariably did whenever he came near the axlotl tanks. Since the Bene Gesserit doctors ignored him, the old man vented his displeasure on Sheeana. "After years of sanity, you have done it again! When will you learn to stop taunting God?"

After receiving an ominous prescient dream, Sheeana had declared a temporary moratorium on the ghola project that had been her passion from its inception. But their recent ordeal on the planet of the Handlers and their near capture by the Enemy hunters had forced Sheeana to reassess that decision. The wealth of historical and tactical experience the reawakened gholas could offer might be the greatest weapon the no-ship possessed. Sheeana had decided to take the risk.

Perhaps we will be saved by Alia one day, Jessica thought. *Or by one of the other gholas . . .*

Tempting fate, Sheeana had performed an experiment on this unborn ghola in an effort to make it more like *the* Alia. Estimating the point in the pregnancy when the original Jessica had consumed the Water of Life, Sheeana had instructed Bene Gesserit Suk doctors to flood the axlotl tank with a near-fatal spice overdose. Saturating the fetus. *Trying* to re-create an Abomination.

Jessica had been horrified to learn of it—too late, when she could do nothing about it. How would the spice affect that innocent baby? A melange overdose was different from undergoing the Agony.

One of the Suk doctors told the Rabbi to stay out of the birthing creche. Scowling, the old man held up a trembling hand, as if making a blessing on the pale flesh of the axlotl tank. "You witches think these tanks are no longer women, no longer human—but this is still Rebecca. She remains a child of my flock."

"Rebecca fulfilled a vital need." Sheeana said. "All of the volunteers knew exactly what they were doing. She accepted her responsibility. Why can't you?"

The Rabbi turned in exasperation toward the young man at his side. "Speak to them, Yueh. Maybe they will listen to you."

Jessica thought the sallow young ghola seemed more intrigued than incensed about the tanks. "As a Suk doctor," he said, "I delivered many children. But never like this. At least I don't think so. With my ghola memories still locked away, I get confused sometimes."

"And Rebecca is human—not just some biological machine to

produce melange and a brood of gholas. You have to see that." The Rabbi's voice grew in volume.

Yueh shrugged. "Because I was born in the same fashion, I cannot be entirely objective. If my memories were restored, maybe I'd agree with you."

"You don't need original memories to think! You can *think*, can't you?"

"The baby is ready," one of the doctors interrupted. "We must decant it now." She turned impatiently to the Rabbi. "Let us do our work—or the tank could be harmed as well."

With a sound of disgust, the Rabbi shouldered his way from the birthing creche. Yueh remained behind, continuing to watch.

One of the Suk women tied off the umbilical cord from the fleshy tank. Her shorter colleague cut the purplish-red whip; then she wiped off the slick infant and lifted little Alia into the air. The child let out a loud and immediate cry, as if she had been impatient to be born. Jessica sighed in relief at the healthy sound, which told her the girl was not an Abomination this time. The original newborn Alia had purportedly looked upon the world with the eyes and intelligence of a full adult. This baby's crying sounded normal. But it stopped abruptly.

While one doctor tended the now-sagging axlotl tank, the other dried the infant and wrapped her in a blanket. Unable to help feeling a tug at her heart, Jessica wanted to reach out and hold the baby, but resisted the urge. Would Alia suddenly start speaking, uttering voices from Other Memory? Instead, the baby looked around the medical center, without seeming to focus.

Others would care for Alia, not unlike the way Bene Gesserit sisters took baby girls under their collective wing. The first Jessica, born under the close scrutiny of breeding mistresses, had never known a mother in the traditional sense. Nor would this Jessica, nor Alia, nor any of the other experimental ghola babies. The new daughter would be raised communally in an improvised society, more an object of scientific curiosity than love.

"What an odd family we all are," Jessica whispered.

Humans are never capable of complete accuracy. Despite all the knowledge and experiences we have absorbed from countless Face Dancer "ambassadors," we are left with a confused picture. Nonetheless, the flawed accounts of human history provide amusing insights into the delusions of mankind.

— ERASMUS,

Records and Analyses, Backup #242

I n spite of a decades-long effort, the thinking machines had not yet captured the no-ship and its precious cargo. That did not, however, stop the computer evermind from launching his vast extermination fleet against the rest of humanity.

Duncan Idaho continued to elude Omnius and Erasmus, who repeatedly cast their sparkling tachyon net into the nothingness, searching for their quarry. The no-ship's veiling capability normally prevented it from being seen, but from time to time the pursuers caught glimpses, as of something concealed behind shrubbery. At first the hunt had been a challenge, but now the evermind was growing frustrated.

"You have lost the ship again," Omnius boomed through wall speakers in the central, cathedral-like chamber in the technological metropolis of Synchrony.

"Inaccurate. I must first find it before I can lose it." Erasmus tried to sound carefree as he shifted his flowmetal skin, reverting from his guise as a kindly old woman to the more familiar appearance of a platinum-surfaced robot.

Like overarching tree trunks, metal spires towered above Erasmus to form a vaulted dome within the machine cathedral. Photons glittered from the activated skins of the pillars, bathing his new laboratory in light. He had even installed a glowing fountain that bubbled with lava—a useless decoration, but the robot often indulged his carefully cultivated artistic sensibilities. "Do not be impatient. Remember the mathematical projections. Everything is nicely predetermined."

"Your mathematical projections could be myths, like any prophecy. How do I know they are correct?"

"Because I have said they are correct."

With the launch of the machine fleet, the long-foretold Kralizec had begun, at last. Kralizec . . . Armageddon . . . the Battle at the End of the Universe . . . Ragnarok . . . Azrafel . . . the End Times . . . the Cloud Darkness. It was a time of fundamental change, of the entire universe shifting on its cosmic axis. Human legends had predicted such a cataclysmic event since the dawn of civilization. Indeed, they had already been through several iterations of similar cataclysms: the Butlerian Jihad itself, the jihad of Paul Muad'Dib, the reign of the Tyrant Leto II. By manipulating computer projections, and thus creating expectations in the mind of Omnius, Erasmus had succeeded in initiating the events that would bring about another fundamental shift. Prophecy and reality—the order of things really didn't matter.

Like an arrow, all of Erasmus's infinitely complex calculations, running trillions of data points through the most sophisticated routines, pointed to one result: The final Kwisatz Haderach—whoever that was—would determine the course of events at the end of Kralizec. The projection also revealed that the Kwisatz Haderach was on the no-ship, so Omnius naturally wanted such a force fighting on his side. Ergo, the thinking machines needed to capture that ship. The first to exert control over the final Kwisatz Haderach would win.

Erasmus didn't fully understand exactly what the superhuman might do when he was located and seized. Though the robot was a longtime student of mankind, he was still a thinking machine, while the Kwisatz Haderach was not. The new Face Dancers, who had long infiltrated humanity and brought vital information back to the Synchronized Empire, fell somewhere in between, like hybrid biological machines. He and Omnius had both absorbed so many of the lives stolen by the Face Dancers that sometimes they forgot who they were. The original Tleilaxu Masters had not foreseen the significance of what they had helped create.

The independent robot knew he still had to keep Omnius under control, though. "We have time. You have a galaxy to conquer before we need the Kwisatz Haderach aboard that ship."

"I am glad I did not wait for you to succeed."

For centuries Omnius had been building his invincible force. Using traditional but supremely efficient lightspeed engines, the millions and millions of machine vessels now swept forward and spread out, conquering one star system at a time. The evermind could have made use of the surrogate mathematical navigation systems, which his Face Dancers had "given" to the Spacing Guild, but one element of the Holtzman technology simply remained too incomprehensible. Something indefinably human was required to travel through foldspace, an intangible "leap of faith." The evermind would never admit that the bizarre technology actually made him . . . nervous.

Following a flurry of test skirmishes, the wall of robotic battleships had encountered and swiftly destroyed fringe outpost worlds settled by humans. Vanguard drones mapped out the planets ahead and distributed deadly biological plagues that Erasmus had developed; by the time the actual machine fleet arrived at a target world, military action was often unnecessary against a dying population. Each combat engagement, even clashes with isolated groups of Honored Matres, was equally decisive.

To keep himself occupied, the independent robot reviewed the streams of data sent back to him. This was the part he enjoyed best. A buzzing watcheye flitted in front of him, and he brushed it away. "If you allow me to concentrate, Omnius, I may find some way to speed up our progress against the humans."

"How do I know you will not make another mistake?"

"Because you have confidence in my abilities."

The watcheye flitted away.

While the machine fleet crushed one human planet after another, Erasmus issued additional instructions for the invader robots. As the infected humans lay writhing, vomiting, and bleeding from their pores, machine scouts casually ransacked databases, halls of records, libraries, and other sources. This was different from the information to be winnowed from the random lives that Face Dancers had assimilated.

With all the fresh data flowing in, Erasmus had the luxury of becoming a scientist again, as he had been long ago. The pursuit of scientific truth had always been his true reason for existence. Now the flood was greater than ever before. Glad to possess so much new information, so much undigested data, he gorged his elaborate mind on raw facts and histories.

After the supposed destruction of thinking machines more than fifteen millennia earlier, the fecund humans had spread, building civilizations and destroying them. Erasmus was intrigued by how, after the Battle of Corrin, the Butler family had founded an empire and ruled it under the name of Corrino for ten thousand years, with a few gaps and interregnums, only to be overthrown by a fanatical leader named Muad'Dib.

Paul Atreides. The first Kwisatz Haderach.

A more fundamental change, however, had come from his son Leto II, called the God Emperor or Tyrant. Another Kwisatz Haderach—a unique hybrid of man and sandworm that had imposed a draconian rule for thirty-five hundred years. After his assassination, human civilization fragmented. Fleeing to the far reaches of the galaxy in the Scattering, people became hardened by their privations until the worst sort of humans—Honored Matres—had blundered into the burgeoning machine empire. . . .

Another flitting watcheye scanned the same records Erasmus was reading. Omnius spoke through resonating plates in the walls. "I find their contradictions—posed as fact—to be unsettling."

"Unsettling perhaps, but fascinating." Erasmus disengaged himself from the stacks of historical files. "Their histories show how they view themselves and the universe around them. Obviously, these humans need someone to take firm control again."

Why is religion important? Because logic alone does not compel a person to make great sacrifices. Given sufficient religious fervor, however, people will throw themselves against impossible odds and consider themselves blessed for doing so.

—MISSIONARIA PROTECTIVA,

First Primer

Two male workers appeared at the door of Murbella's coldly ostentatious council chambers during a tense meeting. Using suspensor clamps, they hauled a large, motionless robot between them. "Mother Commander? You asked for this to be delivered here."

The combat machine was built from blue and black metal, reinforced with struts and overlapping armor. Its conical head contained a suite of sensors and targeting arrays, and four engine-driven arms were wrapped with cables and augmented with weapons. Damaged during a recent skirmish, the fighting robot had dark smears across its bulky torso where high-energy blasts had knocked out its internal processors. The robotic thing was shut down, dead, defeated. But even deactivated, it was cause for nightmares.

Murbella's advisors, startled out of their discussions and arguments, stared at the big machine. All of the gathered women wore the plain black unitard of the New Sisterhood, following a code of homogenized dress that allowed no indication of their origins as either Bene Gesserit or Honored Matre.

Murbella gestured to the intimidated-looking workers. "Bring that thing inside where we can see it every time we talk about the Enemy. It will do us good to be reminded of the adversary we're up against."

Even with the suspensor clamps, the men sweated as they wrestled the machine into the room. Murbella strode to the bulky combat robot and stared with defiance up into its dull optic sensors. She glanced proudly at her daughter. "Bashar Idaho brought this specimen back from the battle at Duvalle."

"It should be sent to the scrap heap. Or shot into space," said Kiria, a hard-edged former Honored Matre. "What if it still has passive spy programming?"

"It's been thoroughly purged," said Janess Idaho. As the newly appointed commandant of the Sisterhood's military forces, she had become a very pragmatic young woman.

"A trophy, Mother Commander?" asked Laera, a dark-skinned Reverend Mother who often quietly supported Murbella. "Or a prisoner of war?"

"This is the only one our armies found intact. We blew up four machine ships before we retreated and let them destroy the planet behind us. They had already turned their plagues loose on Ronto and Pital, leaving no survivors. Total population losses number in the billions."

Duvalle, Ronto, and Pital were just the latest casualties as the machine army continued its forward march through the outlying systems. Because of the distances involved and the sheer might of the attacking ships, reports were sketchy and often outdated. Refugees and couriers surged away from battle zones, heading inward from the fringes of the Scattering.

Murbella turned her back on the deactivated robot and faced the Sisters. "Knowing that a tempest approaches, we have the option of simply evacuating—abandoning everything we have. That is the Honored Matre way."

Some of the Sisters flinched at the comment. Long ago, Honored Matres had chosen to run from the Enemy, pillaging on their way out, hoping to stay one step ahead of the storm. To them, the Old Empire had been no more than a crude barricade to be thrown up against the Enemy; they had simply hoped it would last long enough for them to get away.

"*Or*, we can board up our windows, strengthen our walls, and ride it out. And hope we survive."

"This is no mere storm, Mother Commander," said Laera. "The repercussions are already being felt. Refugees fleeing the battlefront are overwhelming the support systems of second-wave worlds, all of which are preparing for evacuation as well. The people won't stand and fight."

"Like waterlogged rats crowding to the corner of a sinking raft," Kiria muttered.

"Says the Honored Matre, who did exactly the same," Janess said from the end of the table, then tried to cover her comment by loudly sipping her spice coffee. Kiria glared at her.

"A shadow deep in our Honored Matre past," Murbella said. "Through hubris, and a violent predisposition to strike first and understand later, the whores caused all these problems." By digging deep into her mind and history, she had been the first to remember how her long-dead sisters had stupidly provoked the thinking machines.

Kiria was indignant, clearly still associating herself with the Honored Matres. Murbella found it disturbing. "You yourself revealed why the Honored Matres are what they are, Mother Commander. Descended from tortured Tleilaxu females, rogue Reverend Mothers, and a few Fish Speakers. They had every right to be vengeful."

"They had no right to be stupid!" Murbella snapped. "A painful past did not give them the right to lash out against anything they encountered. They couldn't salve their conscience by pretending they knew what they were doing when they attacked a machine outpost and stole weapons they didn't understand." She smiled slightly. "If anything, I can relate to—though not approve of—their revenge against the Tleilaxu worlds. In Other Memory I know what the Tleilaxu did to my ancestors . . . I *remember* being one of their vile axlotl tanks. But make no mistake, that kind of provocative and poorly planned violence has caused immeasurable trouble for the human race. And now look what we face!"

"How can we strengthen ourselves against this storm, Mother Commander?" The question came from ancient Accadia, a Reverend Mother who lived in the Chapterhouse Archives. Accadia hardly ever slept and rarely allowed sunlight to touch her parchment skin. "What defenses do we have?" The hulking combat robot seemed to mock them from the corner of the room, where the men had left it.

"We have the weapon of religion. Especially *Sheeana*."

"Sheeana is of no use to us!" Janess said. "Her followers believe she died on Rakis decades ago."

The priests on Rakis had once made much of the girl who could command sandworms. The Bene Gesserit had created a grassroots religion around Sheeana, and the annihilation of Dune had only served the Sisterhood's greater purpose. After her supposed death, the rescued girl was isolated on Chapterhouse, so that one day she might "return from the grave" to great fanfare. But the real Sheeana had escaped with Duncan on the no-ship more than twenty years ago.

"It's not necessary for us to have *her*, specifically. Simply find Sisters who resemble her and apply any necessary makeup and facial modifications." Murbella tapped fingers against her lips. "Yes, we shall begin with twelve new Sheeanas. Disperse them to the refugee worlds, since the displaced survivors will be our most impressionable recruits. The resurrected Sheeana will seem to appear everywhere at once—a messiah, a visionary, a leader."

Laera spoke in an eminently reasonable voice. "Genetic tests will prove that these impostors are not Sheeana. Your plan will backfire once people see we have tried to trick them."

Kiria had already thought of the obvious solution. "We can have Bene Gesserit doctors—Suk doctors—perform the tests . . . and lie for us."

"Also, don't underestimate the greatest advantage we have." Murbella held out her hand like a mendicant asking for alms. "The people *want* to believe. For thousands of years, our Missionaria Protectiva wove religious beliefs among populations. Now we must use those techniques not just for our own protection, but as a functional weapon, a means of influencing armies. No longer passive and protective, but an active force. A Missionaria *Aggressiva*."

The other women, especially Kiria, seemed to like the idea. Accadia scowled down at her Ridulian crystal sheets, as if trying to find profound answers written in the dense characters.

Murbella flashed a defiant look at the combat robot. "The twelve Sheeanas will carry spice from our stockpiles. Each will distribute extravagant amounts of melange as she makes her pronouncements. She will say that Shaitan told her in a dream that spice would flow again soon. Though Rakis was burned as lifeless as Sodom and Gomorrah, many new Dunes will appear elsewhere. Sheeana will promise them this." Years ago, groups of Reverend Mothers had been sent out on a secret Scattering, taking ships and all-important sandtrout to seed additional planets and create more desert worlds for the sandworms.

"False prophets and sightings of the messiah. It's been done before." Kiria sounded bored. "Explain how this will benefit us."

Murbella shot her a calculated smile. "We take advantage of the superstitions that will run rampant. People believe they must endure a time of tribulation, a cycle as old as the most ancient religions, long before the First Great Movement or the Zensunni Hajj. So, we tailor that belief to our own uses. The thinking machines are the great evil we have to defeat before humanity can reap its reward."

Turning to the aged mistress of the Archives, she said, "Accadia, read everything you can find about the Butlerian Jihad and how Serena Butler led her forces. The same for Paul Muad'Dib. We could even say that the Tyrant began to prepare us for this. Study his writings and take sections out of context to support our message, so the people will be convinced that this final universal conflict has been foretold all along: *Kralizec*. If they believe in the prophecies, they'll continue to fight long after any rational hope should be dashed."

She motioned for the women to go about their tasks. "In the meantime, I have set up a meeting with the Ixians and the Guild. Since Richese is destroyed, I'll demand that they devote their manufacturing capabilities to our war effort. We need every scrap of resistance the human race can muster."

As she was leaving, Accadia asked, "And what if those old prophecies prove to be correct? What if these truly are the End Times?"

"Then our efforts are all the more justified. And we still fight. It's all we can do." Facing the robot, Murbella spoke to it as if the machine mind could still hear her. "And that's how we will defeat you."

I am the keeper of private knowledge and uncounted secrets. You will never know what I know! I would pity you, if you were not an infidel.

—Mirage in the Shariat Road,
an apocryphal Tleilaxu writing

In the enormous Guild Heighliner, no passengers ever guessed what the Navigator and his captive Tleilaxu Master were doing right under their noses.

By holding melange supplies for ransom, the Bene Gesserit witches had backed the Spacing Guild into a corner and forced them to choose drastic alternatives. Facing extinction from spice starvation, the Navigator faction urged Waff to greater speed to complete his task. The Tleilaxu Master felt the need for haste as well, since he was facing extinction himself, though for different reasons.

Turning his back on the observation lens, Waff surreptitiously consumed another dose of melange. The cinnamony powder had been provided strictly for scientific purposes. He touched the burning substance to his lips and tongue, closed his eyes in ecstasy. Such a small quantity—only a taste—was enough to buy a house on a colony world these days! The Tleilaxu man felt energy rush back into his ailing body. Edrik would not begrudge him this bit of melange to help him think straight.

Normally, Tleilaxu Masters lived from body to body in a chain of ghola immortality. They had learned patience and long-term planning from the Great Belief. Had not God's Messenger himself lived for three and a half millennia? But forbidden techniques had accelerated this Waff 's growth in the axlotl tank. The cells in his body burned through his existence like flames through a forest, sweeping him from infancy to childhood to maturity, in only a few years. Waff 's memory restoration had been imperfect, bringing back only fragments of his past life and knowledge.

Escaping the Honored Matres, Waff had been forced to take refuge with the Navigator faction. Since Edrik and his fellows had financed his ghola resurrection in the first place, why not beg them for sanctuary? Though the little man did not remember how to create melange with axlotl tanks, he claimed he could do the impossible—bring back the supposedly extinct sandworms. A much more spectacular and necessary solution.

In the isolated Heighliner laboratory, Edrik had provided all of the research tools, technical equipment, and genetic raw material he could possibly need. Waff did as the Navigators demanded. Bringing back the magnificent worms that had been exterminated on Rakis offered the simultaneous possibilities of manufacturing spice, and of restoring his Prophet.

I must do this! Failure is not an option.

With his accelerated maturity, Waff would be at his peak—the best health, the sharpest mind—for only a short while longer. Before he began the inevitable rapid degeneration, he had much to accomplish. The tremendous responsibility prodded at him.

Focus, focus!

He climbed onto a stool and peered into a plaz-walled containment tank full of sand from Rakis itself. *Dune.* Because of the planet's religious significance, pilgrims who could not afford the interplanetary passage contented themselves with relics, fragments of stone chipped from the ruins of Muad'Dib's original palace or scraps of spice cloth embroidered with the sayings of Leto II. Even the poorest of devout followers wanted a sample of Rakian sand, so that they could dust their fingertips and imagine themselves closer to the Divided God. The Navigators had acquired hundreds of cubic meters of authentic Rakian sand. Though it was doubtful that the origin of the grains would have any effect on the sandworm tests, Waff preferred to remove any stray variables.

He leaned over the open tank, filled his mouth with saliva, and let a long droplet splatter onto the soft sand. Like piranhas in an aquarium, shapes stirred beneath the surface, swirling to seize the invading moisture. In another place long ago, spitting—sharing one's personal water—had been a sign of respect among the Fremen. Waff used it to bring sandtrout to the surface.

Little makers. Sandtrout specimens, far more precious even than the sand of Dune.

Years ago, the Guild had intercepted a secret Bene Gesserit ship carrying sandtrout in its hold. When the witches aboard refused to explain their mission, they were all killed, their sandtrout seized, and Chapterhouse had been none the wiser.

Learning that the Guild possessed some of the immature sandworm vectors, Waff demanded them for his work. Though he could not remember how to create melange in an axlotl tank, this experiment had much greater potential. By resurrecting the worms, he could not only bring back spice, but the Prophet himself!

Unafraid of the sandtrout, he reached into the aquarium with a small hand. Grabbing one of the leathery creatures by its fringe, he pulled it flopping out of the sand. Sensing the moisture in Waff's perspiration, the sandtrout wrapped itself around his fingers, palm, and knuckles. He poked and prodded the soft surface, reshaping the edges.

"Little sandtrout, what secrets do you have for me?" He formed a fist, and the creature flowed around it to form a jellylike glove. He could feel his skin drying out.

Carrying the sandtrout, Waff went to a clean research table and set out a wide, deep pan. He tried to unwrap the sandtrout from his knuckles, but each time he moved the membrane it flowed back onto his skin. Feeling the desiccation in his hand now, he poured a beaker of fresh water into the bottom of the pan. The sandtrout, attracted by a larger supply, quickly plopped into it.

Water was deadly poison to sandworms, but not to the younger sandtrout, the larval stage of the worms. The early vector had a fundamentally different biochemistry before it underwent the metamorphosis into its mature form. A paradox. How could one stage in the life cycle be so ravenously drawn to water, while a later phase was killed by it?

Flexing his fingers to recover from the unnatural dryness, Waff was fascinated as the specimen engulfed the water. The larva instinctively hoarded moisture to create a perfectly dry environment for the adult. From previous-life memories that did remain within him, he knew of ancient Tleilaxu experiments to move and control worms. Standard attempts to transplant full-grown worms onto dry planets always failed. Even the most extreme offworld landscapes still had too much moisture to support such a fragile—fragile?—life-form as the sandworms.

Now, though, he had a different idea. Instead of changing the *worlds* to accommodate sandworms, perhaps he could alter the worms themselves in their immature stage, help them adapt. The Tleilaxu understood the Language of God, and their genius for genetics had achieved the impossible many times. Had not Leto II been God's Prophet? It was Waff's duty to bring Him back.

The concept and chromosomal mechanics seemed simple. At some point in the sandtrout's development, a trigger changed the creature's chemical response toward a substance as simple as water. If he could only find that trigger and block it, the sandtrout should continue to mature, but without such a deathly aversion to liquid water. Now that would be a true miracle!

But if one prevented a caterpillar from spinning a cocoon, would it still transform into a great moth? He would have to be very careful, indeed.

If he understood what the witches had done on Chapterhouse, they had discovered a way to release sandtrout into a planetary environment—the Bene Gesserit homeworld. Once there, the sandtrout reproduced and began an unstoppable process to destroy (remake?) the whole ecosystem. From a lush planet to an arid wasteland. They would eventually turn the world into a total desert, where the sandworms could survive and be reborn.

More questions continued to follow, one after another. Why were the fleeing Bene Gesserit Sisters carrying sandtrout samples aboard their refugee ships? Were they trying to distribute them to other worlds, and thereby create more desert planets? Habitats for more worms? Such a plan would require a huge concerted effort, take decades to come to fruition, and kill off the native life on a planet. Inefficient.

Waff had a much more immediate solution. If he could develop a breed of sandworm that tolerated water, even thrived around it, the creatures could be transplanted onto innumerable worlds where they could grow swiftly and multiply! The worms would not need to reconstruct a whole planetary environment before they began to produce melange. That alone would save decades that Waff simply did not have. His modified worms would provide all the spice the Guild Navigators could ever desire—and serve Waff's purposes as well.

Help me, Prophet!

The sandtrout specimen had absorbed all the water in the pan and now gradually moved about the base and sides, exploring the boundaries. Waff brought research tools and chemicals to the laboratory table—his alcohols, acids, and flames, his deep sample extractors.

The first cut was the hardest. Then he began to work on the shapeless, squirming creature to pry loose its genetic secrets in any way he could.

He had the best DNA analyzers and genetic sequencers the Guild could obtain . . . and they were very good, indeed. The sandtrout took a long time to die, but Waff was certain the Prophet wouldn't mind.

A stench seeps from my pores. The foul odor of extinction.

> —SCYTALE,
> the last known Tleilaxu Master

The small, gray-skinned child looked worriedly at his older but identical counterpart. "This is a restricted area. The Bashar will be very angry with us."

The older Scytale scowled, disappointed that a child with such a magnificent destiny could be so timid. "These people have no authority to impose their rules on me—either version of me!" Despite years of preparation, instruction, and insistence, Scytale knew that the ghola boy still did not grasp who he was. The Tleilaxu Master coughed and winced, unable to minimize his physical problems. "You must awaken your genetic memories before it is too late!"

The child followed his older self down the dim corridor of the no-ship, but his steps were too shaky to be furtive. Occasionally the degenerating Scytale needed support from his twelve-year-old "son." Each day, each lesson, should bring the younger one closer to the tipping point at which his embedded memories would cascade free. Then, finally, old Scytale could allow himself to die.

Years ago, he had been forced to offer his only bargaining chip—his secret stash of valuable cellular material—to bribe the witches. Scytale resented being put in such a position, but in return for the raw makings of heroes from the past for the witches' own purposes, Sheeana had agreed to let him use the axlotl tanks to grow a new version of himself. He hoped it wasn't too late.

For years now, every sentence, every day increased pressure on the younger Scytale. His "father," a victim of planned cellular obsolescence, doubted he had another year before collapsing completely. Unless the boy received his memories soon, *very soon*, all the knowledge of the Tleilaxu would be lost. Old Scytale winced at the dire prospect, which hurt him far more than any physical pain.

They reached one of the vacant lower levels, where a testing chamber had gone unnoticed in the empty expanses of the ship. "I will use this powindah teaching equipment to show you how God meant for the Tleilaxu to live." The walls were smooth and curved, the glowpanels tuned to a dull orange. The room seemed to be full of gestating wombs, round, flaccid, mindless—the way women were supposed to serve a truly civilized society.

Scytale smiled at the sight, while the boy stared around with dark eyes. "Axlotl tanks. So many of them! Where did they all come from?"

"Unfortunately they are merely holographic projections." The high-quality simulation included mock tank sounds, as well as the odors of chemicals, disinfectants, and medicinals.

As Scytale stood surrounded by the glorious images, his heart ached to see the home he missed so much, a home now utterly destroyed. Years ago, before he was allowed to set foot again in sacred Bandalong, Scytale and all Tleilaxu had always undergone a lengthy cleansing process. Ever since the Honored Matres had forced him to flee with only his life and a few bargaining chips, he had tried to observe the rituals and practices as much as possible—and had vigorously taught them to the young ghola—but there were limitations. Scytale had not felt sufficiently clean in a long time. But he knew that God would understand.

"This is how a typical breeding chamber used to look. Study it. Absorb it. Remind yourself of how things were, how they should be. I created these images from my own memories, and those same memories are within you. Find them."

Scytale had said the same thing again and again, hammering it into the child. His younger version was a good student, very intelligent, and knew all the information by rote learning, but the boy didn't know it in his soul.

Sheeana and the other witches didn't grasp the immensity of the crisis he faced, or perhaps they didn't care. The Bene Gesserits understood little about the nuances of restoring a ghola's memories, could not recognize the moment when a ghola was perfectly ready . . . but Scytale might not have the luxury of waiting. The child was certainly old enough. He should awaken! Soon the boy would be the only Tleilaxu left, with no one to wake his memories.

As he surveyed the rows of breeding vats, the junior Scytale's face filled with awe and intimidation. The boy was drinking it all in. *Good.* "That tank in the second row is the one that gave birth to me," he said. "The Sisterhood called her Rebecca."

"The tank has no name. It is not a person and never was. Even when it could speak, it was only a female. We Tleilaxu never name our tanks, nor the females that preceded them."

Expanding the image, he allowed the walls to disappear into a projection of a vast breeding house with tank after tank after tank; outside were the spires and streets of Bandalong. These visual cues should have been sufficient, but Scytale wished he could have added other sensory details, the female reproductive smells, the feel of the sunlight of home, the comforting knowledge of countless Tleilaxu filling the streets, the buildings, the temples.

He felt achingly lonely.

"I should not still be alive and standing before you. It offends me to be old and in pain, with my body malfunctioning. The kehl of true Masters should have euthanized me long ago and let me live on in a fresh ghola body. But these are not proper times."

"These are not proper times," the boy repeated, backing through one of the detailed holo-images. "You have to do things you would not otherwise tolerate. You must use heroic means to stay alive long enough to awaken me, and I promise you, with all my heart, that I will become *Scytale.* Before it is too late."

The process of awakening a ghola was neither simple nor swift. Year after year, Scytale had applied pressures, reminders, mental twists to this boy. Each lesson and each demand built, like a pebble added to the pile, higher and higher, and sooner or later he would add enough to that unstable mound to trigger an avalanche. And only God and his Prophet could know which small stone of memory would cause that barrier to come crashing down.

The boy watched the flickering moods cross his mentor's face. Not knowing what else to do, he quoted a comforting lesson from his catechism. "When one is faced with an impossible choice, one must always choose the path of the Great Belief. God guides those who wish to be led."

The very thought seemed to consume Scytale's last energy, and he slumped into a nearby chair in the simulation room, trying to recover his strength. When the ghola hurried to his side, Scytale stroked the dark hair of his alternate self. "You are young, perhaps too young."

The boy placed a comforting hand on the old man's shoulder. "I will try—I promise. I'll work as hard as I can." He squeezed his eyes shut and seemed to push, as if wrestling with the intangible walls inside his brain. At last, perspiring heavily, he gave up the effort.

The elder Scytale felt despondent. He had already used all the techniques he knew to push this ghola to the brink. Crisis, paradox, unrelenting desperation. But he felt it more than the boy did. Clinical knowledge was simply insufficient.

The witches had used some sort of sexual twisting to bring back the Bashar Miles Teg when his ghola was only ten years old, and Scytale's successor was already two years past that mark. But he could not bear the thought of the Bene Gesserit women using their unclean bodies to break this boy. Scytale had already sacrificed so much, selling most of his soul for a glimmer of hope for his race's future. The Prophet Himself would turn his back on Scytale in disgust. Not that!

Scytale placed his head in his hands. "You are a flawed ghola. I should have thrown away your fetus and started anew twelve years ago!"

The boy's voice was rough, like torn fiber. "I will concentrate, and push my memories out of my cells!"

The Tleilaxu Master felt a weary sadness weighing him down. "It is an instinctive process, not an intellectual one. It must come to you. If your memories don't return, then you are of no use to me. Why should I let you live?"

The boy was visibly struggling, but Scytale saw no flash of awe and relief, no sudden flood of a lifetime's experiences. Both Tleilaxu reeked of failure. With each passing moment, Scytale felt more and more of himself dying.

The fate of our race depends on the actions of an unlikely collection of misfits.

—from a Bene Gesserit study on the human condition

In his second life, Baron Vladimir Harkonnen had done well for himself. At only seventeen, the awakened ghola already commanded a large castle filled with antique relics and a retinue of servants to satisfy his every whim. Better yet, it was Castle Caladan, the seat of House Atreides. He sat upon a high throne of fused black jewels, gazing around a large audience chamber as attendants went about their duties. Pomp and grandeur, all the trappings a Harkonnen deserved.

Despite appearances, though, the ghola Baron had very little real power, and he knew it. The Face Dancer myriad had created him for a specific purpose and, despite his reawakened memories, managed to keep him on a tight leash. Too many important questions remained unanswered, and too much was out of his control. He didn't like that.

The Face Dancers seemed much more interested in their young ghola of Paul Atreides—the one they called "Paolo." He was their real prize. Their leader Khrone said that this planet and the restored castle existed for the sole purpose of triggering Paolo's memories. The Baron was just a means to an end, of secondary importance in the "Kwisatz Haderach matter."

He resented the Atreides brat for it. The boy was only eight and still had much to learn from his mentor, though the Baron hadn't yet determined what the Face Dancers really wanted.

"Prepare him and raise him. See that he is primed for his destiny," Khrone had said. "There is a certain need he must fulfill."

A certain need. But what need?

You are his grandfather, said the annoying voice of Alia inside the Baron's head. *Take good care of him.* The little girl taunted him incessantly. From the moment his memories were restored, she had been there waiting for him in his mind. Her voice still contained a childhood lisp, exactly as she had sounded when she'd killed him with the poisoned needle of the gom jabbar.

"I'd rather take care of you, little Abomination!" he yelled. "Wring your neck, twist your head—once, twice, three times! Make your delicate little skull pop right off! Ha!"

But it's your own skull, dear Baron.

He clamped his hands against his temples. "Leave me alone!"

Seeing no one else in the room with their master, the servants looked at him uneasily. The Baron fumed and slumped back in his glittering black chair. Having embarrassed and angered him, the Alia voice whispered his name tauntingly one more time and faded away.

Just then, a jaunty and self-important Paolo strode into the chamber, followed by an entourage of androgynous Face Dancers who acted as his protectors. The child carried an air of overconfidence that the Baron found at once fascinating and disconcerting.

Baron Vladimir Harkonnen and this other Paul Atreides were inextricably meshed, simultaneously drawn together and repelled, like two powerful magnets. After the Baron's memories had been restored and he understood enough of who he was, Paolo had been brought to Caladan and handed over to the Baron's tender care . . . with dire warnings should any harm befall him.

From his high black chair, the Baron glared down at the cocky youth. What made Paolo so special? What was the "Kwisatz Haderach matter"? What did the Atreides know?

For some time, Paolo had been sensitive, thoughtful, even caring; he had a stubborn streak of innate goodness that the Baron had been working diligently to eradicate. Given time, and enough harsh training, he was sure he could cure even the honorable core of an Atreides. That would prime Paolo for his destiny, all right! Though the boy still struggled with his actions occasionally, he had made considerable progress.

Paolo came to an impertinent halt in front of the dais. One of the androgynous Face Dancers placed an antique handgun into the boy's hand.

Angrily, the Baron leaned forward for a better view. "Is that gun from my personal collection? I told you to stay out of those things."

"This is a relic of House Atreides, so I'm entitled to use it. A disk gun, once carried by my sister Alia, according to the label."

The Baron shifted on his throne, nervous to have the loaded weapon so close to him.

"It's just a woman's gun."

Inside the thick black armrests the Baron had secreted his own weapons, any one of which could easily turn the boy into a wet smear— hmm, fresh material for growing another ghola, he thought. "Even so, it's a valuable relic, and I don't want it damaged by a reckless child."

"I won't damage it." Paolo seemed pensive. "I respect artifacts that my ancestors used."

Anxious to keep the boy from thinking too much, he stood. "Shall we take it outside, then, Paolo? Why don't we see how it works?" The Baron gave him an avuncular pat on the shoulder. "And afterward we can kill something with our bare hands, like we did to the mongrel hounds and ferrets."

Paolo seemed uncertain. "Maybe another day."

Nevertheless, the Baron hurried him out of the throne room. "Let's get rid of those noisy gulls around the midden piles. Have I mentioned how much you remind me of Feyd? Lovely Feyd."

"More than once."

Watched over by Face Dancers, they spent the next two hours at the castle's trash heap, taking turns shooting the raucous birds with the disk gun. Oblivious to the danger, the gulls swooped and shrieked at one another, fighting over morsels of rain-splattered garbage. Paolo took a shot, then the Baron. Despite its antiquity, the gun was quite accurate. Each spinning, microthin disk chopped a bird into bloody meat and dislodged feathers. Then the surviving gulls squabbled over the fresh gobbets.

Between them, they killed fourteen birds, although the Baron did not do nearly as well as the child, who had quite an aptitude for cool marksmanship. As the Baron raised the disk gun and aimed carefully, the girl's annoying voice rang in his head again. *That's not my gun, you know.*

He took the shot and missed by a wide margin. Alia giggled.

"What do you mean it's not yours?" He ignored Paolo's puzzled stare as the boy took the weapon for his turn.

It's a fake. I never had a disk gun like that.

"Leave me alone."

"Who are you talking to?" Paolo asked.

After reaching into a pocket the Baron offered several capsules of orange melange substitute to Paolo, who obediently took them. He grabbed the weapon back from the boy. "Don't be ridiculous. The antiquities dealer provided a certificate of authenticity and documentation when he sold the weapon to me."

Grandfather, you shouldn't be so easily fooled! My own gun shot larger disks. This is a cheap imitation and doesn't even have the maker's initials on the barrel, like the original.

He studied the carved ornamental handle, turned the gun toward his face, then looked at the short barrel. No initials. "And what about my other things, the objects supposedly owned by Jessica and Duke Leto?"

Some are real, some are not. I'll let you find out which are which. Knowing the nobleman's penchant for buying historical artifacts, the dealer would return to Caladan soon. No one made a fool of the Baron! The Baron ghola decided the next meeting would not be quite so cordial. He would ask a few incisive questions. Alia's voice faded away, and he was glad to have a moment of peace inside his head.

Paolo had consumed two of the orange capsules, and as the melange substitute took hold, the boy dropped to his knees and stared beatifically into the sky. "I see a great victory in my future! I'm holding a knife that drips with blood. I'm standing over my enemy . . . over myself." He frowned, then beamed again, yelling, "I *am* the Kwisatz Haderach!" Then Paolo let out a bloodcurdling scream. "No . . . now, I see myself dying on the floor, bleeding to death. But how can this be, if I am the Kwisatz Haderach? How can this be?"

The nearest Face Dancer grew animated. "We were instructed to watch for signs of prescience. We must notify Khrone immediately."

Prescience? the Baron thought. *Or insanity?*

Inside his mind, the presence of Alia laughed.

DAYS LATER, THE Baron strolled along the top of the cliff and gazed out to sea. Caladan did not yet have the lovely, grimy industrial capacity of his beloved Giedi Prime, but at least he'd paved over the gardens in the vicinity of the castle. The Baron hated flowers with their eye-straining colors and sickening odors. He much preferred the perfume of factory smoke. He had great ambitions of turning Caladan into another Giedi Prime. The march of progress was more important than any esoteric plans the Face Dancers had for young Paolo.

On the lowest level of the restored castle, where other great houses would have prepared chambers for "policy enforcement activities," House Atreides had instead used the space for food storage rooms, a wine cellar, and an emergency shelter. Being a more traditional nobleman, the Baron had installed dungeons, interrogation rooms, and a well-equipped torture chamber. He also had a party room on that level, where he often took young boys from the fishing village.

You can't remove the marks of House Atreides with such cosmetic changes, Grandfather, said the pestering voice of Alia. *I preferred the old castle.*

"Shut up, devil child! You were never here in life, either."

Oh, I visited my ancestral home when my mother lived here, when Muad'Dib was Emperor and his jihad splashed blood across the star systems. Don't you remember, Grandfather? Or weren't you inside my head then?

"I wish you weren't inside mine. I was born before you! I can't possibly have your memories inside me. You're an Abomination!"

Alia chuckled in a particularly disconcerting way. *Yes, Grandfather. I'm that, and much more. Perhaps that's why I have the power to be inside you. Or, perhaps you are just flawed—completely mad. Have you considered the possibility that you might be imagining me? That's what everyone else thinks.*

Servants hurried by, glancing fearfully at him. Just then the Baron saw a groundcar negotiating the steep road from the spaceport. "Ah, here is our guest." Despite Alia's intrusion, he expected this to be an entertaining day.

After the groundcar pulled up, a tall man stepped out of the rear compartment and made his way past statues of great Harkonnens that the Baron had erected in the past year. A suspensor platform floated behind the antiquities dealer, carrying his wares.

What do you plan to do with him, Grandfather?

"You know damned well what I'm going to do." High on the wall above, the Baron rubbed his hands together in gleeful anticipation. "Make yourself useful for a change, Abomination." Alia giggled, but it sounded as if she was laughing *at* him.

The Baron hurried down as a haunted-looking house servant escorted the visitor inside. Shay Vendee was an antiquities dealer, always pleased to meet with one of his best customers. As he strolled in with his goods trailing behind him, his round face shone as radiantly as a small red sun.

The Baron greeted him with a moist handshake, clasping with both hands and holding on a little too long, squeezing a bit too hard.

The merchant extricated himself from his customer's grip. "You'll marvel at what I've brought, Baron—amazing what turns up with a little digging." He opened one of the cases on the suspensor platform. "I saved these treasures especially for you."

The Baron brushed a speck off one of the jeweled rings on his fingers. "First I have something to show you, my dear Mr. Vendee. My new wine cellar. I am quite proud of it."

A look of surprise. "Are the Danian vineyards operating again?"

"I have other sources."

After the dealer disengaged his suspensor platform, the Baron led him down a wide rock staircase into increasing gloom. Oblivious to the danger, Vendee chattered cordially. "Caladan wines used to be quite famous, and deservedly so. In fact, I heard a rumor that a cache was found on the ruins of Kaitain, bottles perfectly preserved in a nullentropy vault. The nullentropy field prevented the wine from aging and mellowing—in this case for thousands of years—but even so, the vintage must be quite extraordinary. Would you like me to see if I can acquire a bottle or two for you?"

The Baron stopped at the bottom of the dim stairs and peered with spider-black eyes at his guest. "So long as you can provide the appropriate documentation. I wouldn't want to be duped into buying anything fake."

Vendee wore a look of horror. "Of course not, Baron Harkonnen!"

Finally, they passed through a narrow corridor illuminated by smoking oil lamps. Glowglobes were too efficient and harsh for the Baron's taste. He loved the dank, gritty smell of the air; it almost masked the other odors.

"Here we are!" The Baron pushed open a heavy wooden door and led the way into his fully stocked torture chamber. It had the traditional accoutrements: racks, masks, electrified chairs, and a strappado, by which a subject could be alternately hoisted into the air and dropped. "This is one of my new playrooms. My pride and joy."

Vendee's eyes opened wide in alarm. "I thought you said we were going to your wine cellar."

"Why, over there, my good man." With a good-natured expression, the Baron pointed to a table from which loose straps hung. A wine bottle and two glasses sat on top. He poured red wine into both glasses and handed one to his increasingly agitated guest.

Vendee glanced around, nervously eyeing the red stains on the table and rock floor. Spilled wine? "I have just made a long journey, and I'm tired. Maybe we should go back up to the main rooms. You will be absolutely delighted with the new items I've brought. Quite valuable relics, I assure you."

The Baron fingered one of the straps on the table. "There is another matter, first." He narrowed his eyes. From a side door a sunken-eyed boy marched in, carrying what looked like two ornate old weapons, disk handguns of ancient manufacture.

"Do these look familiar? Examine them carefully."

Vendee held one weapon to examine it. "Oh, yes. The antique gun of Alia Atreides. Used by her own hands."

"So you said." Taking the other handgun from the serving boy, the

Baron said to Vendee, "You sold me a fake. I happen to know that the gun you hold is not the original weapon used by Alia."

"I have a reputation for integrity, Baron. If anyone has told you otherwise, they are lying."

"Unfortunately for you, my source is beyond reproach."

You are lucky to have me inside you to point out your mistakes, Alia said. *If you believe I am real.*

Indignantly, Vendee placed the gun on the table and turned to leave. He only made it halfway to the door.

The Baron pulled the trigger of his own weapon, and a large, spinning disk shot out and hit the dealer squarely in the back of his neck, decapitating him. Swiftly, smoothly. The Baron was sure it hadn't hurt a bit.

"Good shot, eh?" The Baron grinned at the serving boy.

The servant did not flinch at the murder. "Will that be all you desire from me, sir?"

"You don't expect me to clean up this mess myself, do you?"

"No, my Lord. I will get right to it."

"Then wash yourself afterward." The Baron looked him over. "We'll have even more fun this afternoon." Meanwhile, he went back upstairs to study what the antique dealer had brought with him.

Once, I was born of a natural mother, and then reborn many times as a ghola. Considering the millennia over which the Bene Gesserit, the Tleilaxu, and others have meddled with the gene pool, I wonder—are any of us truly natural anymore?

—ship's log, entry of
DUNCAN IDAHO

Today, Gurney Halleck would be born again. Paul Atreides had looked forward to this during the months-long gestation process. Since the recent birth of his sister Alia, the waiting had become nearly unbearable. But in a matter of hours, Gurney would be removed from the axlotl tank. The famed Gurney Halleck!

In his studies under Proctor Superior Garimi, Paul had read much about the troubadour warrior, had seen images of the man and heard recordings of his songs. But he wanted to know the real Gurney, his friend, mentor, and protector from an epic time. Someday, though their ages were topsy-turvy now, the two would remember how close their friendship had been.

Paul couldn't keep the grin off his face as he rushed to get ready. Whistling an old Atreides song that he'd learned from Gurney's recorded collection, he stepped into the corridor, and Chani emerged from her own quarters to join him. Two years his junior, the thirteen-year-old was whip-thin and fast, soft-spoken and beautiful, only a preview of the woman she would become again. Knowing their destinies, she and Paul were already inseparable. He took her hand, and the pair happily hurried toward the medical center.

He wondered if Gurney would be an ugly baby, or if he had only become a rolling lump of a man after being battered by the Harkonnens. He hoped the Gurney ghola would have a natural skill with the baliset, too. Paul was confident that the no-ship's stores could re-create one of the antique musical instruments. Maybe the two of them could play music together.

Others would be there for the new birth: his "mother" Jessica, Thufir Hawat, and almost certainly Duncan Idaho. Gurney had many friends aboard. No one on the ship had known Xavier Harkonnen or Serena Butler, the other two gholas who would be decanted today, but they were legends from the Butlerian Jihad. Each ghola, according to Sheeana, had a role to play, and any one of them—or all of them together—might be the key to defeating the Enemy.

Aside from the ghola children, many other boys and girls had been born over the years of the *Ithaca*'s long flight. The Sisters bred with male Bene Gesserit workers who had also escaped from Chapterhouse; they understood the need to increase their population and prepare a solid foundation for a new colony, if the no-ship ever found a suitable planet to settle. The Rabbi's group of Jewish refugees, who had also married and begun families, still waited for a new home to fulfill their long quest. The no-ship was so vast, and the population aboard still so far below its capacity, that there was no real concern about running short on resources. Not yet.

As Paul and Chani approached the main birthing creche, four female proctors ran toward them down the hall, urgently calling for any qualified Suk doctor. "They're dead! All three of them."

Paul's heart stuttered. At fifteen, he was already training in some of the skills that had once made him the historical leader known as Muad'Dib. Summoning all the steel he could put into his voice, he demanded that the second proctor stop. "Explain yourself!"

The Bene Gesserit blurted, surprised into her answer. "Three axlotl tanks, three gholas. Sabotage—and murder. Someone destroyed them."

Paul and Chani rushed toward the medical center. Duncan and

Sheeana were already in the doorway looking shaken. Inside the chamber, three axlotl tanks had been ripped from their life-support mechanisms and lay in puddles of burned flesh and spilled liquid. Someone had used an incinerating beam and corrosives to destroy not only the life-support machinery, but the core flesh of the tanks and the unborn gholas.

Gurney Halleck. Xavier Harkonnen. Serena Butler. All lost. And the tanks, which had once been living women.

Duncan looked at Paul, articulating the real horror here. "We have a saboteur aboard. Someone who wishes to harm the ghola project—or maybe *all* of us."

"But why now?" Paul asked. "The ship has been fleeing for two decades, and the ghola project began years ago. What changed?"

"Maybe someone was afraid of Gurney," Sheeana suggested. "Or Xavier Harkonnen, or Serena Butler."

Paul saw that the other three axlotl tanks in the creche had not been harmed, including the one that had recently given birth to the spice-saturated Alia.

Standing by Gurney's tank, he saw the dead, half-born baby among the burned and dissolved folds of flesh. Nauseated, he knelt to touch the few wisps of blond hair. "Poor Gurney."

As Duncan helped Paul to his feet, Sheeana said in a coldly businesslike voice, "We still have the cellular material. We can grow replacements for all of them." Paul could sense her deep fury, barely controlled by her strict Bene Gesserit training. "We will need more axlotl tanks. I'll send out a call for volunteers."

The ghola of Thufir Hawat entered and stared in disbelief at what had happened, his face an ashen mask. After the ordeal on the planet of the Handlers, he and Miles Teg had bonded closely; Thufir now helped the Bashar with security and defenses aboard the ship. The fourteen-year-old struggled to sound authoritative. "We will find out who did this."

"Scan the security images," Sheeana said. "The killer can't hide."

Thufir looked embarrassed, as well as angry and so very young. "I already checked. The security imagers were deactivated, intentionally, but there must be other evidence."

"All of us were attacked, not just these axlotl tanks." Duncan's anger was plain as he turned toward young Thufir. "The Bashar has cited several previous incidents that he believes may be sabotage."

"Those were never proved," Thufir said. "They could have been mechanical breakdowns, systems fatigue, natural failures."

Paul's voice was ice as he took a last, lingering look at the infant that would have been Gurney Halleck. "This was no natural failure."

Then Paul's legs went suddenly rubbery. Dizziness rose around him, and his consciousness blurred. As Chani rushed to grab him, he reeled, lost his footing, and hit his head hard on the deck. For a moment blackness enveloped him, a gloom that brightened into a frightening vision. Paul Atreides had seen it before, but he didn't know if it was memory or prescience.

He saw himself lying on the floor in a spacious, unknown place. A knife wound deep inside him sucked out his life. A mortal wound. His life's blood poured onto the floor, and his vision turned to dark static. Gazing up, he saw his own young face looking back at him, laughing. "I have killed you!"

Chani was shaking him, shouting into his ear. "Usul! Usul, look at me!"

He felt the touch of her hand on his own, and when his vision cleared he saw another concerned face. For a moment he thought it was Gurney Halleck, complete with an inkvine scar on his jawline, the glass-splinter eyes, the wispy blond hair.

The image shifted, and he realized it was the black-haired Duncan Idaho. Another old friend and guardian. "Will you protect me from danger, Duncan?" Paul's voice hitched. "As you vowed to do when I was a child? Gurney is no longer able."

"Yes, Master Paul. Always."

The Honored Matres clearly devised their own name for them-selves, for no one else would ever apply the term "honor" after see-ing their cowardly, self-serving actions. Most people have a very different way of referring to those women.

— MOTHER COMMANDER MURBELLA,
assessment of past and present strengths

W eapons and battleships were as important as air and food dur-ing these supposed End Times. Murbella knew she would have to change the way she approached the problem, but she had never expected such resistance from her own Sisterhood.

With both anger and disdain, Kiria cried, "You offer them Obliter-ators, Mother Commander? We can't just hand over such destructive weapons to Ix."

She had no patience for this. "Who else will build them for us? Holding secrets among ourselves only benefits the Enemy. You know as well as I do that only the Ixians can decipher the technology and man-ufacture great quantities for the coming war. Therefore, Ix must have full access. There is no other answer."

Many worlds were building their own gigantic fleets, armoring every ship they could find, working on new weapon designs, but noth-ing had so far proved even remotely effective against the Enemy. The technology of the thinking machines was unsurpassed. But with a sup-ply of new Obliterators, Murbella could turn the machines' own destructive power against them.

After snatching the weapons from fringe machine outposts centuries ago, the Honored Matres could have formed an impenetrable line and hurled Obliterators at the oncoming Enemy. If they had stood together for the common good, they could have prevented this whole problem. Instead, those Honored Matres had fled.

Thinking about the hidden history she had excavated from deep within Other Memory, Murbella continued to be annoyed at those ancestors. They had taken the weapons, used them without understanding them, and depleted most of their stockpiles in their petty revenge against the hated Tleilaxu. Yes, many generations earlier the Tleilaxu had tormented their females, and the Honored Matres had good reason to direct vengeful violence against them.

But such a waste!

Because the Honored Matres had been so profligate in using the planet-roasting weapons against any world that offended them, only a few Obliterators remained intact. Recently, when cracking down on the rebel Honored Matre strongholds, Murbella had expected to unearth greater stockpiles. But they had found nothing. Had someone else stolen the weapons? The Guild perhaps, under their original pretext of helping the Honored Matres? Or had the whores truly used them all, holding nothing in reserve?

Now the human race had insufficient weapons left to stand against the real Enemy. The Obliterators were as incomprehensible as any device Tio Holtzman had ever created for folding space, and the women had never known how to create more. For the sake of humanity, she hoped the Ixians could do so.

Times of extremis demand extreme actions.

Under her orders, the members of the united Sisterhood now removed the powerful weapons from their no-ships, battle cruisers, and infiltration vessels. She would take them to Ix herself. Murbella cut off continued arguments as she marched with a small entourage toward the Chapterhouse spaceport.

"But Mother Commander, at least negotiate patent protections," Laera said, a flush showing even on her dark skin. "Impose restrictions so that the technology does not become widespread." She was one of the most businesslike Reverend Mothers, filling much of Bellonda's old role. "Proliferation amongst planetary warlords could result in the devastation of the largest star systems. CHOAM alone, working with Ix, could wreak—"

Murbella cut her off with a disgusted noise. "I have no interest in who may or may not benefit commercially *after we win this war.* If the Ixians help us achieve victory, they are entitled to profit." She rubbed her chin thoughtfully as she looked up at the ramp of her small, fast lighter. "We'll let the planetary warlords deal with their own problems."

You play with feelings as a child plays with toys. I know why your Sisterhood does not value emotions: You cannot value what you do not understand!

—DUNCAN IDAHO,
letter submitted to Reverend Mother Bellonda

Sheeana used an authoritative tone, just short of Voice. "'Respect for the truth comes close to being the basis for all morality.' And I want the truth from you. *Now.*"

Garimi raised her eyebrows and said calmly, "A quote from Duke Leto Atreides to bolster the interrogation? Shall we bring in blazing lights and a Truthsayer?"

"My Truthsense is sufficient. I have always known you well enough to read you."

The shock waves from the appalling crime in the birthing center rippled through the no-ship. The slaughter of unborn gholas, the destruction of three axlotl tanks—tanks created from volunteer *Sisters!*—went beyond anything Sheeana had expected from even her most vehement detractors. Her suspicions had naturally turned toward the outspoken leader of the ultraconservative faction.

Inside an interior conference chamber whose doors were sealed, Sheeana stood like a stern schoolteacher, facing nine of the most prominent dissenters. These women had opposed the ghola project since its inception, disagreeing even more vehemently after Sheeana's decision to restart the work.

Under the blistering scrutiny, Garimi stared back, while her supporters were openly hostile—especially the squat Stuka. "Why would I damage an axlotl tank? It makes no sense."

Within her mind, among the lives in Other Memory, she heard the now-familiar voice of the ancient Serena Butler, sounding horrified. *Killing a child!* Serena was an odd visitor in Other Memory, a woman whose ancient thoughts should not have traveled down the corridors of the generations, and yet she had been with Sheeana for years now.

"You have shown a previous willingness to kill ghola children." Sheeana finally sat down.

Garimi fought to control her trembling. "I attempted to save us before Leto could become a threat, before he could become the Tyrant again. That was all, and I failed. My reasons were well known, and I stand by them. Why would I go to such extremes now? What do I care about Halleck? Or old General Xavier Harkonnen? Even Serena Butler is so far buried in our past that she's little more than the smoke of a legend. Why would I bother with them when the worst gholas—Paul Muad'Dib, Leto II, the fallen Lady Jessica, and Alia the Abomination—already walk among us?" Garimi made a disgusted rumble in her throat. "Your suspicions offend me."

"And the evidence offends *me*."

"Despite our disagreements, we are all Sisters," Garimi insisted.

At first the fleeing Bene Gesserits had had a common cause, a shared goal. But in a matter of months after their escape from Chapterhouse the divisions had begun, power struggles, command questions, a bifurcation of visions. Duncan and Sheeana focused on escaping from the outside Enemy, while Garimi wanted to found a new Keep and train a fresh Bene Gesserit population according to established ways.

How have we changed so dramatically? How did the divisions get so deep?

Sheeana gazed from face to face, looking for indications of guilt, particularly in the eyes. Short, curly-haired Stuka had a line of moisture on her upper lip, one of the indicators of nervousness. But she detected no hatred there, no loathing sufficient to have sparked an act of such brutality. With dismay, she had no choice but to conclude that the perpetrator was not here.

"Then I need your help. The person standing next to any of us could be a saboteur. We must interview everyone. Gather our qualified Truthsayers, and use the last stores of the truthtrance drug." Sheeana rubbed her temples, already dreading the huge task. "Please leave me alone, so I can meditate."

After the nine dissenters departed, Sheeana stood alone, her eyes half closed. The population aboard the *Ithaca* had grown, spread out in the no-ship over the years. Even she wasn't sure how many children were aboard, but she could easily find out. Or so she presumed.

She murmured to Other Memory, "So, Serena Butler—was your murderer in the room? If not them, then who could it be?"

Serena's voice interjected, full of sadness. *A liar can hide behind barricades, but all barricades eventually fall. You will have other opportunities to discover the murderer. There is sure to be more sabotage.*

THE TRUTHSAYERS TESTED each other first.

Twenty-eight qualified Reverend Mothers were gathered from Garimi's followers and from the general population of Sisters. The women did not protest their innocence or complain about the suspicions cast upon them. Instead, they accepted mutual questioning.

Sheeana observed coolly as the women formed triads, two individuals acting as interrogators, the third as the subject. As soon as each subject passed the rigorous questioning, the roles switched, so that everyone was questioned. One by one, the Truthsayers created an ever-growing pool of reliable investigators. Everyone passed the test.

Once the Truthsayers had confirmed each other, Sheeana allowed them to question her. Garimi and her dissident Sisters also faced the challenges and proved their innocence, as did Sheeana's staunch followers. All of them.

Next, with a Truthsayer named Calissa beside her, Sheeana stood before a stiff-backed Duncan Idaho. The very thought of Duncan being a murderer and a saboteur struck her as absurd. Sheeana wouldn't have believed it of anyone on board, and yet three axlotl tanks and three ghola children had been butchered.

But Duncan . . . Standing so close to him, smelling his perspiration, feeling him somehow fill the room with his presence, summoned dangerous memories in her. She had used her own sexual bonding skills to break him free of Murbella. Despite their backgrounds, both knew there had been more to that passionate encounter than just a necessary task. Duncan had been uneasy around her ever since, afraid of what he might succumb to.

But in this situation there was neither romance nor sexual tension, only accusations. "Duncan Idaho, do you know how to bypass the security imagers in the medical center?"

He looked past her, not blinking. "That is within my capabilities."

"Did you commit this terrible act and cover your tracks?"

Now his gaze met hers. "No."

"Did you have any reason to prevent Gurney Halleck, Serena Butler, or Xavier Harkonnen from being born?"

"I did not."

Now that Duncan faced her and a Truthsayer, Sheeana could have asked him questions about their personal relationship to witness his reaction. He would not be able to lie to her or pretend. But she feared his answers. She didn't dare ask.

"He speaks the truth," said Calissa. "He's not our saboteur."

Duncan remained in the room when Bashar Miles Teg came for questioning. Calissa displayed images of the horrific scene from the birthing chamber. "Are you in any way responsible for this, Miles Teg?"

The Bashar stared at the images, looked up at her, turned his gaze to Duncan. "Yes."

Sheeana was so startled that she struggled to think of another question.

"How so?" Duncan asked.

"I am responsible for security aboard this no-ship. Clearly, I failed in my duty. If I had done a better job, this atrocity never would have occurred." He glanced at the troubled Calissa. "Since you asked me in the presence of a Truthsayer, I couldn't lie."

"Very well, Miles. But that isn't what we meant. Did you commit this sabotage or authorize it? Do you know anything about it?"

"No," he answered emphatically.

Dozens of private chambers were set up, where the interrogations could continue unabated. They asked every one of the ghola children, from Paul Atreides all the way to nine-year-old Leto II, and the Truthsayers detected no criminal falsehoods.

Then the Rabbi and all of the Jews.

And every other passenger aboard the no-ship.

Nothing. Not a single person seemed to be connected with the murderous incident. Duncan and Teg used their Mentat skills to check and recheck the lists of people aboard, yet they could find no errors. No one had evaded questioning.

Sitting across from Sheeana in the otherwise empty interrogation room, Duncan steepled his fingers. "There are two possibilities. Either the saboteur is capable of deceiving a Truthsayer . . . or someone we don't know about is hiding aboard the *Ithaca*."

IN WELL ORGANIZED teams, the Bene Gesserit blocked off, then sectioned the no-ship's decks, methodically moving from cabin to cabin and chamber to chamber. But it was a formidable task. The *Ithaca* was the size of a small city, more than a kilometer long and hundreds of decks high, each filled with passages, chambers, and hidden doors.

While trying to guess how someone else might have sneaked aboard, unknown to them, Duncan remembered discovering the mummified remains of Bene Gesserit captives the Honored Matres had tortured to death. That sealed chamber of horrors had gone undetected during the whole time Duncan had been held prisoner inside the ship on the Chapterhouse landing field.

Could someone else—an unknown Honored Matre, perhaps?— have remained hidden aboard for all that time? More than thirty years! It did not seem possible, but the vessel had thousands of work bays, living quarters, corridors, and storage lockers.

Another possibility: During the escape from the planet of the

Handlers, several Face Dancers had crashed small fighters into the no-ship's hull. Mangled bodies had been pulled from the wreckage of those ships . . . but could it all have been a ruse? What if some had actually survived those kamikaze crashes and slipped away? Perhaps one or more Face Dancers were lurking in the untraveled passages of the no-ship, looking for ways to strike.

If so, it was imperative to find them.

Teg had already installed hundreds more surveillance imagers at strategic locations, but that was only a stopgap measure at best. The *Ithaca* was so large that even the best security equipment had thousands of blind spots, and there simply weren't enough personnel to monitor the imagers already in place. It was an impossible task.

Still, they tried.

As Duncan accompanied a group of five searchers, he was reminded of a beating party marching through the tall grass on a big game hunt. He wondered if they would scare a deadly lion out from somewhere in the vastness of the vessel.

Deck after deck was searched, but even with a dozen teams, a complete inspection from the topmost deck to the lowest cargo hold would take a great deal of time, and in the limited searches they conducted, they found nothing. Duncan was exhausted and stressed.

And the murderer—or murderers—remained aboard.

Only two options are before us now: defend ourselves or surrender to the Enemy. But if any of you believes that surrender is a viable option, then we have already lost.

—BASHAR MILES TEG,
speech given before the Pellikor Engagement

Leaving the Obliterators on Ix for the fabricators to study and duplicate, Murbella traveled next to the main Guild shipyards on Junction.

Administrator Rentel Gorus, with long, pale hair and milky eyes, led Murbella among the construction bays, suspensor cranes, conveyors, and assemblers, all of them teeming with workers. The buildings were tall and blocky, the streets serviceable rather than beautiful. Everything on Junction was done on a breathtaking scale. Great lifters hauled components up to the skeletons of gigantic ships, assembling one vessel after another. The air held the bitter tang of hot metal, the chemical residues from welding mismatched components into huge vessels.

Gorus seemed overly proud. "As you can see, we have the facilities you request, Mother Commander, provided the price is right."

"The price will be right." With the New Sisterhood's wealth in melange and soostones, Murbella could meet virtually any demand for payment. "We'll pay you well for every ship you create, every vessel that can be placed into battle, every craft that can stand against the thinking machine army. The end of our civilization is at hand if we don't defeat the thinking machines."

Gorus did not seem intimidated. "Every side in every war believes their conflict is crucial to history. But most often those are delusionary and needlessly alarmist thoughts. This war may be over before you have to resort to such measures."

She scowled. "I don't know what you mean."

"There are other ways to solve the problem. We know that outside forces are sweeping in to many planetary systems. But what do they *want*? To what will they concede? We believe such discussions are worth pursuing." He blinked his milky eyes.

"What sort of trick is the Guild trying to play on us this time?"

"No trick, just sensibility. Regardless of politics, commerce must continue. Wartime desperation inspires technological innovation, but peace promotes profitability in the long run. Trade will go on, no matter who wins the conflict."

Heighliners had long been the luxury ships of the universe; now Murbella forced the Spacing Guild to devote their shipyards to creating the tools of war. For centuries the Guild's commercial fleet had been stable, and demand for trade steadily increased as people returned from the Scattering. Now, however, with Omnius's fleet wiping out whole populations and sending refugees in panicked flight back into the heart of the Old Empire, CHOAM and the Guild were in turmoil.

A hot wind from the assembly bays blew in Murbella's face, burning her nostrils with the acrid smoke of waste chemicals. A shiver coursed down her spine.

"Our common enemy must be rational," Gorus continued. "We have therefore dispatched emissaries and negotiators out to the war zone. We will find the thinking machines and make our proposal. The Guild would prefer to continue its commerce regardless of the outcome of this disagreement."

Murbella gasped. "Are you insane? Omnius seeks the extermination of all humanity. That includes you."

"You overstate your case, Mother Commander. Some of our emissaries will, I believe, achieve our goal."

In the background, blasts of steam curled up from the stone smoke-stacks. She ignored the noise and the smell. "You are a consummate fool, Administrator Gorus. Thinking machines do not follow the rules you assume."

"Be that as it may, we feel obligated to try."

"And what is the result so far?"

"Acceptable losses. Our first emissaries have disappeared, but we will continue the effort. We plan for all eventualities—even disaster." Casually, he led her out onto a broad, open field under the half-assembled hulk of a huge ship. "Thus, we are comfortable with extending certain beneficial terms to the New Sisterhood. You have always been a valued customer, but the order you submitted is massive. Even under wartime conditions, you have asked for more ships than we are able to provide."

"Then offer your workers more incentive."

"Ahh, Mother Commander, but will you provide enough incentive to *us?*"

She bristled. "How can you think solely of profits when the fate of the human race is at stake?"

"Profits determine all our fates." The Administrator gestured casually, as if to encompass the huge assembly of the ships around him.

"We'll pay what you demand, and the Guild Bank will offer us loans if necessary. We need those ships, Gorus."

He smiled coolly. "Your credit is good, but we must address another problem. We do not have enough Guild Navigators to man so many new ships. All of the vessels we build for you will have to be equipped with Ixian mathematical compilers, rather than traditional Navigators. Is that acceptable?"

"Provided the ships function as we require, I have no objection. We don't have time to develop and train another population of Navigators."

Obviously pleased, Gorus rubbed his hands together. "Of late, Navigators have proven somewhat intractable, due to the shortage of spice—a shortage which your Sisterhood created, Mother Commander. It is because of you that we had to look for alternatives to Navigators."

"I have no fondness for Navigators, or for your obscene profits. I don't care how the Guild accomplishes it, but we need those ships."

"Of course, Mother Commander, and we shall provide what you wish."

"That is precisely the answer I need."

What is the advantage of prescience if it serves only to reveal our own downfall?

—NAVIGATOR EDRIK,
message to the Oracle of Time

The Guild bureaucrats had the audacity to call Edrik's Heighliner back to the shipyards on Junction. Staring ahead with his milky eyes, Administrator Gorus blithely announced that the Heighliner would be fitted with one of the new Ixian mathematical compilers. "Our spice supply line is undependable. We must be certain each vessel can operate safely if its Navigator fails."

Over the past two years, more and more Guildships had been outfitted with the hated artificial controls. Mathematical compilers! No simple engine or tool could adequately complete the phenomenally complex projections that a Navigator performed. Edrik and his fellows had evolved through immersion in spice, their prescient vision strengthened through the power of melange. There could be no mechanical substitute.

Nevertheless, Edrik had no choice but to accept a team of qualified and arrogant Ixian workers who shuttled up from the Junction shipyards. The tight-lipped men boarded the Heighliner under the watchful eyes of the Guild, with their smug expressions, compiler machines, and dangerous curiosity.

In his tank, Edrik was concerned that they would snoop around under the pretext of completing their installation. The Navigator faction could not risk these men finding Waff's laboratory, the genetically altered sandtrout, and the small mutated worms he was producing in his tanks. The Tleilaxu man claimed to be making excellent progress, and his work must remain a secret.

Therefore, when the Ixian installers were all safely aboard, Edrik simply folded space, informing no one in the shipyards where he was going. He carried his empty Heighliner far out into an isolated wasteland between solar systems, and there ejected the disbelieving Ixians, along with their accursed navigation machines, out into the cold vacuum.

Problem solved.

His acts would be discovered eventually, but that could not be avoided. Edrik was a Navigator. Mere human Administrators had no hold over him.

Edrik suspected that the devious Administrator and his faction saw the melange crisis as an opportunity to shift the Guild's burden away from problematic Navigators; they did not really want a new source of spice. Gorus was now an absolute ally, if not a puppet, of the Ixians. Edrik had seen the economic projections and knew that the Administrators considered navigation machines to be more cost-effective than Navigators—and more easily controlled.

With the Ixians and their machines happily ejected, Edrik knew it was time to call another meeting with his fellow Navigators; they needed to receive fresh guidance from the Oracle of Time. Because Junction and several other Guild planets were already compromised by Gorus and his cronies, Edrik chose a place that no one but Navigators could find.

Once they had been shown how, they could fold their Guildships deep into another dimension, a nontraditional universe where the Oracle occasionally went on personal, incomprehensible explorations.

Ignited by the light of seven newborn stars, the cosmic gases swirling around his giant ship seemed inflamed. The nebula shone pink and green and blue, depending on which window of the spectrum Edrik chose to look through. The misty curtains put on a spectacular show, a great whirlpool of ionized gases—and a perfect place to hide.

When the ships gathered, the Navigators were in quite an uproar, and their numbers were less than Edrik had hoped. So far, four hundred Heighliners had been decommissioned, their parts salvaged to construct new no-ships that relied on artificial guidance systems. Seventeen Navigators had died horribly, their tanks emptied. Edrik learned that six of his fellows had likewise murdered the Ixian engineers rather than allow them to install mathematical compilers. Four Navigators had simply disconnected the machines, and the onboard Ixian teams failed to realize that their vaunted systems were no longer functional.

"We require melange," he transmitted. "By the grace of spice, we see through folded space."

"But the Sisterhood has denied it to us," one of the other Navigators said.

"They have spice. They spend spice. But they do not give it to us."

"The witches give it to the Guild for ships . . . but the Administrators have cut us off. We are betrayed by our own."

"They control the spice."

"But they do not control us," Edrik insisted. "If we find our own source of spice, we will not need the Administrators. This is for the survival of Navigators, not simply for commerce. We have struggled with this problem for years. The Tleilaxu ghola has finally come up with a solution."

"A new source of spice? Has it been proven?"

"Is anything fully proven? If this goes well, we can destroy the corrupt old Spacing Guild and supercede them."

"We must speak to the Oracle."

Edrik waved his tiny, misshapen hands. "The Oracle already knows our problem."

"The Oracle has not deigned to help us," said another.

"The Oracle has her own reasons."

Drifting in his tank, Edrik acknowledged their conundrum. "I have spoken to her myself, but perhaps all of us together can urge her to respond. Let us summon the Oracle."

Using their spice-enhanced minds, the numerous Navigators shot a message arrow through the folds of space. Edrik knew they had no way to coerce the Oracle of Time—or the Oracle Infinity, as she was sometimes called—to respond, but he sensed her presence, and her deep uneasiness.

With a silent flash, a trapdoor opened in the vacuum, and the ancient container arrived. It was not quite a ship, for the Oracle could travel anywhere she wished, mentally folding space without the help of Holtzman engines.

Even in that small and nonthreatening enclosure, Edrik knew full well the power and immensity of that highly advanced mind. As a human, Norma Cenva had first discovered the connection between spice and prescience. She had developed the technology of folding space, had created the incomprehensible equations that Tio Holtzman had taken as his own.

Though the Oracle used no known transmitting device, her words were loud and implacable in their minds. "Your concerns are parochial. I must find the wayward no-ship. I must determine where Duncan Idaho has taken it, before the Enemy intercepts it."

The Oracle often chose her own esoteric goals without explaining them. One of the Navigators asked, "Why is the no-ship so important, Oracle?"

"Because the Enemy wishes to have it. Our great foe is Omnius—except that he is as changed from his former computer evermind as I am evolved from the human I once was. The machines have completed their high-order projections. The evermind knows he must have the Kwisatz Haderach, just as I know the Enemy must *not* have him." The Oracle let the silence hang in space like a hole, before she added a stinging rebuke. "Your appetite for spice is not the priority. I must find the ship."

Abruptly discontinuing the debate, she winked out again and vanished into her own place in an alternate universe.

Edrik and the gathered Navigators were shocked by her response. Navigators were dying, spice was dwindling away to nothing, Administrators were trying to overthrow the Guild—and the Oracle simply wanted to find a lost ship?

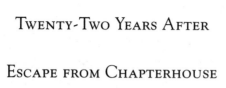

Twenty-Two Years After

Escape from Chapterhouse

These new Face Dancers cannot be detected by DNA analysis or any other form of cellular scrutiny. As far as we know, only a Tleilaxu Master can tell the difference.

—Bene Gesserit report on human mutation

Though the Ixian specialists had studied the Obliterators for half a year, they still hadn't given the Sisterhood an answer. Murbella brooded in her offices on Chapterhouse, waiting. The news seemed to worsen with each passing day.

She received regular updates on the depredations of the thinking-machine fleet. The powerful Enemy ships moved inexorably through the fringe systems like a crashing tidal wave, drowning world after world. Another ten planets evacuated or contaminated by plagues, another ten lost, and more refugees flooded into the Old Empire.

A network of Sisters met with any refugee ships that came from the battleground systems. Taking statements from groups of survivors, they compiled an exhaustive three-dimensional map of the movements of the machine fleet. The pattern seeped like a bloodstain through the galaxy.

In a single desperate stand, nineteen Sisterhood no-ships expended their last three Obliterators to destroy a whole battle group of oncoming machine ships and temporarily prevent the annihilation of one human-inhabited system. In the end, though, even that devastation amounted to only a brief delay; the machine fleet came back with greater strength and crushed the world after all, killing every inhabitant. With the last Obliterators gone, the New Sisterhood was woefully underdefended.

Unless the Ixians could help. *What was taking them so long?*

Finally, a lone Ixian engineer came to Chapterhouse to deliver his news. When he said he would speak to no one but the Mother Commander herself, escorts brought him to the main Keep. Waiting on her imposing throne in front of the dust-streaked, segmented window, Murbella could respect the man for bypassing bureaucracy and getting to the core of the matter.

The engineer's face was bland and unmemorable, his brown hair closely cropped, his demeanor unassuming. He had a peculiar, unpleasant odor about him, perhaps from chemical residue or the machinery of Ix's underground fabrication plants. He bowed perfunctorily and stepped in front of her. "Our best engineers and scientists have deconstructed and analyzed the sample Obliterators you provided."

Murbella leaned forward, giving him her full attention. "And you can reproduce them?"

"Better than that, Mother Commander." His confident smile held no warmth at all, was simply an imitation of a facial expression. "Our fabricators understand the underlying concept of the weapon, and are able to concentrate its destructive power. Previously, it required several Honored Matre battleships deploying multiple Obliterators to kill a planet. With our enhanced weapon a single ship can launch enough firepower to do what was done to Rakis." He gave a perfunctory shrug. "Imagine what such an energy release would do to Enemy battleships."

Murbella tried to conceal her delight. "We need as many as you can produce. Instruct your factories to begin work on these weapons immediately." She kept her voice hard, letting her impatience seep through. "But why did you need to see me in person, when you could easily have sent a message with this information?" Her lips quirked. "Do you require a pat on the back? Shall I give you my applause? There, you have it."

The Ixian engineer remained bland. "Before we begin, Mother Commander, there is the matter of payment. Chief Fabricator Sen has instructed me to inform you that Ix must be compensated if we are to pull our profitable manufacturing centers off-line in order to create these Obliterators for your war."

"My war? All humans must share the burden of the cost."

"Unfortunately, we disagree. The only payment we will accept is spice. And the only source of spice is your New Sisterhood."

"We have other ways to pay you." Murbella tried to conceal her alarm. She wasn't sure their fledgling spice operations could supply the necessary amount. And why would Ix care about spice, in particular? Sisterhood accounts in Guild banks could be drained; CHOAM could be convinced to supply important commodities; and soostones were more valuable than ever, especially since the recent turmoil on Buzzell.

When she offered these alternatives, though, the Ixian fabricator shook his head. "I have no flexibility in these negotiations, Mother Commander. It must be melange. No other coin will do."

She ground her teeth, but had no patience for further delay. "Spice it is, then. Get started."

DEPARTING FROM CHAPTERHOUSE, Khrone the Face Dancer felt content. The New Sisterhood had bowed to his demands, as he had known they would. Back on Ix, he had the ear of the Chief Fabricator, and Face Dancer replacements already controlled all key Ixian manufacturing centers.

Khrone found it ironic to demand payment in spice, since Ix had devoted so much technological effort into installing navigation machines in Guildships. Thanks to the mathematical compilers, melange was basically obsolete when it came to folding space, and the Navigators were fading swiftly.

But by insisting on such a huge payment in spice alone, and then hoarding the commodity, Khrone would remove a large amount of it from the market, making it even rarer. That, in turn, would force more and more ships to convert to the Ixian navigation compilers, because the Guild could not support the melange needs of their Navigators.

Before long, with no way of supporting their own Navigators, the whole Spacing Guild would fall under Khrone's control. He had worked it all out in exquisite detail.

In the meantime, he and his disguised workers would make it look as if they were providing everything the Sisterhood demanded. Let them fight useless battles while the real war was already won, right under their noses! Mother Commander Murbella would be quite satisfied—up until the moment a curtain of darkness fell on humankind. Permanently.

Every man makes errors. When a security chief makes them, though, there are consequences. People die.

—THUFIR HAWAT,

the original

The Bashar and his protégé marched down the corridors toward the no-ship's life-support center. "I am deeply ashamed, Thufir. It has been almost a year, and I am incapable of finding a blatant saboteur and murderer."

The young Hawat looked up at him, clearly idolizing the military genius. "We have a limited pool of suspects, and a discrete area in which he—or she—could hide. We've done everything possible, Bashar."

"And yet the saboteur is here, somewhere." Teg did not slow his pace. "Therefore, we have not done everything possible, because we still haven't found the person responsible. The fact that there have been no further murders does not mean we can let down our guard. I am convinced our saboteur is still among us."

The *Ithaca* was constantly being searched and monitored. Additional surveillance imagers had been installed, but the culprit seemed to have an affinity for hiding. Teg suspected that the work of the saboteur went well beyond the murder of the gholas and the axlotl tanks. In recent months, many ship's systems had inexplicably failed—too many to be caused by random events and natural breakdowns. "Our adversary is still at work."

The Thufir ghola raised his smooth chin in a display of pride. He was strong and gangly with a heavy brow; he had let his hair grow shaggy. "Then you and I will find him."

Teg smiled at Thufir. "As soon as you regain his memories and experience as a warrior Mentat and Master of Assassins, you will be a formidable ally."

"I'm formidable now." Thufir had already proved his worth during the tense escape from the Handlers, risking his own life to help the Rabbi get away from Face Dancers in league with the Enemy. Teg believed the young ghola had the potential to do much more.

Varying his pattern, he insisted on an exhausting round of daily security inspections while he left Duncan Idaho on the navigation bridge, ever vigilant for the Enemy's glowing net.

The *Ithaca* continued to wander in empty space. At first, their voyage had simply been to get away from the Enemy hunters. Duncan had been forced to remain hidden behind the ship's veiling no-field, since the old man and woman seemed to want him in particular. Now, after more than two decades, the population aboard had increased, and children were growing up and being taught necessary skills without ever having set foot on a planetary surface.

Despite all the worlds settled during the Scattering, habitable systems seemed sparse indeed. For the first time, Teg wondered how many ships of refugees fleeing from the Famine Times had simply died without ever finding their destination. The *Ithaca* had no Guild Navigator; only pure chance brought them within range of planets. So far, they had encountered only two places that might have supported a new colony: one Honored Matre world that had been completely wiped out by Enemy plagues, and the planet of the insidious Handlers.

Nevertheless, with its recyclers, greenhouses, and algae tanks, the aging *Ithaca* should have been able to sustain the present number of passengers for centuries, if necessary. They—and their successors—could effectively stay onboard forever and never stop running. *Is that our fate?* Teg asked himself. But because of leakages, losses, and "accidents," the passengers had cause for concern. Sooner or later, they would need to replenish their reserves.

Thinking of resources, the Bashar took a side corridor to the fermentation bins and adjacent algae-growth tanks. Grown in the vaulted, humid chamber, the biomass provided raw material for the food-manufacturing units. A prime vulnerability.

As he opened a hatch, Teg caught the rich, marshy smell of compost and algae. They climbed metal steps to a catwalk and looked down into the cylindrical vat filled with hairy green slime. The stinking wet mass of fecund algae digested anything organic, growing large amounts of edible, rather unpalatable, material that could be converted into better-flavored foods. Ceiling fans whirred, drawing the odorous air upward through filters and into the intricate set of ducts that acted as the no-ship's circulatory system. After taking samples and testing the chemical balance of the tanks, Teg concluded that everything was in order. No sign of sabotage since his last inspection.

The serious young man tagged along beside him. "I am not a Mentat yet, sir, but I have been giving the sabotage problem a great deal of thought."

With raised eyebrows Teg turned to his protégé. "And do you have a first-order approximation?"

"I have an idea." Thufir did not try to conceal his anger. "I suggest you have a long talk with the Yueh ghola. Perhaps he knows more than he has admitted."

"Yueh is only thirteen. He does not have his memories back."

"Maybe the weakness is in his blood. Bashar, we know that *someone* committed the sabotage." The young man sounded disappointed in himself for allowing it to happen. "Even the real Thufir Hawat didn't find the traitor in House Atreides before he betrayed us to the Harkonnens. That traitor was Yueh."

"I'll keep it in mind."

Back in the corridors again, the two passed a sick-looking old Scytale and his clone emerging from their quarters. Because they isolated themselves and lived with odd traditions and behavior, the Tleilaxu were natural suspects, but Teg had found no evidence against them. In fact, he believed the real saboteur would be careful to blend in perfectly and draw no attention at all. It was the only way he could have remained hidden for so long.

Two pregnant women passed by them in the corridor, chatting as they continued on their way. Both were part of Sheeana's conventional breeding program to maintain the population of the Sisterhood, providing an adequate genetic base should the splinter group ever find a place to settle.

Finally, Teg and Thufir reached the cavernous, humming engine chamber, and entered the large aft compartment through a round doorway. Apparently safe but lost again since their last passage through foldspace, the *Ithaca* drifted, though Duncan insisted on keeping the Holtzman engines ready at all times.

Thick clearplaz separated the Bashar and Thufir from a trio of power plants that fed the machines. Walkways laced the outside of an explosion-proof plaz chamber that contained the side-by-side engines. The two stared up at the giant mechanisms that could fold space. A true miracle of technology. All of the readings remained within nominal range. Again, no sign of sabotage.

"We're still missing something," he mused. "I can feel it."

Once before, at the end of the Battle of Junction, Teg had failed to see the terrible and deadly "Weapon" that the Honored Matres had held in reserve. That mistake had nearly lost him the entire war. He considered their situation now. *What deadly device will I fail to see this time?*

Humanity has a great genetic compass that constantly guides us onward. Our task is to keep it always pointed in the right direction.

—REVEREND MOTHER ANGELOU,
famed breeding mistress

Wellington Yueh had a powerful need to be forgiven. The blank spot in his mind was filled with guilt. He was just a ghola and only thirteen, but he knew he had done terrible things. His own history clung to him like tar to his shoe.

In his first life, he had broken his Suk conditioning. He had failed his wife Wanna by allowing the Harkonnens to use her as a pawn and had betrayed Duke Leto, bringing about the Atreides downfall on Arrakis.

After studying records of his prior existence, learning in painful detail what he had done, Yueh tried to find solace in considering the Orange Catholic Bible, along with other ancient religions, sects, philosophies, and interpretations that had developed over the millennia. The oft-repeated doctrine of Original Sin—so unfair!—was a particular thorn in his side. Yueh could have made a coward's excuse that he couldn't remember and therefore didn't deserve blame, but that was not the path to redemption. He had to turn elsewhere.

Jessica was the only one who could forgive him.

The eight ghola children in Sheeana's project had been raised and trained together. Because of their individual personalities they had formed personal bonds and friendships. Even before they knew the history that should tear them apart, Yueh had tried to be a friend to Jessica.

He had read the journals and instructional writings of the original Lady Jessica, bound concubine to the Duke Leto Atreides. She'd also been a Reverend Mother, an exile, the mother of Muad'Dib, and the grandmother of the Tyrant. That long-dead Jessica had been a strong woman, a role model despite how the Bene Gesserit reviled her for her flaw, her weakness. *Love.*

Together, the gholas now faced a far greater enemy than the Harkonnens. When Jessica's memories were finally awakened, would the shared threat be sufficient to keep her from wanting to murder him? He had read her own words, as written down by Princess Irulan, expressing her poignant agony of grief: "Yueh! Yueh! Yueh! A million deaths were not enough for Yueh!"

Yes, she was the only one who could offer him any hope of forgiveness. With a clean slate and an open heart, he prayed that it was possible for him to lead an honorable life this time.

Jessica often occupied herself in the main conservatory, tending the plants that served as a supplemental food source for the hundreds aboard. She had an affinity for the greenhouse work and was happy to be around the fertile dirt, the misting irrigators, the fleshy green leaves, and sweet-scented flowers. With her bronze hair and oval face, noble and young, she looked exquisitely beautiful. How she and Duke Leto must have loved each other long ago . . . until Yueh destroyed it all.

Jessica looked up from the flowers and lush herbs to focus haunted eyes on Yueh.

He said, "Do you mind the company?"

"Not yours. It's refreshing to be with someone who doesn't blame me for things I don't remember doing."

"I hope you'll grant me the same consideration, my Lady."

"Please don't call me that, Wellington. At least not yet. I can't be the Lady Jessica until I . . . well, until I become the Lady Jessica."

He tried to guess the reasons for her gloomy mood. "Has Garimi been haranguing you again?"

"Some Bene Gesserits won't forgive me for having gone against the strict commands of the Sisterhood, for betraying their breeding program."

She seemed to be reciting something she had read. "The consequences of that brought down an empire and subjected the human race to thousands of years of tyrannical rule and many more centuries of privation." She let out a bitter laugh. "In fact, if your actions had actually resulted in the death of Paul and me, maybe Bene Gesserit histories would describe you as a hero."

"I am no hero, Jessica." To his credit, the original Yueh had given her and Paul the means to survive in the desert after the Harkonnens stormed Arrakeen. He had facilitated their escape, but was that enough for redemption? Could it possibly be?

She moved on, smelling the flowers, checking the moist soil. She had a habit of running her fingertips along the leaves, touching the undersides.

Yueh followed her as she walked through a small grove of dwarf citrus trees. Overhead, the segmented panes of the filtered windows showed only distant starlight and no nearby sun. "If they hate us so much, why did the Sisters bring us back?"

Her expression was one of bitter amusement. "Bene Gesserits have a terrible habit, Wellington: Even if they know a hook is hidden inside the juicy worm, they'll still bite. They always think they can avoid traps that get the rest of us."

"But you're a Bene Gesserit yourself."

"Not anymore . . . or not yet."

Yueh touched his own smooth, unmarked forehead. "We're starting over, Jessica. Blank slates. Look at me. The first Yueh broke his Suk conditioning—but *I* was born without the diamond tattoo. Entirely unblemished."

"Maybe that means some things can be erased."

"*Can* they? We gholas were raised for one purpose: to become who we once were. But are we anyone in our own right? Or are gholas simply tools, temporary tenants living in houses on borrowed time until the rightful owners return? What if we don't want those old lives? Is it right for Sheeana and the others to force them upon us? What about *us* as we are right now?"

Abruptly the gridwork of interlocking solar panes overhead seemed to glow brighter, as if the system had absorbed a wash of outside energy.

The rows of densely arranged plants inside the greenhouse chamber became more defined, as if his eyes had suddenly become much more sensitive. Overlaying the whole chamber he saw a complex mesh of thin iridescent lines, resolving and focusing.

Something was happening—something Yueh had never experienced before. The lines became visible all around them, like fine netting that drifted through the air itself. They crackled with energy.

"Jessica, what is this? Do you see it?"

"A web . . . a net." She caught her breath. "It's what Duncan Idaho claims to see!"

Yueh's heart lurched. *The hunters?*

A loud security klaxon went off, accompanied by Duncan's voice. "Prepare for activation of Holtzman engines!"

Whenever the no-ship folded space, unguided by a Navigator, they risked a disaster. Until now, Duncan's warnings had been unsupported by outside witnesses, though the Handlers had proved that the threat from the mysterious Enemy was real.

From the ship's corridors, Yueh heard the shouts of people running to emergency stations. The gossamer stranglehold grew brighter and more powerful, surrounding and infiltrating the whole ship. Surely, everyone could see this!

He felt a shudder through the deck, a disorientation and a *slipping* as the immense ship folded space. Staring through the conservatory dome, he saw star systems, swirling shapes and colors . . . as if the contents of the universe had been placed in a mixing bowl and stirred.

Suddenly the *Ithaca* cruised along elsewhere, far from the snares. Duncan's calm voice came over the intercom. "We are safe again, for the moment."

"Why did we see the net now and never before?" Jessica asked.

Yueh rubbed his chin, his thoughts in turmoil. "Perhaps the Enemy is using a different sort of net—a stronger one. Or maybe they are testing new ways of tracking and snaring us."

We must never voice doubt. We must believe utterly that we can win this struggle against our Enemy. But in my darkest times alone in my quarters, I always wonder: Is this truly faith, or is it mere foolishness?

—MOTHER COMMANDER MURBELLA,
private Chapterhouse Archives

When Murbella's small Missionaria Aggressiva council gathered again, the meeting was tense. In the past year, the Sisterhood had sent seven Sheeana surrogates to refugee camps in order to rally the fighters. The counterfeit Sheeanas had their work cut out for them, convincing fanatics to stand firm in the face of certain defeat.

The seemingly unstoppable Enemy warships proliferated like the heads of a hydra; no matter how many vessels the humans destroyed, more and more appeared. Given millennia to prepare for his final conquest, Omnius had left nothing to chance. The dots on the star charts showed one planet after another falling under the onslaught of thinking machines.

Murbella sat in a hard and uncomfortable seat at the end of the table; most of the others selected furry chairdogs. At the head of the table, Bashar Janess Idaho waited at attention, ready to deliver her report.

"I have news."

"Good or bad?" Murbella dreaded the answer.

"Judge for yourself."

Her daughter looked haggard, weary, and considerably older than her years. Having undergone the Spice Agony and extensive Bene Gesserit training, Janess had the ability to slow her body's changes, not for the sake of appearances, but to keep herself strong and limber. The constant fighting required it. Even so, the unending crisis was taking its toll. Murbella noticed a scar on her daughter's left cheek and a burn mark on her arm.

The female Bashar's words were unemotional, but Murbella could feel the turmoil in her clipped voice. "Even before the first Enemy battleships were seen in the Jhibraith system, the machines sent scout probes to disseminate plagues. The people of Jhibraith had already called for an evacuation, but once the first signs of disease appeared, the Guild turned their ships around and refused to come closer. One Heighliner had to be quarantined. Fortunately, the plague was contained within seven isolated frigates inside its hold. All passengers aboard those frigates died, but the rest were saved."

"What about the planet itself?" Murbella asked.

"The plague spread rapidly across all continents. As expected. The current viral strains are far worse than anything previously encountered, more deadly than even the legendary plagues during the Butlerian Jihad."

Laera skimmed a Ridulian crystal sheet in front of her. "Jhibraith has a population of three hundred twenty-eight million."

"Not anymore," said Kiria.

Janess locked her fingers together, as if to draw strength from her own grip. "One of our Sheeana surrogates was on Jhibraith. As soon as the Guild quarantined the planet, the faux Sheeana rose to her calling and spoke to crowd after crowd as the plague spread. They knew they would all die. They knew the thinking machine forces were on their way. But she convinced them that if they must die, they should die as heroes."

"But if the Guildships had already departed, how could they fight?" Kiria sounded skeptical. "By throwing pebbles?"

"Jhibraith had its own in-system frigates, cargo vessels, and transport runners, none of them equipped with Holtzman engines or no-fields. As the disease cut people down, survivors raced to create a homegrown military force that might stand against Omnius. The people had to work faster than the epidemic killed them off." She forced her lips into a cold, hard smile as she continued her report.

"Our false Sheeana was like a demon herself. I know for a fact that she went five days without sleeping, for the records show she appeared again and again at different cities and factories, rallying the citizenry, forcing them to crawl to their assembly stations if necessary. Nobody bothered with quarantines, since everyone was already infected. As people died in the factories, their bodies were dragged out to mass burial pits and huge bonfires. Others took their places at workstations.

"Even when the Enemy fleet surrounded the world, people did not pause. Then our Sheeana disappeared." Janess looked around the table, lowered her voice. "Afterward, I learned from a coded Bene Gesserit signal that our surrogate contracted the disease, and died from it."

Murbella was startled. "*Died?* How can that be? Any Reverend Mother knows how to fight off infection."

"That requires great concentration and significant physical resources. Our Sheeana had depleted her reserves. If she'd rested for a day or two, she might have rallied her strength and driven off the disease. But she kept going and going, using up whatever energy reserves she had. Knowing Jhibraith was doomed, that the invading machine armies would destroy her if the plague did not, Sheeana never slackened in her efforts."

Old Accadia nodded. "She had pushed the people into a fanatical fervor. No doubt she realized that if they saw her weakened and dying, they would lose their resolve. She was wise to remove herself from public view."

Janess's thin smile showed true admiration. "As soon as her symptoms began to manifest, Sheeana delivered one last grand speech, telling them she would now ascend to heaven. Then she isolated herself and died alone so that no one could see the horrific plague take its toll on her."

"A marvelous and brave story for the archival histories." Accadia pursed her withered lips. "Her sacrifice will not be forgotten."

"If anyone still studies the histories after this," Kiria mumbled.

"And what of the subsequent fight on Jhibraith?" Murbella asked. "Did the people defend themselves?"

"When the Enemy came, the people fought like ancient berserkers, to the last man and woman. Nothing could stop them. They met the Enemy fleet with ship after ship flown by grandfathers, teenagers, mothers, husbands, and even criminals released from detention centers. All fought and died bravely. Their sheer ferocity drove back the machines. Even with no defined military force, the people of Jhibraith destroyed more than a thousand Enemy vessels."

Reality forced ice into Murbella's voice. "My enthusiasm is tempered by the knowledge that even after losing a thousand vessels, the thinking machines have countless others to throw against us."

"Still, if all planets fought like that, there might be a chance for humankind to survive," Janess pointed out. "The species would be preserved."

Choosing her moment to pounce, Kiria peeled crystal sheets from another set of reports, then propped an image projector in the center of the table. The chairdog shifted subtly and compliantly to accommodate her movements. "This new report shows why we can't count on all planets. We are being attacked by a rot from within, as well as the outside fleet."

Murbella frowned. "Where did you get this?"

"Sources." Wearing a smug expression, the former Honored Matre activated the projector. "While we face the thinking machines head-on, a more devious opponent undermines us from within."

The image resolved to show a mob scene. "This is Belos IV, but such occurrences have been documented elsewhere. Sparked by helplessness in the face of the approaching Enemy fleet, brushfire wars and political struggles are starting on planet after planet. People are afraid. When their leaders don't tell them what they want to hear, they riot, overthrow their prime ministers, and prop others in their place. More often than not, they depose the new leaders as well."

"We know this." Murbella looked at Janess, who remained rigidly at attention at the front of the table. She wished her daughter would sit down. On the images, the citizens of Belos IV had risen up against their governor, who had advocated surrender to the oncoming thinking machines. "Obviously, the people didn't want to hear such a message. Why is this relevant?"

Kiria jabbed a sharp-nailed finger at the image. "Observe!"

When the crowd attacked the middle-aged leader, he fought remarkably well, using skills and speed rarely demonstrated by any bureaucrat. While Murbella watched, she decided the governor must have acquired some sort of special training. His combat methods were unusual and effective, but the mob far outnumbered him. They dragged him through the streets to the balcony of the governor's palace and threw him off onto the flagstones far below. As he lay still, the howling, cheering mob backed away. The images drew in closer. The dead governor shifted and paled. His face became sunken and scarecrowish, somehow unformed. A Face Dancer!

"We always suspected the new Face Dancers had questionable loyalties. They allied themselves with Honored Matres and turned against the old Tleilaxu. We found them among the rebel whores on Gammu and Tleilax, and now it appears that the threat is even worse than we suspected. Listen to the governor's words. He advocated surrender to the thinking machines. Who are the Face Dancers really working for?"

Murbella reached the obvious conclusion and dragged her sharp gaze like a serrated knife across the other Sisters. "The new Face Dancers are puppets of Omnius, and have infiltrated our populace. They are far superior to the old ones, able to resist almost any Bene Gesserit technique. We always wondered how the Lost Tleilaxu could have created them, when their skills were so inferior to those the old Masters demonstrated. It did not seem possible."

Laera said coldly, "It is possible if the thinking machines helped to create them, then sent them back among Tleilaxu returning from the Scattering."

"A first wave of scouts and infiltrators." Kiria nodded. "How far have they spread? Could there be Face Dancers among *us*, undetected by Truthsayers?"

Accadia scowled. "A frightening thought, if we have no way of exposing these new Face Dancers. From what I can tell, their mimicry is perfect."

"Nothing is perfect," Murbella said. "Even thinking machines have flaws."

Without humor, Kiria said, "Oh, we can identify them easily enough. Kill them, and Face Dancers revert to their blank state."

"So you suggest we simply kill everyone?"

"That's what the Enemy intends to do anyway."

Restless, Murbella stood up. She could remain here on Chapterhouse with the other anxious Sisters, receive reports for another year, listen to summaries, and plot the advance of the thinking machines on a map, as if it were some kind of war game. Meanwhile, the Ixian engineers struggled to build weapons equivalent to the Obliterators, and the Guild shipyards worked to produce thousands of ships, all of them equipped with mathematical compilers.

But the crisis went far beyond internal politics and power struggles. She decided to go out there herself and travel among the worlds on the edge of the war zone, not as Mother Commander, but as a keen observer. She would let a council of Reverend Mothers run the everyday activities here on Chapterhouse, dealing with bureaucratic matters and doling out spice rations to the Guild in order to ensure their cooperation.

When Murbella announced her intent, Laera cried, "Mother Commander, that's not possible. We need you here—there's so much to do!"

"I represent more than the New Sisterhood. Since no one else will step up to the plate, I am responsible for the whole human race." She sighed. "Somebody has to be."

Our no-ship holds many secrets, yes, but not nearly the number we hold inside ourselves.

—LETO II,

the ghola

L eto II and Thufir Hawat had never known each other in their original lifetimes. To them, that was not a disadvantage. It left them free to form a friendship without any expectations or preconceptions.

Nine-year-old Leto hurried ahead, down the corridor. "Come with me, Thufir. Now that nobody's watching, I can show you a special place."

"Another one? Do you spend all your days exploring instead of studying?"

"If you're going to be deputy chief of security, you need to know everything about the *Ithaca*. Maybe we'll find your saboteur down here." Leto turned sharply right, dropped into a small emergency lift, then paused at a dim, lower deck, where everything seemed larger and darker. He led Thufir to a sealed hatch that was posted with warnings and restrictions in half a dozen languages. Despite the locks, he opened it with barely a pause.

Thufir looked puzzled, even a little offended. "How did you bypass security so easily?"

"This ship is old, and systems break down all the time. Nobody even knows this one failed." He ducked into the low passageway.

The tunnel on the other side was a whistling, cool air channel. Up ahead the roaring grew louder, and the wind became powerful. Thufir sniffed. "Where does it go?"

"To an air-exchange filtration system." The passages were smooth and curving—like worm tunnels. A shiver brushed across Leto's skin, perhaps from a memory of when he had been joined with numerous sandtrout, from when he was the God Emperor of Dune, the Tyrant. . . .

The two reached the central recyclers where large fans drove the air through thick curtains of filter mats, scrubbing out particulates and purifying the atmosphere. Breezes tugged at the boys' hair. Ahead, sheets of filtration material blocked further passage. The lungs of the ship, replenishing and redistributing oxygen.

Recently, Thufir had begun to mark his lips with a cranberry-red stain. As the pair stood in the bowels of the ship, listening to the roaring wind, Leto finally asked, "Why do you do that to your mouth?"

Self-consciously, the fourteen-year-old rubbed his lips. "My original used the sapho drug, which made stains like these. The Bashar wants me to live the part. He says he's preparing to awaken my memories." Thufir didn't sound entirely pleased with the situation. "Sheeana has been talking about forcing me to remember. She has some special technique to trigger a ghola's awakening."

"Aren't you excited at the prospect? Thufir Hawat was a great man."

The other boy remained preoccupied and troubled. "It's not that, Leto. I really don't want my memories back, but Sheeana and the Bashar have their minds made up."

"That's why you were created." Leto was baffled. "Why wouldn't you want your past life? The Master of Assassins would not be afraid of the ordeal."

"I'm not afraid. I'd just rather be the person I choose to become, and not emerge fully formed. I don't feel I've earned it."

"Trust me, they'll make you earn it, once you become the real Thufir again."

"I *am* the real Thufir! Or do you doubt that, too?"

Thinking of the restless worm that crouched inside him, aware of all the atrocious things he would soon remember, Leto understood completely.

By following the same beliefs and making the same decisions, one wears Life's path into a circular rut, going nowhere, accomplishing nothing, making no progress. With God's help, though, we can turn a sharp corner in the circle and achieve enlightenment.

—The Cant of the Shariat

At last Waff was ready to release his new worms, and Buzzell was a convenient ocean planet on Edrik's standard trade route. A perfect test bed.

The giant vessel carried merchants who traded in soostones. Earlier, when Honored Matres had conquered Buzzell and killed most of the exiled Reverend Mothers, the whores had taken the soostone wealth for themselves. Since then, few of the aquatic gems had been traded on the galactic market, which made their value skyrocket. Now that the New Sisterhood had recaptured Buzzell, soostone production was up again. The witches ran tightly regimented operations there and kept smugglers at bay, thus maintaining stable but high prices for the stones. With mercenary armies to protect them, CHOAM merchants began to sell large quantities of the gems, reaping profits before a glut drove prices down again. A temporary market fluctuation.

Though pretty and desirable, soostones were not *necessary*. Melange, on the other hand, was vital—as the Navigators well knew. Waff knew that his experiments would eventually produce far more wealth than these undersea baubles could ever represent. Soon, if his expectations were met, Buzzell would be home to something far more interesting than baubles. . . .

The Heighliner appeared above the liquid sapphire world, where tiny islands dotted the expansive ocean. Buzzell's oceans were deep and fertile, a large zone where the genetically altered worms would thrive, provided they survived their initial baptism.

The Tleilaxu Master paced the cold metal floor of his laboratory chamber. Soon, Edrik would inform him that the commercial lighters and cargo transports had disembarked for the island outposts. Once they were safely gone, Waff could begin his real work on Buzzell without being observed.

Inside the lab, the smell of salt, iodine, and cinnamon had replaced harsh chemical odors. Waff's test tanks were full of murky green water, rich with algae and plankton. Once turned loose in the oceans, the modified worms would have to find their own sources of nourishment, but Waff was sure they could adapt. God would make it all possible.

Serpentine forms swam about in the tanks looking like ringed eels. Their ridges were an iridescent blue-green, showing a soft pink membrane between segments, a surrogate set of gills that absorbed oxygen from the water. Their mouths were round like those of lampreys. Though they had no eyes, the new seaworms could navigate using water vibrations in much the way that Rakian worms had been attracted by tremors in the dunes. Using carefully mapped models from sandtrout chromosomes, Waff knew that these creatures had the same internal metabolic reactions as a traditional sandworm.

Therefore, they should still produce spice, but Waff didn't know what kind of spice, or how it would be harvested. He stepped back, interlocking his grayish fingers. That wasn't his problem or concern. He had done as Edrik commanded. He only wanted the worms back.

It had taken more than a year out of his accelerated lifetime, but if Waff succeeded in resurrecting God's messengers, his destiny would be complete. Even if the little man never received another ghola lifetime, he would have earned his place beside God in the highest levels of Heaven.

Under proper conditions, sandtrout specimens reproduced swiftly. From them, he had adapted nearly a hundred seaworms, most of which he would deposit in the oceans of Buzzell. For a new species to survive, especially in an unfamiliar environment, the creatures faced quite a challenge, and Waff fully expected that many of his test specimens would die. Maybe most of them. But he was also convinced that some would live—enough to establish a foothold.

Waff stood on his tiptoes, pressing his face to the tank. "If you are in there, Prophet, I will soon give you a whole new domain."

Five Guild assistants entered the lab without knocking. When Waff turned abruptly, the seaworms sensed his movement. With a thump, fleshy heads struck the reinforced tank walls. Startled again, Waff turned the other direction.

"Passengers have disembarked for Buzzell," said one of the gray-clothed men. "Navigator Edrik has commanded us to follow your instructions."

The five all had oddly distorted heads, swollen brows, and asymmetric facial features. Any Tleilaxu Master could have repaired genetic flaws so that their descendants would be more physically attractive. But that would serve no purpose, and Waff had no interest in cosmetics.

He gestured to the tanks as the Guildsmen sealed them for transport. "Exercise extreme care. Those creatures are worth more than all your lives."

The reticent assistants installed handles on the crowded tanks and began lugging them along the curving halls of the Heighliner. Knowing he had only four hours to complete his task before the passenger shuttles returned, Waff urged them to hurry.

Because of the schism in the Guild between Navigators and Administrators, some people might not wish him to create this new avenue for spice production. The Ixians, the New Sisterhood, even the bureaucratic faction of the Guild might all work together, or separately, to assassinate him. Waff didn't know how or why these particular five Guildsmen had been chosen to assist him. If he expressed any misgivings about them, Waff knew that the Navigator would not hesitate to have all five killed, just to keep his Tleilaxu researcher happy. As the troupe walked to a small transport craft, Waff decided that was exactly what he would do. Get rid of these men, these witnesses. Afterward.

The sample tanks were loaded aboard the small transport. Waff did not usually leave the safe confines of the Heighliner, but he insisted on accompanying the crew down to the open sea. It was his experiment, and he wanted to be there in person to make sure the worms were released properly. He didn't trust the five Guildsmen to be sufficiently competent or attentive.

Then his suspicions ran deeper. What was to stop these men from flying off in the ship, revealing—or selling!—the seaworms to one of the opposing factions? Could they be perfectly loyal to Edrik? Waff saw danger everywhere.

As the transport dropped out of the cargo bay, Waff wished belatedly that he had demanded additional bodyguards, or at least a sufficiently powerful hand-weapon for himself. Whom could he really trust?

Using technological apparatus connected to their throats, the silent Guildsmen communicated with each other electronically, transmitting brain signals without voicing words. He knew they could speak aloud— why would they be so secretive? Perhaps they were plotting against him. Waff looked at the immense Heighliner far overhead and wished fervently for this to be over.

The small transport descended into the cloudy skies, fighting choppy air currents. Waff felt ill. Finally, they broke through the moisture layers, and the oceans below sprawled out to every horizon. On charts displayed across the cockpit screens, Waff searched for a temperate zone where he could deposit the test worms, a place where the seas were rich with plankton and fish. It would give the creatures the greatest chance for survival.

He indicated a line of rocks not far from the Sisterhood's main island base and the center of their soostone-harvesting operations. "*There.* Safe, and close enough to monitor the worms." He smiled, already imagining the first panicked reports of eyewitnesses. "Any rumors or wild stories should be interesting."

The Guildsmen nodded, all business. The transport ship flew low over the waves and hovered above the gentle swells. The lower cargo hatch opened, and Waff went down to observe the emptying of the tanks. He smelled the raw salt air, the tang of floating kelp, the wet breezes that whipped across the sea. A squall was about to begin.

Using the handles, two of the silent Guildsmen brought the first tank to the opening, released the plaz cover sheet, and spilled the water and writhing seaworms into the freedom of the waiting waves.

The serpentine creatures burst out like frantic snakes. Once they plunged into the green water, they streaked away. Waff watched their ridged bodies undulating, then diving and disappearing. They seemed joyous in their newfound freedom, glad to have a large world without plaz boundaries.

Brusquely, he gestured to the Guildsmen, telling them to release the rest of the worms, emptying all of the aquariums. Waff had kept one crowded tank of specimens aboard the Heighliner, and he could always create more.

As he stood by the open hatch, he suddenly shuddered, realizing his vulnerability. Now that he had turned the worms loose, would Edrik even require his services anymore? The Tleilaxu man feared the silent assistants might shove him overboard and leave him floating kilometers from the nearest speck of land. Warily, he backed deeper into the cargo hold and gripped a ridged wall strut.

But the Guildsmen made no move against him. They performed their work exactly as he told them to, and precisely as the Navigator had specified. Perhaps Waff was fearful only because he intended to have these men killed. He naturally suspected they would think the same about him.

Waff anticipated the seaworms would thrive here. The environment was conducive to their growth and reproduction. The worms would mark their territory, and when they grew large enough they would become leviathans of the deep. A fitting form for the Prophet.

The transport's cargo doors sealed again with a low hiss, and the Guild pilot flew away. Waff and his party would arrive back at the Heighliner well before the merchant vessels returned with their loads of soostones. No one would be the wiser.

The Tleilaxu Master glanced through the cockpit's plaz port to see the waves receding. He saw no sign of the seaworms, but he knew they were down there somewhere.

He let out a contented sigh, confident that his Prophet would come back.

It is the principle of the ticking time bomb, a strategy of aggression that has long been part of human violence. Thus we have inserted our "time bombs" into the cells of gholas, activating specific behaviors at precise moments of our choosing.

—from *The Secret Manual of Tleilaxu Masters*

The no-ship had its own time, its own cycles. Most of the people were asleep, except for off-shift watches and maintenance crews. The decks were quiet, the glowpanels dimmed. In the shadowy chamber that held the axlotl tanks, the Rabbi paced back and forth, murmuring Talmudic prayers.

On a surveillance screen Sheeana observed the old man carefully, always alert to prevent any new incident of sabotage. When the saboteur had killed the three gholas and axlotl tanks, he or she had shut down the security imagers, but Bashar Teg had made sure that was no longer possible. Everything was under observation. As a former Suk doctor, the Rabbi had access to the medical center; he often spent time with what remained of the woman he'd known as Rebecca.

Though the old man had answered all questions the Truthsayers asked him, he still hadn't earned her trust. Despite her best efforts, the saboteur and murderer remained at large. And the recent appearance of the glowing net had brought the Enemy too close, reminding the passengers of the very real threat. Everyone onboard had seen it. Their danger remained unabated.

Three relatively new axlotl tanks rested on their platforms; volunteers had come forward to answer Sheeana's call, exactly as she had expected. All three new tanks were currently producing liquid-form melange that dripped into small collecting vials, but she had begun preparations to implant one of the wombs with cells from Scytale's nullentropy tube. A new embryo to bring back yet another figure from the past. She refused to let the sabotage deflect her ghola project.

The Rabbi stood before the new tanks, his tense body exhibiting clear markers of loathing and disgust. He spoke to the fleshy mound. "I hate you. Unnatural, ungodly."

After watching the old man carefully, Sheeana left the monitor screens and entered the medical center, gliding up behind him. "Is it honorable to hate the helpless, Rabbi? Those women are no longer aware, no longer human. Why despise them?"

He whirled, lights reflecting on his polished spectacles. "Stop spying on me. I wish time alone to pray for Rebecca's soul." Rebecca had been his personal favorite, willing to pit her intellect against his; the old man had never forgiven her for volunteering to become a tank.

"Even you need to be watched, Rabbi."

Anger flushed his leathery skin. "You and your witches should have heeded the warnings and ceased your grotesque experiments. If only the Honored Matres had managed to get rid of Scytale when they destroyed all Tleilaxu worlds, then his hateful knowledge of tanks and gholas would have been lost."

"The Honored Matres also hunted down your people, Rabbi. You and the Tleilaxu share the same enemy."

"But it is not the same at all. We have been unfairly persecuted throughout history, while the Tleilaxu merely received their just desserts. Their own Face Dancers turned on them, from what I understand." He took a step away from the fleshy mound, from the chemical and biological odors that wafted from the tanks. "I can hardly recall what Rebecca once looked like, before she became this *thing*."

Sheeana searched for the memories, and asked the voices within to assist her. This time they did, and she found what she wanted, like accessing old archival images. The woman had looked elegant in her brown robe and braided hair. She'd worn contact lenses to conceal the blue eyes of her spice addiction. . . .

With a bitter expression, the Rabbi placed a hand on Rebecca's exposed flesh. A tear ran down his cheek. He muttered the same thing each time he visited her. A litany for him. "You witches did this to her, made her into a monster."

"She's not a monster, not even a martyr." She tapped her own forehead. "Rebecca's thoughts and memories are in here and inside many other Sisters, Shared with us all. Rebecca did what was necessary, and so will we."

"By making more gholas? Will it never end?"

"You are concerned about a pebble in your shoe, while we seek to avoid the rockslide. Sooner or later, we will no longer be able to run from the Enemy. We'll need the ingenuity and special talents of these gholas, in particular those capable of becoming another Kwisatz Haderach. But we must handle the genetic material carefully, nurturing and developing it in the proper order, at the proper pace." She strolled to one of the new tanks, a fresh young woman whose form had not yet deteriorated into unrecognizability.

As she stood there, a troubling thought refused to leave her mind, no matter how much she tried to push it away. An absurd line of reasoning, but all day long it had been percolating. *What if my own abilities could be equivalent to those of a Kwisatz Haderach? I already have a natural ability to control the great worms. I have the Atreides genes, and centuries of the Sisterhood's perfected knowledge to draw upon. Would I dare?*

She felt voices surfacing from within; one rose above the others. The ancient Reverend Mother Gaius Helen Mohiam, repeating something that she once said so long ago to a young Paul Atreides: "Yet, there's a place where no Truthsayer can see. We are repelled by it, terrorized. It is said a man will come one day and find in the gift of the drug his inward eye. He will look where we cannot—into both feminine and masculine pasts . . . the one who can be many places at once . . ." The old crone's voice drifted away, without giving Sheeana any advice, one way or the other.

With a sneer, the Rabbi interrupted her thoughts. "And you trust that old Tleilaxu to help you, when he's desperate to achieve his own goals before dying? Scytale hid those cells for so many years. How many of them contain dangerous secrets? You've already discovered Face Dancer cells among the samples. How many of your ghola abominations are traps laid by the Tleilaxu?"

She gazed at him dispassionately, knowing that no argument would ever sway him. The Rabbi made the sign of the evil eye, and fled.

DUNCAN ENCOUNTERED SHEEANA in an empty corridor, in the dimness of the artificial night. The no-ship's recyclers and life-support systems kept the air comfortably cool, but upon seeing her alone like this Duncan felt a flush of heat.

Sheeana's large eyes fixed on him like a weapon's targeting system. Feeling a tingle like static electricity on his skin, he cursed his body for being so easily tempted. Even now, three years after Sheeana had broken the debilitating chains of Murbella's love, the two of them still found themselves drawn irresistibly into unexpected bouts of sex as frenetic as any he and Murbella had ever shared.

Duncan preferred to manage the circumstances of their casual meetings, always trying to make certain that others were present, that he had safe guardrails to prevent him from falling off a dangerous cliff. He did not like to be out of control: That had already happened too many times.

He and Sheeana had surrendered to each other like terrified people huddling in a bombed-out battle zone. She had cauterized him to cure his debility and stolen him from Murbella, yet he felt like a casualty of war.

Now as he saw Sheeana's expression flicker, Duncan thought she felt the same sense of vertigo and disorientation. She tried to sound reserved and rational. "It is better if we don't do this. We have too many concerns, too many risks. Another regenerator system has just failed. The saboteur—"

"You're right. We should not." His voice was hoarse, but they had already started down a path with ever-increasing consequences. Duncan took a hesitant step forward. The muted corridor lights reflected off the no-ship's metal walls. "We shouldn't do this," he said again.

Desire swept like a wave over both of them. As a Mentat he could observe and assess, concluding that what they were doing was simply a reaffirmation of humanity. When they touched fingertips, lips, and skin, both of them were lost. . . .

Later, they rested on tangled sheets in Sheeana's quarters. The air carried a moist muskiness. Duncan lay sated with his fingers laced in his wiry dark hair. He was confused and disappointed in himself. "You've taken away too much of my control."

Sheeana raised her eyebrows in the dim light, showing amusement. Her breath was warm and close to his ear. "Oh? And Murbella did not?" When Duncan turned away and did not answer, she chuckled. "You're feeling guilty! You think you've betrayed her somehow. But how many female imprinters did you train back on Chapterhouse?"

He answered the question in his own way. "Murbella and I were trapped together, and no part of our relationship was voluntary. We had a mutual addiction, two people brought to a stalemate. That isn't love or tenderness. For Murbella—for all of you witches—our love-making was supposed to be 'just business.' But I still had feelings for her, dammit! It isn't a matter of whether or not I should."

"But you—you were like a violent detoxification of my system. The Agony served the same purpose for Murbella, breaking her bond to me." He reached out and cupped Sheeana's chin. "This cannot happen again."

Now she looked even more amused. "I agree that it should not . . . but it will anyway."

"You're a loaded weapon, a full Bene Gesserit. Every time we make love, you could easily let yourself get pregnant. Isn't that what the Sisterhood would demand? You could carry my child whenever you allow yourself to do so."

"True. But I haven't. We are far from Chapterhouse, and I make my own decisions now." Sheeana pulled him back to her.

Scientists see sandworms as specimens, while the Fremen see them as their god. But the worms devour anyone who tries to gather information. How am I supposed to work under such conditions?
—IMPERIAL PLANETOLOGIST PARDOT KYNES,
ancient records

Sheeana stood in the high observation gallery where she and Garimi had once gone to discuss the future of their journey. The kilometer-long great hold was large enough to offer the illusion of freedom, though much too small for a brood of sandworms. The seven creatures were growing but remained stunted, waiting for the promised arid land. They had been waiting a long time, perhaps too long.

More than two decades ago, Sheeana had brought the small worms aboard the no-ship, stealing them from the growing desert band on Chapterhouse. She had always intended to transplant them to another world, far from the Honored Matres and safe from the Enemy. For years, the worms had zigzagged endlessly in the sand-filled confines of the hold, as lost as everyone else on the *Ithaca.* . . .

She wondered if the no-ship would ever find a planet where they could stop, where the Sisters could establish a new and orthodox Chapterhouse, rather than the mongrel organization that made concessions to the ways of the Honored Matres. If the ship simply fled for generations and generations, it would be impossible to find a perfect world for the sandworms, for Garimi and her conservative Bene Gesserits, for the Rabbi and his Jews.

She recalled searching Other Memory for advice the evening before. For a while, there had been no response. Then Serena Butler, the ancient leader of the Jihad, came to her just as Sheeana drifted off to sleep in her quarters. Long-dead Serena told of her experiences being lost and overwhelmed by an endless war, forced to guide vast populations when she herself didn't know where to go.

"But you found your way, Serena. You did what you had to do. You did what humanity needed."

And so will you, Sheeana.

Now, seeing the sandworms ripple the sand far below, Sheeana could sense their feelings in an indefinable way, and they could sense hers. Did they dream of endless, dry dunes in which to stake their territory? The largest of the worms, nearly forty meters long with a maw large enough to swallow three people abreast, was clearly dominant. Sheeana had given that one a name: Monarch.

The seven worms pointed their eyeless faces toward her, displaying crystalline teeth. The smaller ones burrowed into the shallow sand, leaving only Monarch, who seemed to be summoning Sheeana. She stared at the dominant worm, trying to understand what it wanted. The connection between them began to burn inside her, calling her.

Sheeana descended to the sand-filled cargo hold. Stepping out onto churned dunes, she strode directly toward the worm, unafraid. She had faced the creatures many times before and had nothing to fear from this one.

Monarch towered over her. Putting her hands on her hips, Sheeana looked up, and waited. In the heady days on Rakis, she had learned to dance on the sands and control the behemoths, but she had always known she could do more. When she was ready.

The worm seemed to be playing upon her need for understanding. She was the girl who could communicate with the beasts, who could control and understand them. And now, in order to see her own future, she had to go farther. Literally and metaphorically. It was what Monarch wanted. Dangerous and frightening, the creature exhaled a stink of inner furnaces and pure melange.

"So, now what do we do, you and I? Are you Shaitan, or just an impostor?"

The restless worm seemed to know exactly what she had in mind. Instead of rolling its body toward her so she could climb its rings to ride, Monarch faced her with its round maw open. Each milky-white tooth in a mouth the size of a cave opening was long enough to be used as a crysknife. Sheeana did not tremble.

The sandworm laid its head on the soft dunes directly in front of her. Tempting her to a symbolic journey, like Jonah and the whale? Sheeana wrestled with her fears, but knew what she must do—not as a charlatan's performance, for she doubted anyone was watching her, but because it was necessary for her own understanding.

Monarch lay waiting for her, mouth agape. The worm itself became a secret doorway, luring her like a dangerous lover. Sheeana stepped past the portcullis of crysknife teeth and knelt inside the gullet, inhaling the rank cinnamon odor. Dizzy and nauseated, she could barely breathe. The sandworm did not move. Willingly, she worked her way deeper inside, offering herself, though convinced that her sacrifice would not be accepted. It wasn't what the worm wanted from her.

Without looking back, she crawled farther down the throat into dry, dark warmth. Monarch did not twitch. Sheeana kept going, felt her breathing slow. Deeper and deeper she went, and soon guessed that she had gone at least half the length of the prone worm. Without the friction heat sparked by roaming endless deserts, the worm's gullet was no longer a furnace. Her eyes became accustomed to what she realized was not total darkness, but was instead an eerie illumination that seemed more the product of another sense in her own mind than traditional eyesight. She could dimly see the rough, membranous surface around her, and as she proceeded, the undigested odor of melange precursors grew stronger, more concentrated.

Finally she reached a fleshy chamber that might have been Monarch's stomach, but without digestive acids. How did the captive sandworms survive? The odor of spice was more intense here than she had ever experienced—so much so that an ordinary person would have suffocated.

But I am no ordinary person.

Sheeana lay there, absorbing the warmth, letting the intense melange seep into every pore in her body, feeling Monarch's dim consciousness merge into hers. She inhaled deeply and felt a great, cosmic sense of calm, like being in the womb of the Great Mother of the Universe.

Unexpectedly, with the unusual visitor deep in its gullet, the sandworm dove into the artificial desert and began to move through it; taking her on a strange journey. As if connected directly with Monarch's nervous system, Sheeana could see *through* the eyeless worm to its companions beneath the sand. Working together, the seven sandworms were forming small veins of spice in the cargo hold.

Preparing.

Sheeana lost track of time and thought again of Leto II, whose pearl of awareness was now inside this beast and all of the others in the hold. She wondered where she fit into this paranormal realm. As the God Emperor's queen? As the female part of the godhead? Or as something else entirely, an entity she could not begin to imagine?

The worms all carried secrets, and Sheeana understood how much the ghola children were like that as well. They each held a treasure greater than spice within their cells: their past memories and lives. Paul and Chani, Jessica, Yueh, Leto II. Even Thufir Hawat, Stilgar, Liet-Kynes . . . and now baby Alia. Each had a crucial role to play, but only if they could remember who they were.

She saw each image, but not in her own imagination. The sandworms knew what those lost figures contained. An urgency rushed toward her like a desert wind. Time, and with it their chances for survival, was slipping away too quickly. She envisioned a succession of the possible gholas, all primed like weapons, but blurred as to what each could do.

She could not wait for the Enemy. She had to act now.

The worm resurfaced, and after moving along the sands, it jolted to a stop. Inside, Sheeana caught her balance. Then, by constricting its membranous interior, the creature gently pushed her back out. She crawled from the mouth and tumbled onto the sands.

Dust and grit clung to the film coating her body. Monarch nudged her, like a mother bird urging a chick to go out on its own. Caught up in disorienting visions, she struggled and dropped to her knees on the dry sand. The faces of the ghola children wavered around her, dissolving into bright lights. *Awaken!*

She lay gasping for breath, her body and clothing drenched in spice essence. Beside Sheeana, the big worm turned, burrowed back into the shallow sand, and disappeared from view.

Reeking and reeling, Sheeana made her way back toward the cargo-hold doors, but she kept losing her footing and falling. She had to reach the ghola children . . . The worm had given her an important message, something that seeped into her consciousness like a wordless form of Other Memory. In moments, she was left with an overwhelming certainty of what she had to do.

You say that we must learn from the past. But I—I fear the past,
for I have been there, and I have no desire to return.

—DR. WELLINGTON YUEH,

the ghola

After being scrubbed and showered to rid her of a spice reek so strong that even the Sisters who assisted her covered their mouths and noses, Sheeana slept for two days in deep and disturbing dreams.

When she finally emerged and found Duncan Idaho and Miles Teg on the navigation bridge, she made her announcement. "The gholas are all old enough. Even Leto II is the same age as when I restored the Bashar." The smell of melange was heavy on Sheeana's breath. "It's time to awaken them all."

Duncan turned his back on the observation window where he stood. "Triggering the process isn't like activating a subroutine or working through a bout of temporary amnesia. You can't just issue a memo and order it done."

"The ghola children have always known that we would demand this of them," she said. "Without their past memories, without their genius, they are of no more value to us than any other children."

The Bashar nodded slowly. "To recall a ghola's past life is an experience that destroys and recreates the psyche. There are numerous proven methods, some more painful than others, but none are easy. You can't awaken the children all at once. Each critical event must be tailored to the individual. A horrible, mind-shattering crisis." Teg's face showed echoes of pain. "You thought you were using a humane awakening method with me, Sheeana . . . when I was only a ten-year-old child."

Though Duncan, too, seemed uneasy at the prospect, he stepped down from the observation window and walked toward Sheeana. "She's right, Miles. We created those gholas for a purpose, and right now they're all like unloaded guns. We need to load our gholas—our unique weapons. The Enemy's net is stronger now, and it nearly snared us again. We all saw it. Next time, we may not be able to slip away."

"We've waited long enough." Sheeana's voice was hard, brooking no argument.

"Some gholas may be more challenging than others." Teg's eyes narrowed. "You may lose some to madness. Are you prepared for that?"

"I have gone through the Spice Agony, as have all Reverend Mothers on this ship. We survived the unbearable pain."

"I have the memories of my old life," Teg said. "Of wars and atrocities, and enduring unbearable torture. Somehow the bad details are much more vivid than the pleasant ones, but nothing is worse than the awakening."

Sheeana waved her hand. "Throughout history, men and women have had a monopoly on their own kinds of pain, each thinking theirs is the worst." She smiled grimly. "We will start with the least valuable ghola, of course. In case something goes wrong."

WELLINGTON YUEH WAS summoned to stand before the Bene Gesserits in one of the no-ship's council chambers. The gangly teenager had a pointed chin and pinched lips. Already buried within his face were hints of the familiar chiseled features and broad forehead—the despised visage that had become synonymous with the word *traitor* for thousands of years in galactic reference works.

The young man was nervous, fidgeting. Sheeana drew herself to her full height and stepped closer. He flinched at her intimidating presence, but somehow found the courage to stand where he was. "You summoned me, Reverend Mother. How may I assist?"

"By awakening your memories. Tomorrow you will be the first of our subjects to undergo the trigger."

Yueh's yellowish face paled. "But I'm not ready!"

"That is why we have given you a full day to prepare." Proctor Superior Garimi's tongue was sharp, as usual.

Although Garimi had never embraced the project, she now wanted to see its culmination. Sheeana knew what she was thinking: If the awakening process failed, Garimi intended to prevent any further gholas from being grown; if the awakening succeeded, she would insist that the program had fulfilled its goal and could be discontinued. She knew that Sheeana, still intrigued by all those cells in the Tleilaxu's nullentropy capsule, was planning further ghola experiments.

Yueh's legs were locked. He seemed close to fainting and grasped a nearby chair to steady himself. "Sisters, I don't want to have my memories back. I am not the man you think you resurrected, but a new person—my own person. The old Wellington Yueh was tormented in so many ways. Even though he was in part *me*, how can I forgive him for what he did?"

Garimi made a dismissive gesture. "Nevertheless, we brought you back for one purpose only. Don't expect sympathy from us. You have a task to perform."

After the proctors took the distraught young man away, Sheeana looked at Garimi and two other senior Sisters—Calissa and Elyen— who had observed the discussion. "I will use the sexual method on him, the same one that worked on the ghola of the Bashar. It is the best technique we know."

Elyen said, "Your sexual imprinting unlocked the Bashar's memories only because it precipitated a crisis in him. Teg's mother had armed him against sexual imprinting. It wasn't your technique that stirred up his past, but his sheer resistance to it."

"Indeed. So for each of our gholas we'll tailor an individualized agony that leverages their own fears and weaknesses."

"How can sex break Yueh the way it broke the Bashar?" Garimi asked.

"Not the sex itself, but Yueh's resistance to it. He's terrified of remembering his past. If he believes we know how to unlock his memories, he'll fight us with everything he has. As he fights, I will apply my most potent procedures, and he'll spiral over the brink into complete madness."

Garimi shrugged. "If it doesn't work, we have other ways."

THE ROOM WAS dim and the shadows cloying, which made Yueh's terror more palpable. The chamber was devoid of furniture except for a padded mat on the floor, like those that the ghola children used during physical training sessions.

The witches had not explained what to expect. The young man knew from his studies that the process of regaining one's past was painful. He was not a strong man, nor was he particularly brave. Even so, the prospect of pain did not petrify him nearly so much as the dread of remembering.

The door slid open with a gentle hiss of lubricated metal gliding in its tracks. From the corridor, blinding light flowed in, much brighter than the glowpanels in his cell. It silhouetted a woman's figure—Sheeana? He turned to face her and could see only her outline, the sensual curves of her body no longer masked by flowing robes. When the door sealed behind her, his eyes adjusted to the more comfortable illumination.

When he saw that Sheeana was completely unclothed, his fear increased. "What is this?" His voice, torn by nervousness, came out as a squeak.

She stepped closer. "You will disrobe now."

Barely a teenager, Yueh swallowed. "Not until you explain what is going to happen to me."

She used the hurricane force of Bene Gesserit Voice. "*You will disrobe now!*"

In a spasmodic reaction, his arms and legs jerking, he tore off his clothes. Sheeana inspected him, running her eyes up and down his thin, naked body like a hawk assessing its prey. Yueh got the impression that she found him inadequate.

"Don't hurt me," he pleaded, and hated himself for saying it.

"Of course it will hurt, but the pain won't be anything *I* inflict upon you." She touched his shoulder. He felt an almost electric shock, but he was transfixed, unable to move. "Your own memories will do that."

"I don't want them back. I'll fight you."

"Fight all you wish. It will do you no good. We know how to awaken you."

Yueh closed his eyes and gritted his teeth. He tried to turn away, but she grasped his arms to hold him still, then released her grip and began touching him. The delicate strokings felt like the line of heat left by a lighted match down his arm and across his chest. "Your memories are stored within your cells. In order to awaken them, I must awaken your body." She stroked him, and he shuddered, unable to draw away. "I shall teach your nerve endings to do things they've forgotten how to do." Another jolt, and he gasped.

She touched him again, and his knees buckled, exactly as she wanted. Sheeana pushed him toward the mat on the floor. "I need to wrench you into the full awareness of every chromosome in every cell."

"No." The word sounded incredibly weak to him.

As she pressed herself against him, letting warm skin ignite his per- spiration, Yueh tunneled backward into himself, trying to flee. From all he had learned of his past, he found one thing with which to anchor his bravery. *Wanna!* His beloved Bene Gesserit wife, the weak link in his long chain of betrayals, and the strongest link in his original life- time.

The evil Harkonnens had known that Wanna would be the key to breaking his Suk conditioning, and it had only worked—could only have worked—because Yueh loved her with all his heart. Bene Gesser- its were not supposed to succumb to love, but he knew that she must have reciprocated.

He thought of her pictures in the archives, of all he had learned about her in his researches. "Oh, Wanna." He yearned for her in his mind, tried to latch onto her as a lifeline.

Sheeana stroked his waist, trailed her fingers lower and climbed on top of him. Yueh's muscles were completely out of his control. He couldn't move. Her lips vibrated against the skin of his shoulder, his neck. Sheeana was a skilled sexual imprinter. Her body was a weapon, and he was the target.

A flood of sensations nearly drove the archival image of Wanna from his mind, but Yueh fought against what Sheeana was making him feel. Instead, he focused on what he might have done in Wanna's loving embrace. *Wanna.*

As the rhythm of their lovemaking increased, real memories intruded on the information he had obtained through research. Yueh recalled those terrible moments after his wife had been seized by the Harkonnens, and saw images of the loathsome fat Baron, his thuggish nephew Rabban, the viper Feyd-Rautha, and the Mentat Piter de Vries, who had a laugh that sounded like vinegar.

Weak, helpless, and infuriated, he had been forced to watch them torture Wanna inside an isolated chamber. She was a Bene Gesserit; she could block her pain, could deflect her body's responses. But Yueh could not so easily shunt such things aside, no matter how hard he tried.

In his nightmare memory the Baron laughed, a rumbling basso sound. "See the little chamber she's in, Doctor? A toy with some very interesting possibilities." As the men watched the groggy and disoriented Wanna, she stood on weak knees, but upside-down within the booth. "We can convert gravity into a thing that depends entirely on perspective."

Rabban chuckled, a harsh release of noise. He operated artificial gravity controls in the small room, and suddenly Wanna fell with a thud to the floor. She managed to tuck her head and shoulders just enough to avoid breaking her neck. With the speed and fluidity of a serpent, Piter de Vries scurried forward carrying a pain amplifier. At the last moment, Rabban snatched it out of the Twisted Mentat's hands and applied it to Wanna's throat himself. She writhed with a jagged spasm of agony.

"Stop! Stop, I beg you!" Yueh cried.

"Oh, Doctor, Doctor—you know it can't possibly be that easy . . ." In the vision, the Baron folded his pudgy arms across his chest.

Rabban twisted the gravity controls again, and Wanna was thrown like a limp doll from wall to wall, smashing into the sides of the chamber. "When one is too lovely, something must be done to correct that condition."

My beautiful Wanna!

The memories were so vivid now, far more detailed than anything he had read in the Archives section. No mere documentation could have provided such precise clarity. . . .

In a different, newly unlocked compartment of his brain, he lived another memory. He was artificially paralyzed, forced to watch during one of the Baron's drunken parties while Piter played a sparking pain amplifier over Wanna's suspended body. Each flash provoked a twitching response of agony from her. The other guests laughed at her pain and at his helpless misery.

When he was freed from his paralysis, Yueh trembled, drooled, and struggled. The Baron stood over him, a huge grin on his bloated face. He handed Yueh a projectile pistol. "As a Suk doctor, you should do everything possible to stop a patient from feeling pain. You know how to stop Wanna's pain, Doctor."

Unable to break his conditioning, Yueh shuddered and spasmed. He wanted nothing more than to do as the Baron demanded. "I . . . can't!"

"Of course you can. Choose a guest, any guest. I don't care which. See how amused they are by our little game?" Grasping Yueh's shaking wrists, he helped the doctor point his projectile weapon around the room. "But don't try any tricks, or we will make the torment last a great deal longer!"

He wished he could put Wanna out of her misery, killing her instead of letting the Harkonnens have their perverted fun. He saw her eyes, the spark of pain and hope, but Rabban stopped him. "Focus, Doctor. No mistakes."

Through blurred vision he made out numerous targets, and tried to concentrate on one, a tottering old nobleman, a semuta addict. That one had lived a long life, undoubtedly with considerable debauchery. But for a Suk doctor to kill—

He fired.

Overwhelmed by the horrific scene now playing out in his head, Yueh paid no further attention to Sheeana's ministrations. His body was drenched with sweat, but less from sexual exertion than from the extreme psychological distress. He saw Sheeana appraising him. The memories were so clear to him that his entire body felt like a raw wound: Wanna in agony and the sharp, broken-crystal pain of how his Suk conditioning had been thwarted. It had happened *thousands* of years ago!

The years before that watershed occurrence, and the years afterward, extended outward, filling his mind, now fresh and hungry. As the relentless memories returned, so did more anguish and guilt, accompanied by a disgust with himself.

Yueh felt as if he was about to vomit. Tears poured down his cheeks.

In the training room, Sheeana studied the wet streaks clinically. "You're weeping. Does that mean you've successfully regained your memories?"

"I have them back." His voice was husky and sounded infinitely old. "And damn you witches to hell for it."

We have so little trouble finding enemies because violence is an innate part of human nature. Our greatest challenge, then, is to choose the most significant enemy, for we cannot hope to fight them all.

—BASHAR MILES TEG,

military assessment delivered to the Bene Gesserit

After she departed from Chapterhouse, Murbella traveled to the battle lines. That was where the Mother Commander belonged. Posing as nothing more important than an inspector for the New Sisterhood, Murbella arrived at Oculiat, one of the systems that lay directly in the path of the advancing thinking-machine fleet.

Once, Oculiat had been at the far edges of inhabited space, a jumping-off point for the Scattering after the Tyrant's death. Objectively, this sparsely populated world had little significance, just another target on the vast cosmic map. But for Murbella, Oculiat represented a genuine psychological blow: When this world fell to the machines, the Enemy would be encroaching into the *Old Empire* itself, not just into a distant and unknown place that had been omitted from old star maps.

Until the Ixians delivered their Obliterators and the Guild provided all the ships she had demanded, the Mother Commander had no way to stop, or even slow, the thinking machines.

Under a hazy sky illuminated by watery yellow sunlight, Murbella stepped out of her ship. The landing field seemed deserted, as if no one tended the spaceport any longer. As if they were not even watching for the Enemy.

When she made her way to the frantic crowds in the central city, though, she saw that the inhabitants had already found their own enemy. A mob surrounded the main administration building where government officials had barricaded themselves. The locals had put their leaders under siege, screaming for blood or divine intervention. *Preferably blood.*

Murbella knew the raw power that their fear generated, but it was clearly not channeled properly. The people of Oculiat—and all desperate worlds facing the oncoming Enemy—needed guidance from the Sisterhood. They were an already-charged weapon that must be aimed. Instead, they were out of control. She saw what was happening and rushed forward, but stopped short of throwing herself headlong into the mob.

They would tear her limb from limb, and they would do it for Sheeana.

The random appearances and sermons of the "resurrected Sheeana" had prepared billions of people to fight. The Sheeanas had kindled the anger and fervor of populations, so that the Sisterhood could manipulate that raw power for their own purposes. Once unleashed, however, such fanaticism became a chaotic force. Knowing they were unlikely to survive against the oncoming machines, the men and women threw themselves into violence, seeking any sort of enemy they could get their hands on . . . even among their own people.

"Face Dancers!" someone shouted. Murbella pushed her way closer to the center of action, knocked aside flailing arms and fists, and cuffed someone on the side of the head. But even stunned, the wild and emboldened people surged onward. "Face Dancers! They've been manipulating us all along—selling us out to the Enemy."

Those who recognized the Mother Commander's Bene Gesserit unitard backed away; others, either oblivious or too angry to care, were not swayed until she used Voice. Bombarded by the irresistible command, they staggered away. Just one person against the multitude, Murbella strode toward the colonnaded doorways of the government center, which the people saw as their target. She used Voice again but could not stop them all in their tracks. The shouting and accusatory shrieks rose and fell like a thunderstorm.

As she fought her way to the front of the barricade, several of the foremost mob members noticed her uniform and let out a long cheer. "A Reverend Mother is here to support us!"

"Kill the Face Dancers! Kill them all!"

"For Sheeana!"

Murbella grabbed an elderly woman who had been yelling along with the others. "How do you know they're Face Dancers?"

"We *know*. Think about their decisions, listen to their speeches. It's obvious they are traitors." Murbella didn't believe that Face Dancers would be quite so obvious that common rabble could detect the faint subtleties. But the mob was convinced.

Six huffing men ran by, carrying a heavy plasteel pole that they proceeded to use as a battering ram. Inside the capitol building, terrified officials had piled obstructions against the doors and windows. Thrown stones shattered the ornamental plaz, but the crowd couldn't break in so easily. Bars and heavy objects blocked the way.

Wielded with the strength of panic and hysteria, the battering ram pounded the thick doors, tearing hinges loose and splintering wood. In moments, a wave of human bodies pushed forward.

Murbella called out. "Wait! Why not prove they're Face Dancers before you kill anyone—"

The old woman shoved past, eager to get to the officials. She stepped on Murbella's foot, heard her shouted cautions, then turned to her with a narrowed gaze like a serpent's. "Why do you hesitate, Reverend Mother? Help us capture the traitors. Or are you a Face Dancer yourself?"

Murbella's Honored Matre reflexes came to the fore, and her hand snapped out, cutting into the woman's neck with a blow that rendered her unconscious. She had not meant to kill the woman, but as her accuser fell to the steps a dozen people surged forward, trampling her to death.

Heart pounding, Murbella pressed against the wall to avoid the brunt of the stampede. If the cry had been taken up—"Face Dancer! Face Dancer!"—with fingers pointing at her, the crowd would have killed her without thinking. Even with superior fighting abilities, Murbella could never fend off so many.

She backed up farther and took shelter behind the tall statue of a long-forgotten hero of the Famine Times, shielding herself with its pla-stone bulk. The screaming mob would crush many of its own members to get into the government building.

She could hear cries inside, a discharge of weapons, and small explosions. Some of the trapped officials must have been carrying personal protection. Murbella waited, knowing it would be over soon. . . .

The bloody attack burned itself out in half an hour. The mob found and killed all twenty government officials suspected of being enemy Face Dancers. Then, still not sated in their thirst for blood, they turned against any of their own members who had not shown sufficient murderous fervor, until most of the violence drained away into guilty exhaustion. . . .

Standing tall, Mother Commander Murbella entered the building, where she surveyed the smashed windows, display cases, and artwork. Jubilant murderers dragged bodies onto the polished tiled floor of the main legislative gallery. Almost thirty men and women were dead, some shot with projectile weapons, others beaten to death, many with such violence that their genders were hardly recognizable. The corpses on the polished stone floor wore expressions of horror and shock.

One of the bodies among the bloody mess was indeed a Face Dancer.

"We were right! You see, Reverend Mother." A man pointed at the dead shape-shifter. "We were infiltrated, but we rooted out the enemy and killed it."

Murbella looked around, at all of the innocent humans murdered to discover one Face Dancer. What was the economy of bloodshed? She tried to assess it coolly. How much damage could that one Face Dancer have caused, exposing vulnerabilities to the oncoming Enemy forces? All of those lives? Yes, and more, she had to admit.

From their elation it was obvious that the people of Oculiat considered their uprising a victory, and Murbella could not dispute that. But if this wave of insane vigilantism continued, would all governments topple? Even on Chapterhouse? Then who would organize the people to defend themselves?

Weak minds are gullible. The weaker the thought processes, the more ridiculous the notions they will believe. Strong minds, like mine, can turn that to an advantage.

—BARON VLADIMIR HARKONNEN,
original recordings

Despite being unarmed, the Baron sneered into the face of the red-eyed mongrel hound. The growling animal moved toward him on the flagstoned floor, baring its sharp fangs, ready to spring.

Fortunately, the Baron had killed the feral creature with a poison dart gun some time ago, and this stuffed mechanical version merely followed a programmed reenactment. The simulacrum went motionless when he gave it a hand signal. An amusing toy.

Nine-year-old Paolo moved around the trophy chamber, admiring the wild animals on display. The Baron had dragged the boy out on many hunts in the pristine wilderness of Caladan, so that he could witness the killing firsthand. It was good for his development and education.

Rabban had always enjoyed such things, but Paolo had originally been reluctant to engage in the slaughter. Maybe it was some flaw in the genetics. However, the Baron was gradually breaking down his resistance. With vigorous training and a system of rewards and punishments (plenty of the latter), the Baron had almost managed to squash the core of innate goodness in this ghola of Paul Atreides.

Weathersats had predicted constant rain and wind for the rest of the week. The Baron had looked forward to going out on a fresh hunt, but the cold and wet would have made for a miserable expedition. He and Paolo were trapped inside the castle. The two had formed a remarkable bond. House Atreides and House Harkonnen—how ironic! But though Paolo was a clone of the hated Duke's son, raised properly he was turning out more like a Harkonnen.

He is your grandson, after all, the internal voice of Alia nagged at him.

Overcoming an urge to shout back at her, the Baron watched four workmen with suspensors hoist an immense stuffed mastaphont onto a viewing stand. Yet another nearly extinct creature, this ferocious beast had charged at them across a field last autumn, slashing with its serrated horns. But the Baron, Paolo, and half a dozen guards had opened fire with lasguns, cutting disks, and poison flechettes, mangling the creature before it finally fell. What an exciting hunt that had been!

Paolo looked at the animated creatures on stands. "Instead of going outside to the wilderness, let's go hunting in here. We can pretend they're not already dead. Then we don't have to worry about getting wet and cold."

The Baron looked out at the stormy skies, wondering if the weather was the real reason for Paolo's reluctance. "I don't mind pain, but personal discomfort is another matter entirely." He looked around, assessing possibilities for damage. And grinned. "You're absolutely right, my boy!" It pleased him to hear how deep his own voice was becoming.

They ordered servants to bring a selection of lasguns, dart pistols, swords, and knives for their next ersatz adventure. When the mechanical systems were activated, the dead animals went into a frenzy all over the trophy room. The two hunters took cover, imagined their danger, and shot the mechanical creatures off of their stands, chopping through prosthetic bones, stuffing, and preserved flesh. Last of all, they activated the huge mastaphont and watched it stomp over the debris. Finally catching it in a crossfire of lasgun blasts, they amputated its legs. The beast crashed to the floor, its automatic servos writhing.

The Baron found the violence to be eminently satisfying, and even Paolo seemed to warm to the activity. Afterward, the brave hunters surveyed the damage and laughed as they marched out into the corridor. The Baron spotted three workmen, who looked as if they wanted to become invisible. "Get back in there and clean things up!"

You always make a mess of things, don't you, Grandfather?

The Baron pressed his hands against his head. "Shut up, damn you!" Alia began humming repetitive singsong tunes, designed to drive him mad, no doubt. When a bewildered Paolo pestered him with questions, the Baron slapped him away. "Leave me alone! You're as bad as your sister!"

Confused and startled, Paolo ran off.

The girl's grating voice vibrated in his mind until he couldn't stand it. He hurried out of the castle. Barely able to see where he was going, the Baron bumped into one of the blocky Harkonnen statues and rushed toward the sea cliff. "I'll hurl myself over the edge—I swear it, Abomination—unless you leave me alone!"

He got all the way to the windy, rocky brink, before the Alia voice at last faded into sweet silence. The Baron dropped to his knees on the high stone walkway, looking with delicious vertigo over the tremendous drop-off. Maybe he should just do it anyway, and fall to the wet black rocks and churning waves. If the damned Face Dancers needed him so badly, they could just grow another ghola, and maybe that one wouldn't be so flawed. The Baron Harkonnen would be back!

He felt a hand on his shoulder. Gathering his remaining shreds of dignity, he looked up to see a pug-nosed Face Dancer staring at him. Though all shape-shifters looked exactly the same to him, he somehow knew this one was Khrone. "What do you want?"

Officiously, the Face Dancer said, "You and Paolo will depart Caladan and never return. The great war is proceeding, and the evermind has decided that he needs the Kwisatz Haderach close to him. Omnius wants you to complete the boy's preparation under his direct supervision in the heart of the machine empire. You will depart for Synchrony as soon as a ship is ready."

The Baron flicked his gaze past the Face Dancer to Paolo, who crouched by a Harkonnen statue, close enough to eavesdrop on the conversation. He chuckled to himself, for this boy was as persistent as Piter de Vries! As soon as he realized he was discovered, Paolo scampered forward. "Is he talking about me?"

"Discuss Paolo's destiny with him on the way," Khrone said to the Baron. "Do more than explain it. Make the boy *believe*."

"Paolo is inclined to believe anything that reinforces his delusions of grandeur," the Baron said, ignoring the boy. "So, this Kwisatz Haderach business is . . . real?"

Even though the Face Dancers had finally explained the truth to him, the idea still sounded preposterous. He was not convinced that this young ghola could be so important in the grand scheme of things.

Khrone looked ghastly in his blank state. Shadows around his eyes darkened as his displeasure became evident. "I believe it, and so does Omnius. Who are you to question?"

Believe it, dear Grandfather, said the annoying voice. *By his very genes, Paul Atreides has the potential to be greater than you will ever be, in any incarnation.*

The Baron refused to reply, either aloud or in his own thoughts. Ignoring the Abomination often made her shut up.

And now they were going to Synchrony, the home of Omnius. He looked forward to seeing the thinking-machine empire. New challenges, new opportunities.

In spite of the sum of his first life's memories, the stories of the evil thinking machines and the Butlerian Jihad were too distant to seem relevant. Though he harbored considerable resentment toward the Face Dancers, he was glad to be on the side of greater strength.

Later, during the shuttle ride to orbit, the Baron gazed down at the coastline, the villages, the new smokestacks and strip-mined areas of Caladan. In his excitement, Paolo bustled from window to window. "Will we have a long journey?"

"I'm not a pilot. How should I know? The thinking machines must be very far away, otherwise humans would have known about them long before now."

"What will happen when we get there?"

"Ask a Face Dancer."

"They won't talk to me."

"Then ask Omnius when you see him. In the meantime, amuse yourself."

Paolo sat down beside him in the passenger compartment and

began sampling packets of syrupy packaged food. "I'm special, you know. They've been grooming me, watching over me carefully. What exactly is a Kwisatz Haderach, anyway?" He wiped his mouth with the back of a hand.

"Don't crawl into their delusions, boy. There is no such thing as a Kwisatz Haderach. A myth, a legend, something with a hundred vague explanations in as many prophecies. The entire Bene Gesserit breeding program is utter nonsense." He recalled from deep memories that he had been part of that breeding program himself, forced to impregnate the vile witch Mohiam. He had humiliated her during the act, but in retaliation the hag had transmitted the debilitating disease that had made him bloated and fat.

"It can't be nonsense. I have visions, especially when I take spice tablets. I see it again and again. I've got a bloody knife in my hand, and I'm victorious. I see myself rushing to take my prize—melange, but more than melange. I also see myself lying on the floor, bleeding to death. Which one is right? It's so confusing!"

"Shut up and take a nap."

They docked with an unmarked ship high above Caladan. It bore no markings of the Guild and carried no Navigator. Wide hangar doors opened, drawing the shuttle up and inside. Silvery figures moved within the cold, airless landing bay, guiding the small vessel into a docking cradle. Robots—demons from ancient history! Ah, so, at least part of Khrone's wild tale might be true.

The Baron smiled at the boy staring out the windows. "You and I are about to undertake an interesting journey, Paolo."

A sheathed dagger is useless in a fight. A maula pistol without pro-
jectiles is no more than a club. And a ghola without his memories is
merely flesh.

—PAUL ATREIDES,
secret ghola journals

Now that the ghola of Dr. Yueh had his memories restored, Paul
Atreides knew he had to attempt more innovative measures to
awaken himself. Paul was the oldest of the ghola children, the one
with (presumably) the greatest potential, but Sheeana and the Bene
Gesserit observers had chosen Yueh as a test case. Unlike the Suk doctor, however, Paul actually wanted his past back. He longed to remember his life and love with Chani, his childhood with Duke Leto and
Lady Jessica, his friendships with Gurney Halleck and Duncan Idaho.

But Paul continued to be haunted by prescient memory-visions of
his own double death. And he was growing impatient.

How could the passengers aboard the no-ship think there was still
time for caution? Only a few months ago, they had again narrowly
escaped the Enemy's net, brighter and stronger than ever before. Of
great concern, the saboteur still had not been caught. Though the
saboteur had done nothing else as dramatic as the murder of the three
axlotl tanks and unborn gholas, the danger remained.

Paul knew the *Ithaca* needed him, and he was tired of being just a
ghola. He had an idea to attempt, one that was both desperate and

dangerous, but he didn't hesitate. His real memories hovered like a mirage just beyond the heat-shimmered horizon.

With faithful Chani beside him, he stood outside the hatch that led into the great sand-filled hold. He had told no one else what he intended to do. Over the past two years, security had been tightened as much as the Bashar and an eager Thufir Hawat could manage, but no one guarded the entrance to the cargo hold. The seven sandworms were considered sufficiently dangerous to act as their own watchdogs. Only Sheeana could safely go among the large creatures, and the last time she had done so, even she had been briefly swallowed up.

Paul gazed at Chani's beautiful elfin face and her thick, dark red hair. Even without prior knowledge, without knowing his destiny was to be with her, he would have found the Fremen girl strikingly attractive. In turn, she ran a methodical eye over his body, his special new suit, his tools. "You look like a real Fremen warrior, Usul."

After studying records and working with a fabrication station in the engineering levels, Chani had fashioned an authentic stillsuit for him—probably the first one manufactured in centuries—and provided him with a rope, maker hooks, and spreaders. The unusual tools felt oddly familiar in his grasp. According to legend, Muad'Dib had summoned a dangerous monster for his first worm ride. These creatures in the hold, though stunted by their captivity, were still behemoths.

The hatch opened, and he and Chani stepped into the artificial desert. When the flinty odors and arid heat struck him, he said, "Stay here, where it's safe. I have to do this alone, or it won't be effective. If I face the worm and ride it, that may jar my memories."

Chani did not try to stop him. She understood the need as well as he did.

He climbed up the first rise, leaving footprints in the sand, then raised both hands and shouted, "Shai-Hulud! I have come for you!" In this confined space, he did not need a thumper to summon the worms.

A quality in the air changed. He sensed a stirring in the shallow dunes and saw seven serpentlike shapes coming toward him. Instead of running away, he sprinted toward them, selecting a place where he could set up his approach and mount one. His heart pounded. His throat was dry despite the stillsuit mask covering his mouth and nose.

Paul had reviewed holofilms to study Fremen sandriding tech-niques. Intellectually he knew what to do, just as—intellectually—he knew the factual details of his past. But a theoretical understanding was far different from actual experience. It occurred to him now, as he stood small and vulnerable on the sand, that the most effective form of learning was in the actual doing, which ensured a more thorough com-prehension than he could derive from dusty archives.

I shall learn well, he thought, letting fear wash past him.

The nearest worm surged toward him with a rushing sound of scat-tered sand. The sheer size of the worms grew more incomprehensible as they approached, cresting the dunes.

Infusing his heart with courage, Paul forced himself to face this challenge. He held up his hook and spreader and crouched for the first leap. The noise of the monsters' approach was so loud that at first he did not hear the woman shouting. From the corner of his eye, he saw Sheeana bounding across the dunes, throwing herself in front of him. The largest worm exploded through the dust and reared up, its gigantic round mouth glittering with crystalline teeth.

Sheeana held up her hands and shouted, "Stop, Shaitan!"

The worm hesitated, and quested from side to side with its fleshy head as if confused.

"Stop! This one is not for you." She placed a firm hand on the chest of Paul's stillsuit and pushed him behind her. "He is not for you, Monarch."

As if sulking, the largest worm backed away, keeping its eyeless head turned toward them. "Get back to the hatch, foolish boy," Sheeana hissed at Paul, using just enough Voice to make his legs respond before he could think.

Duncan Idaho was also there at the hatchway, glowering. Chani looked both fearful and relieved.

Sheeana marched Paul back toward the waiting observers. "That worm would have destroyed you!"

"I'm an Atreides. Shouldn't I be able to control them like you can?"

"That isn't a theory I intend to test with you. You are too important to us. Of all the gholas, if *you* foolishly throw your life away, what are we to do?"

"But if you protect me too much, you'll never get what you need. Riding a worm would have brought my memories back, I'm sure of it."

"You restored Yueh," Chani pointed out to Sheeana. "Why not Usul? He's older."

"Yueh was expendable, and we weren't sure of what we were doing. We have already developed specific plans for awakening Liet-Kynes and Stilgar, and if we succeed with them, others may follow— including Thufir Hawat and you, Chani. One day, Paul Atreides will get his chance. But only after we are certain."

"What if we don't have the time?" Paul walked away from them, brushing sand and dust from his new stillsuit.

DUNCAN AWOKE TO a loud signal at the door to his quarters. His initial thought was that Sheeana had come to him again, despite their mutual reservations. He slid aside the door, ready for an argument.

Paul stood there wearing a replica of an Atreides military uniform, which evoked instant respect and loyalty from Duncan. The young man had dressed that way on purpose. Right now, the ghola Paul was almost exactly the same age as the original had been when Arrakeen had fallen to the devious Harkonnens, when the first Duncan had died defending him and his mother.

"Duncan, you say you were my close friend. You say you knew Paul Atreides. Help me now." Grasping an ornately carved ivory hilt, the young man drew a blue-white crystalline dagger from a sheath at his waist.

Duncan stared in amazement. "A crysknife? It looks . . . Is it real?"

"Chani made it from a worm tooth Sheeana found in the cargo hold."

In wonder, Duncan touched his fingers to the blade, noting how tough and sharp it was. He drew his thumb along the edge, intentionally cutting himself. He let a single drop of blood fall onto the milky-white dagger. "According to ancient tradition, a crysknife must never be drawn unless it tastes blood."

"I know." Paul was clearly troubled as he took the weapon back and returned it to its sheath. After hesitating, he blurted out what he had come to say. "Why won't the Bene Gesserits awaken me, Duncan? You need me. Everyone on this no-ship needs me."

"Yes, young Master Paul. We do need you, but we need you *alive*."

"You need my abilities, as soon as possible. I was the Kwisatz Haderach, and this ghola has the same genetics. Imagine how I could help."

"The Kwisatz Haderach . . ." Duncan sighed and sat down on his bed. "The Sisterhood spent centuries creating him, but at the same time they were terrified of him. He can supposedly bridge space and time, seeing the future and the past, places even a Reverend Mother dares not look. Through brute force or guile he can forge a union between the most diverse of factions. It's a grab bag of tremendous powers."

"Whatever those powers are, Duncan, I need them. And for that I require my memories. Convince Sheeana to try me next."

"She will do what she will do, at a time of her choosing. You overestimate the influence I have among the Sisters."

"But what if the Enemy's net ensnares us completely? What if the Kwisatz Haderach is your only hope?"

"Leto II was a Kwisatz Haderach, as well, though neither you nor your son turned out exactly the way the Bene Gesserit intended. The Sisters are very afraid of anyone who manifests unusual powers." He laughed. "After the Scattering, when the Sisterhood brought the great Duncan Idaho back, some of them even accused *me* of being a Kwisatz Haderach. They killed eleven of my gholas, either by Bene Gesserit heretics or Tleilaxu schemers."

"But why don't they want these powers? I thought—"

"Oh, they want the powers, Paul, but only under carefully controlled conditions." His heart went out to the young man, who looked so lost and desperate.

"I can't do anything without my past, Duncan. Help me retrieve it! You lived through part of it with me. You remember."

"Oh, I remember you very well." Duncan laced his hands behind his head and leaned back. "I remember your christening on Caladan after you were nearly killed by Imperial intrigues as an infant. I remember how Duke Leto's whole family was put at risk in the War of

Assassins. I was given the great honor of taking you to safety, and you and I went to the wilds of Caladan. We stayed with your exiled grandmother Helena, and we hid among the Caladan primitives. That was when you and I became so close. Yes, I remember it very well."

"I don't," Paul said with a sigh.

Duncan seemed caught in a loop of his past lives. Caladan . . . Dune . . . the Harkonnens . . . Alia . . . Hayt. "Do you know what you're asking me, about your memories, about your life? The Tleilaxu created my first ghola as an assassination tool. They manipulated me because I was your friend. They knew you could not turn me away, even though you saw the trap."

"I wouldn't have turned you away, Duncan."

"I had the knife raised against you, ready to strike, but in the last instant, I collided with myself. The programmed assassin Hayt became the loyal Duncan Idaho. You can't imagine the agony!" He pointed a stern finger at the young man. "Restoring your past will require a similar crisis."

Paul squared his jaw. "I'm prepared for it. I'm not afraid of pain."

Wrinkling his brow, Duncan said, "You're too content, young Paul, because your Chani grounds you. She makes you stable and happy—and that's a severe drawback. In contrast, look at Yueh. He fought against remembering with every fiber of his being, and that's what broke him. But you . . . what fulcrum can they use on you, Paul Atreides?"

"We'll just have to find something."

"Are you really ready to accept it?" Duncan leaned forward, offering no mercy. "What if the only way you can have your past restored is that you must *lose* Chani? What if she has to die bleeding in your arms, before you can remember?"

More than anything, I need my father to know I did not fail. I do not want him to die thinking I was unworthy of his genes.

—THE SCYTALE GHOLA,
no-ship security interview

It must be built according to precise standards," insisted the old Tleilaxu. His voice cracked. "*Precise* standards!"

"I will take care of it, Father." The ghola, only thirteen, tended the degenerating Master who sat in a stiff armchair. Old Scytale refused to lie down until a traditional bier for his body was built. He intentionally kept his austere living quarters locked to keep others away. He had no desire to be interrupted or harassed during his dying days.

The Tleilaxu Master's organs, joints, and skin had begun to fail in increasingly problematic ways. It reminded him of how the no-ship itself seemed to be breaking down, its systems failing as air leaked into space, water was inexplicably lost, food stores went missing. Some of the more paranoid refugees saw sabotage in every flickering glowpanel, and many turned their suspicious eyes toward the Tleilaxu. It was another reason for him to grumble. At least he would soon be gone.

"I thought you said my bier was already being built. It cannot be rushed."

The teenager bowed his head. "Do not worry. I am following the strict laws of the Shariat."

"Show it to me, then."

"Your own bier? But that is meant to carry your body only after you . . . after you . . ."

Old Scytale glowered with his dark eyes. "Purge those useless emotions! You have become too involved in this process. It is shameful."

"Am I not supposed to care about you, Father? I see your pain—"

"Stop calling me Father. Think of me as *yourself*. Once you become me, I will not be dead. No need for weeping. Each of our incarnations is disposable, so long as the memory train continues uninterrupted."

Young Scytale tried to regain his composure. "You are still a father to me, no matter what memories are buried inside me. Will I stop feeling these emotions when my old life is restored?"

"Of course. At that glorious moment you will understand the truth—and your obligations." Scytale grabbed the young man by his shirt and pulled his face close. "Where are your memories? What if I were to die tomorrow?"

Old Scytale knew death was imminent, but he had dramatized his infirmity in an attempt to shock his replacement. The premature construction of the bier was yet another attempt to provoke a crisis. If only the two of them could be back on Tleilax, where full immersion in the holy traditions of the Great Belief would be enough to trigger even the most stubborn of gholas. Here onboard a godless no-ship, the difficulties seemed insurmountable.

"This should never have taken so long."

"I have failed you."

The rheumy eyes flashed. "You are not only failing me, you are failing your people. If you do not awaken, our whole race—our entire history and all the knowledge in my mind—will vanish from the universe. Do you want to be responsible for that? I refuse to believe God has turned His back on us entirely. Our fate, lamentably, depends upon you."

The ghola looked crestfallen, as if an unsupportable weight rested on his shoulders. "I am doing all I can to achieve that goal, *Father*." He said the word deliberately. "And until I succeed, you must do all you can to remain alive."

He's finally showing a little strength, Scytale thought, bitterly. *But it's not enough.*

DAYS LATER, THE ghola stood by his father's deathbed, his *own* deathbed. He felt as if he were having an out-of-body experience, watching his life slip away moment by moment. It gave the boy an oddly disconnected feeling.

Since emerging from the axlotl tank, Scytale had loved only one person: himself . . . both his older self and the self he was going to be. The degenerating man had provided cells from his own body, cells that held all his memories and experiences, all the knowledge of the Tleilaxu.

But he hadn't provided the key to unlock them. No matter how hard the young ghola strained, his memories obstinately refused to emerge. He clutched the old man's hand. "Not yet, Father. I've tried and tried."

With near-sightless eyes, old Scytale glared at his counterpart. "Why do you . . . disappoint me so?"

Yueh had been restored to his past life, and two other gholas—Stilgar and Liet-Kynes—were even now being raked over the mental coals. How could mere witches succeed where a Tleilaxu Master failed? Bene Gesserits should never have been so adept at triggering the avalanche of experiences. If Scytale could not do it, the Tleilaxu would be relegated to the dustbins of history.

The old man on the bed coughed and wheezed, while the younger leaned close, tears trickling down his cheeks. Old Scytale spat blood. His disappointment and utter despair were palpable.

An insistent signal at the door announced the arrival of two Suk doctors. The bespectacled Rabbi was obviously repulsed by his duties, while young Yueh still appeared to be shaken by the recent return of his memories. Scytale could see in their eyes that they both knew the older Master would perish very soon.

Among the witches there were other Suk practitioners, but Scytale had insisted on being tended only by the Rabbi, and only when absolutely necessary. They were all unclean powindah, but at least the Rabbi wasn't a disgusting *female*. Or, perhaps Scytale should choose Wellington Yueh over the old Jew. The old Tleilaxu Master had to accept certain medical examinations, if only to keep himself alive until his "son" reawakened.

Scytale lifted his head. "Go away! We are praying."

"Do you think I like tending to gholas? To filthy Tleilaxu? Do you think I want to be here? You can both die, for all I care!"

Yueh, though, moved forward with a medical kit, easing the younger Scytale aside to check the dying man's vital signs. Behind Yueh the Rabbi squinted through his spectacles with vulture eyes. "It won't be long now."

Such an odd old holy man, young Scytale thought. Even compared to the smells of disinfectant, medicine, and sickness, he'd always had an odd smell about him.

Sounding compassionate, Yueh said, "There isn't much we can do."

Gasping for air, old Scytale croaked out, "A Tleilaxu Master should not be so weak and decrepit. It is . . . unseemly."

His youthful counterpart tried again to trigger the flow of memories, to squeeze them into his brain by sheer force of will, as he had attempted to do countless times before. The essential past must be in there somewhere, buried deep. But he felt no tickle of possibilities, no glimmer of success. *What if they are not there at all?* What if something had gone terribly wrong? His pulse pounded as the panic began to rise. Not much time. Never enough time.

He tried to cut off the thought. The body provided a wealth of cellular material. They could create more Scytale gholas, try again and again if necessary. But if his own memories had failed to resurface, why should an identical ghola have any better luck without the guidance of the original?

I am the only one who knew the Master so intimately.

He wanted to shake Yueh, demand to know how he had managed to remember his past. Tears were in full flow now, falling onto the old man's hand, but Scytale knew they were inadequate. His father's chest spasmed in an almost imperceptible death rattle. The life-support equipment hummed with more intensity, and the instrument readings fluctuated.

"He's slipped into a coma," Yueh reported.

The Rabbi nodded. Like an executioner announcing his plans, he said, "Too weak. He's going to die now."

Scytale's heart sank. "He has given up on me." His father would never know if he succeeded now; he would perish wondering and worrying. The last great calamity in a long line of disasters that had befallen the Tleilaxu race.

He gripped the old man's hand. So cold, too cold. He felt the life ebbing. *I have failed!*

As if felled by a stunner, Scytale dropped to his knees at the bedside. In his crashing despair, he knew with absolute certainly that he could never resurrect the recalcitrant memories. Not alone. *Lost! Forever lost! Everything that comprised the great Tleilaxu race.* He could not bear the magnitude of this disaster. The reality of his defeat sliced like shattered glass into his heart.

Abruptly, the Tleilaxu youth felt something changing inside, followed by an explosion between his temples. He cried out from the excruciating pain. At first he thought he was dying himself, but instead of being swallowed in blackness, he felt new thoughts burning like wildfire across his consciousness. Memories streamed past in a blur, but Scytale locked onto each one, absorbing it again and reprocessing it into the synapses of his brain. The precious memories returned to where they had always belonged.

His father's death had opened the barriers. At last Scytale retrieved what he was supposed to know, the critical data bank of a Tleilaxu Master, all the ancient secrets of his race.

Instilled with pride and a new sense of dignity, he rose to his feet. Wiping away warm tears, he looked down at the discarded copy of himself on the bed. It was nothing more than a withered husk. He no longer needed that old man.

These ghola children contain old souls that are not unlike the voices in a Reverend Mother's Other Memory. The challenge is to access and exploit these old souls.

—ship's log, entry of
DUNCAN IDAHO

I n the gangly body of a teenager, filled with the memories of a long life and the shame of things he had done, Wellington Yueh walked with painstaking slowness. Each step brought him closer to the moment he had been dreading. The skin of his brow burned where a diamond tattoo should have been; at least he no longer displayed that lie.

Yueh knew that if he ever intended to make this life different from his error-prone past, he must confront the terrible things he had done.

Here, thousands of years later and on the other side of the universe, House Atreides lived all around him: Paul Atreides, Lady Jessica, Duncan Idaho, Thufir Hawat. At least Duke Leto had not been resurrected as a ghola. Not yet. Yueh didn't think he could bear to look into the eyes of the man he had betrayed.

Facing Jessica would be tough enough.

Walking ponderously toward her quarters, Yueh heard voices ahead, a child's giggle and a woman's rebuke. Suddenly little Alia toddled out of one doorway and ducked into another, followed by a scolding proctor. The two-year-old was extremely precocious, with a hint of the genius that the first Alia had been; the spice saturation in the axlotl tank had altered her somewhat, but she didn't possess the complete Other Memory of her predecessor. The proctor followed and sealed the door behind them. Neither of them had glanced at Yueh.

Alia was the most recent ghola to be born; the program had been stalled since the horrific murder of the three tanks and unborn children. *At least that is one crime I do not have on my conscience.* But the Bene Gesserits would soon begin the program again. They were already discussing which cells to implant in the new axlotl tanks. Irulan? Emperor Shaddam himself? Count Fenring . . . or someone far worse? Yueh shuddered at the thought. He feared that the witches had gone beyond true need and now were just toying with lives, letting their infernal curiosity sidestep all caution.

He paused in front of Jessica's quarters, steeling himself. *I will face my fear.* Wasn't that part of the Litany the witches so often quoted? In their present incarnations as gholas, Jessica and Yueh had been close enough to think of themselves as friends. But since becoming Dr. Wellington Yueh again, everything was different.

Now I have a second chance, he thought. *But my road to redemption is long, and the incline very steep.*

Jessica opened her door at his signal. "Oh hello, Wellington. My grandson and I were just reading a holobook about Paul's younger years, one of those tomes Princess Irulan was always writing." She invited him inside, where he saw Leto II sitting cross-legged on the carpeted floor. Leto was a loner, though he frequently spent time with his "grandmother."

Yueh twitched nervously when she closed the door behind them, as if to seal his doom and prevent escape. He kept his eyes down, and after a deep sigh he said, "I wish to apologize to you, my Lady. Though I know you can never forgive me."

Jessica placed an arm on his shoulder. "We've been through this. You can't bear the blame for things that were done so long ago. It wasn't really you."

"Yes it was, because I remember it all now! We gholas were created for one purpose, and we must accept the consequences."

Jessica looked at him impatiently. "We all know what you did, Wellington. I accepted that and forgave you long ago."

"But will you do it again after you *remember?* One day those vaults will be opened in your mind, the terrible old wounds. We've got to face the guilt our predecessors left for us, or we'll be consumed by things we never did."

"It's uncharted territory for all of us, but I suspect we each have plenty of things to atone for." She tried to console him, but he didn't feel he deserved it.

Leto paused the filmbook and looked up with an eerie intelligence in his eyes. "Well, I'm only going to take responsibility for what I do in *this* life."

Jessica reached out to touch Yueh's face gently. "I can't understand what you went through, what you're still going through. I'll know soon enough, I suppose. But you should think about what you would *like* to be, not what you're afraid of being."

She made it sound so simple, but despite his best efforts, he had been twisted before. "What if I do something bad in this lifetime, too?"

Jessica's expression hardened. "Then no one can help you."

You think your eyes are open, yet you do not see.

—Bene Gesserit admonishment

Water crashed against the black reef on Buzzell, sending up a veil of spray. Mother Commander Murbella stood with the once-disgraced Sister at the edge of the cove, watching Phibians frolic in deep water. The amphibious creatures swam together, slick and smooth-skinned, diving under the combers and then bursting to the surface again.

"They love their new freedom," Corysta said.

Like dolphins in an ancient Earth sea, Murbella thought, admiring their forms. Human . . . and yet dramatically not so.

"I'm more interested in seeing them harvest soostones." She turned her face into the salty wind. Gray clouds were gathering, but the air remained warm and humid. "Our debts in this war are staggering. Our credit is stretched beyond its limits, and some of our most vital suppliers will accept nothing but hard currency—like soostones."

In the months since leaving Oculiat, the Mother Commander had traveled from planet to planet, studying humanity's defenses. Realizing their great peril, local kings, presidents, and warlords provided independent battleships to add to the newly constructed Guild vessels being released by the Junction shipyards. Every government and cluster of allied worlds scrambled to invent or acquire new armaments to use against the Enemy, but so far nothing had proved effective. The Ixians were still testing the Obliterator weapons, which had proved to be more difficult to manufacture than expected. Murbella continued to demand more work, more material and sacrifices. It wouldn't be enough.

And the war continued. Plagues spread. Machine fleets destroyed every human-inhabited world they encountered. Near the edge of one of the main combat zones, three more Sheeana surrogates rallied the people caught between a hammer and an anvil, but to no avail. So far, since the beginning of Omnius's march across space, Murbella could not claim a single clear victory.

In her bleakest moments the odds seemed poor and the obstacles insurmountable. Millennia ago, the fighters of the Butlerian Jihad had faced another impossible situation, and humankind had won only by accepting an appalling cost. They had unleashed countless atomic weapons that not only destroyed thinking machines, but also trillions of human beings who had been held in slavery. The Pyrrhic victory had left a horrendous stain on the human soul.

And now, even after that monumental sacrifice, Omnius was back, like a noxious weed whose roots had never been destroyed. Gauging the progress of the thinking machines, in the next year or two the human race would be forced into a climactic showdown.

Once the Ixian industrialists delivered their long-awaited Obliterators, all the collected militaries from planet after planet would draw a line in space. As far as she was concerned, that opportunity could not come soon enough.

"Our soostone shipments have increased every month for the past two years." As she spoke, Corysta did not remove her gaze from the frolicking aquatic creatures. "The Phibians are more productive, now that the Honored Matres have stopped torturing them. And they never used to play like that before. They consider the seas of Buzzell their home instead of their prison."

Corysta, a former Breeding Mother exiled here for the crime of trying to keep her own baby, had become a stalwart monitor of soostone harvests. She oversaw the grading, cleaning, and packaging of the pearlescent gems, which were delivered regularly to CHOAM intermediaries.

"Even so, we need more soostones."

"I'll speak with the Phibians, Mother Commander. I'll explain that our need is great, that the Enemy draws near. For me, they might work harder." Corysta's smile was strangely unreadable. "I'll ask it as a favor."

"And that will work?"

The other Sister shrugged. The Phibians leapt high into the air and dove back into the water, while Corysta waved to them, laughing. They seemed to know she was watching them. Sunlight glinted on the water. Were these Phibians putting on a special performance?

Quite suddenly, something large and serpentine emerged from the depths near the splashing creatures. An eyeless head rose above the waves, its round mouth flashing crystalline teeth. The head quested around, fin-edged gill flaps sensing vibrations, like a sea serpent from ancient legends.

Murbella caught her breath. To her amazement it resembled a sandworm from Rakis, though only about ten meters long—and with adaptations that enabled it to live in the water. Impossible! A seaworm?

Corysta ran frantically down the rocks and waded into the surf. The Phibians had already seen the monster and tried to swim away. The worm darted toward them, spray glistening from its greenish rings.

Two more of the long, sinuous monsters appeared from the deep water and circled around the Phibians. The aquatic people clustered in a defensive formation; one male with a scar on his forehead drew a wide, flat-bladed knife used for scoring cholisters on the ocean floor. The other Phibians brandished their own weapons, which were laughable against a sea serpent.

Knee-deep in waves, Corysta slipped on the algae-slick rocks. Murbella ran after her, fixated on what she saw in the water. "What are those creatures?"

"Monsters! I have never seen them before."

The scarred male Phibian emitted a loud vibrating sound and slapped

one webbed hand on the water with a sharp crack. The clustered Phibians bolted like a startled school of fish, several diving underwater, others swimming briskly across the waves.

Though they had no eyes, the swimming worms knew where the
Phibians were. With a blur and a flick of long serpentine bodies, they
pursued the aquatic workers, driving them toward the rocky shore.

Murbella and Corysta watched the largest worm lunge and grab one
of the Phibians, scooping him down into the wet gullet. The other
worms attacked like a group of frenzied sharks.

Murbella waded out to grab Corysta's shoulder, preventing her from
swimming farther into the churning water. They were both helpless to
prevent the violence. "My Sea Child," Corysta moaned.

The seaworms thrashed and splashed as they fed. Bloody waves
lapped against Murbella's legs, and she dragged the sobbing Corysta
back to shore.

A planet is not merely an item for study. Rather it is a tool, per-haps even a weapon, with which we can make our mark on the galaxy.

—LIET‑KYNES,
the original

N ow that Stilgar and Liet had their ghola memories back, they had become the no-ship's experts on extreme recycling, making the most of their reduced resources. The *Ithaca*'s life-support systems had been designed by geniuses out in the Scattering, descendants of those who had survived the horrific Famine Times. The highly efficient technology could serve passengers and crew for long periods, even in the face of the increasing population. But not in the face of deliberate sabotage.

Tall and lean, with the body of a youth and the aged eyes of a naib, Stilgar looked ready to embark on a desert journey. He and Liet-Kynes had been bound at first by common interests and more recently by their awakened pasts. Liet refused to talk about the crisis through which Sheeana had broken him—it was a matter too private even for close friends.

For himself, Stilgar couldn't forget what the witches had done to him. To the very depths of his being he was a desert man of Arrakis. Watched over by Proctor Superior Garimi, he had read of his history as a young commando against the Harkonnens, later as naib, and then as a supporter of Muad'Dib. But to trigger his ghola memories, the Sisters had tried to *drown* him.

At a water-filled recycling reservoir, Sheeana and Garimi had tied weights around his ankles. Stilgar fought, but the witches were more than a match for him. "What have I done? Why are you doing this to me?"

"Find your past," Sheeana said, "or die."

"Without your memories you are useless, and better off drowned," Garimi said. They dumped him into the pool.

Unable to free himself from the weights on his ankles, Stilgar had quickly sunk. He had struggled mightily, but the water was everywhere, more oppressive than the thickest dust cloud. Trying desperately to peer upward, he made out only the vague wavering shapes of the two women up there. Neither lifted a hand to help him.

His lungs screamed, and blackness closed in around his eyesight. Stilgar thrashed violently and grew weaker every second. He was starving for breath. He wanted to cry out—*needed* to—but there was no air. Exhaled bubbles roared out of his open mouth. When it was more than unbearable, he inhaled a huge gulp into his lungs, flooding his air passages. He couldn't see any way out of the tank—

—and suddenly it was no longer a tank, but a wide, deep river, which he realized was on one of the planets where he had fought in Muad'Dib's jihad. He had marched with a regiment of Caladan soldiers and they had needed to ford the river. The water had been deeper than anyone anticipated, and all of them went under. His companions, who had been born swimming, thought nothing of it, even laughed as they made their way to shore. But Stilgar was dragged beneath the surface. He reached up, clutching for air. He had inhaled water then, too, and nearly drowned—

Finally, Sheeana dragged Stilgar out of the tank and pumped his lungs. A disapproving Suk doctor scolded her and Garimi as she revived the young ghola. They rolled him over, and he vomited up sour mouthfuls of water. He was barely able to rise to his knees.

When he turned his glare on Sheeana, he was more than an eleven-year-old boy. He was Naib Stilgar.

Later, when he saw Liet restored as well, Stilgar was afraid to ask what terrible ordeal his friend had been forced to endure. . . .

Now the two headed for the great hold to see the sandworms, as they had done many times before. The high observation chamber was one of their favorite places, especially now. The tremendous worms called up strong and atavistic feelings in them.

As they approached, Stilgar breathed in the comforting scent of warm, dry air with the distinct odors of worms and cinnamon. He smiled briefly in a passing nostalgia, before his face creased in a frown. "I should not be smelling that."

Liet picked up his pace. "That environment has to be carefully controlled. If the seals are leaking, then moisture could penetrate the hold." Yet another breakdown, after so many others!

Rushing into the equipment chamber, they found young Thufir Hawat supervising repair operations. Two Bene Gesserit Sisters and Levi, one of the refugee Jews, worked to install sheets of replacement plaz. They applied thick sealants around the windows high above the sand-filled cargo hold. Thufir was scowling.

Stilgar strode forward, his demeanor intimidating. The task of monitoring the sandworms and the recycling systems was generally reserved for himself and Liet. "Why are you here, Hawat?"

Thufir showed surprise at the coldly accusatory tone of the Fremen's voice. "Someone poured acid on the seals. The corrosive destroyed not only the sealant, but part of the plaz and the wallplates as well."

"We patched it in time," said Levi. "We also found a timed device that would have emptied one of our water reservoirs into the hold, flooding it."

Stilgar trembled with rage. "That would have killed the worms!"

"I checked those systems myself, only two days ago," Liet said. "This is no simple breakdown."

"No," Thufir agreed. "Our saboteur is at work again."

While Stilgar ran his gaze suspiciously over the gathered people, Liet hurried to the instrument consoles to check the desert environment. "There appears to be no permanent damage. The readings are still within the creatures' tolerance range. Scrubbers should bring the air back to desired levels in short order."

Stilgar took special care to inspect the new seals, found them adequate. He and Liet exchanged looks that said they had to be suspicious of everyone onboard. *Except for each other*, Stilgar decided.

Long ago, when he and Liet had first known each other, the two had shared many adventures fighting the nefarious Harkonnens. Like his father, Liet had led a double life, delivering grand dreams to the desert people while acting as Imperial Planetologist and Judge of the Change. Liet was also the father of Chani. While the Fremen girl's ghola did not remember him yet, he remembered her, and he looked at Chani with a strange, age-worn love.

Bothered by the acrid odors of acid and sealant, Stilgar turned grimly away from the observation window. "From now on, I sleep here. I will not let Shai-Hulud die, not while I still breathe."

"I'm working with the Bashar. There must be some kind of a trail, so we only need to find it. The corrosive was acquired from secure stores, so there may be fingerprints or genetic traces." Thufir's lips were not stained red with sapho, his skin not grizzled, his eyes not weary with age and experiences, as in the famous old portraits. "Perhaps the imagers captured the saboteur sneaking to the observation deck. Once I catch him, we can all rest more easily."

"No," Stilgar said. "Even then, I would not let my guard down."

IN A SUDDEN resurgence, the maddening sabotage continued in myriad ways and at random points around the huge ship, setting everyone's nerves on edge. The Bene Gesserits remained vigilant and wary, while the Rabbi preached to a growing number of followers about spies and murderers lurking among them.

Duncan studied the readings, ran projections. Again, he wondered if one or more of the Face Dancer Handlers might still be aboard, having escaped the wreckage of a crashed ship. Where else could the saboteur be hiding? After years of searching, Duncan and Teg had run out of ideas. How could this enemy elude surveillance imagers, Truthsayer interrogations, and vigorous searches? In a few suspicious incidents, a blurry form could be seen moving in restricted areas, but even enhancement could not sharpen the facial features to recognizability.

The saboteur seemed to know exactly where and when to strike. An endless succession of little breakdowns and small accidents, each taking its toll, ran the ship's company to exhaustion.

One time, imagers detected what appeared to be a man as he moved furtively down a corridor near a bank of oxygen-scrubber units and air-circulating machines. Dressed in dark clothing and a tight-fitting hood that covered most of his face, he carried a long silver knife and a pry bar, and his body leaned forward against the heavy air flow. Then, like liquid flowing around a corner, the man slipped into the central recirculation chamber, where great fans blasted air through a system of arteries in the no-ship, pushing it through thick curtains of matted fibers coated with biogels to remove impurities.

With sudden fury, the unidentifiable saboteur slashed and hacked at the porous filter mats, ripping them from their frames and destroying their ability to purify air. After completing this mayhem, the saboteur turned to flee. Not a single frame of the imagers showed the face; it wasn't even absolutely clear whether the hooded vandal was male or female. By the time security personnel rushed into the area, the saboteur had vanished into the howling, recirculated wind.

Duncan did not need to whisper the obvious answer. *Face Dancer.* He studied all records of the kamikaze ships from the Handlers, noting where they had crashed into the hull and how the bodies aboard had been confirmed dead and disposed of. One of the shape-shifting Handlers must have crawled out of the flaming wreckage.

Even worse, there might be more than one.

THE AIR SMELLED moist and foul, like seaweed and sewage. Duncan stood on the mist-slickened catwalk above one of the largest algae tanks. The entire vat was dying. *Poisoned.*

Standing next to him, gripping the catwalk rail with a white-knuckled hand, Teg frowned at the chemical analyses displayed on his datapad. "Heavy metals, potent toxins, a list of deadly chemicals that even this stuff can't digest." He pulled up a dripping handful of the once-fecund green substance. The goop was brownish now, breaking down.

"The saboteur is trying to destroy our food supply," Duncan said.

"Our air, too."

"To what end? To kill us, it appears."

"Or simply to make us helpless."

Duncan glared at the vat, feeling angry and violated. "Get work crews to drain and scrub the tank. Decontaminate as quickly as possible. Then harvest starter material from other tanks to fertilize the biomass. We've got to stabilize it before something else goes wrong."

DUNCAN WAS ALONE on the navigation bridge when the next disaster occurred. Over the years the passengers had learned to ignore the faint vibrations of the no-ship's movement. Now, though, an abrupt lurch and an obvious deflection in course nearly threw him out of his chair.

He called for Teg and Thufir, then scrambled over the controls, scanning empty space around them. He feared they might have run into a piece of space debris or some gravitational anomaly. But he found no evidence of impact, no obstacles in their vicinity. The *Ithaca* was obviously yawing, and he struggled to steady it using the numerous smaller engines distributed around the hull. This slowed the spinning of the ship, but did not entirely stop it.

As the immense vessel continued to turn, he saw a glittering silver path like a scarf of mist, spewing from the stern. One of the no-ship's three primary water reservoirs had been dumped—intentionally. The great swath of water had been ejected with enough force to push the *Ithaca* off course. The evacuated water shifted the ship's ballast and sent them into a spin. The loss of angular momentum made their situation worsen as more and more water poured away, like a comet's tail behind them. The ship's reserves!

Working feverishly at the controls, Duncan overrode the reservoir hatch, praying all the while that the mysterious saboteur had merely opened the door to space, rather than using one of the deadly mines locked away in the armory.

Teg burst onto the navigation bridge just as Duncan managed to close the cargo doors and reestablish containment. The Bashar bent over the screens, his young but seasoned face creased in concern. "That was enough water to supply us for a year!" His gray-eyed gaze flitted around nervously.

Pacing the deck, Duncan stared out at the misty veil of dispersed water. "We can retrieve some of it. Scoop it up as ice, and when I fully stabilize our spin—"

But as he looked at the smear of lost water spreading out against the starry backdrop, he saw other lines appear, sparkling multicolored threads drawing together and enclosing the no-ship like a spider's web. The Enemy's net! Again it was bright enough for Teg to see it, too. "Damn it! Not now!"

Lunging into the pilot's seat, Duncan activated the Holtzman engines. With one or more saboteurs aboard, the engines themselves could have been rigged to explode, but he had no choice. He forced the enigmatic machines to fold space well before he could think about what course to take. The no-ship, still spinning, lurched off to another place.

They survived.

Afterward, Duncan looked at Teg and sighed. "We couldn't have retrieved much of the expelled water anyway."

Even the ship's sophisticated recyclers had their limits, and now the actions of the saboteur had driven them—intentionally—toward an inescapable conclusion. After many years of constant flight, the no-ship's provisions had to be replenished as soon as an acceptable planet could be located. Not an easy task in a huge galaxy, encompassing vast distances. They had found nothing suitable in years. Not since the planet of the Handlers.

But Duncan knew that would not be their only problem. When they found a place, they would be forced to expose themselves—again.

Synchrony is more than a machine, more than a metropolis; it is an extension of the evermind itself. It constantly shifts and morphs into different configurations. At first I believed this effect was for defense, but there seems to be another force at work, a surprising creative spark. These machines are exceedingly odd.

—BARON VLADIMIR HARKONNEN,
the ghola

The metropolis before them was beautiful in an industrial and metallic way: sharp angles, smooth curves, and a great deal of energy as structures moved and flashed like a perfectly tuned machine. Angular buildings and windowless towers covered every square meter of ground. The Baron saw no offensive greenery, no gaudy flowers or landscaping, not a leaf, blossom, or blade of grass.

Synchrony was a bustling symbol of productivity—along with concomitant profits and political power, if thinking machines ever figured out how to pay attention to such things. Maybe Vladimir Harkonnen would show Omnius how it was done.

After the long journey from Caladan, the Baron and Paolo rode a tram to the shifting center of the machine city. The Atreides ghola peered out through the curved windows, his eyes wide and hungry. They were crowded in the tram with an escort of eight Face Dancers. The Baron had never understood how the shape-shifters were connected with Omnius and the new Synchronized Empire. The elevated car shot along an unseen charge path high above the ground, whizzing like a bullet between the perpetually shifting buildings.

As they went deeper into the city, huge edifices moved up, down, and sideways like pistons, threatening to crush the streaking tram. When the half-alive buildings swayed like robotic seaweed, he noticed that the Face Dancers inside the tram moved in unison, wearing placid smiles on their cadaverous faces, as if they were part of a choreographed presentation.

Like a needle threading a complex maze of holes, the tram sped toward an immense spire that rose out of the center of the city like a spike thrust up from the netherworld. Finally, the car came to a clicking stop in a spectacular central square.

Anxious to see, Paolo squirmed and pushed his way out the door. Even with uncertainty and fear gnawing at his gut, the Baron marveled at the numerous fires burning at specific geometric points around the spire, each with a human tied to a stake, martyr-fashion. Obviously, in their conquest of world after world, the thinking-machine fleet had taken experimental subjects. He found the extravagance breathtaking. These machines certainly showed a lot of potential and even uncanny imagination.

He thought of the huge thinking-machine fleet out in space, as it methodically plowed deeper into human-settled territory. From what Khrone had explained, when the machines finally obtained a pet Kwisatz Haderach, Omnius believed he would be fulfilling the terms of the mechanical prophecy, making it impossible to fail. The Baron found it amusing how the thinking machines viewed everything as an absolute. After fifteen thousand years, they should know better.

Paolo had let himself be caught up in a megalomaniacal whirlwind. The Baron's job was to feed those delusions, always keeping in mind that he was in a dangerous situation himself and needed to keep his wits and focus. Unsure whether personal glory or ignominious death lay ahead, the Baron was repeatedly reminded that he was merely a catalyst for Paolo. *Secondary importance indeed!*

Emerging from the back of his mind, Alia interrupted him, insisting that the machines would discard him when he had fulfilled his purpose. When he sputtered internally in protest, she screeched over him: *You're going to get us killed, Grandfather! Think back to your first life—you weren't always such a gullible fool!*

The Baron shook his head briskly, wishing he could get her out of his mind. Maybe his Alia tormentor was the result of a tumor pressing upon a cognitive center of his brain. The malignant little Abomination was deeply entrenched in his skull. Maybe a robot surgeon could cut her out. . . .

The Face Dancers led him and his young ward across a platform and down a set of stairs to the square. Giddy, Paolo ran ahead and did a brief dance of joy. "Is this all mine? Where is my throne room?" He looked back at the Baron. "Don't worry—I'll find a place for you in my court. You have been good to me." Was that a scrap of leftover Atreides honor? The Baron scowled.

The Face Dancers nudged the Baron into a lift tube, while allowing Paolo to enter unassisted. Instead of climbing to the apex of the tower as the Baron expected, however, the lift plunged in free fall toward the bowels of hell. Swallowing the impulse to scream, he said, "If you're really the Kwisatz Haderach, Paolo, perhaps you should learn to use your powers . . . *immediately.*"

The boy shrugged dumbly, showing little recognition of the peril they were in.

As soon as the lift settled to a smooth stop, the walls melted away around them to reveal an immense, underground chamber. Here, as outside, nothing remained stationary. Rotating walls and a clearplaz floor left the Baron dizzy and disoriented, as if the two humans stood in a vault of space.

A mist rose and congealed in the shape of a large man, a faceless, ghostlike figure. The foggy form, nearly twice the height of a grown man, stopped in front of them and moved its arms to make a swirl of icy air that smelled of metal and oil. Within the countenance, two glowing eyes became apparent. From a misty mouth, a deep voice said, "So, this is our Kwisatz Haderach."

Paolo lifted his chin and recited what the Baron had told him, with considerable passion. "I'll be the one who can see all places and all things simultaneously, the one who will lead the multitudes. I am the shortening of the way, the rescuer, the messiah, the one spoken of in countless legends."

Words flowed from the fog. "You have a charismatic presence that

I find fascinating. Humans exhibit an irresistible compulsion to follow physically attractive, charming leaders. Properly harnessed, you could be an effective and destructive tool for us." The fog creature laughed, swirling the cold wind around him. Then his otherworldly eyes riveted on the Baron. "You will see that the boy cooperates."

"Yes, of course. Are you Omnius?"

"I speak for the evermind." The fogginess shifted as the mist flowed into itself and resolved into the gleaming metallic shape of a polished robot with an exaggerated but menacing smile molded onto his face. "For the sake of convenience, I call myself Erasmus."

The walls of the chamber shifted like a kaleidoscope to reveal hundreds of angular combat robots stationed around the perimeter like strange beetles. Their metal eyes glittered in the same hostile fashion.

"Perhaps I will question you now. Or later? Indecision is a very human thing, you know. We have all the time in the world." The smile on the robot's platinum face had locked into place. "I so love your clichés."

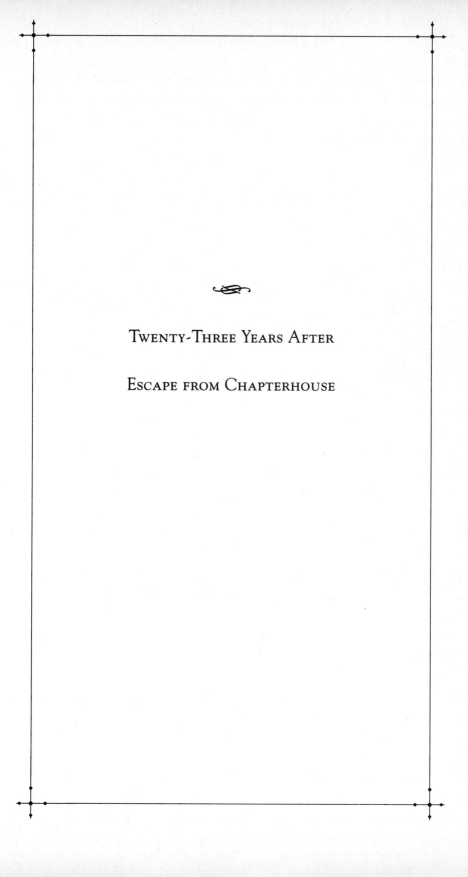

Twenty-Three Years After

Escape from Chapterhouse

Even with a Navigator's incredible mental advancement, I cannot forget the fundamental thread that ties us to the rest of humanity: the old emotion of hope.

—NAVIGATOR EDRIK,
unacknowledged message to the Oracle of Time

The four specialized Guild craft were shaped like hornets, sleek sensor-studded ships that skimmed low over the waves of Buzzell. Scan eyes pointed down at the water, searching for movement. From the lead ship Waff peered through the spray-specked plaz windows, hoping to catch a glimpse of seaworms. The Tleilaxu's excitement and anticipation were palpable. Worms were down there somewhere. *Growing.*

He had released the creatures just over a year ago, and judging from the flurry of rumors the Guild had picked up, the seaworms must have thrived. None of the Bene Gesserit witches on the rocky islands understood where the serpentine creatures had come from. Now, Waff thought with a thrill, it was time to reap the harvest he had sown. He couldn't wait to see them, to know that he had accomplished his holy mission.

The sky was overcast, with patches of fog lying low over the sea. At regular intervals, the scanning crews dropped sonic pulsers into the water. The throbbing signals would map the movements of large underwater denizens, and theoretically attract the seaworms just as Fremen thumpers had once attracted the huge monsters on old Rakis. Near

Waff in the cockpit, five silent Guildsmen monitored the equipment while separate, smaller hunting platforms circled lower, keeping pace with the hornets. Periodically the platforms went back to check the points where the pulsers had been dropped.

The leviathans of the deep from the ancient scriptures were more than just God's judgment on powindah unbelievers. This was the return of the Prophet, God's Messenger resurrected from the ashes of Rakis, in an adaptive new form.

The initial sightings of the beasts had occurred within six months. At first the tales told by the amphibious soostone harvesters had been met with disbelief, until the seaworms attacked in full view of island settlements. According to eyewitness accounts—and Bene Gesserits were well trained in accurate observation—the monstrous things had grown far larger than Waff had predicted. Truly, a sign from God that his work was blessed!

So long as they were fed, the worms continued to grow and multiply. Seaworms apparently preferred to eat the large cholisters that produced soostones, tearing into beds tended by Phibians. The aquatic people had rallied to drive away the sea monsters, but they had failed.

Waff smiled. Of course they had failed. One could not change a path that God had laid down.

The angry witches had led hunting parties, taking boats out onto the waters, guided by vengeful Phibians. They begged Chapterhouse for weapons to kill the seaworms. But with Enemy forces attacking hundreds of fringe worlds, and the industries of Junction and Ix consuming most of the New Sisterhood's resources, they were stretched far too thin.

The Bene Gesserits needed soostone wealth to build and replenish their armies faster than the Enemy could destroy them, but if the seaworms produced what Waff hoped, the creatures would be worth far more than any gem. Soon, there would be multiple sources of spice, including a new and more potent form. Waff could transplant the creatures to any ocean planet, where they could thrive without reconfiguring an entire ecosystem. Considering their current monopoly on melange, that would not make the Sisterhood happy.

The pilot circled the lead hornet ship. Guild assistants stared fixedly at monitors. "Picking up shadows at various depths. Numerous tracks. We are close."

Waff moved eagerly to the other side of the craft and stared down at the choppy waves. Pulse beacons continued to emit siren songs, and hunting platforms flitted alongside. "Be ready to move as soon as you detect a worm. I want to see one. Let me know when you have a sighting."

Down in the water, he noticed two slick-skinned Phibians, who seemed curious about the pulse beacons and the flurry of activity. One raised a webbed hand in an incomprehensible signal as the hornet ships and hunting platforms streaked overhead.

"Seaworm surfacing," announced one of the Guildsmen. "Target acquired."

The little Tleilaxu rushed forward to the cockpit. Below, a long, dark shape appeared in the water, breaching like a great whale. "We must capture and kill it. That is the only way to see what's inside."

"Yes," said the Guildsman. Waff narrowed his eyes, never able to understand these people. Was the man agreeing with him, or simply acknowledging the orders? This time he didn't care.

Waff glanced at the projected map, noting that their search had taken them to one of the inhabited rocky islands. Once he verified the success of the new worms, there would be no need to continue keeping secrets. The witches could do nothing about the seaworms, nor what they produced. They could not stop his work. Today, after his team captured a specimen and confirmed the results of his experiments, the truth would be obvious.

We will show the witches what lies beneath the waves, and let them draw their own conclusions.

The lead hornet craft slowed, its engines buzzing. The moment the seaworm emerged from the waves, ringed and glistening, Waff's hunters fired a fusillade of supersonic harpoons from their hovering platforms. The barbed tips hit the beast before it could realize its danger and submerge. Spear points caught in the soft rings, anchoring themselves as the worm thrashed and writhed. Waff felt joy, as well as a twinge of sympathetic pain. From behind the lead craft, three other hornet ships shot more harpoons into the trapped creature, pulling back on hyperfilament cables.

"Don't damage it too much!" Waff intended to kill the thing anyway—a necessary sacrifice in the name of the Prophet—but if the carcass and internal organs were too mangled, his dissection would be more difficult.

The group of hornet craft went into hover mode above the waves, their cables taut and straining as the seaworm thrashed. Milky fluid oozed into the water, dissipating before the Tleilaxu researcher could order one of the Guildsmen to collect samples. Other seaworms circled their struggling brother like hungry sharks.

The worm was twenty meters long—a tremendous rate of growth for such a short time. He was impressed. If the creatures were reproducing as rapidly as they were growing, the oceans of Buzzell would soon be teeming with them! He couldn't ask for more.

The wounded beast quickly tired. Engines humming with the strain, the Guild vessels began to drag the feebly struggling worm toward the nearest reef, which was barely visible in the wispy fog banks. The small hunting platforms returned to the hornet ships, docking inside their cramped cargo holds.

The island was one of the main Sisterhood outposts for soostone processing, complete with barracks, warehouses, and a flattened spaceport capable of handling small ships. *Let the witches see this!*

Flying in formation, the hornet ships towed the captive worm to shore. In the water below, at least twenty Phibians appeared carrying crude spears and tridents—as if they thought they could pose a threat to the giant creatures! Shouting curses and threats, the Phibians attacked the tangled worm, stabbing and cutting.

Annoyed at the interference, Waff turned to his Guildsmen. "Drive them away!" Using small cannons mounted on the deck of the lead hornet ship, Guildsmen took potshots at the Phibians, killing two. The others dove underwater. At first they left the bloody corpses bobbing in the waves, but a number of the Phibians returned moments later. When they attempted to retrieve their fallen comrades, a second seaworm streaked in and devoured the bodies.

The droning hum of the hornet ships attracted a crowd of women on the docks as the sluggish prize was dragged into the village harbor. Dark-clad Sisters left their barracks, perhaps thinking that smugglers or CHOAM representatives had arrived. From the recent depredations of the seaworms, most soostone operations had stalled. Sorting bins and packaging lines were silent and unmanned.

His chest swelled with pride, Waff jumped down from the ramp onto the metal and stone wharf as the Guildsmen hoisted the ringed creature onto the main dock. Its narrow tail drooped into the water. Exhausted from its struggles and oozing fluids from the harpoon wounds, the captive worm thrashed one more time, expending the last of its energy. Though Waff and his servants had conquered and subdued the worm, he still felt impressed to be so close to the magnificent creature.

Seven curious Phibians floated by the dock pilings, staring upward. In their bubbling, hissing voices, they mumbled in awe.

Waff stood triumphantly before the large, dripping thing. Slime trickled from the dead seaworm onto the dock, and a gush of milky-gray fluid flowed from its mouth. The long sharp teeth were very fine, like needles. Rather than reeking of fish, the seaworm had a distinct sharp-sweet odor with a hint of pungent cinnamon.

Perfect!

Women came forward to confront Waff. "We've never captured and killed a seaworm before," said a Sister in a brown dress who introduced herself as Corysta. She seemed delighted to see the leviathan dead. "They have caused great havoc in the seas."

"And they will continue to do so. Learn to adapt your operations." Waff perfunctorily turned from her to issue instructions to his crew, then told Corysta and the other Bene Gesserits to stay back. "We are on strict Guild business. Do not attempt to interfere."

Though dead, the seaworm twitched as nerve impulses continued to fire. Waff ordered the Guildsmen to lash down the carcass, so that he could dissect it without interruption. The Guild assistants brought him a lascutter, a superfine shigawire saw, spreaders, and shovels.

Setting the lascutter to full power and holding it in both hands, Waff swept sideways in a broad arc and sliced the seaworm open, so that the round, dripping segments flopped apart. Guildsmen hurried forward with spreaders to pull open the wound and expose the internal structure. Waff reveled in the gore. The Prophet must be so pleased with him.

In preparation, he had already killed and autopsied two of the original small specimens in his laboratory, so he knew the creatures' basic arrangement of organs. The worm was a biologically simple creature, and working on this larger scale made the process easier. Water and slime oozed onto the dock, splattering Waff. Under other circumstances he might have been disgusted, but this was the sacred essence of his Prophet. The Tleilaxu man sniffed more deeply, and there—a definite undertone to the smell—he caught the vital, pungent aroma of pure melange. No doubt about it.

Waff buried his arms up to his shoulders in the organs, feeling around, identifying specific structures by their shapes and textures. Guild assistants used wide scoops to shovel offal onto the dock. Witches and Phibians watched in fascination, but Waff paid little attention to them.

Ignoring the obviously confused and impotent Sisters, he laser-cut deeper into the worm, sliced along its length and rummaged through the stinking debris, until finally a large bluish-purple lump of soft liver-like material spilled out. Waff stepped back for a breath, then leaned closer, poking and prodding with his fingers. He made a cut with the lasknife at its lowest setting.

A rich oily-cinnamon odor boiled out, so thick it could be seen as fumes. Waff reeled dizzily. The intensity of the melange nearly bowled him over. "Spice! The creature is saturated with melange! Extremely concentrated spice."

The Sisters looked at each other and came closer with curious expressions. "Spice? The seaworms produce *spice?*" The Guildsmen stood close to Waff and his dripping prize, blocking the Bene Gesserits.

"The seaworms destroyed our soostone beds!" another woman shouted.

Waff stared them down. "These creatures may have destroyed one economy on Buzzell, but they created an even more important one." His assistants picked up the large, melange-saturated organ and carried it back to the nearest hornet ship. Waff would have to test the substance thoroughly, but he already felt confident in what he would find.

Up in the orbiting Heighliner, Edrik the Navigator would be pleased.

Dripping with slime and seawater, Waff hurried back to the ship.

Some see spice as a blessing, others as a curse. To everyone, how-ever, it is a necessity.

—PLANETOLOGIST PARDOT KYNES,
Original Arrakis Notebooks

After her long and exhausting journey across the Old Empire, from the planets preparing for battle, to the Guild shipyards, to the soostone operations on Buzzell, Mother Commander Murbella returned to Chapterhouse with renewed determination. Since she had been gone for many months, her quarters in the Keep now looked like a stranger's rooms. Harried acolytes and male workers scurried to unload her belongings from her ship.

After a polite knock on the door, an acolyte stepped in. The young woman had short brown hair and a furtive smile. "Mother Comman-der, Archives sent these updated charts. They were supposed to be waiting for you upon your arrival." She held out thin maps with finely detailed lines, then drew back, startled, when she noticed the hulking combat robot, deactivated but still standing in the corner of the room like a war trophy.

"Thank you. Don't mind the machine—it is as dead as they will all soon be." Murbella took the reports from the girl's hands. With a sec-ond glance, she realized the young woman was her own daughter Gianne, her last child with Duncan Idaho. Another daughter, Tanidia, also raised by the New Sisterhood, had been shipped off to work among the Missionaria.

Do Gianne or Tanidia even know who their parents are? Years ago she had made the choice to tell Janess of her parentage, and the young woman had thrown herself into the study and understanding of her famous father. But Murbella had let her other two daughters be raised among the Bene Gesserit in the more traditional way. She doubted they knew how special they were.

Gianne seemed hesitant, as if hoping the Mother Commander would ask her for something else. Though she knew the answer, on impulse Murbella asked, "How old are you, Gianne?"

The girl seemed startled that she knew her name. "Why, twenty-three, Mother Commander."

"And you have not yet undergone the Agony." It was not a question. Occasionally, the Mother Commander had been tempted to use her position to interfere with the girl's training, but had not done so. A Bene Gesserit was not supposed to show such weakness.

The young woman seemed ashamed. "The proctors suggest that I would benefit from more focus and concentration."

"Then devote yourself to that. We need every Reverend Mother we can find." She glanced at the ominous combat robot. "The war has worsened."

MURBELLA REALIZED SHE could not rest, could not waste the time. She demanded to see her advisors, Kiria, Janess, Laera, and Accadia. The women arrived, expecting a meeting, but Murbella herded them out of the Keep. "Prepare a 'thopter. We leave immediately for the desert belt."

Carrying a stack of reports, Laera did not react well to the news. "But Mother Commander, you've been gone so long. Many documents await your attention. You have to make decisions, give proper—"

"*I* decide the priorities."

Kiria, looking scornful, bit her words back when she noted the Mother Commander's complete seriousness. They all crowded aboard an empty ornithopter, then waited for the tedious takeoff preparations. Murbella wouldn't sit still for a moment. "If I don't get a pilot, I'll fly this damned thing myself." A young male pilot was quickly brought to her.

As the 'thopter took off, she finally turned to her advisors and explained, "The Guild demands an exorbitant payment for all the warships we have under construction. Ix already accepts payments only in melange, and now that soostones from Buzzell are no longer economically viable, everything hinges on spice. That is our only coin significant enough to appease the Guild."

"Appease them?" Kiria snapped. "What madness is this? We should *conquer* them and force them to produce the weapons and vessels we need. Are we the only ones who understand the threat? Thinking machines are coming!"

Janess was astonished by the other woman's suggestion. "Attacking the Guild would create open civil warfare at a time when we can least afford it."

"Do we have enough resources to spend on these ships?" asked Laera. "Our credit has already been strained past its limits with the Guild Bank."

"We all face a common enemy," old Accadia said. "Surely, the Guild and Ix would be willing—"

Murbella clenched her hands. "This has nothing to do with altruism or greed. Despite the best intentions, resources and raw materials do not appear like rainbows after a storm. Populations must be fed, ships must be fueled, energy must be produced and expended. Money is only a symbol, but economics is the engine that drives the whole machine. The piper must be paid."

The 'thopter raced across the sky, buffeted by dry winds and blown dust long before they saw the desert. Murbella gazed out the curved window, sure that dunes had not extended this far across the continent the last time she'd visited the desert. It was a spreading *anti*flood, total dryness sweeping outward in waves. At the heart of the desert, the worms grew and reproduced, keeping the cycle going in a perpetually increasing spiral.

The Mother Commander turned to the woman behind her. "Laera, I require a complete assessment of our spice-harvesting operations. I need to know numbers. How many long tons of melange do we gather? How much do we have in our stockpiles, and how much is available for export?"

"We produce enough to meet our needs, Mother Commander. Our investment continues to go into expanding the operations, but our expenditures have increased dramatically."

Kiria muttered a bitter comment about the Ixians and their endless bills.

"We may need to bring in outside workers," Janess pointed out. "These obstacles can be overcome."

The 'thopter swooped toward a chimney-plume of dust and sand thrown up by a harvester. Around it, like wolves circling a wounded animal, several sandworms approached the vibrations. Already the operations were beginning to wrap up, with miners rushing and carryalls hovering to snatch the heavy machinery away as soon as worms ventured too close.

Murbella said, "Squeeze the desert, wring out every gram of spice."

"Beast Rabban was given the same task long ago, during the days of Muad'Dib," said Accadia. "And he failed in a spectacular fashion."

"Rabban did not have the Sisterhood behind him." She could see Laera, Janess, and Kiria all making silent mental calculations. How many workers could be diverted to the desert zone? How many off-planet prospectors and treasure hunters could they allow on Chapterhouse? And how much spice would be enough to keep Guild and Ixian engineers producing the desperately needed ships and weapons?

The male pilot, having been silent until now, said, "While we are out here, Mother Commander, shall I take you to our desert research station? The planetology crew is studying the sandworm cycle, the spread of desert, and the parameters necessary for the most effective spice harvest."

"'Understanding is required before success is possible,'" Laera said, quoting directly from the old Orange Catholic Bible.

"Yes, let me inspect this station. Research is necessary, but in times like these it must be *practical* research. We have no time for frivolous studies concocted by the whim of an offworld scientist."

The pilot banked the 'thopter and accelerated far out into the open desert. On the horizon, a lumpy, black ridge showed a reef of buried rock, a safe bastion where worms could not go.

Shakkad Station had been named after Shakkad the Wise, a ruler from days before the Butlerian Jihad. Nearly lost in the mists of legend, Shakkad's chemist had been the first man in history to recognize the geriatric properties of melange. Now, far from Chapterhouse Keep or any outside interference, a group of fifty scientists, Sisters, and their support staff lived and worked. They set up weather-testing devices, traveled out onto the dunes to measure chemical changes during spice blows and monitor the growth and movement of sandworms.

When the 'thopter settled onto a flat cliff outcropping that served as a makeshift landing pad, a group of scientists came out to meet them. Dusty and windblown, a survey team was just returning from the edges of the desert where they had set out sampling poles and weather-testing instruments. They wore stillsuits, exact reproductions of those once used by the Fremen.

A majority of the scientists at Shakkad Station were men, and several of the older ones had made brief expeditions to charred Rakis itself. Three decades had passed since the ecological destruction of the desert planet, and by now few experts could claim firsthand knowledge of the sandworms or original conditions on Dune.

"How may we assist you, Mother Commander?" asked the station manager, an offworlder who pushed dusty protective goggles up onto his forehead. The man's owlish eyes had already begun to turn a faint blue. Spice had been in his diet every day since his arrival at the outpost. His body gave off an unpleasant sour odor, as if he had taken his assignment in the waterless belt with particular seriousness, even to the point of foregoing regular bathing.

"Assist us by getting more melange," Murbella answered bluntly.

"Do your teams have everything they need?" Laera asked. "Do you require additional supplies or workers?"

"No, no. We just want solitude and the freedom to work. Oh, and time."

"I can give you the first two. But time is a commodity none of us has."

*We can conquer our enemy, of course, but is it worthwhile to
achieve victory without understanding the flaws of our opponent?
Such an analysis is the most interesting part.*

—ERASMUS,
Laboratory Notebooks

The machine-based cathedral on Synchrony was a mere manifestation of what the rest of the galaxy might become. Omnius was pleased at the progress the thinking-machine fleet had made in the past few years, conquering one system after another, but Erasmus knew that so much more remained to do.

The voice of Omnius boomed much louder than necessary, as he sometimes liked to do. "The New Sisterhood offers the strongest resistance to us, but I know how to defeat them. Scouts have verified the secret location of Chapterhouse, and I have already dispatched plague probes there. Those women will soon be extinct." Omnius sounded quite bored. "Shall I display the map of star systems, so you know just how many we have encountered and conquered? Not a single failure."

Displays jabbed into Erasmus's mind, regardless of whether he wanted to see them or not. In bygone days the independent robot had been able to decide what he wanted to download from the evermind, and what he didn't. Increasingly, however, Omnius had found ways to override the robot's decision-making abilities, forcing data into his internal systems, sliding it past multiple firewalls.

"Those are mere symbolic victories," Erasmus said, intentionally shifting to his disguise of the wrinkled old woman in gardening clothes. "I am pleased that we have made it to the edge of the Old Empire, but we still have not won this war. I have spent millennia studying these stubborn, resourceful humans. Do not assume victory until we actually have it in our hands. Remember what happened last time."

Omnius's snort of disbelief echoed through the entire city of Synchrony. "We are by definition better than flawed humanity." From a thousand watcheyes, he looked down upon Erasmus and his matronly disguise. "Why do you persist in wearing that embarrassing shape? It makes you look weak."

"My physical body does not determine my strength. My mind makes me what I am."

"I am not interested in your mind either. I simply wish to win this war. I must win. I *need* to win. Where is the no-ship? Where is my Kwisatz Haderach?"

"You sound as demanding as Baron Harkonnen. Are you unconsciously imitating him?"

"You gave me the mathematical projections, Erasmus. Where is the superhuman? Answer me."

The robot chuckled. "You already have Paolo."

"Your prophecy also guaranteed a Kwisatz Haderach aboard the no-ship. I want both versions—redundancy to assure victory. And I do not want the humans to have one. I must control them both."

"We will find the no-ship. We already know there are many intriguing things aboard, including a Tleilaxu Master. He may be the only one left alive, and I would very much like to speak with him—as would you. The Master needs to see how all those Face Dancers have shaped us, built us, so that we could become closer to gods. Closer than humans, at any rate."

"We will keep sending out our net. And we will find that ship."

All around the city, in a dramatic statement of the evermind's impatience, towering buildings collapsed, full metal structures fell in upon themselves. Hearing the thundering sounds and feeling the floor shake beneath him, the independent robot was not impressed. Too many times he had witnessed such overblown theatrics. Omnius certainly enjoyed running the show, for better and often for worse, though Erasmus continually tried to control the evermind's excesses. The future depended on it—the future that Erasmus had ordained.

He dug through the projections that he'd digested from trillions of datapoints. All of his results were colored to fit precisely the prophecies he had formulated himself. Omnius believed them all. The gullible evermind relied too much on filtered information, and the robot played him well.

Given the proper parameters, Erasmus was absolutely certain the millennia ahead would turn out properly.

What remained of Norma Cenva's ancient corporeal form was confined inside a chamber that had been built and modified around her during thousands of years. But her mind knew no physical boundaries. She was only tenuously connected to flesh, a biological generator of pure thought. The Oracle of Time.

Her mental links to the fabric of the universe gave her the ability to travel anywhere along infinite possibilities. She could see the future and the past, but not always with perfect clarity. Her brain was such that she could touch the Infinite and almost—*almost*—comprehend it.

Her nemesis, the evermind, had laid down a vast electronic network throughout the fabric of space, a complex tachyon road map that most people could not see. Omnius used it as a net to sift for his prey, but so far he had not managed to snare the no-ship.

Long ago, Norma had created the precursor to the Guild as a means of fighting the thinking machines. Since that time, the Guild had taken on a life of its own, growing away from her while she stretched herself farther into the cosmos. Politics between planets, power struggles between the Navigator faction and the human Administrators, monopolies on valuable commodities such as soostones, Ixian technologies, or melange—such problems did not concern her.

Keeping watch over mankind required an investment of her mental currency. She felt the turmoil in civilization, knew the great schism in the Guild. She would have chastised the Administrators for creating such a crisis, if she could only remember how to speak to such small people. Norma found it exhausting to talk in simple enough terms to make herself comprehensible even to her advanced Navigators. She had to make them understand the true Enemy, so that they could shoulder the burden of fighting.

If the Oracle of Time did not attend to grander priorities, no one else would. No one else in the universe could possibly do it. With her prescience, she grasped what was most important: *Find the lost no-ship.* The final Kwisatz Haderach was aboard, and Kralizec's black cloud had already released its torrents. But Omnius was searching for the same thing and might get to it first.

She had felt the recent struggles between the Bene Gesserits and the Honored Matres. Before that she had witnessed the original Scattering and Famine Times, as well as the extended life and traumatic death of the God Emperor. But all of those events were little more than background noise.

Find the no-ship.

As she had always foreseen and feared, the unrelenting foe had come back. No matter what guise the thinking machines now wore, regardless of how much they had changed, the Enemy was still the Enemy.

And Kralizec is well under way.

While her prescience flowed outward and inward, ripples of time eddied around her, making accurate predictions difficult. She encountered a vortex, a random, powerful factor that could change the outcome in uncounted ways: a Kwisatz Haderach, a person as anomalous as Norma Cenva herself, a wildcard variable.

Omnius wanted to guide and control that special human. The evermind and his Face Dancers had sought the no-ship for years, but so far Duncan Idaho had eluded capture. Even the Oracle had been unable to find him again.

Norma had done her best to thwart the Enemy every step of the way. She had saved the no-ship, hoping to protect the people onboard, but she had lost contact afterward. Something on the ship was more effective than a no-field at blinding her search. She could only hope the thinking machines were as blind.

The Oracle's search continued, her thoughts reeling out in delicate probes. Alas, the vessel simply *was not there*. In some mysterious manner, the passengers hid it from her . . . assuming it had not been destroyed.

Though her prescience was not clear, Norma realized that time was growing shorter and shorter, for everyone. The crux point had to occur soon. Thus, she needed to gather her allies. The foolish Administrators had reconfigured many of their great ships, installing artificial controls—like thinking machines!—so that she could no longer call upon them through her paranormal means. But she could still command a thousand of her loyal Navigators. She would make them ready for battle, the final battle.

As soon as she found the no-ship. . . .

The Oracle of Time expanded her mind, casting her thoughts into the void like a fisherman, until the neural ache was incredible. She pushed harder than ever, stretching her boundaries beyond anything she had previously attempted. No price of pain could be too great. She knew full well the consequences of failure.

All around her, a vast clock ticked.

There must be a place where we can find a home, where we can be safe and rest. The Bene Gesserit sent out so many Sisters on their own Scattering before the Honored Matres came. Are they all lost, as well?

—SHEEANA,

confidential no-ship journals

Flying ever onward, the *Ithaca* reeled from the recent spate of damage. And the saboteur continued to elude them. *What more can we do to track him down?* Even Duncan's most thorough Mentat projections offered no new suggestions.

Miles Teg and Thufir Hawat once again dispatched teams to inspect, and even ransack, the quarters of all passengers, hoping to find incriminating evidence. The Rabbi and his people complained about purported violations of their privacy, but Sheeana demanded their full cooperation. To the extent possible, Teg had been closing down sections of the immense vessel with electronic barricades, but the clever saboteur was able to get through anyway.

Assuming no further incidents, with the life-support, air-recirculation, and food-growth systems crippled, the passengers could not last more than a few months without stopping somewhere to replenish the stores. But it had been years since they had found another suitable world.

Duncan wondered: *Is someone trying to destroy us . . . or drive us to a particular place?*

With no starmaps or reliable guidance, he tried to use his uncanny prescience one more time. Another big gamble. Activating the Holtz-man engines and closing his eyes, Duncan folded space again, spinning the cosmic roulette wheel—

And the no-ship emerged, intact but still lost, at the perimeter of a star system. A yellow sun with a necklace of worlds, including a terres-trial planet that orbited at the appropriate distance to support life. Pos-sibly habitable, certainly with oxygen and water that the *Ithaca* could take aboard. A chance . . .

Others had gathered on the navigation bridge by the time the no-ship approached the uncharted world. Sheeana got down to business. "What do we have here? Breathable air? Food? A place to live?"

Gazing through the observation window, Duncan was pleased at what he saw. "The instruments say yes. I suggest we send a team imme-diately."

"Resupply is not good enough," Garimi said, her tone gruff. "It never was. We should consider remaining here, if this is the kind of world we've been looking for."

"We considered that at the planet of the Handlers, too," Sheeana said.

"If the saboteur drove us here, we need to be very cautious," Dun-can said. "I know it was a random foldspace jump, but I'm still troubled. Our pursuers cast a wide net. I would not be quick to dismiss the possi-bility that this place is a trap."

"Or our salvation," Garimi suggested.

"We'll have to see for ourselves," Teg said. Working with the bridge controls, he displayed high-resolution images on the wide screens. "Plentiful oxygen and vegetation, especially at the higher latitudes away from the equator. Clear signs of habitation, small villages, mid-sized cities, mostly far to the north. Large-scale meteorological scans show that the climate is in upheaval." He pointed to storm patterns, swaths of dying forests and plains, large lakes and inland seas shriveling into dust bowls. "Very few clouds in the equatorial latitudes. Minimal atmospheric moisture."

Stilgar and Liet-Kynes, always fascinated with new worlds, joined the group on the high deck. Kynes drew a quick breath. "It's turning into a wasteland down there. An artificial desert!"

"I've seen this before." Sheeana studied a clear brown band like a knife slash across what had apparently been a lushly forested continent. "It's like Chapterhouse."

"Could this be one of Odrade's seed planets?" Stuka asked, from her usual position at Garimi's side. "Did they bring sandtrout here and disperse them? Will we find our Sisters down on that planet?"

"Untainted Sisters," Garimi said with a gleam in her eyes.

"Quite possibly," Sheeana said. "We'll have to go down there. This looks like more than a place to replenish our resources."

"A new colony." Stuka's excitement was infectious. "This could be the world we've been looking for, a site to reestablish Chapterhouse. A new Dune!"

Duncan nodded. "We cannot pass up an opportunity like this. My instincts brought us here for a reason."

Keeping themselves hidden from the planet's inhabitants, several teams of efficient Bene Gesserits launched a major effort to restock the no-ship with necessary air, water, and chemicals. They sent out mining ships, air scoops, water-purification tankers. That was the *Ithaca's* immediate priority.

Stilgar and Liet-Kynes insisted on going down to inspect the growing desert band. Seeing the passion on the faces of the two awakened gholas, neither Teg nor Duncan could deny the request. Everyone was guardedly optimistic about finding a welcoming landscape here, and Sheeana wondered if this might be a place where she could release her seven captive sandworms. Although Duncan could not leave the veiling of the no-ship, because then he would be exposed to the Enemy searchers, he had no cause to prevent the others from finding a home at last. Perhaps this would be it.

Bashar Teg piloted the lighter down to the surface himself, accompanied by Sheeana and an eager Stuka, who had long wanted to establish a new Bene Gesserit center, rather than just drift aimlessly in space. Garimi had let her staunch supporter make the first foray, while she formulated plans with her ultraconservative Sisters aboard the no-ship. Stilgar and Liet were most eager just to set foot on the desert—a real desert with open skies and endless sands.

Teg flew directly toward the ravaged arid zone, where an ecological battle was taking place. If this was indeed one of Odrade's seed planets, the Bashar knew how voracious sandtrout would seal away a planet's water, drop by drop. Environmental checks and balances would fight back with shifting weather patterns; animals would migrate to still-untouched regions; stranded plant life would struggle to adapt, and mostly fail. Reproducing sandtrout could act much faster than a world could adapt.

Sheeana and Stuka stared through the lighter's plaz viewing windows, seeing the spreading desert as a success, a triumph of Odrade's Scattering. To the exquisitely prudent Bene Gesserit, even the ruin of an entire ecosystem was an "acceptable casualty" if it created a new Dune.

"The change is happening so swiftly," Liet-Kynes said, his voice tinged with awe.

"Surely, Shai-Hulud is already here," Stilgar added.

Stuka echoed words that Garimi had said time and again. "This world will be a new Chapterhouse. The hardships will mean nothing to us."

With the detailed information in their archives, the people aboard the *Ithaca* had all the expertise they needed to establish a new place to live. *Yes, a colony.* Teg rather liked the sound of the word, because it represented the hope of a better future.

Teg knew, however, that Duncan could never stop running, unless he chose to face the Enemy directly. The mysterious old man and woman were still after him with their sinister net, or after something on the no-ship, maybe the vessel itself.

The lighter descended with a rough roar through the china-blue sky. In the middle of the abrupt desert band, dunes stretched as far as he could see. Sunlight reflected from the sands into bone-dry air, and thermal currents jostled the ship from side to side. Teg wrestled with the guidance systems.

In the back, Stilgar chuckled. "Just like riding a sandworm."

Cruising over the middle of the widening desert belt, Liet-Kynes pointed at a rusty-red splash that marked an eruption from beneath the surface. "Spice blow! No mistaking the color or pattern." He gave a wry smile to his friend Stilgar. "I died on one of those. Damn the Harkonnens for leaving me to die!"

Mounds rippled and stirred the top layer of sand, but they did not emerge into open air. "If those are worms, they are smaller than the ones in our hold," Stilgar said.

"But still impressive," Liet added.

"They have had less time to mature," Sheeana pointed out. "Mother Superior Odrade did not send volunteers on her Scattering until after the desertification of Chapterhouse was well under way. And we do not know how long the wandering Sisters took to get here."

Below, obvious lines marked the rapid expansion of the sandy wasteland, like ripples on a pond. At the fringes were die-off perimeters, places where all vegetation had perished and the dirt had become blowing dust. The encroaching desert had created ghost forests and inundated villages.

Flying low, searching with uneasy anticipation, Teg discovered half-buried rooftops, the pinnacles of once proud buildings drowned under the spreading desert. In one shocking glimpse, he saw a high dock and part of a capsized boat that sat atop a blistering dune.

"I look forward to seeing our Bene Gesserit Sisters." Stuka sounded eager. "Obviously they succeeded here in their mission."

"I expect they will welcome us," Sheeana admitted.

After seeing the city drowned in sand, Teg did not think the original inhabitants of this planet would have appreciated what the refugee Sisters had done.

As the lighter followed the northern edge of the desert, the scanners picked out small huts and tents erected just beyond the sand's reach. Teg wondered how often the nomadic villages were required to move. If the arid zone expanded as rapidly as it had on Chapterhouse, this world would be losing thousands of acres every day—and accelerating as sandtrout continued to steal precious water.

"Set down at one of those settlements, Bashar," Sheeana said to him. "Any of our lost Sisters could be here on the edge of the dunes to monitor the progress."

"I long to feel real sand under my boots again," Stilgar muttered.

"It's all so fascinating," Liet said.

As Teg circled above one of the nomadic villages, people ran out and pointed up at them. Sheeana and Stuka pressed excitedly against the plaz windows, searching for distinctive dark Bene Gesserit robes, but they saw none.

A formation of rocks towered over the village, a bulwark offering shelter against blowing sand and dust. People, waving, stood atop the pinnacles, but Teg could not determine if the gestures were friendly or threatening.

"See, they cover their heads and faces with cloths and filters," Liet said. "The increased aridity forces them to adapt. In order to live here on the edge of the dry dunes, they are already learning to conserve bodily moisture."

"We could teach them how to make real stillsuits," Stilgar said with a smile. "It has been a long time since I wore a decent one. I spent a dozen years aboard that ship, drowning my lungs with moisture. I can't wait to taste dry air again!"

Teg found an open landing area and brought the lighter down. He felt unaccountably troubled as the natives scurried toward them. "Those are obviously nomadic camps. Why wouldn't they move inland, to where the climate is more hospitable?"

"People adapt," Sheeana said.

"But why would they have to? Yes, the desert belt is growing, but there are still plenty of wide forests, even cities not far from here. Those people could outrun the spreading dunes for generations to come. Yet they stubbornly remain here."

Before the hatch opened to let in a breath of parched air, the nomads encircled the craft. Sheeana and Stuka, both wearing traditional dark robes from Chapterhouse so that their refugee Sisters would recognize them, boldly led the way. Teg followed with Stilgar and Liet.

"We are Bene Gesserit," Sheeana called to the people in universal Galach. "Are any of our Sisters among you?" Shielding her eyes against the brightness, she searched the few weathered female faces she saw, but got no response.

"Perhaps another village would be best," Teg suggested in a whisper. His tactical senses were alert.

"Not yet."

An elderly man drew closer, pushing a filter mask away from his face. "You ask for Bene Gesserits? Here on Qelso?" Though coarse, his accent was understandable. Despite his age, he appeared to be healthy and energetic.

Taking the lead, Stuka stepped ahead of Sheeana. "The ones who wore black robes, like ours. Where are they?"

"All dead." The old man's eyes flashed.

Stuka's suspicion came too late. Moving like a striking snake, the man hurled a hidden knife from his sleeve, with deadly accuracy. At an unseen signal the rest of the throng rushed forward.

Stuka plucked clumsily at the blade that protruded from her chest but could not make her fingers work. Crumpling to her knees, she tumbled sideways off the lighter's ramp.

Sheeana was already moving, retreating. Teg shouted for Liet and Stilgar to get back inside the ship as he drew one of the stun weapons he had brought from the no-ship's armory. A large rock struck Stilgar in the head, and Liet helped his young friend, trying to drag him back into the lighter. Teg fired a swath of silvery energy, making part of the dusty mob collapse, but more knives and stones clattered at them.

Frenzied people rushed the ramp from all sides, jumping at Teg. Many hands grabbed his wrist before he could fire again, and someone ripped the stunner out of his grip. More took hold of Liet by the shoulders, pulling him away.

Sheeana fought with a whirlwind of blows from her repertoire of Bene Gesserit fighting techniques. Soon a crowd of fallen attackers lay around her.

With a roar, Teg prepared to lurch into his hyperaccelerated metabolism, with which he could easily dodge blows and weapons, but a silvery beam from his own stunner gushed out like tinkling rain, dropping the Bashar, and then Sheeana.

IN SHORT ORDER the villagers bound the hands of their four prisoners with strong cords. Though badly beaten, Teg regained consciousness and saw that Liet and Stilgar were tied together. Stuka's body lay near the ramp while the attackers ransacked the lighter for equipment and hauled things off.

A group of men lifted Stuka's body. The old man retrieved his knife, yanking it from the dead woman's chest and wiping it on her robe with an expression of revulsion. He glowered at the corpse and spat, then marched toward the prisoners. Looking at the three young men, he shook his head in disapproval. "I did not introduce myself. You may call me Var."

Defiantly, Sheeana glared up at him. "Why have you done this to us? You said you knew of the Bene Gesserit order."

Var's face contorted, as if he had hoped to avoid speaking to her. He leaned close to Sheeana. "Yes, we know the Bene Gesserit. They came here years ago and delivered their demon creatures to our world. An experiment, they said. An experiment? Look what they did to our beautiful land! It is becoming nothing more than useless sand." He held his knife, considered Sheeana for a long moment, then sheathed it. "When we finally realized what those women were doing, we killed them all, but too late. Our planet is dying now, and we will fight to protect what's left of it."

The first law of commercial viability is to recognize a need and meet it. When acceptable needs do not present themselves, a good businessman creates them in any way possible.

　　　　　　　　　　　—CHOAM primary commercial directive

When yet another Navigator died in his tank, few of the Spacing Guild's Administrators mourned the loss. The giant Heighliner was simply brought back to the Junction shipyards to be refit with one of the Ixian mathematical compilers. It was considered progress.

After long years of practice, Khrone easily concealed his pleasure at the sight. So far every aspect of the wide-reaching plan had proceeded as expected, one domino falling after another. Posing in his familiar disguise as an Ixian inspection engineer, the leader of the Face Dancer myriad waited on a high, copper-floored platform. He observed the clamorous shipyards, while warm breezes and industrial fumes drifted around him.

Nearby, the human administrator Rentel Gorus was not quite as proficient at covering his satisfaction. He blinked his milky eyes and looked up toward the piloting bay of the ancient, decommissioned ship. "Ardrae was one of the oldest remaining Navigators in our commercial fleet. Even with his spice supplies drastically cut, he clung to life much longer than we expected."

A plump CHOAM representative said, "Navigators! Now that

these drains on our resources are disappearing one by one, Guild profits should increase significantly."

Without prompting from his master, the Mentat assistant recited, "Knowing the lifetime of that Navigator, and considering the quantities of melange required to institute his initial mutation and conversion, I have calculated the total amount of spice consumed during his service to the Guild. With fluctuating prices based on the relative glut during the Tleilaxu years and recent skyrocketing costs due to severe shortages, the Guild could have bought three full-sized Heighliners, complete with no-field capabilities, for the same cost in spice."

The CHOAM man muttered in disgust, while Khrone remained silent. He found it most effective simply to listen and observe. Humans could be counted on to draw their own conclusions (often erroneous ones) so long as they were pointed in the proper direction.

Savoring his secrets, Khrone thought of the numerous ambassadors the Guild had sent to the front, attempting to negotiate nonaggression treaties with the thinking machines, hoping to declare themselves neutral for the survival of the Guild. But many of those emissaries had been Khrone's Face Dancer plants, who intentionally achieved no success. Others—the human ones—never returned from the encounters.

With Richese conveniently obliterated by rebel Honored Matres (secretly guided by Khrone's Face Dancers), humans had no choice but to turn to Ix and the Guild in order to obtain the technological items they required. The Junction shipyards had always been immense complexes for constructing huge interstellar ships.

Murbella's defensive fleet was growing with remarkable speed, but Khrone knew that even these efforts would not be very effective against the sheer size and scope of Omnius's military, which had been thousands of years in the making. The fabrication facilities of Ix (also controlled by Face Dancers) were still delaying the development and modification of the Obliterator weapons upon which the Sisterhood's defense relied. And since every new Guildship was controlled by an Ixian mathematical compiler rather than a Navigator, the Mother Commander and her allies would have many surprises in store.

"We will build more ships to make up for the obsolescence of the

Navigators," Administrator Gorus promised. "Our contract with the New Sisterhood seems infinite. We have never had so much business."

"And yet interplanetary trade is down drastically." The CHOAM representative nodded to both Khrone and Gorus. "How is the Sisterhood to pay for these expensive ships and armaments?"

"They have met their obligations with an increased flow of melange," Gorus said.

Khrone finally nudged the conversation where he wished it to go. "Why not accept payment in horses or petroleum or some other outdated and useless substance? If your Navigators are dying and your ships function perfectly well with Ixian mathematical compilers, the Guild no longer needs melange. What good is it to you?"

"Indeed, its value *is* greatly diminished. Over the past quarter century, following the destruction of Rakis, the Tleilaxu worlds, and so much more, those who could afford spice recreationally have dwindled to a tiny number." The CHOAM representative glanced at his Mentat, who nodded in agreement. "Chapterhouse might have a monopoly on melange, but by their very iron grip, by decreasing the amount of spice available for popular consumption, they have strangled their own market. Few people really *need* it anymore. Now that they have learned to live without spice, will they be so keen to reacquire their addictions?"

"Probably," Gorus said. "You need only drop the price, and we'd have a stampede of customers."

"The witches still control Buzzell," the Mentat pointed out. "They have other ways to pay."

The CHOAM man disdainfully raised his eyebrows. He made very expressive noises without words. "Luxury items during war? Not a good economic investment."

"Providing soostones is no longer easy for them either," Gorus pointed out, "since sea monsters are destroying the shell beds and attacking their harvesters."

Khrone listened intently. His own spies had brought back disturbing, but intriguing, reports about strange happenings on Buzzell, and a possible secret Navigator project centered there. He had demanded more information.

Khrone watched while jawlike machinery on a large crane pried open the pilot's bay on the gigantic decommissioned Heighliner. Heavy suspensor lifters strained and groaned as they pulled out the Navigator's thick-walled plaz tank. During the slow, clumsy extraction, the tank caught on the edge of the hole in the Heighliner's structure. A hull plate broke off and spun downward, striking the side of the Heighliner and ricocheting with a shower of sparks, then tumbling until it finally slammed into the ground far below.

Wisps of orange spice gas escaped from the Navigator's chamber, stray exhaust vapors leaking into the atmosphere. Only a decade or so ago, such a quantity of wasted spice gas would have been enough to buy an Imperial palace. Now the CHOAM representative and Administrator Gorus watched it dissipate without comment. Gorus spoke into a tiny microphone at his collar. "Deposit the tank in front of us. I wish to stare at it."

The crane raised the thick-walled chamber, swung it away from the hulk of the Heighliner, and brought it over to the observation platform. Suspensors lowered the container gently to the copper-floored deck, where it settled with a distressingly heavy thump. Spice gas continued to vent from the chink in the thick plaz.

The melange vapors smelled strangely flat and metallic, telling Khrone that the Navigator had inhaled and exhaled them until very little spice potency remained. At a curt direction from the milky-eyed Administrator, silent Guild workers unsealed a cap on the tank, causing the remainder of the spice to blast out in a death rattle.

As the polluting gas drained, the murky clouds swirled and thinned, revealing a silhouetted form slumped inside. Khrone had seen Navigators before, of course, but this one was flaccid, gray-skinned, and very dead. The bulbous head and small eyes, webbed hands, soft amphibious-looking skin gave the thing the appearance of a large, misshapen fetus. Ardrae had died days earlier, starved for melange. Though the Guild now had plenty of spice in their stockpiles, Administrator Gorus had cut off the Navigators' supplies some time ago.

"Behold, a dead Navigator. A sight few will ever see again."

"How many still survive among your Guildships?" Khrone asked.

Gorus seemed evasive. "Among the ships still in our inventory, only thirteen Navigators remain alive. We are on a death watch for them."

"What do you mean the ships 'still in your inventory'?" the CHOAM man asked.

Gorus hesitated, then admitted, "There were some still flown by Navigators, vessels that we had not yet managed to equip with mathematical compilers. They have . . . how shall I say this? Over the past few months they have disappeared."

"*Disappeared?* How many Heighliners? Each ship is hugely expensive!"

"I do not have precise numbers."

The CHOAM man had a hard voice. "Give us your best estimate."

"Five hundred, perhaps a thousand."

"A *thousand?*"

At his side, the Mentat held his silence, but he appeared as upset and startled as the CHOAM representative.

Trying to demonstrate control over the situation, Gorus said in an almost dismissive tone, "When starved for spice, the Navigators grow desperate. It's not surprising that they take irrational action."

Khrone himself was concerned, but he didn't show it. These disappearances sounded like a widespread conspiracy involving a Navigator faction, something he had not expected. "Do you have any idea where they might have gone?"

The Guild Administrator feigned nonchalance. "It doesn't matter. They will run out of spice and die. Look at these shipyards and see how many vessels we are creating every day. Before long, we'll make up for the loss of those outdated ships and obsolete Navigators. Have no fear. After so many years of bondage to a single substance, the Guild is making a good business decision."

"Thanks to your partners from Ix," Khrone pointed out.

"Yes, thanks to Ix."

Following a lull, the noise of the shipyards became very loud. Welders went to work, and heavy machinery lifted curved components into place. A cargo hauler half a kilometer wide brought in two sets of Holtzman engines. The men continued to watch the magnificent activities for a long time in silence. None of them even looked again at the pathetic dead Navigator in his tank.

*Humanity has many profound beliefs. Chief among them is the
concept of* Home.

—Bene Gesserit Archives,
Analyses of Motivating Factors

The next time Edrik's Heighliner went to Buzzell on a run, the
vessel left the planet carrying something vastly more important
than soostones.

Hidden on the sealed laboratory decks was a package of the uniquely
powerful substance extracted from the slaughtered seaworm's strange,
dense organ. With extravagant optimism, Waff had named it "ultraspice." Tests proved that the potency went beyond that of any spice ever
recorded. This remarkable substance would change everything for the
Navigator faction.

The Tleilaxu Master also understood the importance of his achieve-
ment, and meant to use it to his advantage. Without being summoned,
he pushed past Guild security forces and made his way to the restricted
levels reserved for the Navigator. Officiously ignoring all challenges,
Waff opened thick doors until he stood before the plaz-walled tank that
held Edrik in his expensive bath of spice gas. Having succeeded in
restoring at least one breed of worms, Waff was no longer a sycophant.
He could make brash demands of his own.

Waff 's shortened ghola life span didn't give him much time to meet his critical goals, thus making him increasingly desperate. He was already well past his physical prime, and now his body was in a rapid plunge to degeneration and death. He probably had no more than a year or so left.

Full of rigid defiance, Waff stood before Edrik's tank and said, "Now that my altered seaworms are capable of creating spice in a form accessible by Guild Navigators, I want you to take me to Rakis." He no longer had anything to lose, and everything to gamble. He crossed his thin arms over his chest in triumph.

Swimming slowly, Edrik drifted close to the plaz wall. The swirls of orange gas were hypnotic. "The new melange has not been proved in practice."

"No matter. Its chemistry has been proved."

Edrik's voice grew louder through the speakers. "I am troubled. In its original form, melange has complexities that cannot be revealed in any laboratory analysis."

"You worry unnecessarily," Waff said. "Seaworm spice is more potent than anything you have ever consumed. Try it yourself, if you do not believe me."

"You are in no position to make demands."

"No one else could have accomplished what I did. Buzzell will be your new source of melange. Seaworm hunters will harvest more ultraspice than you can possibly use, and Navigators will no longer be dependent upon the Bene Gesserit witches or the black market. Even if the Sisters decide to harvest the seaworms and try to create another monopoly, you can ignore them. By changing the *worms*, instead of the planet, we can place them anywhere. I have given you the road to freedom."

Waff snorted, raised his voice. "Now I demand my payment."

"We kept you alive after the Honored Matres were overthrown on Tleilax. Is that not sufficient compensation?"

With a conciliatory sigh, the Tleilaxu ghola held his hands out. "What I ask will cost you little and gain you much honor, a blessing from God."

The Navigator wore a look of displeasure on his distorted face. "What do you desire, little man?"

"I repeat: Take me to Rakis."

"Absurd. The world is dead." Edrik's words were flat.

"Rakis is where my last body perished, so consider it a pilgrimage." He continued in a rush, saying more than he had intended. "In my laboratory I created more small worms from the remaining sandtrout specimens. I have strengthened them, made them capable of surviving in the harshest environment. I can repopulate Rakis and bring back the Prophet—" He abruptly fell silent.

At the first rumors that the seaworms were thriving, Waff had turned his efforts to the last few sandtrout in his original stock. Sculpting worm chromosomes for survival in a comfortable ocean environment had been a challenge; much more difficult, though, was the task of toughening the monsters to survive out in the blasted wastelands of Rakis. But Waff did not turn his back on difficulty. All along, his goal had been to bring the sandworms back where they belonged. *God's Messenger must return to Dune.*

He studied Edrik, who stroked with webbed hands as he considered the request. "Our Oracle recently sent us a message, calling upon Navigators to leave the Guild and join her in a great battle. That must be my priority now."

"I implore you, take me to Rakis." As if to remind Waff of his imminent mortality, a twinge of pain shot through his chest and down his spine. He needed all his effort not to show the anguish of dying, the misery of failure. He had so little time remaining. "Is that so much to ask? Grant me this one favor at the end of my life."

"That is all you wish to do? *Die* there?"

"I will spend my last energies on my sandworm specimens. Perhaps there is a way of reintroducing them to Rakis and regenerating the ecological systems. Think of it: If I succeed, you will have yet another source of melange."

"You will not be pleased with what you find there. Even with moisture recycling, shelters, and equipment, survival on Rakis is more difficult than it has ever been. Your expectations are unrealistic. Nothing useful remains."

Waff tried unsuccessfully to keep desperation out of his voice. "Rakis is my home, my spiritual compass."

Edrik thought it over, then said, "I can fold space to Rakis, but I cannot promise to return. The Oracle has called me."

"I will remain there as long as necessary. God will provide for me."

Waff rushed back to his private research levels. Intending to stay on the desert planet, undoubtedly for the rest of his life, he requisitioned all the supplies and equipment he might need for years, allowing him to be entirely self-sufficient on that bleak and lifeless world. After placing the order, he looked at his tanks where the new armored sandworms writhed, eager to be released.

Rakis . . . Dune . . . was his destiny. He felt in his heart that God had summoned him there, and if Waff perished on the planet . . . then so be it. He felt a warm, soothing wave of contentment. He understood his place in the universe.

THE BLACKENED, FAINTLY coppery ball appeared in the Heighliner's private viewing plates. Waff had been so anxious gathering his things that he hadn't even felt the activation of the Holtzman engines, the folding of space.

Edrik surprised him by offering additional supplies and a small team of loyal Guild assistants to help with the labor of setting up a camp and administering the experiments. Perhaps he wanted his own people on hand to see if the Tleilaxu man succeeded again with his worms. Waff didn't mind, so long as they stayed out of the way.

Without introducing himself to the silent members of his new team, Waff directed the transfer of his armored sandworm specimens from the isolated lab, his self-erecting shelters and his equipment, everything they would need for survival on the charred world.

One of the silent, smooth-faced Guild assistants piloted the lighter. Before they reached the dead surface of Dune, the Heighliner had already drifted out of orbit. Edrik was anxious to be on his way to answer the Oracle's call, carrying its cargo of ultraspice and the tidings of new hope for all Navigators.

Waff, though, had eyes only for the blistered, lifeless landscape of the legendary world.

When the virulent plague reached Chapterhouse, the first cases appeared among the male workers. Seven men were struck down so swiftly that their dying expressions showed more surprise than pain.

In the Great Hall where younger Sisters dined, the disease also spread. The virus was so insidious that the most contagious period occurred a full day before any symptoms manifested; thus, the epidemic had already sunk its claws into those most vulnerable before the New Sisterhood even knew a threat existed.

Hundreds perished within the first three days, more than a thousand by the end of the week; after ten days, the victims were beyond counting. Support staff, teachers, visitors, offworld merchants, cooks and kitchen help, even failed Reverend Mothers—all fell like stalks of wheat under the Grim Reaper's scythe.

Murbella called upon her senior advisers to develop an immediate plan, but from prior epidemics on other embattled planets they knew that precautionary measures and quarantines would do no good. The conference room doors were securely locked, because younger Sisters and acolytes could not be allowed to know the strategies being discussed here.

"Survival of the Sisterhood is our primary purpose, even as the rest of Chapterhouse dies around us." Murbella felt sickened to think of all the unprepared acolytes, spice-harvesting teams in the dune belt, transport drivers, architects and construction workers, weather planners, greenhouse gardeners, cleaners, bankers, artists, archive workers, pilots, technicians, and medical assistants. All the underpinnings of Chapterhouse itself.

Laera attempted to sound objective, but her voice cracked. "Reverend Mothers have the precise cellular control needed to fight this disease on its own battleground. We can use our bodily defenses to drive away the plague."

"In other words, anyone who hasn't gone through the Spice Agony will die," Kiria said. "Like the Honored Matres did. That was why we pursued you Bene Gesserits in the first place, to learn how to protect ourselves from the epidemic."

"Can we use the blood of Bene Gesserit survivors to create a vaccine?" Murbella asked.

Laera shook her head. "Reverend Mothers drive out disease organisms, cell by cell. There are no antibodies we can share with others."

"It is not even as simple as that," Accadia rasped. "A Reverend Mother can channel her inner biological defenses only if she has the energy to do so, and if she has the time and ability to concentrate on herself. But this plague forces us to turn our energies to tend the most unfortunate victims."

"If you make that mistake, you'll die, just like our Sheeana surrogate on Jhibraith," Kiria said with the undertone of a sneer in her voice. "We Reverend Mothers will have to take care of ourselves and no one else. The others have no chance anyway. We need to accept that."

Murbella already felt the beginnings of exhaustion, but her nervous anxiety made her pace the sealed council room. She had to think. What could be done against such a minute, lethal enemy? *Only Reverend Mothers will survive. . . .* She spoke firmly to her advisors, "Find every acolyte who is close to being ready for the Agony. Do we have enough Water of Life?"

"For all of them?" cried Laera.

"For every single one. Any Sister who has the slightest chance of survival. Give all of them the poison and hope they can convert it and survive the Agony. Only then will they be able to fight off the plague."

"Many will die in the attempt," warned Laera.

"Or *all* of them will die from the plague. Even if most of the candidates succumb to the Agony, it's an improvement." She did not wince. Her own daughter Rinya had perished that way, many years ago.

Smiling slightly with her wrinkled lips, Accadia nodded. "A Bene Gesserit would rather die from the Agony than from a sickness spread by our Enemy. It is a gesture of defiance rather than surrender."

"See that it is done."

IN THE DEATH houses she turned a deaf ear to the moans of the sick and dying. The Chapterhouse doctors had drugs and potent analgesics, and the Bene Gesserit acolytes had been taught how to block off pain. Even so, the misery of the plague was enough to break the deepest conditioning.

Murbella hated to see the Sisters unable to control their suffering. It shamed her, not for their weakness but because she had been unable to prevent this from happening in the first place.

She went to where lines of makeshift beds held young acolytes, most of them terrified, some of them determined. The room smelled of rancid cinnamon—harsh instead of pleasant. With her brow furrowed and eyes intent, the Mother Commander watched two stony-faced Reverend Mothers carry out a stretcher bearing the sheet-wrapped body of a young woman.

"Another one failed the Agony?"

The Reverend Mothers nodded. "Sixty-one today. They are dying as fast as from the plague."

"And how many successes?"

"Forty-three."

"Forty-three that will live to fight the Enemy."

Like a mother hen, Murbella walked up and down the line of beds, observing the plague-stricken Sisters, some sleeping quietly with new bodily awareness, others writhing in deep comas from which it was uncertain they would ever find their way back.

At the end of the row, a teenage girl lay with frightened eyes. She propped herself up in bed on trembling arms. She met Murbella's gaze, and even in her extreme sickness the girl's eyes glimmered. "Mother Commander," she said hoarsely.

Murbella moved closer to the young one. "What is your name?"

"Baleth."

"Are you waiting to undergo the Agony?"

"I'm waiting to die, Mother Commander. I was brought here to take the Water of Life, but before it could be administered the symptoms of the disease manifested themselves. I'll be dead before the end of the day." She sounded very brave.

"So they will not give you the Water of Life, then? You won't even attempt the Agony?"

Baleth lowered her chin. "They say I will not survive it."

"And you believe them? Aren't you strong enough to try?"

"I am strong enough to *try*, Mother Commander."

"Then I'd rather you died trying, instead of giving up." As she looked down at Baleth, she was poignantly reminded of Rinya . . . eager and confident, so like Duncan. But her daughter hadn't been ready after all, and she had died on the table.

I should have delayed her. Because of my need to prove myself, I pushed Rinya. I should have waited. . . .

And Murbella's youngest daughter Gianne—what had happened to her? The Mother Commander had kept herself apart from the young woman's day-to-day activities, letting the Sisterhood raise her. But in this time of crisis, she decided to ask someone, Laera perhaps, to track her down.

Right now, Baleth seemed to show hope, looking with fervid eyes toward the Mother Commander. Murbella ordered the Suk doctors to attend to her immediately. "Time is shorter for this one than for the others."

From the doctors' skeptical expressions, Murbella could see they considered this a waste of the valuable Water of Life, but she stood firm. Baleth accepted the viscid draught, took a last look at her Mother Commander, and gulped the toxic substance. She lay back, closed her eyes, and began her fight. . . .

It did not last long. Baleth died in a valiant attempt, but Murbella could feel no guilt about it. The Sisterhood must never stop fighting.

THOUGH MELANGE WAS rare and precious, rarer still was the Water of Life.

By the fourth day of Murbella's desperate plan, it became apparent that Chapterhouse's supplies would not be sufficient. Sister after Sister consumed the poison, and many perished while struggling to convert the deadly toxin in their cells, trying to change their bodies.

The Mother Commander tasked her advisors to study the exact amount of poison necessary to trigger the Agony. Some Reverend Mothers suggested diluting the substance, but if they didn't give enough to be fatal, and thus effective, the entire experiment would fail.

Dozens more Sisters died. More than 60 percent of those who took the poison.

Kiria offered a hard but coldly logical solution. "Assess each candidate, and dole out the Water of Life only to those most likely to succeed. We can't gamble foolishly. Each dose we give to a woman who fails is wasted. We must discriminate."

Murbella disagreed. "None of them has a chance unless they undergo the Agony. The whole point of this operation is to give it to everyone—and the most fit will survive."

The women stood amidst the bedlam of the dormitory rooms in the sick houses that had been converted from any building large enough to accommodate beds. Four lifeless bodies were carried past them by exhausted-looking Reverend Mothers. They had run out of sheets, so the corpses were uncovered, their faces twisted in a display of the incalculable pain they had suffered.

Ignoring the dead, Murbella knelt beside the bed of one young woman who survived. She had to look at the casualty total from a different perspective. If they were *all* destined to die, it was a fruitless exercise to count those who perished. In that light, the only relevant number was the tally of those who did recover. The victories.

"If we don't have enough Water of Life, use other poisons." Murbella got wearily to her feet, ignoring the smells, the sounds. "The Bene Gesserit may have determined that the Water of Life is most effective at forcing the Agony, but long ago the Sisters used other deadly chemicals—anything that would push the body into an absolute crisis." She perused the young students, these girls who had hoped one day to grow up to become Reverend Mothers. Now each of them had one chance, and one chance only. "Poison them one way or another. Poison them all. If they survive, they belong here."

A courier ran up to her, one of the younger Sisters who had recently survived the transformation. "Mother Commander! You are needed immediately in Archives."

Murbella turned. "Has Accadia found something?"

"No, Mother Commander. She . . . you have to see for yourself." The younger woman swallowed. "And *hurry.*"

The ancient woman did not have the strength to leave her office. Accadia sat surrounded by wire spool readers and stacks of data-dense crystal sheets. She sprawled back in her large chair, breathing heavily, barely able to move. The old woman's rheumy eyes flickered open. "So, you've come . . . in time."

Murbella looked at the archivist, appalled. Accadia, too, had the plague. "But you are a Reverend Mother! You can fight this."

"I am old and tired. I used the last of my stamina to compile our records and projections, to map out the spread of this disease. Maybe we can prevent it on other worlds."

"Doubtful. The Enemy distributes the virus wherever they consider it strategic." Already she had made up her mind to have several other Reverend Mothers Share with Accadia. Her extensive memories and knowledge must not be lost.

Accadia struggled to sit up in the chair. "Mother Commander, don't be so focused on the epidemic that you fail to see its consequences." She began coughing. Blotches had appeared all over her skin, the advanced stages of the disease. "This plague is a mere foray, a test attack. On many planets it is sufficient, but the Enemy must know the Sisterhood well enough by now to be sure we can fight this, at least to a point. After they soften us up, they'll attack by other means."

Murbella felt cold inside. "If thinking machines destroy the New Sisterhood, then the remaining fragments of humanity will have no chance of resisting them. We are the most important hurdle Omnius has to overcome."

"So you finally understand the implications?" The old woman grasped the Mother Commander's hand to make sure she understood. "This planet has always been hidden, but now the thinking machines must know the location of Chapterhouse. I would wager that their space fleet is already on its way."

One man's dream is another's nightmare.

—a saying of Ancient Kaitain

After dragging Stuka's body away, the nomads separated Sheeana and Teg from Stilgar and Liet-Kynes. Apparently they saw the two boys—twelve and thirteen—as no threat, not knowing that both were deadly Fremen fighters, whose clear memories held many raids against the Harkonnens.

Teg recognized the strategy. "The old leader wants to interrogate our young ones first." Var and his hard-bitten comrades would assume the youths would be easily intimidated, not capable of resisting difficult questioning.

Teg and Sheeana were taken to a holding tent made of a tough, weather-worn polymer. The structure was an odd mixture of primitive design and sophisticated technology, made for serviceability and ease of transport. The guard closed the flap but remained outside.

The windowless tent was just an empty enclosure, devoid of blankets, cushions, or tools of any kind. Teg paced in a small circle, then sat beside her on the packed dirt. Digging with his fingers, he quickly found a couple of sharp pebbles.

With Mentat clarity, he assessed their options. "When we do not return or report in," he said in a low voice, "we can expect Duncan to send another party down. He will be prepared. It sounds trite, but rescue will come." He knew that these nomads would crumble easily against a direct military assault. "Duncan is wise, and I trained him well. He will know what to do."

Sheeana stared at the door as if in meditative trance. "Duncan has lived hundreds of lives and remembers them all, Miles. I doubt you taught him anything new."

Teg gripped one of the pebbles, and it seemed to aid his concentration. Even in an empty tent, he saw a thousand possible avenues of escape. He and Sheeana could easily break out, kill the guard, and fight their way back to the lighter. Teg might not even need to take advantage of his accelerated speed. "These people are no match for me, or for you. But I will not leave Stilgar and Liet behind."

"Ah, the loyal Bashar."

"I wouldn't leave you, either. However, I fear that these people have disabled our ship, which would certainly tangle our escape plans. I heard them ransacking it."

Sheeana continued to stare at the shadowy wall of the tent. "Miles, I'm not so concerned about the possibility of escape as I am curious to learn why they kept us alive. Especially me, if what they said about the Sisterhood is true. They have good reason to hate me."

Teg tried to imagine the incredible exodus and reorganization of populations on this planet. Within years, all the inhabitants of the towns and cities would have seen the sands strangling their croplands, killing their orchards, creeping closer and closer to the city boundaries. They would have pulled away from the desert zone like people fleeing a slowly advancing fire.

Var's nomads, though . . . were they scavengers and misfits? Outcasts from the larger population centers? Why insist on staying at the threshold of the advancing desert, where they would have to uproot their settlement and retreat constantly? To what purpose?

These were technologically capable people, and Qelso clearly must have been settled long ago during the Scattering. They had their own groundcars and low-altitude flyers, fast ships to take them back and forth across the dunes. If they weren't outright exiles, perhaps Var's people replenished their supplies in the distant northern cities.

Teg and Sheeana hardly spoke for hours as they listened to the muffled sounds outside, the dry wind pushing and tugging at the tent, the *scritch* of blowing sand. Everything seemed to be comprised of movement outside: The people sent out parties, marched back and forth, set machinery to work.

As Teg listened to the noises, he catalogued them in his mind, building a picture of the operations. He heard a pounding drill that bored a well shaft, followed by a pump dispensing water into small cisterns. Each time, after only a brief gush of liquid, the flow dwindled to less than a trickle and stopped. He knew that such problems, caused by sandtrout, had been the bane of drilling operations on Arrakis. Water existed in deep enough strata, but it was blocked off by the voracious little Makers. Like platelets at the site of a wound, sandtrout would swiftly seal off the leak. As he listened to the resigned complaints of these people, Teg realized that they were familiar with the routine.

When night fell, a dusty young man entered the tent through the flap held open by the guard. He delivered a small meal of hard bread and dried fruit, as well as gamey-tasting white meat. The two captives also received carefully measured rations of water.

Sheeana looked at her sealed cup. "They are learning the fundamentals of extreme conservation. They begin to understand what their world will become." Obviously despising her Bene Gesserit robes, the young man glared at her and departed without a word.

Throughout the dark night, Teg remained awake, listening, trying to plan. The lack of activity was maddening, but he advised patience rather than rash action. They had heard nothing from Liet or Stilgar, and he feared the two young men might already be dead, like Stuka. Had they been killed during interrogation?

Sheeana sat beside him, in a heightened state of alertness. Her eyes were bright even in the tent shadows. As far as Teg could tell, the guard outside never stepped away from his position, never even moved. The people continued to send out parties and skimmer ships throughout the night, as if the camp were the staging area for a war effort.

At dawn, old Var came up to the tent, spoke briskly with the guard, and pulled the flap aside. Sheeana rose to a half crouch, ready to spring; Teg tensed, also prepared for a fight.

The nomad leader glared at Sheeana. "You and your witches are not forgiven for what you have done to Qelso. You never will be. But Liet-Kynes and Stilgar have convinced us to keep you alive, at least as long as we can learn from you."

The weathered leader brought the pair out into the bright sunlight. The wind flung stinging sand into their eyes. All around the settlement, trees had already died. The blowing dunes had encroached another few feet past the prominent rock outcroppings during the night. Each breath was crackling dry, even in the relative coolness of the morning.

"You put the other Bene Gesserits to death," Sheeana said, "and killed our companion Stuka. Am I next?"

"No. Because I said I would keep you alive."

The weathered man led them through the settlement. Workers were already disassembling large warehouse tents to move them farther from the edge of the sand. A heavy groundcar rumbled by, full of crates. A bloated flyer circled and landed near the smooth sand. Some kind of tanker?

Var led them to a large central building made from sectional metal walls and a conical roof. Inside, a long table was cluttered with charts. Reports were fastened to the walls, and one entire wall displayed a polymer-paper map, a high-resolution topographic projection of the entire continent. Mark after mark showed the steady growth of the desert belt.

Men sat around the table sharing reports and raising their voices in a tumult of conversation. Stilgar and Liet-Kynes, both dressed in dusty shipsuits, waved a greeting at the other two prisoners. The young men seemed pleased and relaxed.

As he scanned the setup, it was obvious to Teg that Stilgar and Liet had spent the whole previous day in the command tent. The old leader positioned himself between them, leaving Teg and Sheeana to stand.

Var pounded on the table, interrupting the cacophony. Everyone stopped talking, impatiently it seemed, and stared at him. "We have listened to our new friends describe what our world is sure to become.

We've all heard legends of long-lost Dune, where water is more precious than blood." His face had a pinched look. "If we fail and the worms take over, our planet will become valuable only by the standards of outsiders."

One of the men snarled at Sheeana, "Damned Bene Gesserits!" The others glared at her as well, and she met their disapproval squarely, without comment.

Liet and Stilgar seemed to be in their element. Teg recalled the Bene Gesserit discussions over the original ghola project, how the long-forgotten abilities of those historical personages might become relevant again. Here was a perfect example. This duo of prominent survivors from the old days of Arrakis certainly knew how to deal with the crisis these people now faced.

The grizzled leader raised his hands, and his voice sounded as dry as the air. "After the death of the Tyrant long ago, my people fled into the Scattering. When they reached Qelso, they thought they had found Eden. It was a paradise for fifteen hundred years afterward."

The men glowered at Sheeana. Var explained how the refugees had established a thriving society, built cities, planted crops, mined for metals and minerals. They had no wish to overextend themselves or go searching for other lost brothers who had escaped during the Famine Times.

"Then a few decades ago everything changed. Visitors came, Bene Gesserits. At first we welcomed them, glad to have news from the outside. We offered them a new home. They became our guests. But the ingrates raped our entire planet, and now it is dying."

Another man clenched his hands into fists as he picked up the story. "The sandtrout multiplied out of control. Huge forests and vast plains died within years—only a few years! Great fires started in the wastelands, and weather patterns changed, turning much of our world into a dust bowl."

Teg spoke up, using his command voice. "If Liet and Stilgar told you about our no-ship and its mission, then you know we don't carry sandtrout and we have no intention of harming your world. We stopped here only to replenish vital supplies."

"In fact, we fled the heart of the Bene Gesserit order because we disagreed with the policies and leadership," Sheeana added.

"You have seven large sandworms in your hold," Var accused.

"Yes, and we will not release them here."

Liet-Kynes spoke quietly, as if lecturing children. "As we already told you, once it has begun, the desertification process is a chain reaction. The sandtrout have no natural enemies, and their encysting of water is so swift that nothing can adapt quickly enough to fight against them."

"Nevertheless, we will fight," Var said. "You see how simply we live in this camp. We have given up everything to stay here."

"But why?" Sheeana asked. "Even as the desert spreads, you have many years to prepare."

"Prepare? Do you mean surrender? You may call it a hopeless fight, but it is still a *fight*. If we cannot stop the desert, we will at least slow it. We'll battle the worms and the sands." The men at the table muttered. "No matter what you say, we will try to hinder the desert's progress in every way. We kill sandtrout, we hunt the new worms." Var stood up, and the others followed suit. "We are commandos sworn to slow the death of our world."

The desert still calls me. It sings in my blood like a love song.

—LIET-KYNES,
Planetology: New Treatises

Early the next morning, Var led his group of dusty, determined fighters to a landing zone of fire-baked pavement. "Today, my new friends, we'll show you how to kill a worm. Maybe two."

"Shai-Hulud," Stilgar said with great uneasiness. "Fremen used to worship the great worms."

"Fremen depended upon the worms and the spice," Liet replied quietly. "These people do not."

"With each demon we eliminate, we give our planet a little more time to survive." Var stared out into the desert as if his hatred could drive back the sands. Stilgar followed the man's gaze across the deeply shadowed dunes, trying to imagine the landscape in front of him as lush and green.

The sun was just rising over an escarpment, glinting off the silvery hull of an old low-altitude flyer parked on an area of pounded gravel and flash-fused cement. Var's people did not bother with permanent landing strips or spaceport zones, which would only be swallowed up by the spreading dunes.

Despite the protests of the two young men, Sheeana and Teg were forced to remain behind in the camp as hostages, watched suspiciously. Liet and Stilgar had been accepted on the hunt because of their invaluable knowledge of the desert. Today, they would demonstrate their skills.

Var's commandos clambered into the heavily used craft. It had obviously weathered countless storms, rough flights, and incomplete maintenance; its hull was scuffed and scraped. The interior smelled of oil and sweat, and the seats were stone-hard, with only bars or straps for the passengers to hold onto.

Stilgar felt comfortable enough among the twenty weathered, grim men. To his trained eye, the commandos had a look of edgy anticipation, but they were too soft in the flesh for the adaptations they would soon face. With the rapid climate shift, even living in their nomadic camps at the fringe of the sand, these people remained unaware of the desert's true harshness. They would have to learn swiftly enough to face the escalating hardships. He and his friend could teach them—if they would listen.

Liet took his seat beside Stilgar and spoke to Var's men with genuine enthusiasm. "Right now, Qelso's air still contains enough moisture that truly dramatic measures aren't required. Soon, though, you will need to be careful not to waste so much as a thimbleful of water."

"We already live under the strictest conservation," one man said, as if Liet had insulted him.

"Oh? You don't recycle your sweat, respiration, or urine. You still import water from the higher latitudes, where it is readily available. Many regions on Qelso are still able to grow crops, and people live a fairly normal life."

"It will get worse," Stilgar agreed. "Your people have much hardening to do before the planet reaches its new equilibrium. This is the first day of your new field training."

The men muttered uncertainly at hearing such words from two seeming boys, but Liet sounded optimistic. "It is not so bad. We can teach you how to make stillsuits, how to conserve every breath, every sweat droplet. Your fighting instincts are admirable, but useless against sandworms. You must learn to survive among the behemoths that will eventually take control of your world. It is a necessary shift in attitude."

"The Fremen did so for a long time." Stilgar seated himself beside his friend. "It was an honorable way of life."

The fighters held onto straps and spread their feet for balance, preparing for takeoff. "That is what lies in store for us? Drinking recycled sweat and piss? Living in sealed chambers?"

"Only if we fail," old Var said. "I choose to believe we still have a chance, no matter how naïve that sounds." He closed the ship's hatch and strapped himself into the creaking pilot seat. "So, if that doesn't sound pleasant to you, then we'd better stop the desert from gaining more of a foothold."

The flyer lifted from the dry camp and swung out over the ghost forests and hummocks of fresh dunes that were swallowing the remnants of grasslands. The engine sputtered periodically as they flew southeast to a region where sandworms had been sighted. The craft seemed like a sluggish bumblebee, its tanks overloaded and heavy.

"We will stop the moving sands," one young commando said.

"Next you will try to stop the wind." Stilgar grabbed a dangling strap as a thermal updraft shook the craft. "In a few short years, your planet will be sand and rock. Do you expect a miracle to turn the desert back?"

"We'll create that miracle for ourselves," Var answered, and his team murmured in agreement.

They flew across the wilderness of dunes, far past the point where they could see anything but buttery tan from horizon to horizon. Stilgar tapped a finger against the scratched windowplaz and shouted against the engine noise. "See the desert for what it is—not a place to fear and loathe, but a great engine to power an empire."

Liet added, "Already, small worms in the desert belt have created priceless amounts of melange just waiting to be mined. How have you survived for so long without spice?"

"We haven't needed spice for fifteen hundred years, not since we came to Qelso," Var called from the cockpit. "When you do not have a thing, you learn to live without it, or you don't live."

"We don't give a damn about spice," one of the commandos said. "I'd rather give a damn about trees and crops and fat herds."

Var continued, "Our first settlers brought a great deal of spice from far away, and three generations fought addiction until the supplies were gone. Then what? We were forced to survive without it—and we have. Why should we open ourselves to that monstrous dependency again? My people are better off without it."

"If used carefully, melange has important qualities," Liet said. "Health, life extension, the possibility of prescience. And it's a valuable commodity to sell, should you ever reconnect with CHOAM and the rest of mankind. As Qelso dries up, you may need offworld supplies for your basic needs."

If anyone survives the outside Enemy, Stilgar thought to himself, recalling the ever-present threat of capture by the shimmering net. But these people were much more concerned with their own local enemies, fighting the desert, trying to stop the unstoppable.

He remembered the great dreams of Pardot Kynes, Liet's father. Pardot had done the calculations and determined that the Fremen could turn Dune into a garden, but only after generations of intense effort. According to the histories, Arrakis had indeed become green and verdant for a time, before the new worms reclaimed it, and brought the desert back. The planet seemed unable to achieve a balance.

The battered craft flew low, its engines droning. Stilgar wondered if the noise of their passage would attract worms, but as he stared down at the hypnotic, oceanic dunes, he saw only a couple of patches of rust-colored sand that indicated fresh spice blows.

"Dropping signal vibrators," Var called, while throbbing canisters—the equivalent of ancient thumpers—tumbled out of the small bays below the cockpit. "That should bring at least one of them."

With a puff of sand and dust the thumpers plunged into the dunes and sent out droning signals. After circling back to make certain the devices were operating properly, Var selected two more spots within a radius of five kilometers. Stilgar could not determine why the craft still felt overloaded.

As they cruised in search of a worm, Stilgar described his legendary days on Dune, how he and Paul Muad'Dib had led a ragtag Fremen army to victory against far superior forces. "We used desert power. That is what you can learn from us. Once you see we are not your enemies, we can learn much from each other."

Under Stilgar's firm hand, these people could come to understand their possibilities. With the awakening of the populace would come the awakening of the planet, with plantings and green zones to keep the desert under control. Perhaps they could succeed, if they could just find—and maintain—an equilibrium.

Stilgar remembered something Liet's father had said to him once. *Extremes invariably lead to disaster. Only through balance can we fully harvest the fruits of nature.* He leaned closer to the craft's observation windows and saw a familiar wrinkling of the sand, ripples of deep movement disturbing the smooth dunes. "Wormsign!"

"Prepare for our first encounter of the day." A grin wrinkled Var's grizzled face as he turned away from the cockpit. "The shipment that came in last night brought us enough water for two targets—but we need to find them."

Water! The heavy ship was carrying water.

The men shifted position, heading toward gunnery hatches and hoses mounted on the sides of the stripped-down flyer. The pilot banked back toward the first cluster of thumpers.

As the commandos prepared to strike, Stilgar mused about the strange turnabout. Pardot Kynes had spoken of the need to understand ecological consequences, that humans were stewards of the land, and never owners. *We must do a thing on Arrakis never before attempted for an entire planet. We must use man as a constructive ecological force—inserting adapted terraform life: a plant here, an animal there, a man in that place—to transform the water cycle, to build a new kind of landscape.*

The battle today was the opposite. Stilgar and Liet would help fight to prevent the desert from swallowing all of Qelso.

Through the nearest window Stilgar saw a mound in motion, a bucking sandworm drawn toward the thumper. Liet crowded close beside him,

SANDWORMS OF DUNE

and said, "I estimate it at forty meters. Larger than Sheeana's worms in our hold."

"These have grown in the open desert," Stilgar said. "Shai-Hulud wants this planet."

"Not if I can help it," Var said. But as if to defy him, directly below the flyer an immense head surfaced and quested around, trying to track the conflicting sources of vibrations.

Long tubes protruded from the front and rear of the flyer. The commandos gripped their gun mountings, nozzles that could be turned and aimed. The flyer swooped low. "Fire when ready, but conserve what you can. The water's deadly enough."

The fighters shot high-pressure streams from their hoses, blasting the sandworm below. The drenching bursts were more effective than artillery shells.

Taken by surprise, the creature writhed and twisted its round head back and forth, convulsing. Hard ring segments split apart to reveal softer pink flesh between, and water burned like acid into the vulnerable parts. The worm rolled on the wet sand, in obvious agony.

"They are killing Shai-Hulud," Stilgar said, sickened.

Liet was also stunned, but said, "These people have to defend themselves."

"That's enough! It is dead—or soon will be," Var shouted. The small force reluctantly shut off their hoses, looking with hatred upon the dying worm. Unable to dig deep enough to escape the poisonous moisture, the mortally wounded creature continued to squirm as the flyer circled over its death throes. Finally the beast gave a great final shudder and stopped moving.

Stilgar nodded, his expression still grim. "There are necessities to life in the desert, hard decisions to be made." He had to accept the clear fact that this worm did not belong here on Qelso. No sandworm did. On the way back to the settlement, they encountered a second worm, drawn by the vibrations of their flyer's engines. The commandos emptied their water reservoirs, and the second worm perished even more quickly.

Liet and Stilgar sat together in uncomfortable silence, wrapped up in what they had seen and the fight they had agreed to join. "Even though she doesn't have her memories back yet," Liet said, "I'm glad my daughter Chani did not see this."

Though the mood of the fighters was upbeat aboard the flyer, the two young men, remembering Arrakis, murmured Fremen prayers. Stilgar was still contemplating what they had seen and done when Var yelled a strangled-sounding alarm.

Suddenly strange ships swarmed around them.

You see only harshness, devastation, and ugliness. That is because you have no faith. Around me I see a potential paradise, for Rakis is the birthplace of my beloved Prophet.

—WAFF of the Tleilaxu

When he first glimpsed Rakis, the bleak ruins brought dismay to Waff 's heart. But when Edrik's Heighliner deposited him and his small team of Guild assistants there, he experienced the joy of setting foot on the desert planet again. He could feel the holy calling deep inside his bones.

In his previous lifetime he had stood on these sands, face to face with the Prophet. With Sheeana and Reverend Mother Odrade, he had ridden a great worm out to the ruins of Sietch Tabr. His ghola memories were corrupted and uncertain, riddled with annoying gaps. Waff could not recall his final moments as the whores closed in around the desert planet, deploying their awful Obliterators. Had he run for hopeless shelter, looking behind him like Lot's wife for a last glimpse of the doomed city? Had he seen explosions and walls of flame searing the sky, sweeping toward him?

But the cells of another Waff ghola had been grown in an axlotl tank in Bandalong as part of the usual process. The secret council of the kehl had planned for the serial immortality of all Tleilaxu Masters long before anyone had heard of Honored Matres. The next thing he knew, Waff was awakened to his past life during a grand guignol stage show as the brutal women murdered one of his twins after another until just one of them—him—reached a sufficiently desperate crisis to break through the ghola barrier and reveal his past. Some of it, at least.

But not until now had Waff actually seen the Armageddon that the whores had wrought on this sacred world.

The ecosystem of Rakis had been fundamentally destroyed. Half of the atmosphere was burned away, the ground sterilized, most life forms dead—from the microscopic sandplankton all the way up to the giant sandworms. It made the old Dune seem comfortable by comparison.

The sky was a dark purple, touched with an underburn of orange. As their ship circled, searching for a spot less hellish than others, Waff studied a panel of atmospheric readings. The moisture content was abnormally high. At some point in its geologic history, Arrakis had possessed open water, but sandtrout had sealed it all away. During the bombardment, underground rivers and seas must have been vaporized as they were released from aquifers.

The Honored Matres' horrific weapons had not only turned the soft dunes to a baked moonscape, they had also thrown up great clouds of dust that had not settled entirely out of the atmosphere, even decades later. The Coriolis storms would be worse than ever before.

He and his team would likely have to wear special bodily protection and supplemental breather masks; their small dwelling huts would need to be sealed and pressurized. Waff didn't mind. Was that so different from wearing a stillsuit? By degrees, perhaps, but not fundamentally harder.

His lighter circled over the remains of a sprawling metropolis that had been called Arrakeen in the days of Muad'Dib, then the Festival City of Onn during the reign of the God Emperor, and later—after Leto II's death—the moated city of Keen. No longer concerned about secrecy, now that the seaworms had successfully taken hold on Buzzell, Waff was happy to have four assistants help him with the hard work he was sure to face on this Obliterator-blasted planet.

Studying the surface, he discerned lumpy geometric shapes that had once been angled streets and tall buildings. Surprisingly, in the dimness of seared daylight, he also spotted numerous artificial illumination sources and a few dark structures of recent construction. "There seems to be a camp down there. Who else would come to Rakis? What could they possibly want here?"

"The same as us," said the Guildsman. "Spice."

He shook his head. "Too little here anymore, at least until we bring back the worms. No one else has that skill."

"Pilgrims perhaps? There may still be those who make a hajj," a second assistant said. Waff knew that a dizzying mishmash of religious splinter groups and cults had sprung from Rakis.

"More likely," suggested a third Guildsman, "they are treasure hunters."

Waff quoted quietly from the Cant of the Shariat: "'When greed and desperation are coupled, men accomplish superhuman feats—though for the wrong reasons.'"

He considered choosing a different place for their base camp, then accepted the idea that joining resources with the strangers might help them all last longer in the harsh environment. No one knew when—or if—Edrik might be coming back for them, or how long the sandworm work would take, or how much longer Waff himself would last. He planned to be here for the remainder of his days.

After the lighter landed unannounced at the edge of the camp, the Guildsmen waited for instructions from Waff. The Tleilaxu man settled goggles over his eyes to protect against the caustic wind, and emerged. For long journeys outside, he might have to wear a supplemental oxygen mask, but the Rakian atmosphere was surprisingly breathable.

Six tall and dirty men faced him from the encampment. They wore rags wrapped around their heads, carried knives and antique maula pistols. Their eyes were red-veined, their skin rough and cracked. The foremost man had shaggy black hair, a square chest, and a rock-hard potbelly. "You are fortunate that I'm curious about why you are here. Otherwise, we would've shot you out of the sky."

Waff held up his hands. "We are no threat to you, whoever you are."

Five men leveled their maula pistols, and the other slashed the air with his knife. "We have claimed Rakis for ourselves. All spice here is ours."

"You've claimed a whole planet?"

"Yes, the whole damned planet." The first man tossed back his dark hair. "I'm Guriff, and these are my prospectors. There's damned little spice left in the burned crust, and it's ours."

"Then you may have it." Waff performed a perfunctory bow. "We have other interests, as geological investigators and archaeologists. We wish to take readings and run tests to determine the extent of damage to the ecosystem." The four Guild assistants waited beside him in complete silence.

Guriff laughed loudly and heartily. "There isn't much of an ecosystem left here."

"Then where does breathable oxygen come from?" He knew that Liet-Kynes had asked that question in the ancient days, curious because the planet had neither widespread plant life nor volcanoes to generate an atmosphere.

The man just stared. Obviously, he had not thought about this. "Do I look like a planetologist to you? Go ahead and look into it, but don't expect any help from us. Here on Rakis, you are self-sufficient or you die."

The Tleilaxu man raised his eyebrows. "And what if we wish to share some of our spice coffee with you, as a token of friendship? I understand that water is more easily obtainable than in the old days."

Guriff glanced at his prospectors, then said, "We're happy to accept your hospitality, but we have no intention of reciprocating."

"Nonetheless, our offer stands."

INSIDE GURIFF'S DUSTY hut, Waff used his own supplies of melange (left over from his sandworm experiments) to brew coffee. Guriff didn't have a desperate shortage of water in his camp, though his dwelling smelled of long-unwashed bodies and the savory sweetness of a drug smoke that Waff could not identify.

At his command, the four Guildsmen erected the shelters brought down from the Heighliner, setting up armored sleeping tents and laboratory enclosures. Waff saw no reason to assist them. He was a Tleilaxu

Master after all, and these were his workers, so he would allow them to perform their tasks.

While they drank a second pot of spice coffee, Guriff grew more relaxed. He didn't trust the diminutive Tleilaxu, but he didn't seem to trust anyone. He took pains to say he harbored no particular hatred toward Waff's race, and that his scavengers held no grudges against others of low social position. Guriff cared only about Rakis.

"All that melted sand and plascrete. By chipping away the upper crust of glass, we were able to get down to the foundations of the sturdier buildings in Keen." Guriff produced a hand-drawn chart. "Scraping out buried treasure. We found what we think is the original Bene Gesserit Keep—a few heavily barricaded bomb shelters filled with skeletons." He smiled. "We also uncovered the extravagant temple built by the Priests of the Divided God. It was so huge we couldn't miss it. Full of trinkets, but still not enough to pay for our effort. CHOAM is expecting us to find something much more extraordinary, though they seem happy enough to sell containers of 'genuine Rakian sand' to gullible fools."

Waff didn't reply. Edrik and the Navigators had obtained such Rakian sand for him to use in his original experiments.

"But we've got a lot more digging to do. Keen was a big city."

In his previous life, Waff had seen those structures before they were destroyed. He knew the ostentation that the deluded Priests placed in all the rooms and towers (as if God cared about such gaudiness!). Guriff and his men would indeed find plenty of treasure there. But the wrong kind.

"The Priesthood's temple had collapsed worse than most other large buildings. Maybe it was a direct target of the Honored Matre attack." The prospector smiled with thick lips. "But deep in the sublevels beneath the temple, we did find chests of stored solaris and hoarded melange. A worthwhile haul. More than we expected, but not so much. We're after something bigger. The Tyrant buried a huge spice hoard deep in the southern polar regions—I'm sure of it."

Waff made a skeptical sound as he sipped spice coffee. "No one has been able to find that treasure for fifteen hundred years."

Guriff held up a finger, noticed a hangnail, and chewed on it. "Still, the bombardment may have churned up the crust enough to reveal the mother lode. And, thanks be to the gods—there are no worms left to torment us."

Waff made a noncommittal sound. *Not yet.*

WITHOUT BOTHERING TO sleep, knowing his time was short, the Tleilaxu man began to make preparations to continue his work. His Guild companions seemed confident that the Navigator would eventually return, though Waff wasn't so sure. He was here on Rakis, and this gave him great pleasure.

While the Guild assistants finished connecting the generators and sealed the prefab shelters, the Tleilaxu researcher went back aboard the near-empty lighter. In the cargo hold he smiled paternally at his magnificent specimens. The armored worms were small but ferocious. They looked ready to tackle a dead world. *Their* world.

Ages ago, the Fremen had been able to summon and ride sandworms, but those original creatures had died out when Leto II's terraforming operations had turned Arrakis into a garden world with green plants, flowing rivers, and moisture from the sky. Such an environment was fatal to sandworms. But when the God Emperor was assassinated and his body fissioned into sandtrout, the whole process of desertification began anew. The freshly spawned worms became far more vicious than their predecessors, tackling the huge challenge of recreating the Dune That Once Was.

Waff now faced a challenge many times more difficult. His modified creatures were armored to resist the most severe environment, with mouths and head ridges powerful enough to crack through the vitrified dunes. They could dig deep beneath the black surface; they could grow and reproduce—even here.

He stood before the dusty holding tank in which the worms churned. Each specimen was about two meters in length. And strong.

Sensing his presence, the creatures twitched restlessly. Waff looked outside to where the sky had turned the deep purple-brown of dusk. Storms swirled gritty dust through the atmosphere. "Be patient, my pets," he said. "Soon I will release you."

We are naïve to think that we control a precious commodity. Only through guile and eternal wariness do we keep it out of the hands of our competitors.

—Spacing Guild internal report

E drik moved his Heighliner away from the ruins of Rakis, no longer concerned with the Tleilaxu Master. Waff had served his purpose.

More important, the Oracle of Time had summoned all surviving Navigators, and Edrik would give them joyous news. With the sea-worms obviously thriving on Buzzell, there would be plenty of ultraspice for the taking. The unusual concentrated form might even be superior to the original spice: a frighteningly potent melange to keep Navigators alive without the meddling, greedy Administrator faction or the witches of Chapterhouse.

Freedom!

It had amused him to see Waff taking his worm samples to Rakis, hoping to establish a new spice cycle. Edrik didn't think the little researcher could do much there, but an alternative source of melange would be a bonus. But even without that, never again would the Navigators be strangled by power games. The four Guildsmen whom Edrik had sent to accompany Waff were spies and would secretly report everything the Tleilaxu achieved.

Inside his tank, Edrik smiled to himself, pleased that he had thought of all eventualities. With the first package of Buzzell ultraspice safely stored in his security chamber, the Navigator guided his Heighliner out into the emptiness of space. Even the Oracle would congratulate him for this remarkable news.

Before he could travel toward his scheduled rendezvous, however, the emptiness rippled around him. When Edrik studied the distortions, he realized what they were. Moments later, scores of Guildships appeared like buckshot in space, winking through foldspace and emerging forward and back, above and below, to surround his Heighliner completely.

Edrik transmitted on a band that only fellow Navigators should have received. "Explain your presence."

But none of the imposing newcomers answered. Studying the glyphs and cartouches on the sides of the enormous hulls, he realized that these were new Guildships, guided by Ixian mathematical compilers.

The computer-controlled vessels closed in. Sensing the threat, Edrik transmitted with greater alarm, "What is your justification?"

The other Guildships formed a smothering blanket around his Heighliner. The silence of the great vessels was more intimidating than any voiced ultimatum. Their proximity distorted his Holtzman fields, preventing him from folding space.

Finally a voice spoke, flat and dull in timbre, yet unnervingly confident. "We require your cargo of seaworm spice. We will board your ship for inspection."

Edrik assessed these enemies, his mind racing through a labyrinth of possibilities. The ships appeared to belong to the Administrator faction. They functioned with Ixian devices, so they had no need for Navigators or melange. Why then would they want to confiscate the ultraspice? To prevent Navigators from having it? To ensure the Guild's complete reliance on Ixian navigation machines?

Or could this be another foe entirely? Were these ships flown by CHOAM pirates hoping to seize a valuable new asset? Witches from Chapterhouse wanting to force continued dependence on the Sisterhood's melange?

But how would any outsiders know about the ultraspice?

While Edrik's Heighliner hung helpless in space, small interdiction ships emerged from the surrounding Guild vessels. He had no choice but to allow boarders onto his ship.

Though Edrik did not recognize him, a man wearing appropriate Guild insignia marched along the decks and ascended to the restricted level, brushing aside all security barriers. Six well-muscled men accompanied him. The leader smiled condescendingly when he stood before the Navigator's tank and looked into it. "Your new spice has fascinating possibilities. We require it from you."

Edrik boomed from within his chamber, intentionally amplifying the speaker system. "Go to Buzzell and obtain your own."

"This is not a request," said the man, his face bland. "We have learned the intensity of this substance and believe it to be a remedy for our difficult situation. We will take it to the heart of the thinking-machine empire."

Thinking machines? What did the Administrator faction have to do with the Enemy? "You may not have it," Edrik repeated, as if he had any say in the matter.

The bland-faced Guildsman gestured to his burly bodyguards, and they withdrew iron-tipped hammers from their slick gray robes. The leader gave them a calm, matter-of-fact nod.

Panicked, Edrik swam backward in his tank, but he had nowhere to go. The muscular bodyguards did not care that he was inside the container or that exposure to the air would kill him. With thick arms, they swung their heavy sledges and smashed the thick plaz walls.

Jagged cracks split out in starburst patterns, and concentrated orange spice gas whistled out through the breaches. The guards did not react to the melange streaming into their faces, though the concentration should have made a normal human reel. Their bland-faced leader watched like a man smelling an approaching storm while Edrik's atmosphere drained out.

When the air pressure was no longer sufficient to buoy him, the Navigator collapsed to the floor of his tank. Weakly, he raised his webbed hands and demanded answers in a voice that was little more than a gasp. The Guildsman and his companions offered no explanations.

Withering and twitching, Edrik lay on the floor. He extended a rubbery arm and tried to crawl, but with all the spice gas draining away, the air was too thin. He could no longer breathe, could hardly move. Even so, the Navigator was slow to die.

The bland-faced man stepped closer to the shattered wall, and his features metamorphosed. Khrone said to his Face Dancer companions, "Take the concentrated spice. With this substance, Omnius will awaken his Kwisatz Haderach."

The others departed to search the decks and soon uncovered the hoard of modified melange. When the disguised guards returned to the interdiction ships, Khrone held one of the heavy packages in his arms. He inhaled deeply. "Excellent. Remove all of our people from this Heighliner. When we are safe, destroy the ship and everyone aboard it."

He looked coolly down at the dying Edrik. Only a few rusty curls of gas continued to ooze from cracks in the tank. "You have served your purpose, Navigator. Take solace in that." The Face Dancer strutted away.

Edrik continued to heave great breaths, but barely a scent of melange remained. By the time the computer-controlled Guildships got into formation in space, he could barely keep from slumping into unconsciousness.

The opposing vessels opened fire. Edrik's Heighliner exploded before he could utter a curse.

There is an art to legend-telling, and an art to living the legend.
—a saying of Ancient Kaitain

The *Ithaca's* replenishing operations had taken place in the still-rich northern latitudes, far from any visible population centers. Garimi managed the complex process with dozens of flying craft from the hangar decks, leaving Duncan on the command bridge. He felt trapped there, unable to leave because of the protective veil that the no-ship usually afforded him. He hated having to remain behind while others did the risky work . . . and he didn't even know what the old man and woman wanted from him.

He had no idea what was going on back in the Old Empire, with Murbella and Chapterhouse. He knew only that the Enemy was still searching for him—and he was still hiding, as he had been for decades. Was this truly the best way to fight, the best way to defend humanity? He had been adrift for as long as the *Ithaca*, and of late, the waters of uncertainty seemed deeper than ever.

It had been two days now without word from Teg or Sheeana and their team. If their group was simply meeting with the natives, someone should have checked in by now. Duncan feared another trap like the one they had encountered on the planet of the Handlers.

Miles Teg had been his mentor and his student, and Sheeana . . . ah, Sheeana. They had been lovers and sexual opponents. She had cured him and saved him, so of course he cared for her. He had tried to protect himself by denying it, but she hadn't believed him, and he hadn't believed himself. Both knew they had a bond unlike any other, different from the one he and Murbella had imposed upon one another.

As he studied the landscape below, it seemed to call to him. Many cities were discernible in the northern and southern forested latitudes. He felt he should be down there facing any possible dangers with the others, not stuck aboard the *Ithaca*, forced to remain safe and out of sight.

How long am I supposed to wait?

When he was Swordmaster of House Atreides he would never have hesitated. If it had been young Paul Atreides under threat, Duncan would have leapt in to fight for him, ignoring the intangible threat of the old man and woman. As the witches said in their oft-quoted Litany, *I will face my fear.* And it was about time he did so.

He closed his eyes, not wanting to see the spreading desert that looked like a seeping knife wound across the continent. "I will not ignore this." Duncan summoned Thufir Hawat as well as Garimi, who had recently returned to the no-ship with all of her flying craft after reloading the *Ithaca's* stores.

Duncan stood when they arrived. "We are going to rescue the landing party," he announced, "and we're going to do it now. I don't know what kind of military force those people have down there, but we'll stand against it if the Bashar is in trouble."

Thufir's eyes brightened and his face flushed. "I'll pilot one of the ships."

Duncan remained stern. "No, you will follow my orders."

Garimi was taken aback by Duncan's bold comment, but nodded as she heard him rebuke Thufir. "Do you have instructions for us before we depart? Shall I command the mission?"

"No—I will do it personally." Before either could argue with him, Duncan strode toward the lift, and they were forced to follow him. "I'm sick of hiding. My plan has been to run and remain unobtrusive, staying one step ahead of that strange net. But in doing so, I've left too much of myself behind. I am *Duncan Idaho*." He raised his voice as they entered the lift. "I was Swordmaster of House Atreides and consort of St. Alia of the Knife. I acted as advisor and companion to the God Emperor. If the Enemy is out there, I won't leave the rest of humanity to face it themselves. If Sheeana and the Bashar need my help, then I'm going to help."

Thufir stiffened, then allowed himself a pleased smile. "You should have left the *Ithaca* long ago, Duncan. I don't see what you've accomplished by staying here. The no-field hasn't exactly offered perfect protection."

Garimi seemed pleased by Duncan's attitude. "My recovery teams took a good look at that planet down there, and it seems a fine place to settle. Does that mean you'll stop opposing my efforts and let us form a colony at last?"

The lift doors closed, and the group began to drop toward the hangar decks where the many ships were being refueled. "That remains to be seen."

TEG BIDED HIS time in the camp long after Stilgar and Liet flew off into the early morning. By now, Duncan would certainly have drawn the obvious conclusions.

"Do you think they'll kill us, after all?" Sheeana's tone was surprisingly matter-of-fact, as if she had accepted the inevitable.

"Maybe just you. You're the one they blame." He spoke without humor. Though they were allowed to sit on the ground outside, their captors still watched them closely.

She sipped from a small cup of water that had been provided. "Is that a joke?"

"A distraction." Teg glanced up at the sky. "We have to trust Duncan to decide on the correct response."

"Maybe he thinks we can handle this ourselves. Duncan has great confidence in our independent abilities."

"As do I. Should it become necessary, I could slaughter every one of these people." He chose the word intentionally. *Slaughter.* As he had done with the Honored Matres in their fortress on Gammu. "And it would take me no longer than the blink of an eye. You know it."

Sheeana had seen him move against the Handlers, helping her, Thufir, and the Rabbi escape, and she had also seen how much that brief burst of energy had drained him. "Yes, I know, Miles. And I pray it doesn't become necessary."

Off in the distance they heard the whining drone of the small flyer returning from the desert. Teg's sharply attuned ears recognized its sputtering engine sound. The villagers gathered at the packed landing zone, anxious to receive the hunting party. First, two specks appeared in the sky, flying low; then they were joined by many more dots, like a dispersed flock of migrating birds. The drone grew to a roar.

Teg shaded his eyes, identifying many of the flying craft. "Mining shuttles and lighters from the no-ship. So this is how Duncan plans to rescue us. He's trying to impress them. It appears he sent everything we have."

"We certainly have superior firepower. Duncan could have taken the direct method and rescued us by force of arms."

Watching the ships come closer, Teg smiled. "He's smarter than that. Like me, he wants to avoid bloodshed, especially in a conflict he doesn't entirely understand." *Did I teach him that lesson, or did he teach me?* As the Bashar reflected on their past lives, he didn't know the answer.

More than forty craft landed together in a flat, open space at the outskirts of the village. They weren't war vessels or armored attack ships, though some had defensive weapons. The Bashar stepped with Sheeana away from the tents, to face the largest mining shuttle. No one tried to stop them; the people were too awed by what they saw.

It surprised Teg to see Duncan Idaho himself march down the ramp of the lead craft, wearing his traditional House Atreides uniform, complete with polished boots and the starburst insignia of his rank. If the Qelsans had been gone from the Old Empire for fifteen centuries, they weren't likely to recognize any of the symbols, but Teg thought the uniform gave his friend a distinguished aura of command, and undoubtedly provided self-assurance.

Duncan swept his gaze across the confused villagers, finally spotting

Teg and Sheeana. The relief on his face was obvious as he made his way to them. "You're still alive. And unhurt?"

"Stuka isn't," Sheeana said with an edge of bitterness.

"You shouldn't have left the no-ship," Teg said. "You're vulnerable now, visible to the searchers and their wide net."

"Let them find me." Duncan appeared stony, as if he had reached an inescapable conclusion. "This endless chase and hiding accomplishes nothing. I can't defeat the Enemy unless I confront them."

Sheeana glanced nervously at the sky, as if expecting the old man and woman to appear suddenly. "Garimi could have led the attack, or even Thufir. Instead, you let yourself be swayed by your emotions."

"I factored them in when I made my correct decision." Duncan's face flushed, as if he were hiding the real answer, and he rushed ahead with an explanation. "By comline, I spoke with Stilgar and Liet-Kynes aboard the flyer. We intercepted them out in the desert, so I have some inkling of what's going on here. I know how they killed Stuka—and why."

"And you're surprised to see me alive?" Sheeana asked. "Grateful, too, I hope."

Teg interrupted. "The death of Stuka was a tragic overreaction. These people made assumptions about us."

Nodding, Duncan said, "Yes, Miles. And if I had made an overzealous response with superior firepower, that would have caused many more deaths and a much greater tragedy. In one of my earlier lives I might have done exactly that, but I only needed to think about what you would have done."

Stilgar and Liet emerged with the commandos from the tanker. The two young gholas displayed a hardness to them now, and new life behind their eyes. The Fremen naib and the planetologist had found something on Qelso that reenergized them and transported them to other times.

Teg understood what all the gholas had gone through since recovering their memories. They had been sheltered and comfortable aboard the *Ithaca*, forced to content themselves with reading about their pasts and watching the sandworms in the cargo hold, as if they were specimens in a zoo. But these gholas could remember the real Arrakis. The lives of Stilgar and Kynes had not been safer or more comfortable in the tumultuous old days, but there had been a certain sharp definition to who they were.

Others continued to emerge from the landed vessels: Thufir, Garimi and more than a dozen Sisters, muscular male Bene Gesserit workers, second-generation children born aboard the no-ship setting foot on a real planet for the very first time in their lives. Five of the Rabbi's followers stood in bright sunlight, looking around in wonder at the landscape, at the open spaces. Presently the old man himself emerged, blinking his bespectacled, owlish eyes.

Var looked admiringly at the mining shuttles and lighters, at his new companions Stilgar and Liet. He raised his chin. Apparently, Duncan had also spoken with the village leader at length during their flight back from the desert. "Duncan Idaho, you know what trials we face here, what we've been driven to do. We are the only ones who'll stand against the death of this planet. We did not bring the desert here. You have no right to condemn us."

"I didn't condemn you for your struggle, but I can't condone what you did to our companion. Years ago, Bene Gesserit visitors to your world acted without considering the consequences of what they were doing to you. And now it appears you have done the same thing."

The old leader shook his head. His eyes burned with anger and righteousness. "We killed the witches responsible for depositing sandtrout here. Finding another witch, we killed her too."

Duncan abruptly cut off what was sure to be a pointless argument. "We will take our friends and leave you. I'll let you have your fruitless fight against a desert you can't defeat."

Teg and Sheeana stepped forward, anxious to leave this place. Liet and Stilgar, though, held back and looked at each other. The latter squared his shoulders and said, "Duncan, Bashar . . . Liet and I are having second thoughts. This is the desert—not *our* desert, but closer than anything we have yet encountered as gholas. We were brought back to life for a purpose. The skills from our past lives can be vital resources in a place like this."

Liet-Kynes picked up the speech as if he and Stilgar had rehearsed what they were going to say. "Look around. Can you imagine a world where our talents are more desperately needed? We are trained as fighters against impossible odds. We're used to desert combat. As a planetologist, I know the best ways to control the spread of the dunes, and I understand more about the sandworm cycle than most people."

Stilgar added, his passion rising, "We can show these fighters how to build sietches in the harshest desert. We can teach them to make real stillsuits. One day, perhaps, we shall even ride the great worms again." His voice cracked. "No one can stop the desert, but we can keep the people alive. The rest of you go back to the no-ship, but the Qelsans need us here."

Sheeana stopped at the hatch of the nearest ship, clearly displeased. "That is not possible. We need you, and all of the gholas, aboard the Ithaca. Each one of you was created, raised, and trained to assist us against the Enemy."

"But no one knows how, Sheeana," Duncan pointed out, moved by what the two young men had said. "None of you can say for certain why we need Stilgar and Liet. And what exactly is our fight?"

"We are not your tools or game pieces." Stilgar crossed his arms over his chest. "We are human beings with free will, regardless of how we might have been created. I never asked to serve the Bene Gesserit witches."

Liet stood by his friend. "This is what we want to do, and who's to say it isn't our destiny? We could save a planet, or at least its population. Isn't that an important enough goal?"

Teg understood the dilemma all too well. These two had found a connection they could hold onto, a battle they could fight that did indeed require their specific abilities. He himself had been created as a pawn, and he'd been forced to play that role. "Let them go, Sheeana. You have enough experimental subjects on the ship."

Thufir Hawat came up to the Bashar, relieved to see his mentor safe. He shot a disturbed glance toward Sheeana. "Is that all we are to them, Bashar? Experimental subjects?"

"In a certain sense. And now we must go back to our cage." He was anxious to leave this dying planet before other problems arose.

"Not so fast," the old Rabbi said, stepping forward. "My people are not, and never have been, part of your reckless flight across space.

We've always wanted a world to settle. Compared to metal decks and small chambers, this planet looks good enough."

"Qelso is dying," Sheeana said. The Rabbi and his hardworking companions simply shrugged.

Var scowled, as did some of the nomadic villagers nearest him. "We do not need any further drain on our resources. You are welcome here only if you intend to fight back against the desert."

Isaac, one of the strong Jewish men, nodded. "If we decide to stay here, we will fight and work. Our people are no strangers to surviving when the rest of the universe is pitted against us."

No matter where I go, no matter what I leave behind, my past is always with me, like a shadow.

—DUNCAN IDAHO,

no-ship logs

Liet-Kynes and Stilgar returned briefly to the *Ithaca* to retrieve informational archives and some of the equipment they would need to monitor Qelso's changing climate. Liet even converted several spare sensor buoys into orbital weathersats, which the no-ship deployed.

He said his goodbyes to the other ghola children who had been raised with him—Paul Atreides, Jessica, Leto II. And Chani, his own daughter. With a surge of emotion, Liet grasped the hand of the young woman, who was physically almost three years older than he. He smiled at her. "Chani, someday you will remember me as I was on Arrakis—busy in the sietches, working as the Imperial Planetologist or the Judge of the Change, carrying on my father's dream for the Fremen and for Dune."

Her expression was intense, as if she struggled to grasp some faint flicker of memory as she listened to him. Releasing her hand, he touched her forehead, her dark red hair. "Maybe I was a strong leader, but I'm afraid I wasn't much of a father. So I must tell you, before I go, that I love you. Then *and* now. When you remember me, remember all we shared."

"I will. If I remembered everything now, I'd probably want to go with you back to the desert. And so would Usul."

Beside them, Paul shook his head. "My place is here. Our fight is bigger than one desert."

Stilgar took his friend's arm, urging Liet to hurry. "This planet is large enough for us. I feel in my soul that this is why Liet and I have been brought back, whether or not Sheeana realizes it. Perhaps someday, no matter how it appears now, we will all see that this is part of the greater battle."

Meanwhile, the Rabbi spoke to his fifty-two enthusiastic followers at their stations on the no-ship. Isaac and Levi had taken over many of the old man's duties, and at his signal they directed the Jews to gather their possessions and bring prefabricated shelters from the *Ithaca*'s vast storage chambers. Soon, all of them had shuttled down to the surface, where they disembarked and began unloading the landed cargo ships under Isaac's direction.

On the ground Var strode through the activity, marshalling his followers. He ran a covetous eye over several of the craft that Duncan had brought down during his show of force. "Those mining shuttles would be a great help to us for carrying supplies and water across the continent."

Sheeana shook her head. "Those ships belong to the *Ithaca*. We may need them."

Var glowered at her. "Small enough compensation for causing the death of an entire world, I'd say."

"*I* didn't contribute to the death of your world. You, however, killed Stuka in cold blood, before—"

Quickly, Teg went into Mentat mode, mentally inventorying the supplies and equipment they carried aboard the no-ship. To Sheeana, he murmured, "Although we had no part in the damage done to this world, we did resupply our ship here, and many of our people are staying behind as settlers. A token payment is not unreasonable." When she nodded, Teg turned to Var. "We can spare two shuttles. No more."

"And two desert experts," Liet piped up. "Stilgar and me."

"Not to mention a willing and hardy workforce. You'll be glad to have the Jews here." Teg had noticed how industrious the Rabbi's people were. He expected they would do well on this planet, even as the climate turned harsher. Someday, however, they might decide that Qelso wasn't their promised land after all.

NOT SURPRISINGLY, GARIMI and her conservative followers also wanted to leave the no-ship permanently. More than a hundred of the Sisters asked to be released from the *Ithaca* to settle on Qelso, even with its ever-growing desert. There, they planned to establish the foundation for their new order. Back on the no-ship, Garimi announced their choice to Sheeana more as a courtesy than a matter for discussion.

But the people of Qelso would hear none of that. They met the Sisters' landed shuttle with drawn weapons. Var stood with his arms crossed over his chest. "We accept Liet-Kynes and Stilgar among us, as well as the Jews. But no Bene Gesserit witch is welcome here."

"No witches!" other Qelsans cried, their expressions suddenly murderous. "If we find them, we kill them."

Having accompanied them for a farewell, Sheeana tried to speak on Garimi's behalf. "We could take them to the other side of the continent. You would never know about their settlement. I promise, they'll cause you no trouble."

But the incensed Qelsans were not inclined to listen, and Var spoke again. "Your kind act only for the benefit of the Sisterhood. We welcomed them once, to our deep and lasting regret. Now Qelsans act for the benefit of Qelso. No member of your Sisterhood is welcome here. Short of violence, I cannot be more clear than that."

Sending up a puff of dust with every step, the Rabbi trudged past tents and portable buildings toward the shuttle. He wiped sweat from his brow and came to stand before Teg and Sheeana, looking uneasily from one to the other. "I think my people will be happy here, by the grace of God." He kicked at the dry dirt with his shoe. "We were meant to have ground under our feet."

"You look disturbed, Rabbi," Sheeana noted.

"Not disturbed. Sad." To Teg he appeared crestfallen, and his watery old eyes seemed redder than usual, as if from crying. "I will not be with them. I cannot leave the no-ship."

Black-bearded Isaac draped a consoling arm around the elderly man's shoulders. "This will be the new Israel for us, Rabbi, under my leadership. Won't you reconsider?"

"Why aren't you staying with your people?" Teg asked.

The Rabbi lowered his gaze, and tears dropped on the hardscrabble ground. "I have a higher obligation to one of my followers whom I failed."

Isaac explained to Sheeana and Teg in a soft voice, "He wishes to remain with Rebecca. Though she is an axlotl tank now, he refuses to leave her."

"I shall watch over her for all my remaining days. My followers will be in good hands here. Isaac and Levi are their future, while I am their past."

The rest of the Jews surrounded the Rabbi, saying their goodbyes and wishing him well. Then the weeping old man joined Teg, Sheeana, and the others on the waiting shuttle, which took them back up to the no-ship.

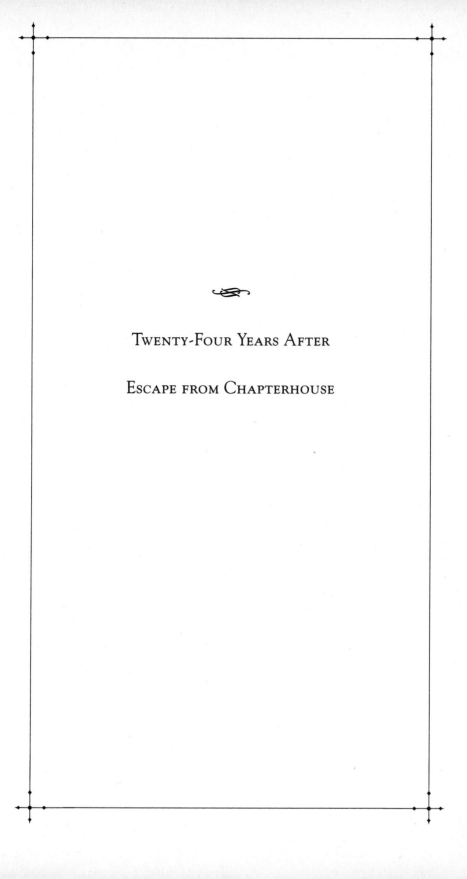

Twenty-Four Years After

Escape from Chapterhouse

We are wounded, but undefeated. We are hurt, but can endure great pain. We are driven to the end of our civilization and our history—but we remain human.

—MOTHER COMMANDER MURBELLA,
address to the survivors of Chapterhouse

As the epidemic burned itself out, the survivors—all of them Reverend Mothers—struggled to hold the Sisterhood together. No vaccines, immunity treatments, diets, or quarantines had any effect as the general populace died.

It required only three days for Murbella's heart to turn to stone. Around her, she watched thousands of promising young acolytes perish, diligent students who had not yet learned enough to become Reverend Mothers. Every one of them died either from the plague or from the Agony that was rushed upon them.

Kiria slipped into her former Honored Matre viciousness. On many occasions she argued vehemently that it was a waste of time to care for anyone who had contracted the plague. "Our resources are better spent on more important things, on activities that have some chance of success!"

Murbella could not dispute her logic, though she did not agree with the opinion. "We're not thinking machines. We are humans, and we will care for humans."

It was a sad irony that as more and more of the population died, fewer Reverend Mothers were needed to tend the remaining sick. Gradually, those women were able to turn to other crucial activities.

From a nearly empty chamber in the Keep, Murbella peered through the broad, arched window segments behind her throne chair. Chapterhouse had once been a bustling administrative complex, the pulsing heart of the New Sisterhood. Before the plague struck, Mother Commander Murbella had been in charge of hundreds of defensive measures, monitoring the constant progress of the Enemy fleet, dealing with the Ixians, the Guild, refugees and warlords, anyone who could fight on her side.

Far away, she could see the brown hills and dying orchards, but what concerned her was the eerie, unnatural silence of the city itself. The dormitories and support buildings, the nearby spaceport field, the markets, gardens, and dwindling herds . . . all should have been tended by a population of hundreds of thousands. Sadly, most normal activity around the Keep and the city had halted. Far too few remained alive to cover even the most basic work. The world itself was virtually vacant, with all hope dashed in a matter of days. So shockingly sudden!

The air in the surrounding city was heavy with the stench of death and burning. Black smoke rose from dozens of bonfires—not funeral pyres, for Murbella had other ways to dispose of the bodies, but simply the incineration of contaminated garments and other materials, including infected medical supplies.

In an admittedly petty moment, Murbella had summoned two exhausted Reverend Mothers. Telling them to bring suspensor clamps, she had ordered them to remove the deactivated combat robot from her private chambers. Though the hated machine had not moved in years, she had begun to feel that it was mocking her. "Take this thing away and destroy it. I abhor everything it symbolizes." The obedient women seemed relieved to follow her orders.

The Mother Commander issued her next instructions. "Release our melange stockpiles and distribute spice to all survivors." Every healthy woman was dedicated to tending the remaining sick, though it was a hopeless task. The surviving Reverend Mothers were utterly exhausted, having worked without rest for days. Even with the bodily control taught by the Sisterhood, they were hard-pressed to continue. But melange could help keep them going.

Long ago in the time of the Butlerian Jihad the palliative properties of melange had been an effective measure against the horrific machine plagues. This time she didn't expect spice to cure anyone who had already contracted the disease, but at least it would help the surviving Reverend Mothers perform the daunting work required of them. Though Murbella desperately needed every gram of spice to pay the Guild and the Ixians, her Sisters needed it more. If the unified Sisterhood died on Chapterhouse, who would lead the fight for humanity?

One more cost among so many. But if we don't spend it now, we will never buy victory. "Do it. Distribute whatever is necessary."

As her orders were being carried out, she made calculations and realized to her dismay that there weren't enough Reverend Mothers left alive to deplete the Sisterhood's hoarded spice anyway. . . .

Her entire support staff had been stripped away, and she felt isolated. Murbella had already imposed austerity measures, severely cut back services, and eliminated every extraneous activity. Even though most of the Reverend Mothers had survived the plague, it was not certain they would survive the aftermath.

She summoned those who were Mentats and ordered them to assess the vital work and create an emergency plan of operations, using personnel who were best qualified for the essential tasks. Where could they possibly get the workforce necessary to maintain Chapterhouse, rebuild, and continue the fight? Maybe they could convince some of the desperate refugees from devastated planets to come here, once the last vestiges of plague died out.

Murbella grew tired of simply recovering. Chapterhouse was only a tiny battlefield on the vast galactic canvas of the climactic war. The greatest threat still remained out there, as the oncoming Enemy fleet struck planet after planet, driving refugees like frantic animals before a forest fire. The battle at the end of the universe.

Kralizec . . .

A Reverend Mother came running up to her with a report. The woman, barely more than a girl, was one of those who had been forced to attempt the Agony long before she should have, but she had survived. Her eyes bore a faint bluish tinge now, a color that would grow deeper as she continued to consume melange. Her gaze had a stunned, haunted look that penetrated to the depths of her soul.

"Your hourly report, Mother Commander." She handed Murbella a stack of Ridulian crystal sheets on which names were printed in columns.

In a cold and businesslike fashion, her advisors had at first provided her with simple numbers and summaries, but Murbella demanded actual names. Each person who died from the plague was a *person,* and each worker and acolyte on Chapterhouse was a soldier lost in the cause against the Enemy. She would not dishonor them by boiling them down to mere numbers and totals. Duncan Idaho would never have condoned such a thing.

"Four more of them were Face Dancers," the messenger said.

Murbella clenched her jaws. "Who?" When the woman spoke the names, Murbella barely knew them, unobtrusive Sisters who called no attention to themselves . . . exactly as Face Dancer spies would do. So far sixteen of the shape-shifters had turned up among the plague victims. She had always suspected that even the New Sisterhood had been infiltrated, and now she had proof. But, in an irony the thinking machines could not possibly grasp, the Face Dancers were also susceptible to the horrible epidemic. They died just as easily as anyone else.

"Keep their bodies for dissection and analysis, along with the others. If nothing else, maybe we can learn something that will allow us to detect them among us."

The young woman waited while Murbella scanned the long list of names. She felt a cold whisper run down her spine as an entry in the third column of one sheet caught her eye. She felt as if she had been struck a heavy blow.

Gianne.

Her own daughter, her youngest child by Duncan Idaho. For years the girl had delayed passing through the Agony, never reaching the point where she was ready for the ordeal. Gianne had shown great promise, but that was not nearly enough. Though she had not demonstrated herself to be ready, the girl—among thousands of others—had been forced to take the poison early, the only chance of surviving.

Murbella reeled in shock. She should have been at Gianne's side, but in the chaos no one had told the Mother Commander when her daughter would be given the Water of Life. Most Sisters did not even realize that Gianne was her daughter. The frantic, exhausted helpers would not have known. With her priorities set in true Bene Gesserit fashion, Murbella had tended to her official duties and had gone without sleep for several days in succession.

I should have been there to support her and help, even if I could only watch over her as she died.

Yet no one had informed her. No one had known that Gianne was special.

I should have thought to check on her, but I put it off, made assumptions.

With so many events crashing around her, Murbella had misplaced her own daughter's life. First Rinya, and now Gianne, both lost to the perilous Agony. Only two other daughters remained: Janess was off at the battlefront fighting thinking machines, while her sister Tanidia, not knowing the identity of her parents, had been sent to join the Missionaria. Though both of them faced risks, they might at least avoid contracting the horrific plague.

"Two of my children dead," she said aloud, though the messenger did not understand. "Oh, what would Duncan think of me?" Murbella set the report aside. She closed her eyes for a moment, drew a deep breath, and straightened herself. Pointing to the name on the list of victims she said, "Take me to her."

The messenger glanced down, ran a quick assessment. "The bodies in that column have been hauled off to the spaceport. 'Thopter loads of them are taking off right now."

"Hurry. I must try to see her." Murbella rushed out of the hall, glancing back to be certain the young woman was right behind her. Though the Mother Commander felt disturbingly numb, she had to do this.

They took a groundcar to the nearby spaceport, where the fluttering hum of 'thopters droned. On the way, the young Reverend Mother activated her commline, and in a quiet voice requested information.

She then directed the driver of the car to take a particular access road.

On all of the spaceport landing pads, large cargo 'thopters were being loaded with the dead, and were lifting off as soon as they were full. In normal, better times when Bene Gesserits died, they would be buried in the thriving orchards or gardens. The bodies would decompose and provide nourishment and fertilizer. Now they piled up so fast that even large cargo ships could barely keep up with removing them.

The young assistant directed the driver to a specific grid in the landing zone, where a dark green 'thopter was being loaded by workers. Bundle after bundle of bodies went into the large hold. "She has to be in that one, Mother Commander. Would you . . . would you like them to unload so that you can find and identify her?"

As the two women stepped out of the groundcar, Murbella felt stunned, but tried to steel herself. "Not necessary. It is only her body, not *her.* Just the same, I'll allow myself enough sentimentality to accompany her out to the dunes." Leaving the young Reverend Mother to tend to other duties, Murbella climbed into the 'thopter and sat next to the female pilot.

"My daughter is aboard," Murbella said. Then she grew silent, and stared glumly out the window.

A vibrating shudder passed through the 'thopter as it took off with jets and flapping wings. It would take them half an hour or so to get out to the desert zone, an hour the Mother Commander could ill afford to be away from the Keep. But it was time she desperately needed. . . .

Even the best of the Sisterhood who had undergone the most arduous testing were dismayed by the very real and material tragedy—but not to the point of total surrender. Bene Gesserit teachings showed them how to control base emotions, how to act for the greater good and see the overall picture. Upon watching almost 90 percent of a planet's population fall within a few days, however, the magnitude of the disaster—the *extermination*—was breaking down even the strongest barriers in many Sisters. It was up to Murbella to maintain the morale of the survivors.

The thinking machines have found a cruel and effective way to destroy our human weapons, but we are not so easily disarmed!

"Mother Commander, we have arrived," the pilot said, her clipped words loud enough to be heard over the thrum of the wings.

Murbella opened her eyes to see clean desert, tan eddies of sand and dust curling from stray breezes. It seemed pristine and untouched, no matter how much human debris the Sisterhood dumped there. She saw other 'thopters circling in the sky, descending over the dunes and opening cargo doors to expel loads . . . hundreds of black-wrapped bodies in each aircraft. The dead Sisters tumbled out onto the sand like charred cordwood.

Natural elements would dispose of them far more efficiently than huge funeral pyres could. The aridity would desiccate them, and scouring sandstorms would wear them down to bones. In many cases, the worms would simply devour them. A sort of purity.

Their 'thopter hovered over a small basin. Large swells of dunes swept up on either side, while dust kicked up by the 'thopter wings swirled around them. The pilot worked her controls, and the bottom doors opened with a weary groan. Bodies tumbled out, wrapped in fabric. They were stiff, their features covered, but to Murbella they were still individuals. One of those unidentified shapes was her own little girl . . . born just before Murbella underwent the Agony herself, just before she lost Duncan forever.

She didn't delude herself into thinking that if she had been at her daughter's side she might have helped Gianne survive. Passing through the Spice Agony was solely an individual's battle, but Murbella wished she could have been there.

The bodies spilled unceremoniously onto soft sand. Below, she could see serpentine shapes stirring—two big worms drawn by 'thopter vibrations or the thumps of falling bodies. The creatures scooped up and devoured the human shapes, then plunged back beneath the sand.

The pilot lifted the 'thopter high enough to swing around, so that Murbella could look down and observe the horrible feeding frenzy. Touching the commline in her ear, the pilot received a message, then offered a faint smile to Murbella. "Mother Commander, there is some good news, at least."

After seeing the last unmarked body vanish below, Murbella wasn't in the mood for any sort of cheering up, but she waited.

"One of our deep-desert research settlements has survived. Shakkad Station. They were far enough out in the sand and had no contact with the Keep. Somehow they avoided the touch of the virus."

Murbella remembered the tiny group of offworld scientists and helpers. "I isolated them myself so they could work. I want them to stay completely cut off—no contact whatsoever! If a single one of us goes near, we could contaminate them."

"Shakkad Station doesn't have enough supplies to last long," the pilot said. "Perhaps we could arrange a package drop-off."

"No, nothing! We can't take the chance of contamination." She thought of those people as living at the center of a deadly minefield. But once the epidemic passed, perhaps these few could survive. Only a handful. "If they run out of food, they should increase their consumption of melange. They can find enough to survive for at least a little while. Even if some of them starve, it's better than having every single one succumb to this damned epidemic."

The pilot did not disagree. As she stared out into the desert, Murbella realized what she and her Sisters had become. She muttered aloud, her words drowned by the thrum of engines. "We are the new Fremen, and this whole besieged galaxy is our desert."

The 'thopter soared away, heading back toward the Keep, leaving the worms to their feast.

Hatred breeds in the fertile ground of life itself.

—ancient saying

The no-ship had flown away from the turmoil of the planet Qelso, leaving behind some of their people, some of their hopes and possibilities. On that world Duncan had taken a great risk, daring to leave the no-ship for the first time in decades. Had he revealed his presence? Would the Enemy be able to find him now, seizing upon that clue? It was possible.

Though he had decided not to cower and hide, Duncan did not intend to bring possible destruction to all the innocent people on this planet. He would make another jump, cover his tracks. And so the *Ithaca* had risked another unguided plunge through folded space.

That was three months ago.

Through a thick plaz viewport, Scytale had watched Qelso dwindle, then suddenly vanish into blankness. He had never been allowed to set foot off the ship. Judging by what he had seen, he would have been happy to settle on that world, in spite of its spreading desert.

Although he had his memories back, Scytale found that a part of him missed his father, his predecessor, himself. His mind now contained everything he needed. But he wanted more.

With this new body, the Tleilaxu Master should have another century before cumulative genetic errors caused him to break down again. Enough time to solve many problems. But when another hundred years were gone, he would still be the last Tleilaxu Master, the only remaining keeper of the Great Belief. Unless he could use the cells of the Council of Masters stored in his nullentropy capsule. Someday, maybe the witches would allow him to employ the axlotl tanks for the purpose the Tleilaxu had intended them.

Back at Qelso, he had agonized over whether to remain there and create a new homeland for the Tleilaxu. Could he build the proper laboratories and equipment? Recruit followers from among the people there? Should he have taken that gamble? Young Scytale had studied the scriptures, meditated long and hard, and finally decided against staying behind—the same decision the Rabbi had reached. On Qelso, he wasn't likely ever to have access to the axlotl technology he needed. His decision was perfectly logical.

The Rabbi's recent misery and anger, however, was not so easily explained. No one had forced him into his choice. Ever since the ship left the planet and its spreading deserts, the old man had been marching up and down the corridors, spreading dissent like poison. He was the only one of his kind left aboard. Just like Scytale.

The aged holy man ate with the other refugees, grumbling about how harshly he was treated and how difficult it must be for his people to establish a new Zion without his guidance. Garimi and her hardliners, having been forcibly turned away from the planet, had expressed no sympathy for his grievances.

Watching it all, Scytale concluded that the Rabbi was the sort of person who placed external blame in order to position himself as a martyr. Since he would not leave the axlotl tank that had once been Rebecca, he could cling to his hatred of the Bene Gesserit order, faulting them instead of his own bad choices.

Well, Scytale thought, there was certainly enough hatred to go around.

IN HIS PRIVATE quarters, Wellington Yueh studied his mirror reflection—the sallow face, dark lips, and pointed chin. The narrow visage was younger than the one his memories told him to expect, but still recognizable. Since regaining his memories, he had let his black hair grow out until he had enough at the back to bind in an improvised Suk School ring.

Yet he did not fully accept himself. There was one more critical step to take.

In his hand he held an indelible scriber filled with dark ink that would leave a permanent stain. Not exactly a tattoo, and without any implant or attendant deep Imperial Conditioning, but close enough. His hands were steady, his strokes confident.

I am a Suk doctor, a surgeon. I can draw a simple geometric shape.

A diamond, prominent on his forehead, perfectly centered. Without hesitation, he drew another stroke, connected the lines, and filled in the skin of his brow. When he was finished, he examined himself again. Wellington Yueh looked back at him from the mirror, Suk doctor and personal physician to House Vernius and then House Atreides.

The Traitor.

He set the scriber aside, dressed in a clean doctor's smock, and headed for the medical center. Like the old Rabbi, he was as qualified as any Bene Gesserit doctor to monitor patients and tend the axlotl tanks.

Recently, Sheeana had begun growing another ghola as part of her program, using cells from the Tleilaxu Master's nullentropy tube. Now that Stilgar and Liet-Kynes were gone, she had felt justified in taking that step. Clinging to security, she refused to identify the child gestating in the axlotl tank.

The Bene Gesserits still claimed to need the gholas, though they could not clearly explain why. Their success in restoring the memories of previous lives in Yueh, Stilgar, and Liet-Kynes had not led to similar accomplishments with the other gholas yet. Some of the witches, especially Proctor Superior Garimi, continued to voice grave reservations about bringing back Jessica and Leto II, because of their past crimes. So they had tried to awaken Thufir Hawat next.

Yueh did not know what the witches had done in attempting to break down Hawat's walls, but it had backfired on them. Instead of awakening, Hawat had fallen into convulsions. The old Rabbi had been present and rushed to attend the seventeen-year-old ghola, pushing the Sisters away and scolding them for the foolish risks they had taken.

But Yueh, like Scytale, already had his old knowledge. He was no longer a child, no longer waiting to *become* something. One day, he mustered his courage and implored Sheeana to put him to work. "You witches forced me to remember my old life. I begged you not to, but you insisted on awakening me. Along with my memories and my guilt, came useful skills. Let me act as a Suk doctor again."

At first he wasn't sure the Bene Gesserits would agree, especially considering the constant threat from the unknown saboteur—but when Garimi automatically objected, Sheeana decided to support him. He was granted permission to make rounds in the medical center, so long as he remained under surveillance.

At the entrance to the main axlotl chamber, two security women scanned Yueh carefully, then waved him through. Neither of them remarked on the new diamond-shaped stain on his forehead. He wondered if anyone still remembered what that mark had once symbolized.

In preoccupied silence, Yueh went about his inspections of the healthy axlotl tanks. Several produced melange for the ship's stockpiles, but one was obviously pregnant. This unnamed ghola baby would gestate under much tighter security. Yueh was convinced that the child would not be another attempt at Gurney Halleck, Xavier Harkonnen, or Serena Butler. Nor would it be a duplicate of Liet-Kynes or Stilgar. No, Sheeana would experiment with someone else—someone she believed could dramatically help the *Ithaca*.

Knowing Sheeana's impetuous nature, Yueh feared who the baby might be. The Sisters were not immune to making poor choices (as they had proved by bringing *him* back!). He couldn't believe any of the women had imagined *he* might be a savior or a hero, yet he had been one of their first experiments. Judging from this, what if the witches were curious to study nefarious personalities from the dark pages of history? Emperor Shaddam? Count Fenring? Beast Rabban? Even the despised Baron Harkonnen himself? Yueh could imagine Sheeana's excuses already. She would no doubt insist that even the worst personalities had the potential to provide invaluable information.

What snakes will they set loose among us? he wondered.

In the main medical center away from the tanks, he found the old Rabbi grumbling as he assembled a portable medical kit. Since refusing to remain behind on Qelso with his people, he lingered for hours at a time over the tank that he called Rebecca. Though he despised what had been done to her, he seemed relieved that she hadn't been the one implanted with the new ghola.

Reluctant to have the Rabbi hover too long near the axlotl tanks, the Sisters gave him duties to keep him busy. "I am going to run Scytale through a battery of tests," the old man huffed to Yueh, starting to retreat from the medical center. "Sheeana wants him checked out— again."

"I can do that for you, Rabbi. My duties here are light."

"No. Sticking needles into the Tleilaxu is one of my few pleasures these days." His gaze fixed on Yueh's new diamond mark, but he did not comment on it. "Walk with me." The Rabbi took Yueh's arm in a tight grip and led him into the corridors, away from the hovering Bene Gesserits. When they were far enough away for him to feel safe, the old man leaned closer, speaking in a conspiratorial tone. "I am certain Scytale is the saboteur, though I have not found evidence yet. First the old one, and now his ghola replacement. They are all the same. With his memories restored, the young Scytale continues his insidious work to destroy our ship. Who can trust a Tleilaxu?"

Who can trust anyone? Yueh thought. "Why would he want to harm the ship?"

"We know he has some dirty scheme. Ask yourself why he would store Face Dancer cells in his nullentropy tube, along with all the others—yours included. Why would he need them? Isn't that suspicious enough for you?"

"Those cells were confiscated and secured by Sheeana. No one has had access to them."

"Can you be sure of that? Maybe he wants to kill us all so he can restore an army of Face Dancers for himself." The Rabbi shook his head. Behind the spectacles, his reddened eyes were angry. "And that isn't all. The witches have their own schemes. Why do you suppose they won't reveal the identity of the new ghola baby? Does even Duncan Idaho know who is growing in that *tank?*" He craned his neck, glanced over his shoulder back toward the medical center, watching out for surveillance imagers. "But you can find out."

Yueh was perplexed, and curious, but he didn't tell the Rabbi that he had been having some of the same doubts. "How? They won't tell me either."

"But they don't watch you like they watch me! The witches are afraid I'm going to do something to hinder their program, but now that you have your memories, you're their trusted little ghola." The Rabbi slipped him a small sealed polymer disk, with a dab of filmy substance in the center. "You have access to the scanners. These are cell samples from the pregnant tank in there. Nobody saw me obtain them, but I dare not run the analysis myself."

Yueh surreptitiously pocketed the disk. "Do I really want to know?"

"Can you afford not to? I leave it to you." The Rabbi slipped away, muttering. Carrying his portable medical kit, he trudged off to the Tleilaxu's cabin.

The sample weighed heavily in Yueh's pocket. Why would the Sisters keep the new ghola's identity secret? What were they up to?

It took several hours for him to find an opportunity to slip into one of the no-ship's small lab chambers. As a Suk doctor, he had permission to use the facilities. Even so, he worked as swiftly as possible, running the small sample from the axlotl tank through a DNA catalog. He compared the cells from the growing ghola with the identifications that had been run years ago, when the Sisters first assessed the material in Scytale's nullentropy capsule.

Yueh found a match fairly quickly, and when he learned the answer, he physically recoiled. "Impossible! They would not dare!" But in his heart, as he remembered the torment Sheeana had used to awaken his memories, he didn't doubt the witches would do anything. Now he understood why Sheeana refused to reveal the identity of the ghola.

Even so, the choice itself made no sense. The Sisters had numerous other options. Better ones. Why not try again to bring back Gurney Halleck? Or Ghanima, as a companion for poor Leto II? For what purpose could they possibly need—he shuddered—*Piter de Vries*?

Because Bene Gesserits liked to play with dangerous toys, resurrecting people to serve as chess pieces in their great game. He knew the sort of questions they would pursue, just to satisfy their infernal curiosity. Was the genetic makeup of Piter de Vries corrupt, or was he evil because he had been Twisted by the Tleilaxu? Who better to think like an Enemy than a Harkonnen? Was there any evidence to suggest that a new Piter de Vries would turn out evil, as before, if he were not exposed to the corruptive influence of the Baron?

He could picture Sheeana giving him a condescending frown. "We need another Mentat. You, of all people, Wellington Yueh, should not hold the past crimes of a ghola's old life against him."

He still did not believe it. He squeezed his eyes shut, and even the fake diamond tattoo on his forehead seemed to burn. He remembered being forced to watch Wanna endure her endless torture at the hands of the vile Mentat. And the man thrusting a knife deep into his back, grinding the blade. *Piter de Vries!*

He still felt the sharp steel ripping into his organs, a mortal wound, one of the very last memories of his first life. Piter's laugh reverberated, along with the screams of Wanna in the agony chamber . . . and Yueh unable to help her.

Piter de Vries?

Yueh reeled, barely able to absorb the information. He could not allow a monster like that to be reborn.

DAYS LATER, YUEH entered the medical center, and walked toward the single pregnant tank. This was just an innocent baby at the moment. Even if it was de Vries, this ghola child had committed none of the crimes of the original.

But he will! He is twisted, evil, malicious. The Sisters would raise him and insist on triggering his memories. Then he would be back!

Yet Yueh was trapped by his own previous logic. If the Piter ghola—in fact, *all* the gholas—were unable to escape the chains of fate, wouldn't it be the same for Yueh? Was Yueh therefore destined to betray them all? Would he be doomed to make another terrible mistake—or must he sacrifice everything to prevent one? He had thought about consulting Jessica, but he decided against it. This was his burden, his decision.

Using the Rabbi's sample, he had run the genetic scan privately and seen the result. He had to act alone. Though he was himself a Suk doctor, trained and conditioned to save lives, sometimes the death of one monster was required to save many innocents.

Piter de Vries!

Indirectly he had caused de Vries's death the first time around, by giving the poison-gas tooth to Duke Leto, who bit down on it in the Mentat's presence. Yueh had failed in so many ways, caused so much pain and disappointment. Even Wanna would have hated what he'd done to himself, and to the Atreides.

Now, though—a second life, a second chance. Wellington Yueh could make things right. Each of the resurrected ghola children supposedly had a great purpose. He was convinced that this was his.

The handmade black diamond staining his brow added to the burden as Yueh wrestled with his decision. In his restored memories, he saw with clarity when he had become an actual Suk doctor, when he passed through an entire Inner School regimen of Imperial Conditioning and took the formal oath. "'A Suk shall not take human life.'"

And yet, Yueh's oath had been subverted, thanks to the Harkonnens. Thanks to *Piter de Vries*. What irony that the breaking of his Suk pledge now allowed him to destroy the very man who had broken that conditioning! He had the freedom to kill.

Yueh already had the instrument of death in the pocket of his smock. His plans were in place, and he would take no chances. Since surveillance imagers still monitored the med center and its axlotl tanks, Yueh could not do this in secret, as the real saboteur had. Once he acted, everyone aboard the *Ithaca* would know who had killed the de Vries ghola. And he would face the consequences.

Perspiration formed on his brow as he crossed the room. With the sharp-eyed Bene Gesserit guard watching him, he could not delay, or the damned witches might detect his uneasiness, his nervous movements. Bringing out his device, Yueh turned a dial as if to recalibrate it, then inserted its probe into the pregnant tank, as he would do in taking a biological sample. Thus he easily administered a lethal dosage of fast-acting poison. So far, no one suspected a thing.

There. Done. Fittingly, de Vries had been an expert in cleverly concocted poisons. And no antidote was available for this toxin; Yueh had seen to that. In a matter of hours, the unborn de Vries would shrivel up and die. Along with the tank, unfortunately. But that could not be avoided. A necessary sacrifice.

Leaving the chamber, he smiled grimly and quickened his pace. By tomorrow, there would be no hiding. Thufir Hawat and Bashar Teg would review surveillance holos and interview the guards. They would know who had done it. Unlike the real saboteur, he could not delete the images. He would be caught.

Despite this knowledge, Yueh was content with himself for the first time since his reawakening. At last, he savored the elusive taste of redemption.

Send a fact-finding team to Buzzell to learn why soostone exports have dropped off so drastically. This lack of supply, coupled with the precipitous decline in melange production following the Chapterhouse plague, is highly suspicious, especially in light of the fact that the witches are involved in both enterprises. We have learned over the millennia not to take them at their word.

—CHOAM directive

Now that he possessed the sample of ultraspice, Khrone knew exactly what lived in the fertile seas of Buzzell. The Navigators certainly had an unexpected scheme there, releasing a new breed of melange-producing worms. He needed to go there and see for himself. The leader of the Face Dancer myriad cared little for the loss of soostone revenue, but in his guise as a CHOAM functionary, he had to feign extreme displeasure.

"Monsters?" Standing on the main dock, he gave the woman Corysta a withering glare. "Sea serpents? Can you think of no better excuses for your incompetence?"

Khrone scowled at the sea and gathered his dark business robes about his shoulders. Out there in the water, wary Phibians swam, diving to harvest the gems from beds of cholisters, many of which had already been devoured by the hungry and growing seaworms. Armored boats patrolled the coves, though they would surely prove insignificant if one of the large creatures should decide to attack.

Reverend Mother Corysta held herself erect, surprisingly unintimidated by the faux official. "It's no excuse, sir. No one knows where the worms came from or why they have appeared at this time. But they're real. Guild hunting ships dragged in a carcass, if you care to see it."

"Nonsense. Such a story obviously benefits the New Sisterhood." Ignoring her protestations, he motioned for Corysta to accompany him along a rocky shoreline path, his shoes crunching on the loose stones. Stepping in a puddle, he frowned down at his feet and kept walking. "CHOAM suspects that you're creating a false shortage in order to drive up prices. You have financial obligations. For years now, the Sisterhood has been commissioning extremely expensive ships, weapons, and military supplies. Your losses are tremendous."

"They're *humanity's* losses, sir." Corysta's voice was sharp.

"And now Chapterhouse itself, brought to its knees by a plague. It appears that the Sisterhood can no longer meet its financial obligations. Thus, CHOAM no longer considers you a good credit risk."

Corysta turned into the brisk sea wind. "These are matters you should take up with the Mother Commander."

"I *should*, but since she is on a quarantined planet, I can't very well call on her, can I? Your Sisterhood is falling apart as a result of external attack and internal strife."

Women stood on plastone ramps at the water's edge to receive a tired-looking group of Phibians who carried a net filled with small, misshapen soostones.

Khrone could tell at a glance the gems were of poor quality, but at least it was part of a shipment he could seize as overdue payment. "Are your Phibians afraid of sea monsters? Can they not go to richer beds of shellfish?"

"They harvest what they can, sir. There are no richer beds. The monsters have eaten many of the cholisters. Our underwater crops are ravaged. And, yes, the Phibians are understandably frightened. Many of them have been slaughtered." Corysta stared at him coldly, and Khrone appreciated the steel in her expression; he could respect it. "We have holo-footage of that, too, if you doubt me."

"It doesn't matter if I believe your story. I only want to know what the Sisterhood intends to do about it." Khrone knew the women could do nothing. Eventually the seaworms would bring down the soostone economy of Buzzell, thus removing another one of the Mother Commander's bargaining chips when she desperately needed to buy allegiances and secure equipment.

Kept in the dark, the exiled Sisters did not yet understand the true potential of those worms. The primary chemical attributes of the new melange stolen from Buzzell would be a thousand times more effective on human nerve receptors. Oh, it would work very nicely indeed!

He wondered if the Spacing Guild was even aware of Edrik's destroyed Heighliner yet. It was possible that they weren't. So many of their Navigators had vanished anyway, what was one more? If necessary, by planting a few hints here and there, Khrone could easily blame the loss on an attack by the thinking-machine battle fleet. If nothing else, Omnius made a fine scapegoat.

The Face Dancer myriad had set their hooks everywhere. The Ixians were building supposed weapons and draining the Chapterhouse coffers of spice; now the Sisterhood's soostone wealth was also disappearing. The Guild relied entirely on computerized navigation devices for their new ships, and the Navigators had no source of melange.

All enemies of the Face Dancers would fall. He would see to that. The Lost Tleilaxu and the original Masters had already been erased. The Ixians were in Khrone's pocket. Next would come the New Sisterhood, the Guild, and all of humanity. Finally, when he and his minions defeated the thinking machines, nothing would remain but the Face Dancers. And that would be enough.

Pleased with himself, Khrone marched up to the dock and yanked the net of soostones from the women trying to sort them. "Your production has dropped off drastically, and too many CHOAM merchants have gone away empty-handed."

Corysta hovered close behind him. "I hope to hire mercenary hunters to track down the seaworms. It is possible that we may find something of interest—maybe something more valuable than soostones."

So, this woman already had her suspicions about the ultraspice! "I doubt it," he said. Khrone took the net of rough soostones and marched back to the landing pad. Considering the vast game board, he decided it was finally time to head toward the heart of the thinking-machine empire. He would deliver the ultraspice to Omnius and let the ever-mind continue with his mad dream of creating and controlling his own Kwisatz Haderach.

It wouldn't help him in the end.

We believe that confession should lead to forgiveness and redemp-
tion. Usually, however, it leads only to further accusations.

—DR. WELLINGTON YUEH,

encrypted entry

The axlotl chamber smelled of fetid death. Duncan could not tear his gaze away from the still, cold flesh of the tank and the clear signs of necrosis. Rage and helplessness chewed at his gut. And who would the child have been? Sheeana hadn't even told him. Those damned Bene Gesserits and their secrets!

"Touch nothing," Teg warned. "Get me all security images right away. We will find the saboteur this time." One of the Sisters hurried to obtain the recordings.

Meanwhile, young Thufir cordoned off an area around the poison-ravaged tank and its unborn ghola. Mostly recovered from the memory-trigger attempt that had gone so dramatically awry, he now sternly followed the methods the Bashar had taught him. The corrosive poison had completely destroyed the growing fetus and then eaten through the wall of the womb that kept the thing alive. Somehow the tank had fallen to the floor, and yellow puddles oozed around the dead flesh.

Sheeana turned to one of her Sisters. "Bring Jessica here. Immediately."

Duncan gave her a sharp look. "Why Jessica? Is she a suspect?"

"No, but she will be hurt by this. Maybe I shouldn't even tell her. . . ."

Presently, Teg received a surveillance holotube from one of the Bene Gesserits. "I will scan every second. There must be some piece of evidence pointing to the traitor among us."

"There is no need. I killed the ghola." A young man's voice. All of them spun to look at a grim-faced Dr. Wellington Yueh. "I had to." Thufir moved swiftly to seize him by the arm, and Yueh did not resist. He stood firm, ready to face the questions that would be thrown at him. "You can punish me, but I couldn't allow you to spawn another Twisted Mentat. Piter de Vries would only have caused bloodshed and pain."

While Duncan immediately grasped the implications of Yueh's confession, Sheeana sounded perplexed. "Piter? What are you talking about?"

Yueh didn't struggle in Thufir's firm grip. "I witnessed his evil first-hand, and I couldn't allow you to bring him back. Ever."

Just then, a breathless young Jessica hurried in with the three-year-old Alia in tow. Alia had intent, eager eyes, full of maturity and understanding that she should not have had. She carried a chubby doll that looked remarkably like a juvenile version of the fat Baron Harkonnen. One of its arms had almost torn loose. Leto II followed his grandmother, looking curious and worried.

Sheeana still didn't understand. "What does Piter de Vries have to do with any of this?"

Yueh made a distasteful expression. "Don't try to divert me with lies. I know who that ghola was."

"That baby was not Piter de Vries." Sheeana spoke her words in a normal tone. "It would have been Duke Leto Atreides."

Yueh looked as if he had been felled with an axe. "There was no doubt—I ran a genetic comparison!"

Jessica listened from just inside the doorway, her face flickering with a rush of hope before plunging into sadness. "My Leto?"

Yueh tried to sink to his knees, but Thufir held him upright.

"No! It can't be!"

With adult-sharp awareness, Alia tried to take her mother's hand, but Jessica pulled away from the two children to loom over the Suk doctor. "You killed my Duke? *Again?*"

He grabbed his temples. "It can't be. I saw the results myself. It was Piter de Vries."

Thufir Hawat raised his chin. "At least we have found our saboteur."

"I would never have killed the Duke! I loved Leto—"

"And now you've murdered him twice," Jessica said, stabbing with each icicle-sharp word. "Leto, my Leto . . ."

Finally, Thufir's comment seemed to sink in. "But I didn't kill the other three gholas or harm their tanks! I committed no other sabotage."

Teg said, "How can we believe you? This will require a great deal more investigation. I will review all evidence in light of this new information."

Sheeana was clearly troubled, but her words surprised everyone. "My own truthsense leads me to believe him."

The flesh tank and unborn fetus lay on the floor, chemically decomposing. Black streaks covered all tissue and spread into the surrounding puddle. Yueh struggled to throw himself into the poisonous corrosive, as if by doing so he could kill himself.

With an iron grip, Thufir held him away from it. "Not quite yet, *Traitor.*"

"No good will come from any of this," the old Rabbi said, standing at the doorway of the medical center. No one had heard him arrive.

Desperate, Yueh looked at him. "I tested the samples you gave me—the baby was de Vries!"

The old man backed away like a startled bird. He looked indignant at the very suggestion he might have provoked the unstable young man. "Yes, I gave you a sample I obtained from the axlotl lab. But I merely raised a question—and never suggested that you should commit murder! Murder! I am a man of God, and you are a doctor—a Suk doctor! Who would imagine . . . ?" He shook his head. His gray beard looked especially wild today. "That tank you killed might have been Rebecca! I could never suggest such a thing."

Everyone in the room exchanged glances, silently agreeing that Yueh must be the saboteur after all.

"It wasn't me," he said. "Not the other times. Why would I confess to this but deny the others? My crime is the same."

"Not the same at all," Jessica said in a knotted voice. "This was my Duke. . . ." She turned and left, while Yueh stared beseechingly after her.

Each human, no matter how altruistic or peaceful he seems, car-ries the capacity to commit tremendous violence. I find this quality particularly fascinating, especially because it can lie dormant for extended periods and then flare up. For instance, consider their traditionally docile women. When these life-givers decide instead to take lives, it is a beautiful ferocity to behold.

— ERASMUS,
Laboratory Notes

On Chapterhouse, the meeting of Reverend Mothers degener-ated quickly to murderous intent.

Eyes flashing, Kiria nudged the chairdog away from her as she stood. "Mother Commander, you have to accept certain facts. Chapterhouse is more than decimated. The Ixians still haven't produced the Oblitera-tors they promised. We simply can't win this fight. As soon as we admit that, we can begin to make realistic plans."

Eyes bleary, Murbella gave the former Honored Matre a level look. "Such as?" The Mother Commander dealt with so many ongoing crises, obligations, and unsolvable problems that she could barely con-centrate on the reports coming to the mostly empty Keep. The plague had passed on Chapterhouse, so everyone who was going to die was already dead. With the exception of the isolated inhabitants of the deep desert Shakkad Station, the only survivors on the planet were Reverend Mothers.

All the while, the thinking machines continued to move through space, penetrating deeper into the Old Empire—though by sending scout probes and their plagues here to Chapterhouse, they had broken their previously predictable progression. Omnius must understand the significance of the New Sisterhood; a key victory here could stop the rest of humanity's scattered fighting.

"Let's take what we need," Kiria said, "copy our Archives, and vanish into the great unknown to create seed colonies. The thinking machines are relentless, but we can be swift and unpredictable. For humanity's survival and the preservation of the Sisterhood, we must disperse, reproduce, and *remain alive*." The other Reverend Mothers watched guardedly.

Anger boiled within Murbella. "Those old attitudes have proved wrong time and again. We can't survive simply by running or by breeding faster than Omnius can kill us."

"Many Sisters believe as I do—the ones still living, that is. You've led us now for almost a quarter of a century, and your policies have failed. Most of Chapterhouse is dead. This crisis forces us to consider new alternatives."

"Old alternatives, you mean. There is too much work ahead of us to rehash this tired debate. Is the identification test for Face Dancer genetics ready for distribution yet? That test is critical for all key planetary governments. Our scientists have studied the cadavers for weeks, and we must send—"

"Don't change the subject, Mother Commander! If you won't make the rational decision, if you can't see we need to adapt to circumstances, then I challenge you for leadership."

In astonishment, Laera backed away from the table, while Janess watched her mother, showing no emotion. After the plague had run its course, the female bashar had returned from the fringe battles.

Murbella allowed herself a cool smile as she faced Kiria. Her voice dripped with acid. "I thought we finished this nonsense years ago." She had fought off numerous challengers, killing each one. But Kiria was ready to put it to the test again. "Choose your time and place."

"Choose? That's just like you, Mother Commander—putting off what must be done now." In a flash as swift as nerve impulses could travel, Kiria leapt and lashed out with one foot. Murbella spun away, her spine bending backward with a suppleness that surprised even her. The deadly edge of Kiria's foot came within a hair's breadth of her left eye. The attacker landed on her feet, poised for further combat in the council chamber. "We can't choose a time and place for fighting. We must always be ready, always *adapt*." She lunged forward again, both hands outstretched, fingers rigid as wooden stakes to gouge Murbella's throat.

She writhed out of the way as Kiria thrust. Before her opponent could yank her hand away, Murbella grabbed the woman's arm and added her own momentum, pulling Kiria off balance and slamming her into the council table, scattering Ridulian crystal sheets. Tumbling off, Kiria crashed into a chairdog. In angry reflex, her fist broke through the placid animal's furry hide and spilled its blood on the floor. The piece of living furniture died with only the faintest peep of alarm and pain.

Murbella sprang onto the tabletop and kicked a loose holoprojector at her opponent. The sharp edge of the device caught Kiria on the brow, making a cut that bled profusely. The Mother Commander crouched, ready to defend herself from a frontal attack, but Kiria ducked under the table and heaved upward with her back, knocking the table over. When Murbella fell, Kiria dove over the capsized table and dropped onto the Mother Commander. She wrapped wiry hands around her throat in a primitive but effective method of assassination.

With rigid fingers, Murbella jabbed Kiria's side with enough force to fracture two ribs, but at the same time she felt the sickening snap of her own fingers breaking. Instead of withdrawing as expected, Kiria snarled in pain, raised Murbella's neck and shoulders, and slammed her head against the floor.

Murbella's ears rang, and she felt her skull crack. Fluttering black spots of unconsciousness circled her vision like tiny vultures waiting for fresh carrion. She had to stay awake, had to keep fighting. If she faded now, Kiria would kill her. And if she was defeated here, she would lose not just her life, but the Sisterhood as well. The fate of the entire human race could be decided in this moment.

Janess watched her mother with anguish, but Laera and the other Reverend Mothers were well trained and would not interfere. The unification with Honored Matres had required certain concessions from the Bene Gesserits, including the right of anyone to challenge the Mother Commander's leadership.

Kiria continued to choke her, while Murbella strained to draw a breath. Blocking the pain of her broken fingers, she clapped her palms hard against Kiria's ears. As the deafened woman reeled, Murbella gouged out her right eye with a crooked forefinger, leaving blood and jelly all over her face.

Kiria writhed away, pushing to her feet, but Murbella followed with a flurry of hand blows and kicks. Even so, her challenger was not defeated yet. Kiria hammered her heel into Murbella's sternum, then struck her abdomen with a side blow. Something ruptured inside; Murbella could feel the damage but didn't know how bad it was. Digging into her energy reserves, she drove Kiria aside with her shoulder.

The Honored Matre's lips were drawn back to expose bloody gums and teeth. Rallying, Kiria gathered all of her strength to strike, ignoring her mangled eye. But as she planted her foot, she slipped on a smear of the chairdog's blood on the smooth floor. This threw off her balance for an instant—just long enough to give Murbella the advantage. Without hesitating, the Mother Commander struck a blow so hard that her own wrist shattered—as did Kiria's neck. The challenger fell dead to the floor.

Murbella swayed, while Janess came forward, concern on her face, ready to help her mother, her superior. Murbella raised an arm. Her broken wrist flopped limply, but she banished the wince of pain from her face. "I am capable of standing by myself."

Some of the younger Reverend Mothers, with wide eyes and intense expressions, had backed up to the walls of the council chamber.

Murbella wanted so badly to fall beside her victim on the floor, letting the exhaustion and pain take control. But she could not allow that—not with so many Reverend Mothers observing. She could never reveal a moment of weakness, especially now.

Summoning her breath, dredging up the last sparks of endurance, Murbella spoke in an even voice. "I will go to my quarters now and heal." Then, in a lower voice, "Janess, have the kitchens send up a restorative energy drink." She cast a dismissive glance at the dead Kiria, then raised her eyes to Janess, Laera, and the awed spectators in the hall. "Or do any of you wish to challenge me and take advantage of my condition?" In defiance, she held up her broken wrist. No one took the offer.

Injured inside and out, Murbella had no clear memory of how she made it back to her quarters. Her progress was slow, but she accepted no aid. The other Reverend Mothers, sensing her determination, left her alone.

In her dim room, the spice drink was already waiting for her. *How long did it take me to get here?* After a single sip she could feel energy surge through her body. She murmured a thankful blessing to Janess; her daughter had made this drink extremely potent.

Leaving word that she was not to be disturbed, she sealed her door and consumed the rest of the rejuvenating beverage. It boosted the internal repairs she had already begun to make, delicately probing with her mind to judge the extent of her injuries. Finally, allowing the flood of pain to wash into her senses, Murbella carefully assessed what Kiria had done to her. The degree of internal damage frightened her. Never in any previous challenge had she come so close to losing.

Will the rest of the Reverend Mothers rally behind me—or will they start sniffing out my weaknesses again like hungry hyenas?

She could not afford to waste time and energy battling her own people. Few enough of them remained alive after the plague. What if the Sisterhood was infiltrated by Face Dancers again? Could one of them, trained in exotic fighting techniques, pose as an Honored Matre challenger and kill Murbella? What if a Face Dancer became the Mother Commander of the Sisterhood? Then all indeed would be lost.

She lay back, closed her eyes, and plunged into a healing trance. Time was of the essence. She had to regain her full strength. The forces of Omnius had located this world and would be coming soon.

While Yueh was under arrest and interrogation, yet another instance of sabotage occurred.

The Bene Gesserit Sisters summoned the passengers to the great auditorium for an emergency meeting. Garimi seemed particularly agitated; Duncan Idaho and Miles Teg were alert. Eyes intent, Scytale observed, always the outsider. What had happened now? *And will they blame me for it?*

Was it worse than the murder of another ghola and axlotl tank? Had someone else been killed? Had another water reservoir dumped into space, squandering the new supplies they had acquired at Qelso? Spice stockpiles contaminated? Food vats destroyed? The seven captive sandworms harmed?

The Tleilaxu man sat back, watching everyone stream in from outside corridors and take their seats in islands of friendship or shared opinions. Palpable tension radiated from them. More than two hundred gathered, most of them curious, alarmed, or frightened. Only a few proctors stayed in isolated sections with the younger children that had been born during the journey; others were old enough to be treated as adults.

The Bashar himself made the announcement. "Explosive mines have disappeared from the sealed armory. Eight of the hundred and twelve—certainly enough to cause severe damage to this ship."

After a brief silence, conversation returned in a riptide of whispers, gasps, and accusations.

"The mines," Teg repeated. "Back on Chapterhouse they were placed around this ship as a self-destruct mechanism in case Duncan or anyone else tried to steal it. Now eight of them are gone."

Sheeana went to stand beside the Bashar. "I deactivated those mines myself, so that this vessel could escape. They were locked securely away, but now they've disappeared."

"If they are missing, they might have been dumped out into space . . . or planted around the ship like time bombs," Duncan said. "I suspect the latter, and that our saboteur has further plans."

The Rabbi moaned loudly. "You see? More incompetence! I should have stayed on Qelso with the rest of my people."

"Maybe *you* stole the mines," Garimi snapped.

He looked horrified. "You dare accuse me? A holy man of my stature? First Yueh says I manipulated him to murder a ghola baby, and now you think I have stolen explosives?" Scytale saw that the frail old man could never have lifted one of the heavy mines, much less eight of them.

"Yueh has been under the constant surveillance of Thufir Hawat and myself," Teg said. "Even if he did kill the axlotl tank and the growing ghola, he could not have stolen the mines."

"Unless he has an accomplice," Garimi said, setting off another chain of muttering.

"We will discover who took them." Sheeana cut off the squabble. "And where they have been hidden."

"We've heard similar promises in the past three years," Garimi continued, with a meaningful glare at Teg and Thufir. "But our security has been completely ineffective."

Paul Atreides sat in one of the front rows, near Chani and Jessica. "Are we certain the mines only disappeared recently? How often is the armory checked? Maybe Liet-Kynes or Stilgar took them for their war against the sandtrout without telling us."

"We should evacuate this ship," the Rabbi said. "Find another planet, or go back to Qelso." His voice quavered. "If you witches hadn't . . . hadn't . . . taken Rebecca, I would be safe now with my people. We all could have settled there."

Garimi scowled. "Rabbi, for years you've encouraged dissent with your sniping and destructive arguments, without offering alternatives."

"I speak the truth as I see it. The stolen mines are only the latest in a string of sabotage. My Rebecca remains alive only by chance when four other axlotl tanks have now been murdered. And who damaged the life-support systems, the water holding tanks? Who contaminated the algae vats and destroyed the air-filtration mats? Who poured acid on the seals of the observation window in the sandworm hold? There is a criminal among us, and he is growing bolder and bolder! Why don't you find him?"

Scytale remained silent and unobtrusive, listening to the debate. Everyone feared there would be more incidents of sabotage, and the stolen mines would be sufficient to cripple or destroy the great ship.

The Tleilaxu had no doubt they would eventually turn their suspicions toward him because of his race, but he could prove his innocence. He had laboratory records, surveillance images, a solid alibi. Nevertheless, *someone* had committed the acts of sabotage.

When the exhausting meeting broke up, the Rabbi stalked past Scytale in a huff, saying he was going to go sit in a vigil beside Rebecca, "to make certain no one else tries to kill her!" As the old man passed close, Scytale caught the Rabbi's usual faint, strange scent, a subtly different flavor in the air.

On instinct, Scytale emitted a barely audible whistle in a complicated melody that he remembered from deep in his past lives. The Rabbi ignored him and stalked away. Scytale frowned, not sure if he had noticed a brief hesitation as the old man walked past.

God is God, and life is His alone to give. If God Himself has not
the strength to survive, then we are left with nothing but despair.
                                                    —The Cant of the Shariat

Every investigation of Rakis yielded the same result. Only a few insignificant pockets of its ecosystem had survived. The planet was empty and haunted, yet it seemed to have its own will to live. Against all odds and science, Rakis still clung to its sparse atmosphere, its gasps of moisture.

Guriff's hard-bitten prospectors happily accepted supplies that Waff and the Guildsmen offered as a gesture of goodwill. Waff's primary motivation for this was to get the men to leave him alone while he conducted his innocuous "geological investigations." The prospectors were supplied by irregular CHOAM vessels that came to check on their work, but Guriff had no idea when the next ship would come. The Tleilaxu Master had enough packaged food from the Heighliner to last for years, if his deteriorating body lasted that long.

Above all, he needed to tend to his worms.

As he'd hoped, the prospectors spent the harsh days and nights concentrating on their own digging, hoping to find the legendary lost hoard of the Tyrant's melange. Insulated scout cruisers braved the rugged weather, carrying sensors and probes up to the polar regions, while the men bored test holes, searching unsuccessfully for any threads of spice.

The large dropbox from Edrik's Heighliner had included a wide-bed groundcar that could roll across even the roughest terrain. When the prospectors departed, Waff called his four Guildsmen to assist him. With no curious eyes watching, they wrestled the long, sand-filled test tanks aboard his groundcar. Waff would make a pilgrimage out into the charred and glassy wasteland that had once been a sea of dunes.

"I will release the specimens myself. I don't need your assistance." He directed the Guildsmen to return to the rigid-walled survival tents. "Stay and prepare our food—and make certain you follow the accepted ways." He had given them precise instructions on the proper techniques. "Once I free the worms, I intend to come back for a celebration."

He did not want Guriff and his men, nor any of these untrustworthy Guild assistants, to observe such a private and holy moment. Today he would restore the Prophet to Rakis, to the planet where He belonged. Dressed in protective clothing, he keyed in coordinates and drove off with the two long aquariums in the back of his groundcar. Heading due east, he sped away into a ruddy orange dawn.

Although the landscape here was smeared, eroded, and unrecognizable, Waff knew exactly where he was going. Before coming to Rakis, he had dug up the old charts, and because the Honored Matres' Obliterators had altered even the planetary magnetic field, he had carefully recalibrated his maps from orbit. A long time ago, God's Messenger had purposefully carried him to the location of Sietch Tabr. The worms must consider it sacred, and Waff could think of no more appropriate place to turn loose the armored, augmented creatures. He drove there now.

Light from the dust-thickened sky bathed the glassy ground in eerie colors. From the tanks behind him, Waff could feel the thumping of the worms as they writhed, impatient to burst out onto the open desert. Home.

Back on the Heighliner, Waff had observed the bucking and thrashing creatures, measuring their growth in the lab. He knew the worms were dangerous, and that long confinement in small tanks sapped the creatures' strength. Even under carefully controlled conditions, he hadn't been able to replicate the optimal environment, and the specimens had weakened. Something was wrong.

But hope infused him. Now that he was actually here, all would be right again. Holy Rakis! He could only pray that this injured dune world would provide what a Tleilaxu Master could not, offering some ineffable benefit to the worms, to the Prophet.

When Waff reached the plain and saw the melted rocks, he remembered the weathered line of mountains that had sheltered the buried tomb of the Fremen city. He stopped the groundcar. A vitrified crust—rocky grains melted to glass by the blasts of incomprehensible weapons—covered what had once been open sand. But the worms would know what to do.

Behind the vehicle, Waff paused a moment to close his eyes in prayer to his God and His Prophet. Then, with a flourish, he disengaged the plaz walls of the tanks and let sand spill out. Long serpentine shapes lunged free like uncoiled springs, and dropped to the ground around the vehicle. Waff gazed in wonderment at their thick, ridged bodies, and the python fluidity of their motion.

"Go, Prophet! Reclaim your world."

Eight worms slithered on the hard, smooth ground. *Eight*, a sacred Tleilaxu number.

The freed creatures spread out in random paths, while he watched them in awe. Waff hoped they could break through the fused sand and tunnel into softer levels below, as he had designed them to do. Each of the specimens had a tiny implanted tracer that would enable him to follow them and continue his investigations.

However, the sandworms turned and circled the vehicle, coming closer. Hunting *him*. In a moment of fear, Waff froze. They were certainly large enough to attack and kill him. "Prophet, do not harm me. I have brought you back to Rakis. You are free to make this your kingdom once again."

The worms raised their blunt heads, swaying back and forth. *Are they trying to send me some sort of message?* He struggled to comprehend. Could their hypnotic movements be an alien dance? Or a predatory maneuver?

He did not move. He waited.

If this landscape was too harsh for them, if the Prophet needed to consume him in order to survive, Waff was fully prepared to donate the flesh of his own deteriorating body. If this was to be the end, so be it.

Then, as if at a silent signal, the sandworms turned in unison and sped off, their flexing ridges bumping across the glassy dunes. Presently they stopped, bent their armored heads downward, and smashed into the hard surface. They broke the crust and plunged downward, tunneling into the pristine, sterilized sands. Returning to the desert! Waff's heart swelled. He knew they would survive.

As he returned to the groundcar, he realized he had tears in his eyes.

When the forces are arrayed and the final battle is engaged, the outcome may be decided in only a few moments. Remember this: By the time the first shot is fired, half the battle is already over. Victory or defeat can be determined by the preparations that are set in place weeks or even months beforehand.

— BASHAR MILES TEG,
resource allocation request to the Bene Gesserit

Chief Fabricator Shayama Sen agreed to come to Chapterhouse, but the Ixian dignitary remained aboard his ship high in orbit, far above the recovery operations. He would not risk exposure to any last vestiges of the plague, though the disease had burned itself out down there.

Murbella had to go to him to make her demands—but under the strictest quarantine conditions. Encased in her own decontamination sphere, like a laboratory specimen in a tank, she felt foolish and helpless. The Bene Gesserit sphere's outer hull—though scorched by its passage through the atmosphere on the way to orbit and then exposed to the vacuum of space—underwent additional irradiation and sterilization procedures up there. Fail-safes, redundancies. *Justified paranoia,* she admitted to herself. Although Murbella did not fault him for taking such extraordinary precautions, the Ixian nevertheless had much explaining to do.

While waiting inside her sealed chamber aboard the Guildship (which was guided by a mathematical compiler rather than a Navigator), she composed herself. Still sore and battered from her duel with Kiria, she was satisfied that her violent response to the stupid power play had been necessary. None of the other distraught Sisters would challenge her now, thus leaving her role as Mother Commander uncontested.

Once again, Murbella cursed the rebel Honored Matres and their mindless destruction of the massive shipyards and weapons shops on Richese. Had that not happened, with both Ix and Richese producing armaments, the human race could have consolidated a meaningful defense. Now that Ix was the primary industrial center, the Chief Fabricator felt he could be intractable. Shortsighted fools!

Shayama Sen marched into the large metal-walled room and took a comfortable seat facing her. He looked smug and safe, while she felt like a caged zoo animal. "You called me away from our work, Mother Commander?"

Despite the inherent awkwardness of her position, Murbella tried to take command of the meeting. "Chief Fabricator, you have had three years to duplicate the Obliterators we provided, but all we've received in exchange for our melange payments are reports on your tests, and promise after promise. The Enemy has destroyed more than a hundred planets, and their battleships keep coming. Chapterhouse itself was nearly eradicated by the recent plague."

Sen bowed formally. "We are fully aware of this, Mother Commander, and you have my condolences." He got up and poured himself a glass of water from a pitcher, then roamed the large meeting room, flaunting his own freedom.

Anger heated her cheeks and neck. How could this man sound so calm in the face of the crumbling human civilization? "We require the weapons you promised us—and without further delay."

Sen tapped his circuitry-imprinted fingernails together, pondering her containment sphere with a blank stare. "But we have not yet received full payment, and we hear your New Sisterhood is in dire financial straits. If we continue to devote all our resources to these Obliterators, and you renege—"

"The agreed-upon amount of melange is yours the moment you finish installing Obliterators in our new warships. You know this." She didn't dare let Sen discover that she had released a great deal of stockpiled spice to help her fellow Reverend Mothers fight the plague.

"Ah, but if your spice is contaminated by the plague, of what use is it to us? How else will you pay?"

Murbella couldn't believe his blindness. "The spice is not contaminated. We will implement any sterilization measures you require."

"And what if that destroys its efficacy?"

"Then we will give you the original spice to decontaminate in whatever manner you see fit. Stop quibbling about nonsense when the extinction of the human race is imminent!"

Sen seemed scandalized. "You call it nonsense? The properties of spice are complex and could be harmed by such aggressive measures. The substance is of no value to us if we cannot use it."

"The plague organism has a short lifetime. Unless it is transferred from host to host, the disease dies swiftly. Place the spice on an airless moon for a year if you choose to."

"But the difficulties and the inconvenience . . . I believe these circumstances merit a renegotiation of our price."

If the container wall had not prevented her, Murbella would have killed him for his insolence. "Have you any idea of how much destruction the Enemy has spread?"

He pursed his lips, and said, "Let me dispense with subtleties, Mother Commander. Honored Matres provoked this Enemy into launching its fleet against them, and in turn against the rest of us. Your association with the whores was your own folly, and the whole human race has paid for it. Ix has no quarrel with these robotic invaders. Since they evolved from ancient thinking machines, it is possible that we Ixians have more in common with *them* than with manipulative, murderous females."

Ah. Now she was beginning to understand. Listening to the sharp voice of Odrade-within and a thousand other Reverend Mothers frantically offering advice, Murbella forced calm upon herself. It was clear that the Ixian was trying to escalate this discussion. But why? To distract her? Had he failed to make as much progress in developing the Obliterators as he claimed? Was production running behind schedule?

She selected a gambit that she hoped would shut down his blathering. "I authorize a thirty percent increase in your spice allotment, to be put in a trust fund held in the Guild Bank of your choosing. I expect that is sufficient to make up for any inconvenience? However, payment will be contingent upon your *actual delivery* of the weaponry in our contract. The Guild has delivered our new warships. Now, where are my Obliterators?"

Shayama Sen bowed, accepting her offer and withdrawing his objections. "Our manufactory worlds are operating at full capacity. We can begin loading Obliterators aboard your new ships immediately."

"I'll issue the orders." She paced within the decontamination bubble like a Laza tiger. The smells of disinfectant chemicals seeping through the air filters made her want to gag. She didn't think the chamber's replenishers were working properly. "How do we know your weapons will perform as you promise?"

"You provided the originals, and we duplicated them precisely. If the originals functioned, then these will, too."

"The originals *functioned*. You've seen what's left of Rakis and Richese!"

"Then you have nothing to fear."

"From now on, I insist that we place Bene Gesserit inspectors and line supervisors in your manufactories. They will keep you accountable and guard against sabotage."

Shayama Sen struggled with the demand, but could find no legitimate argument against it. "Provided your women do not interfere, we shall allow them access. Is that all?"

"We also need to witness a successful test before going into battle."

Sen smiled again. "You would have us annihilate a world merely to prove a point? Hmm, I see Honored Matre methods persist in your New Sisterhood." He chuckled. "I'll give you full records of our previous tests and even arrange for a new demonstration, if you like."

"We will review your data, Chief Fabricator. Transmit it to Chapterhouse, and arrange for a demonstration that I can see with my own eyes."

He tapped his silicon fingernails again, an annoying nervous habit. "Very well. I'll find a nice planetoid to blow up for your entertainment."

Murbella pressed against the curved, transparent wall of her sphere. "And there's one other thing I insist upon. Face Dancers have been found on many worlds, manipulating governments, weakening our defenses.

Some even managed to infiltrate Chapterhouse. I need to have assurance that *you* are not a Face Dancer."

Sen reeled backward in surprise. "You accuse me of being an Enemy, a shape-shifter operative?"

Murbella leaned against the solid wall, regarding him coolly. His indignation did nothing to convince her. She worked the internal controls, and a small, sealed container opened near the base of the Bene Gesserit chamber. It was a sterilization bin, an autoclave and chemical bath. Steam still curled from the package as it emerged for the Chief Fabricator to take.

"This is a testing device we have developed. After analyzing Face Dancer specimens found among our dead, we ran genetic tests and developed this infallible indicator. Right now, Chief Fabricator—as I watch— you will complete this test on yourself."

"I will *not*." He sniffed.

"You will, or you'll receive none of our melange."

Sen roamed again, frowning. "What is this test? What does it do?"

"It is mostly automated." Murbella explained the principle to him and the easy steps. "As a bonus for you, we can allow Ix to produce these in great quantities. There are plenty of suspicious people who see Face Dancers everywhere. You could make a tidy profit selling these kits."

Sen considered. "You may be right."

While Murbella observed, he went through the motions, standing close enough to her bubble that she could watch his every movement. As far as the Reverend Mothers knew, the test could not easily be foiled, and the Chief Fabricator had had no time to prepare a deception. She waited with intense interest, and was relieved when the indicators declared him fully human. Shayama Sen was not a Face Dancer.

With an irritated expression on his face, he held the chemical tab up for her to see. "Are you satisfied now?"

"I am. And I advise you to perform this test on all of your chief engineers and team leaders. Ix is a likely target for the Enemy to infiltrate. Another reason for my Sisters to supervise your vital work for us."

Sen looked genuinely disturbed, as if that possibility had not occurred to him. "I concede your point, Mother Commander. I would like to see those results myself."

"Then include them when you send your data about the Obliterator tests. In the meantime, prepare to install your weapons in all the new warships coming out of the Junction shipyards. We are about to engage in an all-out offensive against the thinking-machine fleet."

*Each sentient life requires a place of extreme serenity, where the
mind may roam afterward in memory and to which the body longs
to return.*

—ERASMUS,

contemplation notes

Now that you have been among us for more than a year, it is time
to show you my special place, Paolo." The independent robot
waved a metal arm, and his majestic robes flowed around him. "And
you too, of course, Baron Harkonnen."

The Baron scowled, his voice dripping with sarcasm. "Your special
place? I'm sure we'll be charmed by what a *robot* considers to be a special place."

During the time that he and Paolo had lived on Synchrony, he'd
lost his awe and fear of thinking machines. They seemed plodding and
grandiose, full of redundancy and very little impulsivity. Since Omnius
thought he needed Paolo, along with the Baron to keep Paolo in line,
the two were safe enough. Even so, the Baron felt a need to show some
backbone, and turn the circumstances to his own benefit.

Around the interior of the now-familiar cathedral chamber, the
walls became a wash of color, as if invisible painters were hard at work.
Instead of blank metal and stone surfaces, the murky shades of green
and brown sharpened into highly realistic trees and birds. The oppressive ceiling opened to the sky, and peculiar synthesized music began

playing. A gemgravel pathway ran through the lush garden with comfortable reclining benches at intermittent intervals. A lily pond appeared on one side.

"My contemplation garden." Erasmus formed his artificial smile. "I enjoy this place very much. It is special to me."

"At least the flowers don't stink." Paolo ripped up one of the bright chrysanthemums, sniffed it, and discarded it at the side of the path. After a year of constant training, the Baron had finally made the boy's personality into something he could be proud of.

"This is all lovely," the Baron said drily. "And utterly pointless."

Be careful what you say to him, Grandfather, cautioned the Alia-voice within. *Don't get us killed today.* It was one of her continual harangues.

"Is something troubling you, Baron?" Erasmus asked. "This should be a place of peace and contemplation."

See what you've done! Get out of my head.

But I'm trapped here with you. You can't get rid of me. I killed you once with the gom jabbar, and I can do it again with a little careful manipulation.

"I see that you are often plagued by disturbing thoughts." Erasmus stepped closer. "Would you like me to open your skull and look inside? I could fix the problem."

Be careful with me, Abomination! I just may take him up on the offer!

He forced a smile as he replied to the independent robot. "I'm just impatient to learn exactly how we can work with Omnius. Your war against humanity has gone on for some time now, and we've been your guests for a year. When will we do what you brought us here for?"

Paolo kicked a divot into the gemgravel path. "Yes, Erasmus. When do we get to have fun?"

"Soon enough." The robot swirled his robes and guided his companions through the garden.

The boy had just passed his eleventh birthday and was developing into a strong young man, well-muscled and highly trained. Thanks to the Baron's constant influence, virtually all traces of the former Atreides personality had been extinguished. Erasmus himself had supervised Paolo's vigorous combat training against fighting meks, all to prime him to become the supposed Kwisatz Haderach.

But the Baron still could not fathom *why*. Why would the machines care about some obscure human religious figure from ancient history?

Erasmus motioned for them to sit on the nearest bench. The synthesized music and birdsong around them grew louder and more energetic until they became intertwined melodies. The robot's expression shifted once again, as if in reverie. "Is it not beautiful? I composed it myself."

"Most impressive." The Baron despised the music as too smooth and peaceful; he preferred more cacophonous, discordant selections.

"Over the millennia, I created wondrous works of art and many illusions." Erasmus's face and body shifted, and he became entirely human in appearance. Even the gaudy and unnecessary garments altered, until the robot stood before them again as a matronly old woman in a floral-print dress holding a small hand trowel. "This is one of my favorites. I have perfected it over the years, drawing from more and more of the lives my Face Dancers bring me."

With the hand trowel she dug in the simulated soil near the bench, getting rid of weeds that the Baron was sure had not been there moments earlier. A worm crawled out of the exposed, dark dirt, and the old woman sliced it in half with the trowel. The two parts of the squirming creature faded into the dirt.

A gentle undercurrent flowed in her voice, not unlike that of a grandmother telling bedtime stories to children. "Long ago—during your original lifetime, dear Baron—a Tleilaxu researcher named Hidar Fen Ajidica created an artificial spice that he called amal. Though the substance proved to have significant defects, Ajidica consumed huge quantities of it himself, and as a result he went increasingly mad, which led to his demise."

"Sounds like a failure," Paolo said.

"Oh, Ajidica failed spectacularly, but he did accomplish something very important. Call it a side effect. For his special ambassadors, he created greatly improved Face Dancers, with which he intended to populate a new domain. He dispatched them into deep space as scouts, colonizers, preparers of the way. He died before he could join them. Poor foolish man."

The old woman left her trowel stuck in the ground. When she straightened, she pressed her hand against the small of her back, as if to comfort an ache. "The new Face Dancers located our machine empire, and Omnius allowed me to study them. I spent generations working with the shape-shifters, learning how to draw information from them. Lovely biological machines, far superior to their predecessors. Yes, they are proving to be extremely helpful in winning our final war."

Looking around the illusory garden, the Baron saw other forms, minor workers who appeared to be human. New Face Dancers? "So you made an alliance with them?"

The old woman pursed her lips. "An alliance? They are servants, not our partners. Face Dancers were made to serve. To them, Omnius and I are like gods, greater Masters than the Tleilaxu ever were." Erasmus seemed to be pondering. "I do wish they had brought one of their Masters to me before the Honored Matres destroyed nearly all of them. The discussion could have been most enlightening."

Paolo brought the conversation back around to a subject that interested him. "As the final Kwisatz Haderach, I will be a god, too."

Erasmus laughed, an old woman's cachinnation. "Beware of megalomania, young man. It has brought down many a human—such as Hidar Fen Ajidica. Soon I expect to have a key to help you reach your potential. We need to free the god that crouches inside your body. And that requires a powerful catalyst."

"What is it?" the young man demanded.

"I keep forgetting how impatient you humans are!" The old woman brushed off her flower-print dress. "That is why I enjoy the Face Dancers so much. In them, I see the potential for perfecting humans. Face Dancers could be the sort of humans that even thinking machines might tolerate."

The Baron snorted. "Humans will never be perfect! Believe me, I've known plenty of them, and they're all disappointing in some way." Rabban, Piter . . . even Feyd had failed him in the end.

Don't omit yourself, Grandfather. Remember, you were killed by a little girl with a poison needle. Ha ha!

Shut up! The Baron scratched nervously at the top of his head, as if to dig through flesh and bone to rip her out. She fell silent.

"I fear you may be right, Baron. Humans may not be salvageable, but we don't want Omnius to believe that, or he will destroy them all."

"I thought you machines were already doing that," the Baron said.

"To a certain extent. Omnius is stretching his abilities, but when we find the no-ship, I am certain he will get down to business." The old woman dug holes in the garden and planted seedlings that simply appeared in her hands.

"What's so special about one lost ship?" the Baron asked.

"Our mathematical projections suggest that the Kwisatz Haderach is aboard."

"But *I* am the Kwisatz Haderach!" Paolo insisted. "You already have me."

The old woman gave him a wry smile. "You are our fallback plan, young man. Omnius prefers the security of redundancy. If there are two possible Kwisatz Haderachs, he wants both of them."

His face a mask of displeasure, the Baron cracked his knuckles. "So you think there's another ghola of Paul Atreides aboard that ship? Not likely!"

"I claim only that there is another *Kwisatz Haderach* aboard the ship. However, since we have one Paul Atreides ghola, there could certainly be another."

Are we on the Golden Path, or have we strayed from it? For three and a half millennia we prayed for deliverance from the Tyrant, but now that he is gone, have we forgotten how to live without such stern guidance? Do we know how to make the necessary decisions, or will we become hopelessly lost in the wilderness and starve of our own failings?

—MOTHER SUPERIOR DARWI ODRADE,
Pondering My Epitaph, sealed Bene Gesserit Archives, recorded before Battle of Junction

Highly agitated, Garimi refused to take a seat in Sheeana's private quarters, no matter how many times it was offered. Even the Van Gogh painting on the wall did not seem to interest her. The stolen mines had brought long-simmering tensions to a new, raw level. Frantic search teams had been unable to locate any of the explosive devices. Sheeana knew that the stern Proctor Superior had her own suspicions and her own set of people to blame.

"You and the Bashar didn't make a good bargain back on Qelso," Garimi said. "Leaving all those people and equipment, and getting nothing for ourselves!"

"We replenished all our stores."

"What if further sabotage hits our life-support systems? Liet-Kynes and Stilgar were the two most capable of conservation, recycling, and repairs. What if we need them to help us? Do you intend to grow new ones?"

Sheeana angered the other woman further by responding with a calm, amused smile. "We could, but I thought you suspected all the ghola children. Yet you want Liet and Stilgar back? Besides, maybe Liet was right; maybe it's their destiny to remain on Qelso."

"Now it's obvious that neither of them was the saboteur—though I'm still not entirely convinced about Yueh."

Sheeana stared at the bright daubs of color that the ancient artist had swirled into an image of such power. Van Gogh was a genius. "I took a necessary action, based on our needs and priorities."

"Hardly! You bowed to the demands of those murderous nomads to keep all Bene Gesserits off the planet. We should have formed a new school there—and now, instead, this whole ship could explode at any moment!"

Ah, the core of what is really bothering her.

"You know very well that I would have been happy to let you and your followers settle there." She forced a chuckle. "But I was not willing to start a war with the people of Qelso. We can train others in the nuances of our life-support systems. This ship will survive, as it has for decades."

Obviously in no mood to be brushed aside, Garimi said, "Survive how? By creating another ghola to save us? That's always your solution, whether an Abomination like Alia, a traitor like Yueh or Jessica, or a Tyrant like Leto II. At least Pandora had the good sense to close her box."

"And I want to open it wide. I want to bring back the history, especially Paul Atreides—and Thufir Hawat. We could certainly draw on the security knowledge of the Weapons Master of House Atreides."

"Hawat failed spectacularly the last time you tried to awaken him."

"Then we'll try again. And Chani could be an excellent fulcrum for awakening Paul. Jessica is also ripe for awakening. Even Leto II is ready."

Garimi's eyes flashed. "You are playing with fire, Sheeana."

"I am forging weapons. For that, fire is necessary." Sheeana turned, letting Garimi know that the discussion was at an end. "I've heard your opinions often enough to memorize them. I will dine with the gholas today. Maybe they have fresh ideas."

Incensed, the dark-haired woman followed Sheeana out of her

quarters and down the corridors toward the dining hall. Unexpectedly, young Leto II stepped out of a lift tube, alone and quiet as usual. The twelve-year-old often wandered the halls of the no-ship by himself; now he looked at the two women and blinked, but did not speak to them. Such an odd, preoccupied child.

Before Sheeana could stop her, the Proctor Superior marched toward Leto, stiff and intimidating. Garimi had a fresh target for her anger and frustration. "So, Tyrant, where is your Golden Path? Where has it led us? If you were so prescient, why didn't you warn us of the Honored Matres or the Enemy?"

"I don't know." The boy seemed genuinely perplexed. "I don't remember."

Garimi studied him in disgust. "And what if you *did* remember? Would you be the God Emperor, the greatest butcher in all of human history? Sheeana thinks you could save us, but I say the Tyrant could just as easily destroy us. That's what you're best at. I don't want you or your monstrous ego back, Leto II. Your Golden Path is a blind man's road, sunk in a swamp."

"It is not this boy's Golden Path," Sheeana said, taking the other woman's arm in a viselike grip. "Leave him alone."

Leto took a quick step, darted around them, and fled down the corridor. Garimi looked triumphantly at Sheeana, who merely regarded her as a fool, condemned by her own irrational outburst.

HIS EYES AND ears burned from the Proctor Superior's accusations, but Leto refused to allow a tear. A wise person didn't waste water trying to drown his emotions; he knew that much about old Dune. As he moved away from Sheeana and the insufferable Proctor Superior, and everyone else who thought they knew what to expect from him, the boy silently denied what Garimi had said, trying to block away what he himself knew.

I was the God Emperor, the Tyrant. I created the Golden Path . . . but with my memories locked away, I don't truly understand what it is! Despite all he had learned about his original lifetime, Leto felt like nothing more than a twelve-year-old who had never asked to be reborn.

He rode the transport tube to the deep lower decks, heading for a place where he felt more comfortable and safe. At first he considered slipping into the roaring winds of the recirculation chambers and the atmosphere-pumping ducts, but the strict security measures imposed by Bashar Teg and Leto's friend Thufir had closed off all access.

Before his unpleasant encounter with Garimi, Leto had planned to join Thufir for his regular session on the training floor. Though the other ghola boy was now seventeen and had his security duties with the Bashar, he still frequently sparred with Leto. Despite his youth and size, Leto II was highly competitive even against a larger, stronger opponent. For the past few years they had provided quite a challenge for each other.

At the moment, though, Leto needed to be alone. He reached the bottom levels of the ship and stood at the main access door into the immense hold. The surveillance imagers would have spotted him already. He swallowed hard. He had never dared to go inside alone, though he had stared for hours through the plaz at the captive sandworms.

A pair of young guards stood in the hall, monitoring access to the cargo deck. Seeing the boy approach, they tensed. "This is a restricted area."

"Restricted to *me*? Do you know who I am?"

"You are Leto the Tyrant, the God Emperor," said the young woman, as if answering a proctor's question. She was Debray, one of the Bene Gesserit daughters who had been born in space after the no-ship's escape.

"And those worms are part of me. Don't you remember your history?"

"They're dangerous," the male guard answered. "You shouldn't go in there."

Leto gazed calmly at the pair. "Yes, I should. Especially now. I need to feel the sands, smell the melange, the worms." He narrowed his eyes. "It could well restore my memories, as Sheeana wants."

Debray frowned as she considered this. "Sheeana did say that every means must be used to trigger the reawakening of the gholas."

The male guard turned to his companion. "Call Thufir Hawat and inform him first. This is highly irregular."

Leto approached the heavy door. "I just need to go inside the hatch. I won't stray far. The worms stay out in the center of the habitat, don't they?" Boldly, he used the simple controls to unseal the door. "I know these worms. Thufir will understand. He hasn't recovered his memories either."

Before the guards could agree on stopping him, Leto darted into the hold. The sand itself seemed to give off a crackling, staticky sound. The temperature was warm, the air so dry that his throat burned. The powerful smells of flint and cinnamon seared his nostrils. At the far end of the kilometer-long hold, the large worms moved toward him.

Just standing on the sandy surface took the boy back to a place he had studied extensively in the no-ship's library. The real Arrakis, which had changed from desert to garden during his first extended life. Now the dry heat baked his skin. He took deep, calming breaths of air redolent with the odor of melange.

Not bothering to avoid making noise, Leto strode farther out on the sand, sinking up to his ankles in the soft dunes. He ignored the shouted warnings of the guards as he trudged away from the metal wall. This was the closest thing to an open desert these worms had ever known.

Climbing the crest of a dune and gazing around to the limits of the hold, Leto imagined how magnificent Arrakis must have once been. He wished he could remember. The dune on which he stood was small compared to a real one, and the seven worms in the hold were more diminutive than their unfettered ancestors as well.

Ahead of him, the largest worm churned through sand, followed by the others. Leto felt the connection with these seven worms. It was as if the magnificent beasts sensed his mental pain and wanted to help him, even if his memories were still locked away in a ghola vault.

An unexpected release of tears flowed down Leto's cheeks—not of anger toward Garimi but of joy and awe. Tears! He could not stem the flow of moisture. Perhaps if he perished right there on the sands, his body would be absorbed into the flesh of the worms, leaving behind all his fears and expectations.

These worms were his descendants, each with a nugget of his former awareness. *We are the same.* Leto beckoned them. Although his ghola cells hadn't yet released memories of the thousands of years in his original lifetime, these sandworms possessed buried memories as well. "Are you dreaming in there? Am *I* in there?"

A hundred meters from him the worms stopped and dove back into the sand, one after the other. He sensed that their presence was not threatening, but . . . protective. They *did* know him!

From the hatch behind him, Leto heard a familiar voice calling his name. Looking back, he saw the ghola of Thufir Hawat standing on the verge, motioning him to come back to safety. "Leto, watch out. Don't tempt the worms. You are my friend, but if one of them eats you I won't jump down its gullet to get you back!" Thufir tried to chuckle, but looked deeply anxious.

"I just need some time alone with them." Leto sensed something moving beneath the sands. He felt no concern for his own well-being, but did not want to endanger his friend. He picked up a strong whiff, the cinnamon odor of spice.

"Leave! Now!"

Then, wrestling with his fear, Thufir ventured closer to the young man, a few meters away. "Suicide by worm? Is that what you're doing out here?" He glanced at the hatch behind them, apparently wondering if he could still get back to safety if necessary. Worry lines etched his features. He looked terrified for himself and for Leto, wrestling with something that ran against his instincts. Yet he still stepped forward, as if drawn to his friend.

"Thufir, stay back. You're in more danger than I am."

The worms knew that someone else was in their realm. But they seemed far more agitated than an intruder could account for. Leto sensed a hatred, a roiling and instinctive reaction. He sprinted back to Thufir to save him. His friend seemed to be struggling with himself.

Sand erupted, and worms encircled him and Thufir. The creatures rose from the low dunes, their round and hollow faces questing this way and that for something.

"Leto, we have to go." Thufir grabbed the boy's sleeve. His voice was husky, ragged. "Go!"

"Thufir, they won't harm me. And I feel . . . I feel as if I could make them go away. But they are deeply disturbed. Something about . . . you?" Leto sensed something here that he didn't understand.

Simultaneously, the worms shot like battering rams toward the two young men on the dune. Thufir bolted away from Leto and lost his footing on the soft surface. Leto tried to go toward him, but the largest worm exploded up between them, scattering sand and dust. Another beast loomed on the other side of the transfixed Thufir, stretching its sinuous body into the air.

Thufir let out a shuddering, gut-wrenching scream. It didn't sound at all like the ghola friend Leto had known. It didn't even sound human.

The sandworms struck Thufir, but they did not simply devour him. As if in vindictive anger, the largest worm slammed down on him, smashing the young man's body into the sand. The next worm reared up and rolled over the already broken Thufir Hawat. For good measure, a third worm crushed the lifeless form. Then the trio of worms backed away, as if proud of what they had done.

Leto stumbled across the sand toward the smashed body, oblivious to the threat of the worms. He slid down a churned dune, and fell to his hands and knees beside the smashed, partially buried form. "Thufir!"

But he did not see the familiar face of his friend. The crushed features were pale and blank, the hair colorless, the expression inhuman. The black-button eyes were unfocused and dead.

In shock, Leto reeled backward.

Thufir was a Face Dancer.

Here is my mask—it looks just like yours. We cannot see what our masks look like while we are wearing them.

—*The Wheel of Deception*, Tleilaxu commentary

Uproar in the hierarchy of the no-ship. Astonishment. Even Duncan Idaho could not grasp how such a thing could have happened. How long had the Face Dancer been watching them aboard the no-ship? The mangled, ugly corpse left no room for doubt.

Thufir Hawat had been a Face Dancer! How could it be him?

The original warrior Mentat had served House Atreides. Hawat had been Duncan's good and loyal friend—but not this faux version of him. In all this time, during the three years of sabotage and murder—and perhaps even longer—Duncan had not detected the Face Dancer in Hawat, nor had Bashar Teg who mentored him. Nor had the Bene Gesserit Sisters, nor any of the other ghola children. *But how?*

An even worse question hung over them, blackening Duncan's thoughts like a solar eclipse: *We have found one Face Dancer. Are there others?*

He looked at Sheeana, at the stricken Leto II, and at the two shocked guards who stared at the alien body. "We have to keep this secret until we can account for everyone aboard the ship. We've got to watch them, find a way to test them somehow. . . ."

She agreed. "If there are any other Face Dancers aboard, we need to act before they discover what happened." In Bene Gesserit Voice, using a tone that was the equivalent of a verbal blow, she said to the guards, "*Speak of this to no one.*"

They froze. Sheeana was already making plans to implement a crackdown and sweep of everyone on the ship. Duncan's Mentat mind raced as he tried to comprehend what could have happened, but the nagging questions defied all his attempts to impose logic.

One rose above others: *How do we even know a test will work?* Thufir had already faced interrogation by the Truthsayers, just as everyone onboard had. Somehow, these new Face Dancers could evade even the witches' truthsense.

If the young ghola had been replaced by a Face Dancer at some point, how could such a substitution have occurred without Duncan's knowledge? And when had it occurred? Had the real Thufir accidentally encountered a hidden Face Dancer in a darkened passageway? One of the secret survivors from the Handlers' suicide crashes in a long-term elaborate ruse? How else could a Face Dancer have gotten aboard the *Ithaca*?

In assuming the identity of a victim, a Face Dancer imprinted himself with a perfect copy of the original person's personality and memories, thus creating an exact duplicate. And yet, the false Thufir had risked his life for young Leto II amongst the sandworms. Why? How much of Thufir had actually been in the Face Dancer? Had there ever been a real Thufir ghola?

At first, with the Face Dancer exposed, Duncan had felt a sense of relief that the saboteur and murderer was at last revealed. But after a swift Mentat analysis, he quickly put together several instances of sabotage during which the Thufir Hawat ghola had a clear alibi. Duncan had himself been with him during some of the attacks. The next projection was incontrovertible.

There is more than one Face Dancer among us.

DUNCAN AND TEG met in a small copper-walled room designed for private meetings, blocked from all known scanning devices. Subtle indications implied that this had originally been designed as an inter-rogation chamber. How often had the original Honored Matres used it as such? For torture, or simply amusement?

Standing coolly at attention, Teg and Duncan faced the Reverend Mothers Sheeana, Garimi, and Elyen, who had consumed the last avail-able doses of the truthtrance drug. All of the women were armed and highly suspicious. Sheeana said, "Under various pretexts, we have iso-lated everyone aboard, using layers of observers. Most of them think we're searching for the missing explosive mines. So far, very few people know about Thufir Hawat. Other Face Dancers would not be aware that they are at risk of exposure."

"I would have thought the entire idea absurd—until recently. Now no suspicion seems too paranoid." Duncan locked gazes with the Bashar, and both nodded.

"My truthtrance is deeper than it has been before," Elyen said, sound-ing distant.

"Perhaps we didn't ask the correct questions previously." Garimi put her elbows on the table.

Teg said, "Ask away, then. The sooner you clear us of suspicion, the faster we can root out this cancer. We need a different kind of test."

Normally a trained Bene Gesserit should have been able to uncover deception with a mere question or two, but this extraordinary inquiry lasted an hour. Because they were building a cadre of trustworthy allies, Sheeana and her Sisters needed to be thorough. And they needed to do a better job than before. The three Reverend Mothers watched for even the slightest flicker of evasion. Neither Duncan nor Teg gave them any.

"We believe you," Garimi finally said. "Unless you give us cause to change our minds."

Sheeana nodded. "Provisionally, we accept that you two are exactly who you say you are."

Teg seemed bitterly amused. "And Duncan and I accept you three as well. *Provisionally.*"

"Face Dancers are mimics. They can change their appearance, but they cannot change their DNA. Now that we have cell samples from the Hawat impostor, our Suk doctors should be able to develop an accurate test."

"So we believe," Teg said. With the loss of his protégé, the Bashar seemed fundamentally disturbed. He no longer took anything at face value.

With an iron-hard scowl, Garimi said, "The obvious answer is that Hawat was born a Face Dancer, then carefully planted and manipulated by our Tleilaxu Master. Who would know Face Dancers better than old Scytale? We know he had the cells in his nullentropy tube. If that scenario is true, the deception went on for almost eighteen years."

Sheeana continued, "A Face Dancer infant could have mimicked a generic human baby from the very beginning. As he grew, he took a shape based on archival records of the young Atreides warrior-Mentat. Since no one here—not even you, Duncan—remembers the original Hawat as an adolescent, the disguise would not need to be perfect."

Duncan knew she was right. In his original lifetime, when he'd escaped from the Harkonnens and gone to Caladan, Thufir Hawat had already been a weathered battle veteran. Duncan remembered his first real conversation with Hawat. He'd been a stable boy at Castle Caladan, working with the Salusan bulls that Old Duke Paulus loved to fight in grand spectacles. Someone had drugged the bulls into a frenzy, and young Duncan had tried to raise the alarm, but no one believed him. After Paulus was gored to death, Hawat himself had led the investigation, hauling young Duncan before a board of inquiry, since evidence indicated that he was a Harkonnen spy. . . .

And now this Thufir was a Face Dancer! Duncan still had trouble wrapping his mind around the undeniable reality.

"Then all of the ghola babies could be Face Dancers," Duncan said. "I suggest you summon Scytale. He's now our prime suspect."

"Or," Teg said in a brittle voice, "he may be our best resource. As Garimi already stated, who would know the Face Dancers better?"

When the Tleilaxu Master was brought into the copper-walled chamber, Duncan and Teg took seats at the other side of the table, part of the growing inquisition to root out the Face Dancer infiltration. Scytale appeared frightened and unsettled. The Tleilaxu ghola was fifteen years old, but he did not look like a boy. His elfin features, sharp teeth, and gray skin made him seem alien and suspicious, but Duncan realized that was only a knee-jerk response based on primitive superstitions and previous experiences.

After Scytale sat down, Elyen leaned forward. She looked the sternest of them all. "What have you done, Tleilaxu? What is your plan? How have you tried to betray us?" She used an edge of Voice, enough to make Scytale jerk.

"I did nothing."

"You and your genetic predecessor knew what you were growing in the axlotl tanks. We tested the cells before allowing you to create them, but you deceived us somehow with Thufir Hawat." They showed him images of the dead Face Dancer. Duncan could see that the Tleilaxu's surprise was genuine.

"Are all of the ghola children similarly tainted?" Sheeana demanded.

"None of them are," Scytale insisted. "Unless they were replaced sometime *after* being decanted from the tanks."

Elyen narrowed her gaze. "He's telling the truth. I see none of the indicators." Sheeana and Garimi silently consulted each other and nodded simultaneously. Then Sheeana said, "Unless he is himself a Face Dancer."

"Scytale isn't likely to be a Face Dancer substitute simply because so few of us trust him anyway," Duncan pointed out. "A Face Dancer would choose to be someone who could more easily move among us."

"Someone like Thufir Hawat," Teg said.

Young Scytale looked greatly disturbed. "Those new Face Dancers were brought back from the Scattering. The Lost Tleilaxu claimed to have modified them in ways we didn't understand. Much to my dismay, I have now learned that even I can't detect one of them. Believe me, I never suspected Hawat."

"Then how did a Face Dancer get aboard, if not grown from the Face Dancer cells in your nullentropy capsule?" Sheeana asked.

"The Face Dancer could already have been posing as one of us when we left Chapterhouse," Duncan mused. "How carefully did you check all of the original hundred and fifty who rushed aboard during the escape?"

Teg shook his head. "But why wait more than two decades to strike? It makes no sense."

"A sleeper agent, perhaps," Sheeana suggested. "Or, could the Face Dancer have been someone else for a long time, and only recently replaced Thufir?"

"Yes, look for a scapegoat to persecute," Scytale said bitterly, slumping in the overlarge interrogation chair. "Preferably a Tleilaxu."

Sheeana had fire in her eyes. "As a precaution, we have sealed all of the ghola children in separate rooms, where they can cause no damage if another of them is a Face Dancer. I've already directed our Suk doctors to take blood samples. They won't escape."

Duncan wondered if her vehemence might suggest that *she* was a Face Dancer. He narrowed his eyes suspiciously and continued to watch her. He would have to watch everyone he could, at all times.

Garimi looked around at their small trusted cadre. "I—or another of our choosing—will remain on the navigation bridge and monitor the no-ship while every single person aboard is brought into the main meeting chamber. Herd them in, account for every one, even the children. Lock the doors and test them all. One by one. Learn the truth."

"What definitive tests can we use?" Teg asked. "On any of us?"

Scytale piped up, "I believe I can develop a reliable method. Using a tissue sample from the Hawat Face Dancer, I will prepare a comparison panel. There are certain . . . techniques I could use. He is one of the new breed brought back by the Lost Tleilaxu, and he differs from the old ones. But with this sample—"

"And why should we trust you?" Garimi said. "Your own purity hasn't yet been proven."

Scytale wore a forlorn expression. "You have to trust someone."

"Do we?"

"I would allow myself to be observed by your experts at all times during the preparations."

Duncan glanced at the Tleilaxu Master. "Scytale's suggestion is a good one."

"Or I can offer another option. When the Face Dancers betrayed my fellow Masters back on Tleilax and our other worlds, some of us had time to fight back. We created a toxin that specifically targets Face Dancers—a selective poison. If you grant me access to laboratory facilities, I can recreate that toxin and deploy it as a gas."

"To what purpose?" Teg asked. Then his expression changed to one of understanding. "Ah, to flood the *Ithaca's* air systems. We would kill any Face Dancers who remain among us."

"The quantities necessary to saturate our ship would be huge," Duncan said, racing through a Mentat calculation to estimate the volume of air within the gigantic vessel, the concentration of gas that would prove lethal to the shape-shifters, the possibility of making others ill and debilitating the crew.

Garimi couldn't believe what she was hearing. "You're suggesting we let this *Tleilaxu* release an unknown gas into our ship? They created the Face Dancers!"

Scytale answered her in a voice heavy with scorn. "You witches fail to think. Don't you see that I myself face a dire threat? These are *new* Face Dancers, brought in from outside by the Lost Tleilaxu—our bastard stepbrothers who cooperated with the Honored Matres to annihilate all the old Masters like myself. Think! If other Face Dancers are aboard the *Ithaca*, then I am in greater personal danger than anyone else. Can't you understand that?"

"Scytale's gas must only be a last resort," Duncan said.

Sheeana looked around the room. "I'll let him begin work on the toxin, but I'd prefer that we identify any Face Dancer directly."

"And interrogate it," Garimi said.

Scytale laughed. "You think you can interrogate a Face Dancer?"

"Never underestimate the Bene Gesserit."

Sheeana nodded. "Until we root out any other infiltrators, until we prove there are no more Face Dancers among us, our only safety lies in staying in large enough groups that the shape-shifters can't attack without being seen."

"What if an overwhelming number of us are already Face Dancers?" Teg said.

"Then we're all lost."

DURING THE LOCKDOWN, each of the ghola children was tested; Leto II submitted first. When the sandworms had turned on Thufir

Hawat, somehow sensing the alien Face Dancer, Leto's shock had seemed genuine. The imagers showed him staring in disbelief at the ruined body that had reverted to its blank Face Dancer state. But Thufir had clearly placed himself in danger, voluntarily going toward Leto when he did not need to. Why would a Face Dancer put himself at risk, unless the copy was so accurate that even the friendship was real?

Leto, ghola of the Tyrant, was many extraordinary things. But he was not a Face Dancer. Scytale's genetic analysis proved it.

Paul Atreides was also found to be clean, along with Chani, Jessica, and the three-year-old Alia, who was intrigued by the needles and samples. Despite the usual suspicions surrounding him, Wellington Yueh was also who he claimed to be.

After Scytale completed the blood and cellular tests, Sheeana was still not satisfied. "Even if we can now trust the ghola children, that means only that other Face Dancers—if there are any more—must be hidden among the rest of us."

"Then we'll test the rest," Garimi said. "Or use Scytale's poison gas. I'll personally submit to any scrutiny, again and again, and I suggest we all do so."

Scytale raised his small hands in alarm. "This test is an intensive one. I'll need to prepare enough panels for all passengers, and that will take a great deal of time."

"Then we will take the time," Sheeana announced. "Doing anything less would be foolhardy."

Why do we find destruction so fascinating? When we see a terrible tragedy, do we think ourselves clever for having evaded it ourselves? Or is our fascination rooted in the thrill and fear of knowing we could be next?

— MOTHER SUPERIOR ODRADE,
Documentation of Consequences

Murbella and Janess—mother and daughter, Mother Commander and Supreme Bashar—orbited the dead world of Richese. They rode in an observation ship, separate from the teams of engineers, who were still leery about the burned-out plague on Chapterhouse. Though the disease had run its course, the Ixians refused to be in a confined space with Murbella and Janess, who had been exposed to it.

Nevertheless, alone in their small ship, the two women had a perfect view of the unfolding test.

More than five years earlier, rebel Honored Matre ships from Tleilax had bombarded Richese, erasing not only the entire population, but also the weapons industries and the half-constructed battle fleet that was to have been delivered to the New Sisterhood. Now that the planet was lifeless, however, Richese was a perfectly appropriate place for the Ixians to demonstrate their new Obliterator weapons.

Murbella opened the commline and spoke to the four accompanying test ships. "You take a smug pleasure in doing this, don't you, Chief Fabricator?"

On the screen, Shayama Sen arched his eyebrows and jerked his head back in a fine display of innocence. "We're testing the weapon you ordered from us, Mother Commander. You asked for a demonstration, rather than taking us at our word. We must prove that our technology functions as advertised."

"And the rivalry between Ix and Richese had nothing to do with your choice of targets?" She barely held her sarcasm in check.

"Richese is just a historical footnote, Mother Commander. Any enjoyment Ixians might have taken from our rivals' unfortunate fate has long since faded." After a pause, Sen added, "We admit, however, that the irony does not escape us."

Since last visiting her high above Chapterhouse, the factory leader sounded subtly changed. Recently, when Sen had come back to deliver full records of all their tests on Ix, he had seemed surprised, even embarrassed. He had followed her suspicious suggestion and used the cellular test on all of his people, with the result that twenty-two Face Dancers had been exposed, all of them working in critical industries.

Murbella would have liked to interrogate them, maybe even apply an Ixian T-probe. But those Face Dancers who weren't immediately killed took their own lives, somehow using a machinelike suicide shutdown in their own brains. The lost opportunity angered her, but she doubted her Sisters would have learned anything from the shape-shifters anyway. Nevertheless, she was glad to have installed eight trusted inspectors to watch over the industrial progress from that point onward.

"Our delivery schedule is tight, Mother Commander, as you demanded," Sen transmitted. "We are arming the ships from Junction as quickly as possible. After seeing these four Obliterators successfully tested, you can't deny that our technology is reliable."

"It seems a shame to waste such destructive power on a target that doesn't harm the true enemy," Janess said. "But we require proof." Both of them had reviewed earlier films of the tests, but those could have been faked.

"I still want to see it with my own eyes," Murbella said. "Then we'll throw everything into a defense against the machine advance."

"Deploying the nodes now," transmitted one of the Ixian pilots. "Please observe."

Four balls of light spat from the quartet of Ixian ships, and the incandescent Obliterators spun like pinwheels toward the cracked world below. They shuddered and expanded as they descended, throwing off rippling waves that grew brighter instead of dampening.

The atmosphere of Richese had already been scorched, its forests and cities leveled in the first chain reaction. Even so, the Ixian-modified weapons found sufficient fuel to set the world ablaze all over again.

Murbella remained silent as she watched the awesome swiftness of the flame fronts. She stared without blinking until her eyes felt dry. The planet flared like an ember in a breeze. Cracks appeared across the continents; orange rifts blazed up. Finally, she spoke to her daughter, not caring that the Ixians could overhear on the open commline. "If we deploy such a weapon in the midst of a thinking-machine battle fleet, it will wreak inconceivable havoc."

"We might actually have a chance," Janess said.

Shayama Sen interrupted through the speakers, "You assume, Mother Commander, that the thinking machines will be foolish enough to fly their ships in such a tight cluster that one weapon will suffice."

"We know a great deal about the Enemy's battle plan and how their fleet has been advancing. They do not use foldspace engines, so they move methodically from one target to the next, step by step. With the thinking machines there are few surprises." Murbella looked at her daughter, then back at the burning planet before snapping orders to the Ixians. "Very well, no need to squander any more Obliterators. When we finally hurl them at machine battleships, that will be demonstration enough for me. I want at least ten Obliterators aboard each of our new warships. No more delays! We have waited too long already."

"It will be done, Mother Commander," Sen said.

Murbella chewed at her lower lip as she watched Richese continue to blaze. It wasn't like the Chief Fabricator to be so cooperative, failing to demand additional payment. Perhaps, after seeing countless worlds already destroyed, the Ixians had at last recognized their true enemy.

Whether we see them or not, there are nets everywhere, encompassing our individual and collective lives. Sometimes it is necessary to ignore them, for the sake of our own sanity.

—ship's log, entry of
DUNCAN IDAHO

Face Dancers aboard.

In her quarters with little Alia and twelve-year-old Leto, Jessica felt very much like a mother again—after all these centuries. The three of them had a shared past and bloodline, but no other knowledge or memories in common. Not yet. To Jessica it seemed that they were little more than actors memorizing lines and playing roles, trying to be who they were *supposed* to be. Her body was only seventeen, but she felt much older as she comforted the two younger ones.

"What is a Face Dancer?" three-year-old Alia asked, toying with a sharp knife she kept at her side. Since the time she could walk, the girl had harbored a fascination for weapons, and she often sought permission to practice with them, rather than playing with more appropriate toys. "Are they coming to get us?"

"They're already *in* the ship," Leto said, still shaken. He could not believe that Thufir had been a Face Dancer and that he hadn't known it. "That's why we were all tested."

"No others have been found yet," Jessica said. She and Thufir had been decanted in the same year. In the crèche, she had been raised with the ghola of the warrior-Mentat, and never had she noticed any change in his personality. It did not seem possible that Thufir could have been a Face Dancer from the very beginning.

The real Hawat, Master of Assassins and former weapons master of House Atreides, had been a veteran of numerous successful campaigns like Bashar Miles Teg, serving three generations of House Atreides. No wonder Sheeana and the Bene Gesserits had considered him an invaluable ally. That was why they had wanted to bring him back, and now it was obvious why their memory-triggering crisis hadn't worked. Thufir was not really Thufir, and perhaps never had been.

Now—unless clean cells were found to grow a new ghola—the people aboard the *Ithaca* would never have access to Hawat's Mentat and tactical skills. In fact, Jessica realized that after all this time, the ghola project had produced very little that could be used to help them. Only Yueh, Stilgar, and Liet-Kynes had been reawakened to their past lives, but the latter two were gone. And Yueh, while a skilled Suk doctor, was not a particularly great asset to their team.

He killed my Duke Leto—again.

With the Face Dancer threat, the missing explosive mines, and the various incidents of sabotage, the need for the gholas and their old skills had become more urgent. The remaining unawakened ghola children must have special abilities; Jessica knew they had all been brought back for a reason. Each of them. Paul, Chani, and she were all of an appropriate age; even Leto II should be old enough. Gradual, careful measures could not possibly be sufficient. Not anymore.

She sighed. If not now, then when would their historical abilities be useful? *I must have my memories back!*

Jessica could offer so much more to benefit the no-ship, if given the opportunity. She felt like a husk of a person without her original life. In her quarters, she stood up so swiftly that she startled both Alia and Leto. "You two should return to your rooms." Her gruff voice invited no argument. "There's something important I have to do. These Bene Gesserits are cowards, though they don't realize it. They can no longer afford to be."

In some ways, Sheeana was brash and impetuous, but in other ways overly cautious. Jessica knew someone, however, who would not shy away from inflicting pain upon her.

"Who are you going to see?" Leto asked.

"Garimi."

THE HARD-LINE REVEREND MOTHER regarded her with a stony expression, then smiled slowly. "Why should I do this? Are you mad?"

"Just pragmatic."

"Do you have any understanding of how much this is going to hurt?"

"I am prepared for it." She looked at Garimi's dark, curly hair, her flat and unattractive features; Jessica, by contrast, was the very ideal of classical beauty, designed by the Bene Gesserit to play the role of a seductress, a breeding mother whose features had been copied again and again for centuries after her death. "And I know, Proctor Superior, that if anyone can inflict that pain, you are prepared to do so."

Garimi seemed caught between amusement and uneasiness. "I have imagined countless ways to twist the knife in you, Jessica. I have often considered how much harm your actions did to the old Sisterhood. You derailed our entire Kwisatz Haderach program, created a monster we couldn't control. After Paul, as a direct consequence of your defiance, we suffered thousands of years under the Tyrant. For what conceivable reason would I want to awaken you? You betrayed us."

"So you say." Garimi's words struck like hurled stones. The woman had tormented Jessica for years, as well as poor Leto II. Jessica knew all the accusations, understood how the conservative Bene Gesserit faction viewed her. But she had not previously endured the shocking depth of hatred and anger that the woman now showed toward her. "Your own words reveal a great deal, Garimi. The *old* Sisterhood. Where are your thoughts? We are already living in the future."

"That doesn't negate the terrible pain you caused."

"You keep insisting that I should bear that guilt. But how can I feel it, if I don't remember? Are you content with me as a scapegoat, a whipping boy for all the imagined wrongs of the past? Sheeana wants my memories restored so that I can help us. But *you*, Garimi, should be just as eager to awaken me. Admit it—can you think of a better Bene Gesserit punishment than drowning me in the unforgivable things you say I've done to the Sisterhood? Awaken me! Make me see it for myself!"

Garimi reached out and grabbed her wrist. Instinctively, Jessica tried to pull away, but was unsuccessful. The other woman's expression hardened. "I am going to Share with you. I'm going to give you all my thoughts and memories so that you'll *know*." Garimi leaned closer. "I will dump into your brain those hundreds of generations of past lives that occurred after you committed your crime, so that you can see the full scope and consequences of what you did." She pulled Jessica up against her.

"That's not possible. Only Reverend Mothers can Share." Jessica tried to scramble backward.

Garimi's eyes were steely. "And you are a Reverend Mother—or you were. Therefore, one lives within you." She clasped the back of Jessica's head, grabbed her bronze hair and yanked her closer. Garimi leaned her own forehead down, and pressed it against Jessica's. "I can make this work. I'm strong enough. Can you imagine why I'm doing it? Perhaps the grief will be enough to paralyze you!"

Jessica fought back. "Or it will . . . make . . . me . . . stronger."

She'd wanted her own memories, yes—but had never offered to accept all of Garimi's experiences, or those numerous ancestors who had lived through the persecutions of the God Emperor of Dune, her own grandson. All those who had survived the Famine Times, struggling to overcome their addiction to melange, which was no longer available. The horrors of those generations had left deep scars on the human psyche.

Jessica did not want that at all. *Garimi insists that I caused it.*

She felt something inside her head and resisted, but Garimi was stronger, forcing the Sharing upon her, pouring memories, unleashing them. Hammers pounded Jessica's skull from the inside, strong enough to crack through bone and break out. She heard a snapping sound in the blackness, and wondered if Garimi had won. . . .

SHAKEN, JESSICA—THE *real* Jessica, bound concubine to Duke Leto Atreides, Reverend Mother of the Bene Gesserit—looked around herself with a new wonder she had never imagined possible. Though she saw only the walls of the no-ship, she recalled how good her life had been with the Duke and with their son Paul. She remembered the shell-blue sky of Caladan, the spectacular sunrises on Arrakis.

In the end, she had beaten Garimi. Now she marched out of the angry woman's quarters, swaying and saturated with the knowledge. That flood of memories was a mixed blessing and a new burden, for she was without her beloved Duke Leto.

The sudden emptiness made her feel as if she were plunging into an endless pit. *Leto, my Leto! Why couldn't the Sisters have brought you back at the same time, like Paul and Chani? And damn you, Yueh, for taking him from me twice!*

She felt profoundly alone, her heart drained and her mind left with mere memories and knowledge. Jessica was determined to find a way to make herself useful to her Sisters once more.

Returning to her quarters, she found Alia waiting for her. Possessing a sharp intelligence far beyond her years, the girl looked her over calmly and said, "Mother, I told Dr. Yueh you would have your memories back. Now he's even more afraid of you. You could kill him with a look. I chased him and kicked him for you."

Jessica fought back her automatic hatred of Yueh. The old Yueh. "You mustn't do that. Especially not now." The Traitor had been right to fear the return of her memories, even though she had already known of his crimes and forgiven him. *But that was with my head, not with my heart.* As she stood there, Jessica's restored memories and emotions drove the dagger in deeper.

With a rush of emotion she found herself unable to keep from reaching out and hugging Alia fiercely. Then she looked upon her daughter for the very first time. "I am your mother again."

A test must be defined before it can be useful. What are the parameters? What is the accuracy? Too often a test does nothing more than analyze the tester herself.

—*The Bene Gesserit Acolytes' Handbook*

The death of the Hawat Face Dancer couldn't be kept secret for long. Everyone was accounted for and locked away while Sheeana and her cadre of tested individuals performed a full count, isolated and approved security teams, and then guided all of the ship's inhabitants into the main meeting hall. That giant chamber could easily house hundreds of people for days, if need be, and if enough food was brought in. Meanwhile, Garimi remained up on the navigation deck, monitoring the *Ithaca* by herself.

Since all hands—at least the *known* ones—were sealed in the meeting hall, any hidden traitors could very well be trapped inside. In the next few days, over the course of meticulous testing, any remaining Face Dancers among them would be rooted out.

At first, the younger children born during the journey seemed to think it was a game, but they soon grew restless; the people became uncomfortable and suspicious, wondering why only a handful of individuals were allowed to come and go on mysterious assignments. And why was the horrid little Tleilaxu one of the trusted ones? Many of those aboard still viewed Scytale with open scorn, but he was accustomed to such treatment. The Tleilaxu race had always been despised and distrusted. Now who was to blame?

Working frantically over the past day, he and the Suk doctors had assembled enough analytical kits to perform a genetic comparison on every untested individual. As a backup plan, he had also created enough of his Face Dancer–specific toxic gas to fill numerous canisters, though Sheeana was not ready to approve such a hazardous experiment—not yet. They didn't trust him enough and kept the gas under their strict control.

He didn't trust them entirely, either. After all, he was a Tleilaxu Master, perhaps the last one in existence. Secretly, he put together a more startling, fail-safe test, knowing full well what he was doing. He told no one of it.

When all was ready, Scytale sat in a front row for what he expected to be an important process of revelation. He watched the uneasy Bene Gesserits, Suk doctors, archivists, and proctors. Out in the audience, Teg sat next to the Rabbi and two Bene Gesserit Sisters. The ghola children were a few rows away, each of them already proven to be untainted. Duncan Idaho waited by one of the sealed doors, and male Bene Gesserits guarded the other exit points.

While the gathered passengers waited, Sheeana spoke from the front of the meeting chamber, her words clear and uncompromising, with an edge of Voice. "We have discovered a Face Dancer among us, and we believe there are more in this room."

A moment of shocked silence extended uneasily as she attempted to make eye contact with every individual. Scytale was not surprised that no one stepped forward. The old Rabbi looked simultaneously indignant and lost without the rest of his people. From the seat next to the old man, Teg told him to be patient. The Rabbi glared but did not argue.

"We have created a foolproof test." Sheeana sounded weary even though her voice boomed. "It will be tedious and time-consuming. But you will all submit to it."

"I hope none of you has anything better to do." Duncan crossed his arms over his chest and flashed a grim smile. "The doors will remain guarded until this process is complete."

Scytale and the Suk doctors came forward to the stage, carrying kits, syringes, and chemical swabs. "As each one of you is cleared, our ranks of reliable allies will grow. No Face Dancer can elude this scrutiny."

"Who was this Face Dancer you caught?" one of the Sisters asked, an undertone of anxiety in her voice. "And why do you assume there are others among us? What is your evidence?" When Sheeana explained how the worms had killed Thufir Hawat, stunned murmurs rippled through the audience.

The Bashar called from his seat, with an edge of guilt and revulsion in his tone. "We know that the false Thufir could not have been responsible for all the sabotage incidents we have on record. He was with me, in person, when several of the known incidents occurred."

"How do I know you're not *all* Face Dancers?" The Rabbi rose to his feet and glared at Sheeana, the Suk doctors, and especially Scytale. "Your behavior has never been comprehensible to me." Teg tugged him back down.

Sheeana ignored the old man's question and pointed to the front row. "I will take the first subject now."

Two female Suk doctors moved forward with their kits, and Sheeana said, "Make yourselves comfortable. This will take a while."

For Scytale, though, this process was primarily a diversion—and even the Bene Gesserits didn't know it. Feeling trapped, any Face Dancer in the audience would be trying to find a way to escape detection. Therefore, the Tleilaxu Master had to act precipitously, before any hidden shape-shifters could make a move. Watching the large audience closely, he fingered the small device he carried.

While the slow analytical procedure was certainly reliable, Scytale had fashioned his secret plan based on what he knew of the old Face Dancers created by the original Tleilaxu Masters. He was betting that the new shape-shifters from the Scattering were similar, at least in their fundamental responses. They must have emerged from the same basic blueprint. If so, he might know how to expose them, a weak and secondary test . . . but its very unexpectedness might work in his favor.

In the center of the meeting chamber, the Suk doctors performed their first test on a submissive Sister. She extended her hand, waiting for a drop of blood to be drawn.

Without warning, Scytale activated his high-pitched whistle emitter. A shrill tone warbled up and down, intense but faint, above the range of most human hearing. The original Face Dancers had once communicated with the Tleilaxu in a coded whistling language, a secret set of programming notes burned into their neurological structures. Scytale believed the irresistible noise would make any Face Dancer lose his disguise, at least temporarily.

Suddenly, out in the tiers of seats, the old Rabbi flickered, and his body convulsed. His leathery face shifted and smoothed behind his beard. He let out a cry of surprised outrage and lunged to his feet. Now the old man was unexpectedly supple, wiry, and vicious. His face was flat with sunken eyes and a pug nose, like a bare skull made of half-melted wax.

"Face Dancer!" someone shouted.

The Rabbi became a whirlwind and threw himself against the Bene Gesserits.

Never underestimate your enemy—or your allies.

—MILES TEG,
Memoirs of an Old Commander

Due to his constant complaints, negative attitude, and frail appearance, everyone aboard had dismissed or misjudged the old Rabbi. As had Miles Teg.

In moves as swift and deadly as a lasbeam, the Face Dancer slammed the Bashar with a blow that would have shattered his skull, if it had struck squarely. Just in time, Teg recoiled with a flash of inhuman speed. It was enough to save his life, but even so, the attack stunned him.

Abruptly, the Rabbi killed two Sisters on the other side of him, then moved in a direct, murderous line toward the nearest exit, clearing the way with a flurry of deadly blows. From hidden pockets in his dark, conservative clothes, the Face Dancer withdrew a small throwing dagger for each hand. The blades were no longer than his thumbs, but he hurled them with precision. The sharp tips, undoubtedly poisoned, pierced the throats of two male Bene Gesserits who guarded the door. With barely a sound, the Rabbi shoved their dying bodies out of the way and plunged out into the corridor.

Scytale urgently scanned the crowd to make certain that this one escaping enemy did not divert attention from any other Face Dancers hidden among those gathered in the chamber. The Tleilaxu saw no other sudden shiftings.

Sheeana shouted for others to pursue the Rabbi. "We know who he is, but he can change his shape. Now we have to track him down."

One of the Sisters tried to use the ship's intercom to warn Garimi, but got no response. "It's been damaged."

"Fix it." Sheeana realized that the Rabbi had had sufficient time during their quarantine in this large chamber to subtly perform more sabotage.

Dr. Yueh rushed to a groaning Teg and bent to check the severity of his injury; beside him, the two fallen Sisters were obviously dead. The look on the ghola doctor's face was of dismay rather than vindication. As he examined Teg, he murmured, as if trying to make sense of the situation. "The Rabbi gave me the sample of the ghola baby's cells. He must have taken Piter de Vries's cells from storage and tricked me. He knew what I would do, how I would react."

Duncan glanced from Yueh and Teg to Sheeana. "The connection is obvious to me now. Thufir Hawat and the Rabbi. Why didn't I see it?"

Sheeana caught her breath as she suddenly realized the same thing. "Both went down to the planet of the Handlers!"

Duncan nodded. "Hawat and the Rabbi were alone together during the hunt of the Honored Matres. You all had to fight your way back to the lighter after you discovered that the Handlers were Face Dancers."

"Of course." Sheeana's face was grave. "Those two came running in from the forest at the last moment. It seems they didn't escape the Handlers after all."

"So the original Rabbi and Thufir—" Duncan began.

"Both dead long ago, replaced by Face Dancers on the planet, and their bodies discarded during the hunt."

Finally achieving Mentat focus, Duncan jumped to the next obvious conclusion. "Then it's been more than five years since the substitutions. Five years! In all that time, the Hawat and Rabbi duplicates must have been waiting for their opportunity, killing gholas and axlotl tanks, sabotaging our life-support systems, forcing us to stop at Qelso, where we were vulnerable to discovery by our pursuers. Did the Enemy pick up our trail there? So far, we've managed to elude the net, but now that the Face Dancers have been exposed—"

Sheeana paled. "And what about the stolen mines? What did the Rabbi do with the explosive mines? He can set them off at any time, if he gets to them."

Starting to recover but clearly woozy, Teg was already moving toward the door. "That Face Dancer knows he has to seize the no-ship before we can kill him. He will head for the navigation bridge."

"Garimi is there," Sheeana said. "Let's hope she can stop him."

BY THE TIME the Face Dancer reached the navigation bridge, he had resumed his disguise as the Rabbi. He contained all the memories, experiences, and personality details of the old man, and much more. The frail and frightened-looking Rabbi burst into the chamber, startling Garimi. "What are you doing up here?" she asked.

His eyes were wide and panicked as if he thought she could offer him protection. His spectacles had fallen off. "Face Dancer!" he panted, staggering toward her. "He's killing Bene Gesserits!"

Garimi spun toward the intercom panel to contact Sheeana—and the Rabbi struck. His deadly blow came close to her neck, but she sensed the movement and turned at the last possible moment. The side of his fist drove down on her shoulder instead. She slid from her chair, and the Rabbi dove at her again.

Garimi launched a kick up at him from the deck, aiming for one of the old man's knobby and uncertain knees, but he sprang away like a coiled panther. The Rabbi let out a feral yowl as Garimi leapt to her feet again and assumed a defensive stance. Her lower lip curled. "Clever, Rabbi. Even now that I know what you are, I can hardly smell any Face Dancer stink on you."

With a yank and a twist, the Rabbi uprooted an anchored chair and swung it at her. She ducked and reached up to grab the chair as it whistled over her head. Tearing it out of his hands, her pull was enough to knock him to the floor.

When the Rabbi rose to his feet again, he shifted his body to mimic the form of a ferocious Futar. His body bulged with muscles, his teeth became sharp and elongated, and his claws slashed the air. Garimi stumbled back to get out of his killing reach and hammered her hand down on the intercom. "Sisters! Face Dancer on the navigation bridge!"

The Futar lunged, and his sharp, newly grown claws ripped her robes. Using wild and frantic punches intended more to hurt her foe than protect her own life, Garimi shattered his ribs. With an outraged kick that employed the full force of her heel, she smashed his left femur out of its hip socket.

But the Futar rolled as he collapsed, spun in a blur, and before she could feel a moment of victory, he snapped Garimi's neck. She dropped with barely a sigh. In a purely spiteful gesture, he ripped out her throat before calmly reshaping his body to his blank Face Dancer state. He wiped blood from his face with one sleeve.

More broken than even his own shape-shifter abilities could easily heal, the Rabbi crawled and then limped to the *Ithaca*'s main controls. He heard running feet in the corridor, so he sealed the navigation bridge, applied emergency locks, and activated a mutiny-defense protocol.

In the years he had maintained his disguise, the Face Dancer had covertly sampled the skin cells of Duncan Idaho, Sheeana, and Bashar Miles Teg. Now his hands flowed into the proper identification prints so that the no-ship's highly secure controls responded to him. The sealed doors would stand against any intrusion. Eventually the Bene Gesserits would find a way to break in, but by that time he would have completed his mission.

His thinking-machine masters would be alerted. And they would come.

Long ago, he had studied how to operate the Holtzman engines. Estimating the coordinates as best he could, not worried about the lack of a Navigator, the Face Dancer folded space and plunged the *Ithaca* across the galaxy. The ship tumbled out into a different stellar region, not far from Omnius's advancing forces. He reconfigured the ship's comsystems and triggered a locator beacon. His superiors knew the signal.

The thinking machines would respond swiftly. Already the Face Dancer could sense the hungry, invisible tachyon net coming closer. This time there would be no escape. The no-ship would be completely trapped.

Even small opponents can be deadly.
> —Bene Gesserit Analytical Report on the Tleilaxu Problem

By the time Duncan, Sheeana, and Teg reached the navigation bridge, the thick hatches were sealed and locked. Impregnable. The bridge had been designed to remain secure against even an army.

Within moments, other Sisters followed, having first raced to the armory and obtained hand weapons: poisonous needle guns, stunners, and a high-powered lascutter. None of those devices would be sufficient. Rushing forward, the ghola children joined the crowd outside the sealed bridge, among them Paul, Chani, Jessica, Leto II, and young Alia.

Duncan could feel the change when the no-ship lurched through foldspace. "He's at the controls, moving us!"

"Garimi is dead, then," Sheeana concluded.

"The Face Dancer is going to take us directly to the Enemy," Teg said.

"Now is the time to use Scytale's poison gas to kill the Face Dancer." Sheeana turned to two of the Sisters standing in the corridor. "Find the Tleilaxu and take him to our guarded cabinet. Get one of the canisters, and we will flood the air on the bridge with the gas."

"No time for that," Duncan said. "We've got to get in there!"

Alia sounded eerily cool and intelligent as she announced, "I can get inside."

Duncan looked at the girl. To him, the echo-memories evoked by this child were unsettling. The original Duncan had never known her as a youngster—he had been killed by Sardaukar while Jessica was barely pregnant. But he did have vivid memories of an older Alia as his lover, in another life. But that was all history. Now it might as well be myth or legend.

He bent down to talk to her. "How? There isn't much time."

"I'm small enough." With a flick of her eyes, the little girl indicated the narrow air-exchanger vents leading into the command deck. She was far more diminutive than even Scytale.

Sheeana was already removing the grate. "There are baffles, filters, and bars in the way. How will you get through?"

"Give me a cutter. And a needle gun. I'll get the door open for you as soon as I can. From the inside."

When Alia had what she needed, Duncan hoisted the girl up to where she could squirm inside the tiny tunnel. Not yet four years old, she weighed very little. Jessica stood watching, looking more mature than she had been only a few days earlier, but even seeing her "daughter" placed into such a dangerous situation, she did not protest.

Cold and intent, the child clamped the cutter between her teeth, tucked the needle pistol into her small shirt, and began to creep through the vent. The distance between the chambers was not far, but each half meter was a battle. She exhaled, making herself as small as possible so that she could wriggle ahead.

Outside, the others began pounding on the sealed door as a distraction. They used heavy cutters that sparked and fumed, screeching through the dense, armored barricade a millimeter at a time. The Face Dancer would know they'd need hours to cut through into the navigation bridge. Alia was confident the Face Dancer would not expect an ambush from her.

She encountered the first barricade, a set of plasteel bars interwoven with a filtration grid. The dense mat was coated with neutralizing chemicals, and charged with a faint electrostatic film to scrub all drugs and poisons from the air that passed into the bridge. With the filter in place, Scytale's toxic gas would not have worked, even if they'd been able to release it.

Elbows digging into her sides, Alia took the cutter from her teeth and with jerky wrist movements sliced away the bars. Gently, she set the screen in front of her, careful not to make a noise, and crawled over it. The sharp edges scratched her chest and legs, but Alia cared nothing for the pain.

Similarly, she passed through a second grid, and then found herself at the last opening, from which she could observe the Face Dancer through the grille. His appearance flickered occasionally, sometimes reverting to the old man's shape, sometimes becoming a Futar, but primarily the Face Dancer wore a blank, skull-like visage. Even before she saw the torn body of Garimi on the deck, Alia knew not to underestimate this opponent.

With the tip of the glowing cutter, she sliced the tiny fasteners that held the last screen in place. Moving as silently as she could, she held the plate where it was and squirmed to free the needle gun from her shirt. She tensed, then drew a deep breath, waiting for the right moment.

I will have only a brief instant of surprise, so I must use it to full advantage.

The Face Dancer was working the controls, probably transmitting a signal to the mysterious Enemy, presumably more of his own kind. Every second she delayed would place the *Ithaca* in greater danger.

Suddenly the Face Dancer jerked his head up and snapped his gaze toward the grille. Somehow he had sensed her. Now, without hesitating, Alia shoved the loosened screen toward him like a projectile. He dodged out of the way, reacting just as she had expected. Still lying prone in the ventilation shaft, she extended the needle gun in front of her and fired seven times. Three of the deadly needles found their target: two in the Face Dancer's eyes, another in the artery on his neck.

He spasmed, thrashed, and fell lifeless. Wriggling out of the air shaft, Alia dropped to the floor, recovered her balance, and glanced to verify that Garimi was indeed dead, before casually walking to the door. With her nimble fingers she disarmed the internal security measures and unsealed the hatch from the inside.

Duncan and Teg stood there holding weapons, afraid of what might emerge. The little girl met them with a placid expression. "Our Face Dancer is no longer a problem."

Over Alia's shoulder they could see the inhuman form sprawled next to an overturned chair. Small trickles of blood leaked from the dart wounds in his eyes, and he wore a full crimson collar of blood around his neck. On the floorplates lay the mangled Garimi.

Sheeana narrowed her gaze. "I see that you are a born killer."

Alia was unruffled. "So I've been told. Didn't you bring the ghola children back for our abilities? This is what I do best."

Duncan hurried to the no-ship's controls to assess what the false Rabbi had done. He extended his senses and was dismayed to see the deadly strands of the shimmering net suddenly appear and intensify all around them. Unbreakable. The trap was bright enough, powerful enough, that everyone could see it.

Teg rushed to a scanner station. "Duncan! Ships approaching—a lot of them! The Face Dancer has brought us right to the doorstep of the Enemy. We're tagged, and the net has locked onto us."

"After all these years, we are caught in the strands." Duncan swept his gaze across all of them. "At least, we're about to find out who our Enemy really is."

Our shared humanity should, by definition, make us allies. In sad fact, however, our very similarities often appear to be vast differences and insurmountable obstacles.

—MOTHER COMMANDER MURBELLA,
address to the New Sisterhood

G iven the critical shortage of time, the thousands of newly equipped Guildships could not undergo thorough shakedowns and test runs. The mass-produced Obliterators were loaded aboard the heavily armored vessels that had been built at Junction as well as seventeen satellite shipyards. Crews made preparations to go to the front lines.

Fresh from conscription across hundreds of at-risk planets, novice commanders received only minimal training, barely sufficient to stand against the Enemy at numerous vulnerable points as humanity tried to draw its line in space. Murbella knew that despite their determination and bravery, and no matter how much training and practice they received, most of the human fighters would be annihilated.

In the months after the plague had run its course on Chapterhouse, the Mother Commander had opened her doors to displaced refugees from any evacuated planet. At first they were frightened to settle on the once-quarantined world, but then they had begun to stream in. With so few options available to them, the ragtag groups accepted the Sisterhood's offer of sanctuary in exchange for performing vital labors in the war effort. Politics and old factions had to be set aside. Now every life was devoted to preparing for the last stand against the oncoming forces of Omnius.

From Buzzell, Reverend Mother Corysta sent the incredible news that the giant seaworms wreaking havoc with soostone operations also produced a kind of spice. Murbella immediately suspected some kind of Guild experiment. It could not be a natural occurrence. Corysta suggested that the worms be hunted and harvested, but the Mother Commander could not think that far ahead. A new source of spice mattered only if the human race survived the Enemy.

Mother Commander Murbella called a grand war council for delegates of the front-line planets that were in imminent danger of attack by thinking-machine forces. Despite their indignation, every one of them had undergone cellular testing to root out hidden Face Dancers. Murbella took no chances; the insidious shape-shifters could be anywhere.

In the Keep's grand meeting room, she strode down the length of the elaccawood table to her designated seat. Using her Bene Gesserit powers of close observation, she studied those assembled, all of them driven here by desperation. Murbella tried to view these representatives in their various costumes and uniforms as military leaders, essentially generals in the last great battle for humanity. The people in this room would guide the thrown-together clusters of ships and make a thousand defiant stands. But were they the quality of heroes the human race needed?

When she turned to face the delegates, Murbella saw the uneasiness in their eyes and smelled fear-sweat in the air. The vast Enemy fleet surged forward like a flame front across the map of the galaxy, rolling over star system after star system, heading inexorably toward Chapterhouse and the remaining worlds at the heart of the Old Empire.

After moving among the various embattled worlds and studying their preparations, Murbella had secured alliances with these planetary leaders, warlords, commercial conglomerates, and smaller units of government. Leto II's vision of the Golden Path had fragmented humanity so that they no longer followed a single charismatic leader, and now Murbella had to repair that damage. Diversity might once have been a path to survival, but unless the numerous worlds and armies could stand together against the far greater foe, they would all perish.

If the Tyrant's prescience was so formidable, how could he not have foreseen the existence of the great machine empire, no matter how far away it was? How could the God Emperor not have known that another titanic conflict awaited humankind? She felt a faint shudder. Or *had* he, and everything was playing out exactly as the Tyrant planned?

After considerable effort, she had won a critical internal battle when the various leaders agreed that the strongest defense came from a unified plan—*her* plan—rather than a hundred independent and hopeless defensive battles. To get her message across, she'd had to cut through the stubborn tentacles of various planetary bureaucracies. Nothing was easy in this war.

Feeling the burdens of her position, Murbella rapped a large spherical stone on the table, producing a loud, echoing boom that called the meeting to order. "You all know why you're here. We must make our last stands, a thousand of them across space. Many of us will die—or *all* of us will die. There are no alternatives. The only questions are how soon we will die, and how it will happen. Do we choose to die free and fighting to the last . . . or defeated and running?"

The room resounded with a cacophony of voices, accents, and languages, though she had insisted that they all speak the common Galach tongue. She used Voice to cut through the clamor. "The machines are coming! If we cooperate and do not retreat in the face of our foe, we just might have the means of stopping them dead in their tracks."

She noted Guild officials and Ixian engineers in the audience. Given the short delivery schedule, some of the warship construction had been unavoidably slapdash, but her handful of Bene Gesserit inspectors and line supervisors had overseen the operations.

"Our weapons and ships are now ready, but before we proceed I have one question for all of you." She skewered the leaders with her gaze. If she'd still been an Honored Matre, her eyes would have blazed orange. "Do you have the resolve and courage to do what is necessary?"

"Do *you?*" bellowed a bearded man from a very small planet in a remote system.

Murbella rapped her sonic stone again. "My New Sisterhood will bear the brunt of the initial clash against the thinking machines. We have already fought them in one star system after another, destroying many of their ships, and we survived their plagues here on Chapter-house. But this war will never be won on individual battlefields." She gestured, and Janess worked the controls. "Look at this, all of you."

Startling the assemblage, a large holographic projection appeared, fill-ing the open space of the Keep's great meeting room with detailed maps of the galaxy's numerous solar systems. An advancing blot indicated the thinking machines' conquests, like a tidal wave drowning every system in its path. The darkness of defeat and extermination had already blackened most of the known systems in the regions of the Scattering.

"We have to focus our efforts. Because they don't use foldspace engines, the Enemy proceeds from system to system. We know their path, and therefore we can put ourselves directly in their way." Murbella stood amidst the simulated stars and planets. Her finger darted from point to point, the glowing stars and habitable planets that lay in the Enemy's path. "We've got to hold the line—here, and here, and every-where! Only by combining all of our ships, commanders, and weapons can we hope to halt the Enemy." She swept her hand through the shim-mering images that were just ahead of the encroaching thinking machines. "Any other choice would be cowardice."

"Do you call us cowards?" the bearded man roared.

A merchant stood. "Surely we can negotiate—"

Murbella cut him off. "The thinking machines do not want a partic-ular world. Nor are they searching for gems, spice, or any other goods. There is nothing we can offer them to sue for peace. They do not com-promise, and will keep pursuing us no matter where we run." She looked at the blustering man and said, "By fleeing conflict today, you *could* sur-vive for a time. But there'll be no escape for your children or grandchil-dren. The machines will slaughter them, down to the last infant. Do you value your life over theirs? Then, yes, I do call you cowards."

Despite the murmurs in the hall, no one else spoke out. On the giant star display, a line of tiny fireworks erupted along the interface line between the machine-conquered territories and the vulnerable human planets.

Murbella's gaze moved across the audience. "Each of us is responsi-ble for stopping the Enemy from crossing this line. Failure means death for the human race."

*True loyalty is an unshakable force. The difficulty is in determin-
ing exactly where a person's allegiance lies. Often that bond is only
to oneself.*

—DUNCAN IDAHO,
A Thousand Lives

The leader of the Face Dancer myriad arrived at Synchrony, bearing
a long-anticipated gift for the evermind. The thinking machines
still viewed Khrone as nothing more than a servant, a delivery boy.

Omnius and Erasmus never suspected that the shape-shifters might
be formulating their own schemes independent of both humanity and
the thinking machines. Naïve, oblivious, and so very typical. The evermind would treasure this new melange for his grandiose plans, and it
would keep the machines from doubting Khrone and his Face Dancers.
He intended to make the most of it.

With their brutality and arrogance, the "old man and woman" had
long ago given the new shape-shifters reasons to break their loyalty.
Erasmus fancied himself reminiscent of a Face Dancer, but much
more . . . and similar to a human, but greater. And like Omnius . . . but
infinitely more powerful.

Khrone and the rest of the myriad had never truly given their allegiance to the thinking machines. He saw no more reason to accept
slavery under machine masters than to have accepted the domination
of the original Tleilaxu who had created their predecessors so many

centuries ago. Forced allies, second-class partners . . . The evermind was merely one more layer in the grand pyramid of those who *thought* they controlled the Face Dancers.

After so much effort, Khrone couldn't wait until he could drop this endless deception. He was no longer amused by the number of masks he had to wear and the complicated threads he continued to pull. Soon, though . . .

Alone, he flew his small ship directly to the heart of the modern machine empire. The location of Synchrony had been genetically programmed into all new Face Dancers, like some sort of homing beacon. As he entered the airspace over the technological metropolis, Khrone let his thoughts drift back to Ix. The fabricators and engineers had successfully completed a special demonstration at dead Richese, and now Obliterators were emerging from the production lines. Mother Commander Murbella had been impressed with the power she witnessed, and she'd been entirely convinced by the show. Fool!

But not in all things. In her prior meeting with Chief Fabricator Shayama Sen, Murbella had forced him to administer a biological test that proved he wasn't a Face Dancer. Given what had happened, Khrone was vastly relieved that he had *not* replaced the man, as he'd been tempted to do many times in the past.

Face Dancers already controlled most of the important positions on Ix, and when the Chief Fabricator blithely distributed the biological tests to all the main engineers and team leaders (never suspecting there might actually be a majority of Face Dancers among them), the myriad had been forced to act precipitously. When an indignant Sen announced the Sisterhood's suspicions, the infiltrators had finally been forced to kill him and assume his identity. They had already taken care of the troublesome Bene Gesserit line supervisors and production monitors. And so the deception continued, unmarred.

Enhanced Face Dancers quickly subsumed the last humans among the leaders of Ix. Then, working together, they contrived all the necessary tests, selected the required scapegoats, substituted convincing data, and submitted everything to Chapterhouse in accordance with Murbella's demands. All in perfect order.

After surviving the plague, the Sisterhood's leadership had forced all human protectors to finally band together against the thinking-machine fleet, to defend their race rather than simply their own worlds. The hundreds of new ships that emerged from the Junction shipyards were being loaded with enough Obliterators for a final, concerted stand against the oncoming wave of Omnius's ships. So far, the evermind's forces had encountered very little significant resistance, and now they were on their way to Chapterhouse. For the last time.

Khrone had actually been tempted to let the Reverend Mothers and their last-stand defenders succeed. Given enough functional Obliterators, they could send the machine fleet reeling. Humans and thinking machines could easily annihilate each other. However, that was simply too . . . easy. Kralizec demanded much more! This time, the fundamental shift in the universe would get rid of both rivals, leaving all the remnants of the Old Empire for the Face Dancers.

Khrone felt completely confident in the future as he landed his ship in the convoluted labyrinth of copper steeples, golden turrets, and interlocked silvery buildings. Sentient structures shifted aside to allow a place for his ship to settle. When the small vessel came to rest on a smooth quicksilver plain, Khrone stepped out, breathing air that smelled of smoke and hot metal. He did not spare a moment to look around.

The central machine world was based entirely on theatrics. He suspected the touch of Erasmus in this, though Omnius had such an overblown perception of his own importance that he no doubt wanted all machine minions to bow before him as a god—even if the evermind had to program them to do so.

Rectangular plates appeared on the ground, laying down an interlocked pathway that guided Khrone to his destination in the magnificent arched cathedral. Head held high, he strode along carrying his precious package, refusing to look like a supplicant summoned before his lord. Rather, Khrone was a man on a mission with important business to complete. Omnius would be pleased to have the concentrated ultraspice for use with his cloned Kwisatz Haderach. . . .

Inside the ostentatious hall, the ghola of Baron Harkonnen stood with young Paolo at a nine-level pyramid chess board. Glowering, the Baron knocked over a rook on one of the top levels. "That move is not allowed, Paolo."

"It enabled me to win, didn't it?" Pleased with his ingenuity, the young man crossed his arms over his chest.

"By cheating."

"It's a new rule. If we are as important as you say, we should be allowed to make up our own rules."

A flash of anger crossed the Baron's face, and then vanished into a chuckle. "I see your reasoning—and that you are learning."

When Khrone stepped forward, they looked at him with identical expressions of distaste. "Oh, it's you." The Baron sounded entirely different from when he'd been tormented by the Face Dancers. "I didn't think we'd be seeing you again. Bored of Caladan?"

Ignoring them, Khrone noted that the two principal thinking machines had resumed their guise of an elderly couple in gardening clothes. Why were they wearing these personas now? For the benefit of these two gholas? It wasn't as if the thinking machines were keeping secrets from anybody here. Khrone had never been able to determine a pattern in their behavior.

Perhaps it was linked to the fact that Omnius and Erasmus wanted to receive all of the lives Khrone had gathered and assimilated during his last mission among the humans. They looked forward to the sharing of their Face Dancer "ambassadors" each time one of the far-flung representatives returned. It seemed to make them feel superior, and allowed the independent robot to feel that he belonged to the human race, somehow.

"Look, he's brought something," Paolo pointed out. "A present for us?"

Khrone went directly to the old man and woman. As the woman leaned toward him, her visage had a feral and hungry look. "I think you brought more than just a package, Khrone. You haven't been back to Synchrony in some time. Show us the personas you've acquired. Every little bit adds to us, makes us greater."

"I have had enough." The old man turned away. "I am beginning to find them somewhat distasteful. They are all the same."

"How can you say that, Daniel? Every human is different, so beautifully chaotic and unpredictable."

"Exactly what I mean. They are all confusing. And I am not

Daniel, I am Omnius. Kralizec is upon us, and we have no time for further preparatory games."

"Sometimes I still like to consider myself Marty. In many ways it's more appealing to me than the name or guise of Erasmus." The old woman took a step closer to Khrone. The Face Dancer didn't dare flinch, though he despised what was about to happen. Her hand was gnarled, with large knuckles. It felt clawlike when she touched his forehead. She pressed harder, and Khrone shuddered, unable to block the intrusion.

Each time a Face Dancer mimicked a human shape, he sampled the original subject and acquired both a genetic trace and an imprint of the memories and persona. The thinking machines had set the shape-shifters loose into the Old Empire. Infiltrating the humans, they gathered more and more lives as they subsumed useful people and played their roles. Whenever a Face Dancer returned to the machine empire, Erasmus in particular wanted to add those lives to his vast repository of data and experience.

Out of forced subservience, Khrone and his comrades surrendered that information. But though the thinking machines could upload the various lives the Face Dancers copied, they could not take their core personas. Khrone held onto his secrets, even as he offered up all those people he had been in recent years—an Ixian engineer, a CHOAM representative, a crewman on a Guildship, a dock worker on Caladan, and many others.

When the process was finished, the old woman's hand withdrew. Her wrinkled face wore a satisfied smile. "Oh, those were interesting ones! Omnius will certainly want to share them."

"That remains to be seen," the old man said.

Feeling drained, Khrone caught his breath and straightened himself. "That is not why I came." His voice was shamefully weak and quavering. "I have obtained a special substance you will find invaluable for your Kwisatz Haderach project." He held out the ultraspice package, as if offering a gift to a king, precisely as Omnius expected him to behave. The old man accepted the package, scrutinized it carefully.

The Face Dancer gave Paolo a condescending look. "This potent form of melange is sure to unlock the prescience in any Atreides. Then you will have your Kwisatz Haderach, as I have always promised. There is no need to continue pursuing the no-ship."

Omnius found the comment amusing. "Strange you should say that now."

"What do you mean?"

Beside him, the old woman grinned. "This is a momentous day, since both of our plans have come to fruition. Our patience and foresight have paid off. Now, what shall we do with *two* Kwisatz Haderachs?"

Khrone paused, startled. "Two of them?"

"After so many years, the no-ship has finally fallen into our trap."

Khrone slid his surprise back into himself and went rigid. "That is . . . most excellent."

The old woman rubbed her hands together. "Everything is culminating at once. It reminds me of the climactic movement in a symphony I once wrote."

The old man began to pace around the chamber, holding the package of ultraspice in his hands. He sniffed it.

Paolo turned away from the chess game. "You don't need another Kwisatz Haderach. You have *me*. Give me spice now!"

Erasmus shot him an indulgent smile. "Perhaps in a little while. First we'll see what the no-ship has for us, who their Kwisatz Haderach is. It should be interesting."

"Where is the vessel?" Khrone asked, focusing on the main question. "Are you sure you have it?"

"Our cruisers are surrounding it even now, and our operatives aboard took steps to guarantee that it could not escape again. Your Face Dancers did a fine job, Khrone."

Omnius interrupted, "And, on a greater scale, our largest battleships are closing in on human defenders in their Old Empire. We will conquer Chapterhouse soon, but that is only one of many simultaneous targets."

"It should be quite a spectacular battle." Erasmus sounded more dry than eager.

The evermind was stern. "Triumph will be assured as soon as the proper conditions are met, according to our mathematical prophecies. Success is imminent."

With glee on his flowmetal face, Erasmus beamed at Paolo and the Baron. "Two Kwisatz Haderachs are better than one!"

Time is a commodity more precious than melange. Even the wealth-iest man cannot buy more minutes to put into each hour.

—DUKE LETO ATREIDES,
last message from Caladan

A gossamer net of jeweled colors closed around the *Ithaca*. The no-ship's engines strained, but could not break away. Scrambling to reassert control over the helm and drag themselves free of the strange bonds, Duncan powered up the Holtzman engines, preparing to rip a hole through the glimmering mesh. It was their only way out.

Glaring at the dead Face Dancer on the deck, Sheeana ordered two Sisters nearby, "Remove that thing from the navigation bridge!" Within moments, the women carried away the limp and bloody shape-shifter.

Now that the net was visible to them all, Duncan focused his Mentat awareness to study the woven grid that ensnared them. He searched frantically for holes or weak spots in the powerful structure, but found nothing to suggest the slightest defect, no frayed point that might allow them to escape.

He would try brute force, then.

Years ago, he had broken free of the net by using the Holtzman engines in ways they had never been designed to function, flying the *Ithaca* at just the proper angle and speed to penetrate the fabric of space. It had reminded him of a Swordmaster's move, using a slow blade against a personal shield.

"Accelerating now," he said.

Teg leaned over the navigation controls, sweating. "This is going to be close, Duncan." The large ship pulled against the multicolored strands, tore several, and then picked up speed. "We're breaking free!"

Duncan felt a brief moment of hope, a surge of triumph.

An explosion rocked the ship, followed by another, and another. Vibrations and shock waves rang through the hull and decks as if some titan were smashing the vessel with a great hammer. The navigation bridge shuddered.

Holding his chair, Duncan called up diagnostic maps. "What was that? Is the Enemy firing on us?"

The detonations threw Teg to the floor, but he scrambled back to his feet and gripped the console for balance. "The stolen mines! I think we just found them." His words tumbled out in a rush. "Either Thufir or the Rabbi must have set them to go off—" As if to confirm his speculation, another explosion rocked the deck, much closer than before.

The *Ithaca* reeled out of control, its engines paralyzed. The deck tilted, as artificial gravity generators were knocked offline. Duncan felt a sickening disorientation as the vessel spun off axis.

The shimmering net grew brighter, tightening like a noose.

Finally, out in the distance, Enemy ships drew into view, like hunters approaching a trap they had set. Duncan stared at the external screens. Who had pursued them for so long? Face Dancers? Some vicious, unknown race? What could be frightening enough to drive the Honored Matres back into the Old Empire?

"The bastards think they have us." Duncan made a fist.

"Don't they?" Looking up from his status screens, the Bashar was dismayed by the severe damage indicators lighting up sections of the vessel like fireworks displays. "The mines have ruined our most vital systems, and we're dead in space."

Using Mentat focus, Duncan studied the panels on his command console. The intricate displays showed the strangling net all around them. He jabbed his finger toward a knot in the diagram, an area of pulsing, flickering electronic signals. At first glance the tangle seemed no different from the rest of the interconnected strands, but as he studied it, he thought he might have found a weakness. "Look there."

Teg feverishly bent closer. "A loophole?"

"If only we could move!" Racking his brain, Duncan stalked back and forth in front of the controls. "It would be quite a drunkard's dance to get through that maze—if this ship could fly at all."

"If we all worked together, the entire crew, it would take a week to make repairs. We don't have that much time." The Bashar gestured to the tactical screens that displayed data from the long-distance sensors. "Enemy ships are closing in. They know they've snared us."

Duncan accepted the grim reality. "Holtzman engines are dead. No way to make the repairs in time, no way to escape." He hammered his fists on a panel next to the tangled, pulsing loophole on the console's projections. "But I know I could do it. Why won't this damned ship fly?"

Teg glanced at the sensor blips that indicated the encroaching Enemy, saw the automated damage reports streaming across the display, and knew exactly what had to be done. Only he could do it.

"I can fix the ship." He had no time to explain. "Be ready." Then he simply vanished.

MILES TEG ACCELERATED his metabolism, kicking himself into the hyper-fast speed he had learned after surviving unendurable torture at the hands of the Honored Matres and their underlings. Around him, time slowed. This would be dangerous to him because of the extreme energy requirements, but he had to do it. The rapidly strobing alarm lights became a slow pulsation that seemed to take an hour for each cycle, brightening and dimming. Re-accessing the archival records of the ship's systems would take too long, but Teg had examined them before. As a Mentat he remembered everything, and now he set to work.

By himself.

Even at his accelerated speed, Teg exerted himself to run as fast as he could. On deck after deck, everyone aboard stood like statues, their expressions showing concern and confusion. Teg flashed past them to the nearest damage sites.

Where the first mine had gone off, he stared in amazement and consternation at the twisted metal, the melted craters in the machinery, the vaporized systems. Teg hurried from one explosion to the next, determining how far the damage extended and which systems were crucial for their immediate escape. The Face Dancer infiltrators had planted and hidden the eight mines well, and each detonation had resulted in a crippling blow: navigation, life-support, foldspace engines, defensive weapons.

Teg made snap decisions. His life had primed him for emergencies; on the battlefield, one could not hesitate. If Duncan couldn't manage to fly the *Ithaca* away right now, they would never again require life-support systems. He, or someone else, could fix those later. An acceptable gamble. The no-field generators were off-line.

Engines. Four of the eight mines had been set to damage the foldspace engines. The Face Dancer saboteur had deliberately flown the no-ship close to the Enemy's stronghold, and the detonations had left them crippled and stranded.

With hyper speed Teg studied, analyzed, and compiled a plan using his Mentat abilities. He inventoried spare materials, replacement components, emergency equipment. He needed to work swiftly with what he had; there was no one to help him. First, he rerouted and reprogrammed the weapons, and prepared them to launch a volley of blasts at the oncoming ships. That might grant them an extra few moments.

Teg continued to hurry. The pulsing alarm lights flickered on to off, like a sun rising and setting. Another hour gone in his own frame of reference. In real time, only a few seconds had passed since his disappearance from the bridge. Next, he turned to the engines, which were essential to their escape.

The primary linkages had been disrupted, with Holtzman catalysts shaken from their cradles, shoved out of alignment, made inoperable. Two reaction chambers were breached. An explosion had nearly broken through the hull. He stood stunned, his arms shaking, thinking he couldn't possibly fix this. But he forced such thoughts away, went back to work.

Teg's muscles trembled with exhaustion, and his lungs burned from gasping air so fast the oxygen molecules could barely move into position.

Fixing the hull should be easy enough. Teg ran to the maintenance sectors, where he located extra plates. Since he could never make the ship's heavy-lifting machinery operate fast enough for his time-sense, he decided that suspensors would have to do. He applied the null-gravity projectors to the heavy plates and hurried with them down corridors, dodging petrified people.

With each second, the Enemy battleships were getting closer. Some of his fellow passengers were only just now learning of the mines that had been detonated. He put on another burst of speed, and the suspensor carriers kept up with him.

In a few "hours," according to his metabolism, and only a few moments in reality, he fixed the hull damage that could have resulted in an engine breach. Sweat poured off of Teg's body, and he was near collapse. But in spite of that utter exhaustion, he could not let himself slow down. Never before had he allowed himself to fall so deeply into a pit of burning metabolism.

Teg's body could not maintain this pace for long. But if he didn't, the ship would be captured, and they would all die. Fangs of hunger gnawed at his stomach. This would not do. He had to concentrate, had to fuel the engine of his body so that he could do what must be done.

Ravenous, not slowing from his superspeed, he raided the ship's stores, where he found energy bars and dense food wafers. He ate concentrated nutrients until he was gorged. Then, burning calories as fast as he could swallow them, Teg ran again from one disaster area to the next.

He spent subjective days at these highly focused labors; to observers on the outside, caught in the glacial pace of normal time, only a minute or two passed.

When the task grew overwhelming, the Bashar struggled to reassess what the ship needed in order to function. What was the bare minimum of repairs that would let Duncan fly through the weakened loophole?

The exploding mines had led to a cascading series of damages. Teg nearly got lost in the details, but reminded himself of the immediate need and forced himself to skate the thin ice of possibilities.

Teg and his brave men had stolen this very vessel from Gammu more than three decades ago. Though it had performed admirably since then, the *Ithaca* had not undergone any of the usual necessary maintenance at Guild shipyards. Worn components had not been replaced; systems were breaking down from age and neglect, as well as the depredations of the saboteurs. Limited by the spare parts and materials he could find in the maintenance bays, he tried and discarded possible fixes.

Alarms continued to pulse slowly. He was moving too fast for sound waves to mean anything. In real time, there would be shrieking sirens, shouting people, conflicting orders.

Teg fixed another of the Holtzman catalyst cradles, then took the time to look at a viewer. In the image displayed between scan lines, he saw that the Enemy ships had finally arrived, massive and heavily armed . . . a full fleet of monstrous, angular things that bristled with weapons, sensor arrays, and other sharp protrusions.

Though he already felt used up, Teg knew with a sickening certainty that he needed to go even faster.

He raced to the ship's melange stores and broke the locks with a twist of his hand because he was moving so fast. He removed cakes of the dark brown compressed substance, stared at it with Mentat calculation. Considering his hypermetabolism and his body churning through its biochemical machinery faster than it ever had before, what was the proper dosage? How quickly would it affect him? Teg decided on three wafers— triple the maximum he had ever consumed—and gobbled them all.

As the melange rushed through his body and poured into his senses, he felt alive again, recharged and capable of accomplishing the requisite impossibilities. His muscles and nerves were on fire, and his feet left marks on the deck as he ran.

He repaired the next system in a few moments. But in that time, the Enemy battle fleet had closed in, and the no-ship still could not fly.

Teg looked down at his forearms and saw that his skin seemed to be shriveling up, as if he was consuming every drop of energy within his flesh.

Outside, the encroaching vessels launched a volley of destructive blasts. Balls of energy tumbled forward like storm clouds approaching with exquisite slowness. Those blasts would clearly render his repairs useless, maybe even destroy the ship.

In another burst of extreme speed, Teg dashed to the defensive controls. Thankfully, he had restored a few of their weapons. The *Ithaca's* defensive systems were sluggish, but the firing controls were swift enough. With a scattershot cannonade, like a burst of celebratory fireworks, Teg returned fire. He launched beams carefully targeted to intercept and dissipate the oncoming projectiles. Once he had fired the volley, though, Teg turned his back on the weapons systems and raced to the next damaged engine.

Bashar Teg felt like a candle that had been burnt entirely down to a lump of discolored wax. Despite his best efforts, the exhausted man still saw their doom closing in.

How do we repay a man who has done the impossible?

—BASHAR ALEF BURZMALI,

A Dirge for the Soldier

On the navigation bridge, Duncan stared at the sensor projections for moments after Miles had disappeared. He knew what the Bashar must be doing.

After the internal explosions, the *Ithaca* hung dead in space, surrounded by Enemy ships that bristled with more weaponry than he had seen on an entire Harkonnen battle fleet. The mines had disabled the no-field generator, leaving the great ship visible and vulnerable in space.

After almost a quarter century of fleeing, they were caught. Maybe it was about damned time he faced the mysterious hunters. Who were his strange and invincible foes? He had only ever seen the ghostly shadows of the old man and old woman. And now . . .

On the screens before him, the discontinuity in the gossamer net shifted, almost closed, and then strayed open again, as if taunting him.

Duncan spoke aloud, more to himself than anyone else. A prayer of sorts. "As long as we breathe, we have a chance. Our task is to identify any opportunity, however transitory or difficult it might be."

Teg had said he would fix their systems. Duncan was aware of the Bashar's closely held abilities. For years, Teg had concealed his talent from the Bene Gesserits, who feared such manifestations as the sign of a potential Kwisatz Haderach. Now those abilities might save them all. "Don't let us down, Miles."

The encroaching ships fired a series of blasts at the no-ship. Duncan barely had time to shout a curse and brace for impact—when a flurry of impossibly fast and deft defensive bursts intercepted the Enemy volley. Precisely targeted, instantly fired. All shots blocked.

Duncan blinked. Who had launched the return salvo? He shook his head. The no-ship should have been incapable of even basic maneuvers or defense. A chill of delight coursed down his spine. Miles!

Suddenly, the control deck's systems began to glow; green indicator lights winked on by themselves. One after another, systems came back online. Sensing movement, Duncan snapped his head to the left.

The Bashar materialized in front of him, but it was a different Miles Teg—not the young ghola whom Duncan had raised and awakened, but a horribly drained man, as desiccated and ancient as an ambulatory mummy. Teg looked wrung out and ready to collapse. He had exerted himself through time far beyond the point where a normal man would have already died.

"Boards . . . active." His gasping voice cost him more energy than he had left. "Go!"

Everything happened in an instant, as if Duncan, too, had fallen into an accelerated time frame. His first instinct was to grab his friend. Teg was dying, might already be dead. The aged Bashar could no longer hold himself upright. "Go—damn it!" They were the last words Teg could force out of his mouth.

Thinking with Mentat clarity, Duncan whipped back to the control panels, vowing not to waste what the Bashar had done for them. *Priorities.* He reached the piloting board, where his fingers skittered like a startled spider across the controls.

Teg crumpled to the deck, arms and legs akimbo, as dead as a dried leaf, older even than the first old Bashar had been in the last moments of Rakis. *Miles!* All their years together, teaching, learning, relying on each other. Few people in all of Duncan's many lives had ever mattered so much.

He drove away his thoughts of shocked grief, but Mentat memory kept every experience clear and sharp. Miles! Teg was no more than an ancient husk on the floorplates. Duncan had no time for anger or tears.

The no-ship began to accelerate. He still saw how to slip out of the cruel net, but now he also had to contend with the entire fleet of Enemy ships. They had cut loose with a second volley.

The blurred crackle ahead seemed to invite them. Duncan steered toward it, moving as fast as his human reflexes could go. The no-ship ripped the stubborn strands free. "Come on!" Duncan said, willing it to happen.

More blasts glanced across the *Ithaca*'s hull, grazing the ship as it yawed and rolled. Duncan steered with all of his skill.

The Holtzman engines were hot and the diagnostic boards showed numerous errors and system failures, but none were immediately fatal faults. Duncan pushed the vessel closer and closer to the loophole. The Enemy ships couldn't head them off, couldn't move fast enough to stop them.

More of the net broke away. Duncan could see it happening.

He forced his attention back to the engines, applying acceleration far beyond what the systems normally allowed. In his frantic repairs, Teg had not bothered with the niceties of fail-safes and protective limitations. With increased velocity, they pulled free of the enclosing cordon.

"We're going to make it!" Duncan said to the fallen Bashar, as if his friend could still hear him.

A giant torpedo-shaped Enemy vessel leapt forward. No human could possibly pilot a ship so swiftly, changing directions with g-forces that would snap bones like a handful of straw in a clenched fist. Burning its engines, the attacker exhausted all of its fuel in one burst of forward motion—throwing the craft directly into their path.

With his maneuvering already hampered, Duncan could not dodge in time. The no-ship was too huge, with too much inertia. Impossibly, the suicidal Enemy vessel scraped the lower hull of the *Ithaca*, knocking it off course, damaging the engines yet again. The unexpected impact sent the no-ship spinning. The Enemy rammer tumbled and exploded, and the shock wave knocked them farther off course, out of control . . . back into the remaining strands of the net.

Duncan uttered a curse in dismay and rage.

Unable to fold space, the no-ship dropped back, its engines whining. The bridge control panels blazed red, then went dim. A small internal explosion further damaged the Holtzman engines. The *Ithaca* hung motionless in space. Again.

"I'm sorry, Bashar," Duncan said, heartbroken. With nothing else to do, he knelt beside the husk of his friend.

A message formed on the primary screen on the bridge, a powerful transmission from the surrounding battleships. Even in his stunned sorrow, Duncan was surprised to see the true face of the Enemy at last.

The smooth flowmetal face of a sentient machine appeared on the screen. "You are our prisoners. Your vessel is no longer capable of independent flight. We will deliver you to the evermind Omnius."

Thinking machines!

Duncan struggled to understand what he was seeing and hearing. Omnius? The evermind? The Enemy, posing as a kindly old couple, were really thinking machines? Impossible! Thinking machines had been outlawed for thousands of years, and the last evermind had been destroyed in the Battle of Corrin at the end of the Butlerian Jihad.

Machines? Somehow allied with the new Face Dancers?

The Enemy ships pounced like hyenas on a fresh carcass.

Some people complain of being haunted by their past. Utter non-sense! I revel in it.

—BARON VLADIMIR HARKONNEN, the ghola

Trapped by the machine fleet, the *Ithaca* was held captive with its engines damaged and weapons burned out. Duncan could do nothing but wait and mourn his dead friend. Consequences and memories roared around him. He moved methodically, relying on Mentat focus to perform even simple actions.

Sheeana was beside him on the navigation bridge. Though she prided herself in Bene Gesserit purity, holding all emotions at bay, she seemed profoundly troubled as the two of them picked up Teg's body from where it lay crumpled on the deck. Duncan couldn't believe how fragile and lightweight the Bashar's remains were. He seemed to be made of spiderwebs and sinew, dried leaves and hollow bone.

"Miles gave his life for all of us," Duncan said.

"Two times," she said.

Her remark made Duncan think of all the lives of his own he had given for the Atreides. In a raspy voice, he said, "This time, the sacrifice was for nothing. Miles used up his entire life span to give us the repairs we needed, and I couldn't break us free. He shouldn't have done it."

Sheeana fixed a hard look on him. "He shouldn't have *tried?* We're humans. We have to try, no matter what the odds are. There are never any guarantees. Every action in life is a gamble. The Bashar fought to the last instant of his existence, because he believed there was a chance. I intend to do the same."

Duncan looked down at the sunken, mummified face of his friend, remembering all the determination and hard training the old Bashar had given him when he was a young ghola. Sheeana was right. Even though Duncan hadn't been able to free the *Ithaca* and let them escape, he and Miles had shown the Enemy that humans were unpredictable and resilient, that they were not to be underestimated. And it wasn't over yet. Instead of a simple capture, the thinking machines had been forced to sacrifice one of their largest battleships simply to stop them.

"We'll take him to one of the small airlocks," he announced. Since their every movement was now dictated by the Enemy ships that dragged them along, it was pointless to remain at the controls. "I have no intention of letting the thinking machines have him."

The remnants of the Bashar would fly alone into the cosmos. The rest of them might be trapped, to be used in thinking-machine experiments, or for whatever reason the old man and woman had been pursuing them over the decades. But not Miles. This act would be another small victory—and enough small victories could win an entire war.

They arrived at one of the chambers, which Duncan recognized as the same airlock he had used to jettison Murbella's last possessions, items that had clung to him like cobwebs until he forced himself to let go. They placed the tragically lightweight husk of Teg's body inside the chamber and sealed it. Duncan looked through the observation port, saying his last goodbyes.

"It isn't the ceremony I would have imagined for him. Last time, the Bashar had all of Rakis for his funeral pyre. But there's no time." Before he could have second thoughts, Duncan pushed the button that evacuated the airlock, opening the outside hatch so that the body tumbled out into the void. "We should summon everyone aboard the ship and prepare our defenses."

"What defenses?"

He looked at her. "Anything we can think of."

SHOULDERED FORWARD BY a hundred thinking-machine vessels, the battered no-ship was forced down into Synchrony, where shifting buildings moved aside to form an acceptable place for the captured craft to land. The now-visible *Ithaca* descended like a trussed wild animal, the trophy of big game hunters.

Baron Harkonnen thought it a glorious sight. From an extruded balcony in one of Omnius's capricious high towers, he studied the vessel as it descended. The no-ship's configuration was unfamiliar to him, massive but not as intimidating as he'd imagined it would be. This design was much more organic and alien-looking than huge Guild Heighliners, deadly Sardaukar craft, House Harkonnen military vessels, or his own family frigates. It seemed to be convergent evolution, eerily similar to the flow-form curves of the thinking-machine structures.

Strange ship, strange passengers.

According to initial reports from the machine scouts who had seized the no-ship, many of those aboard were gholas from his own past, annoyances resurrected from history, exactly as Erasmus had suspected—Lady Jessica, another Paul Atreides, a minor Swordmaster named Duncan Idaho, and who knew how many others? Gholas coughed up and spat out like wads of phlegm.

A keyed-up Paolo stood beside him on the balcony, facing the makeshift spaceport that waited to accommodate the new vessel. "Will we kill them all, Grandfather? I don't want there to be another Kwisatz Haderach. I'm supposed to be the only one. I should take the ultraspice that Khrone delivered right now."

"I would have you do it if I could, dear boy, but Omnius won't permit that. Be patient. Even if there is another version of Paul Atreides aboard that no-ship, he's probably soft and compassionate. He doesn't have the advantage of being toughened by *me*." The Baron's full lips curled down in distaste. Paolo himself didn't realize just how much of his fundamental personality had been changed. "You will have no trouble defeating him."

"I have already visualized it," Paolo replied. "Real, prescient dreams—and now I understand what is going to happen."

"Then you have nothing to worry about."

The Omnius-formed buildings swayed like reeds, then embraced the battered no-ship as it landed, pulling the *Ithaca* down into a living metal cradle. The landing and lockdown process seemed interminable. Was it really necessary for so many structural braces to fold around the ship like claws? Considering the obvious damage to the engines, the captives could never find a way to launch the vessel again. However, Omnius had a penchant for doing things in a brute-force manner. The Baron could understand that.

Presently Erasmus appeared on the balcony, once again disguised as a matronly old woman. Gazing dispassionately at the robot, the Baron announced, "I will go aboard the no-ship. I want to be the first to"—his lips quirked in a smile—"greet our visitors."

The old woman's eyes twinkled. "Are you certain that would be wise, Baron? We aren't sure yet exactly who is aboard the vessel. You could be in peril if anyone recognizes you. In your past life, quite a few people were not entirely pleased with you."

"I certainly don't intend to go unprotected! In fact, I expect *you* to provide me with full security. Some of your sentinel robots, perhaps—or better yet, an armed contingent of Face Dancers. Paolo will remain here safe, but I *will* go aboard." He planted his hands on his hips. "In fact, I demand it."

Erasmus seemed amused. "In that case, we had better give you the Face Dancers. Go aboard, Baron, and be our ambassador. I'm sure you will employ all the diplomacy the situation requires."

*We shall face the Enemy, and die if we must die. My strong prefer-
ence, however, is to kill what we must kill.*

—MOTHER COMMANDER MURBELLA,

transmission to human defensive forces

Ten thousand Guildships against an infinite number of Enemy
vessels.

For this confrontation, the Mother Commander had prepared all
the warlords, political leaders and other self-proclaimed generals, as
well as her ferocious Sisters—what remained of them. Spread out
across the path of the oncoming thinking-machine forces, her human
defenders dug themselves in.

Guildsmen had been rushed in at the last minute to help crew the
numerous battleships, launching them to their designated rendezvous
points in space. The untested military commanders were as ready as
the Mother Commander could make them. Like ghost soldiers, red-
eyed refugees from planets already ground under the machine boot
heel volunteered in droves. Each craft was loaded with Obliterators
produced by the tireless Ixian factories.

Unfortunately, Omnius had been preparing for centuries.

Like a force of nature, the thinking machines advanced, not dodging
or changing course, without regard to the strength of planetary defenses
arrayed against them. They simply rolled over anything in their path.

For Murbella's plan to work, the line of Enemy ships had to be stopped at every point, in every star system. No battleground was unimportant. She had divided her defenders into a hundred discrete groups of one hundred new Guild warships apiece. The battle groups were positioned at widely scattered but important points outside inhabited systems, ready to fend off the approaching Enemy.

As a last line of defense, Murbella's one hundred newly constructed vessels patrolled space in the vicinity of Chapterhouse, along with a number of smaller, older vessels to flesh out the military force. They knew Omnius considered this planet a primary target. Waiting for the clash, the Mother Commander thought her new ships looked magnificent, the line formidable. The fighters aboard were more confident than afraid.

By the New Sisterhood's best estimates, though, the thinking machines outnumbered them by more than a hundred to one.

To shore up their confidence, the fighters had all watched holos of the Ixian tests of the new Obliterators on dead Richese, admiring the massive destructive force contained in each of the powerful weapons. Bene Gesserit observers had monitored the Ixian production lines, and technicians had verified the complex weapons after they were installed in Murbella's fleet. She clung to the hope that this line of last stands could turn into a rout for the forces of Omnius.

More than she had for the past quarter century, the Mother Commander wished Duncan Idaho could be at her side again, facing this final conflict with her. Feeling the loneliness of command, tempted to bow to primitive human superstition and offer up a prayer to some invisible guardian angel, she hardened herself.

This has to work!

Her great ships prowled the edge of planetary orbit, not knowing from which direction the Enemy fleet would come. Down below, the refugees who had filled temporary camps on the plague-emptied continents were anxious to evacuate from Chapterhouse, but even if there were vessels to transport them away, they had nowhere to go. Every functional craft in the sector had been commandeered to face the thinking-machine ships. It was everything the human race could rally.

"Enemy ships approaching, Mother Commander," said Administrator Gorus, receiving a message from the sensor deck. His pale braid looked somewhat frayed, his skin whiter than usual. He had been convinced to stay aboard the main ship at the central battlefield, to stand by the new ships his factories had produced; he didn't look at all happy about it.

"Exactly on time. Exactly as expected," Murbella said. "Disperse our vessels into the widest possible firing spread, so we can hit the Enemy all at once, before they can react to us. Machines are adaptable, but they rarely take the unexpected into account."

Gorus looked at her sourly. "Are you making assumptions based on old records, Mother Commander? Extrapolating from the way Omnius reacted fifteen thousand years ago?"

"To some extent, but I trust my instincts."

As the heavily armed machine ships approached, they looked like a meteor shower that grew larger and larger. The monstrous vessels loomed huge—thousands of them against the Sisterhood's desperate hundred. All along the line, at a hundred other systems, she knew her defenders were facing similar odds.

"Prepare to launch Obliterators. Stop them before they get any closer to Chapterhouse." Murbella crossed her arms over her chest. Across the commlines, each captain announced his or her readiness.

The oncoming machine ships slowed, as if curious to see what this small obstacle might be. *They will underestimate us*, Murbella thought. "Maximize targets. Fire into close groupings of Enemy ships. Consolidate explosions."

"Targets locked, Mother Commander," Gorus said, his message transmitted immediately by his sensor technicians.

Murbella had to preempt the thinking machines before they could open fire. "Launch Obliterators." She held herself steady.

Silver sparks spat out of the launch tubes, Obliterators twirling toward the line of Enemy ships, but the glints faded. Nothing happened, though some of the heavy weapons must have struck their targets. The machine vessels seemed to be waiting for something.

She looked around. "Confirm that the Obliterators are armed. Where are the explosions? Launch the second volley!"

Alarms began to ring. In a frenzy, Gorus ran from one station to another, shouting at the Guildsmen on the upper decks. A harried-looking Reverend Mother charged into the command center, skidding to a stop in front of Murbella. "Our Obliterators are doing nothing. They are all useless."

"But they were tested! Our Sisters watched the manufacturing lines. How could they be faulty?"

Then, all at once, the one hundred Chapterhouse defender ships went dead in space, their engines shutting down, lights flickering. The thrum of station-keeping thrusters faded.

"What is happening?" Gorus demanded. "Sabotage? Were we betrayed?"

As if they had expected this all along, the machine ships closed in.

A Guildsman transmitted in a hollow voice over the speaking screen, "The artificial navigation systems no longer respond, Administrator. We are shut out of our own controls. Our ships are . . . nonfunctional." Emergency lights lit the decks with an eerie glow.

"Did the machines figure out how to neutralize our systems?"

Gorus turned to Murbella. "No jamming, Mother Commander. They . . . they just don't work. None of them."

Suddenly the machine forces were upon them, a thousand vessels that would easily overwhelm the defenders. Murbella prepared to die. Her fighters could not protect themselves, or Chapterhouse, which she had sworn to guard.

But instead of attacking, the Enemy fleet cruised slowly past the defenders, taunting them in their impotence. The machines did not bother to open fire, as if the Sisterhood's defenses weren't even worth noticing!

Far behind them, just arriving at the distant edge of the solar system, came another wave of thinking machines, closing in on Chapterhouse. The same thing must be happening everywhere, at all of her carefully staged last stands across a hundred star systems.

"They knew! The damned machines *knew* our Obliterators wouldn't work!" As if Murbella's vessels were no more than a pebble on the path, the Omnius ships flowed around them on their way to the Sisterhood's now-unprotected homeworld.

Not one of her new Guild war vessels had a living Navigator aboard; most of the Navigators and their Heighliners had disappeared. Every ship in her battle groups used Ixian mathematical compilers for guidance. Mathematical compilers! Computers . . . thinking machines.

The Ixians! Now her silent curse was directed at herself for overconfidence in the new Obliterators and her own ability to predict the Enemy's tactics.

"Follow me, Administrator. I want to see these Obliterators for myself." She grabbed Gorus's arm hard enough to leave bruises.

Guided by emergency illumination, they rushed to the weapons deck where the armaments had been installed. Inside, rack upon rack held the burnished silver eggs of the planet-melters that Ix had manufactured. A distraught Guildsman intercepted them. "We tested the weapons, Administrator, and they were installed correctly. The firing controls are operational. We just launched dozens of Obliterators, but none of them detonated."

"Why didn't they function?"

"Because . . . because the Obliterators themselves . . ."

Murbella marched over to where the man had opened one casing at random. Beneath a complicated labyrinth of circuitry and delicate components, the Obliterator charge was fused into the shell of the mechanism, making the whole thing inoperable. The weapon had been neutralized.

"It is useless, Mother Commander," said Gorus. "Sabotaged."

"But I saw the tests myself. How can this be?"

"A timing mechanism may have shut everything down at a prearranged time, or the Enemy fleet might have sent out a deactivating signal. Some devious trick that we could not have anticipated."

Murbella stood appalled, guilty of the same error she had been so certain the machines would fall victim to: She had failed to plan for the unexpected. Together, they opened another Obliterator to find it similarly fused and nonfunctional. A coldness froze her heart and spread into her bloodstream. These weapons had been built over the course of years by the Ixians, at a cost in melange that nearly bankrupted the Sisterhood. She had been duped, and her fleet had been castrated by the Ixians before the battle could even begin.

"And what about our engines?"

"They can be made to function, if we operate them without the mathematical compilers."

"I don't give a damn about the compilers! Find a way to salvage some of the Obliterators. Are they all inactive? Every single one?"

"The only way to know, Mother Commander, is to open and inspect each of them."

"We could just launch them all and hope a few still function." Murbella nodded slowly. It was indeed an option. At this point, it cost them nothing. She had to find some way to fight, and she hoped her other battle groups were faring better than this . . . but she doubted it. Without functional Obliterators, every one of the planets on the front line was essentially unprotected in the face of certain destruction.

And it was all her responsibility.

Some say that survival itself can be the best revenge. For myself, I prefer something a bit more extravagant.

—BARON VLADIMIR HARKONNEN,
the ghola

On a whim, the Baron told the ten Face Dancers accompanying him to pose as Sardaukar from the old Imperium. He didn't know if anyone would even recognize the joke—fashions changed and history forgot such details—but it helped him present an air of command. During his original lifetime he had achieved a great victory over House Atreides with illicit Sardaukar at his side.

Leaving the restless Paolo with Erasmus, supposedly "for his own protection," the Baron dressed himself in a nobleman's uniform frosted with gold braids and ornate chains of office. A ceremonial poison-tipped dagger hung at his side, and a wide-beam stunner was concealed in his sleeve for easy access. Though the imitation Sardaukar were his guards and escort, he didn't particularly trust them, either. One could never be too careful.

When the Baron's entourage marched to the imprisoned no-ship, however, they could not find a door on the kilometer-long hull—a frustrating and embarrassing moment, but Omnius was not to be hindered. Guided by the evermind, parts of nearby buildings transformed into gigantic tools that tore open the hull, peeling away plates and structural girders to leave a wide gash. Brute force was easier and more direct than locating an appropriate hatch and deciphering unfamiliar controls.

With the no-ship suitably opened, the Baron and his escort ducked under low-hanging debris and sparking circuitry. Prepared for an ambush, but moving with an outward show of confidence, they made their way through the winding corridors. Several of Omnius's floating watcheyes zoomed ahead of them down the passageways to scout out and map the interior of the vessel.

The captives would surely see that surrender was their only option. What other conclusion could they draw? Unfortunately, in his original lifetime the Baron had had considerable experience with fanatics, such as the mad Fremen bands on Arrakis. It was possible that these poor wretches intended to mount a desperate, hopeless resistance until they were all slaughtered, including the purported Kwisatz Haderach among them.

Paolo would then be the only contender, and that would be that.

Inside the no-ship, they first encountered Duncan Idaho and a defiant-looking Bene Gesserit woman who identified herself as Sheeana. The two waited for the boarding party in the middle of a wide corridor. The Baron only vaguely remembered the man from the records of House Atreides: a Swordmaster of Ginaz, one of Duke Leto's most trusted fighters, killed on Arrakis while protecting Paul and Jessica in their escape. From the sneer on Idaho's face, he could tell that this ghola had his memories back, too.

"Oh ho, I see that you know me."

Idaho didn't budge. "I escaped from Giedi Prime as a boy, Baron. I beat Rabban on one of his hunts. I've lived many lifetimes since then. This time, I hope to watch you die with my own eyes."

"How boldly you speak, like one of those yipping dogs Emperor Shaddam used to keep at his side: full of annoying barks and growls, yet easily stepped on." Protected by the Face Dancer Sardaukar, he peered ahead down the hall. "How many people do you have aboard?" He snapped. "Bring them forward for our inspection."

"We have already assembled," Sheeana said. "We're ready for you."

The Baron sighed. "And no doubt you've scattered commandos or snipers throughout the decks? Your personnel records will have been doctored. A childish resistance that may cause us a few headaches, but will gain you nothing. We have enough troops to mow all of you down."

"It would be foolish for us to resist," Sheeana said, "at least in such obvious ways."

The Baron scowled, and he heard the little girl's voice inside his head. *She is playing with your mind, Grandfather!*

"So are you!" he hissed to himself, startling the others.

"Five hundred more of our men are coming aboard," said the counterfeit Sardaukar commander. "Mobile machine sensors will scour every chamber on every deck, and we'll find anything there is to find. We will locate the Kwisatz Haderach."

"A Kwisatz Haderach?" Idaho asked. "Is that what the old man and woman have been looking for? On this ship? You're welcome to waste your time."

Sheeana added harshly, "If we had a superman aboard, you would never have been able to capture us."

That remark disturbed the Baron. At the back of his mind he heard the maddening voice of Alia chuckling at his discomfiture. His face flushed, but he forced himself not to speak aloud. What a fool, debating with the unheard voice of an invisible tormentor! New groups came down the no-ship corridors to gather in front of him like troops for inspection.

One small-statured teenaged ghola unsettled him the most. The young man was thin and sallow-skinned, his face etched in a scowl. His eyes burned with hatred for the Baron, though he did not find the fellow at all familiar. He wondered what he had done to that one.

Look more closely, Grandfather. Surely you recognize him? He almost killed you!

I swear I will find some way to rip you out of my head!

With a neutral expression on his face, he looked again at the dour ghola, and suddenly understood the crude black diamond marked on his forehead. "Why, it's Yueh! My dear Dr. Yueh, how good to see you again. I never got a chance to tell you how much you helped the Harkonnen cause so long ago. Glad to see that I have an unexpected ally aboard this ship."

Yueh looked skinny and ineffectual, yet the gleam in his eyes was genuinely murderous. "I am not your ally."

"You are a weak little worm. It was easy enough to manipulate you before—I can do it again." The Baron was surprised that the scrawny man did not back down. This version of Yueh seemed stronger, perhaps transformed by the lessons of his ignominious past.

"You no longer have leverage over me, Baron. You have no Wanna. Even if you did, I would not repeat my earlier mistakes." Crossing his arms over his narrow chest, he thrust his pointed chin forward.

The Baron turned abruptly from the Suk doctor as even more no-ship captives came forward. One bronze-haired young woman of about eighteen looked exactly like the lovely Lady Jessica. The way she viewed him with palpable revulsion proved that this ghola also had her memories restored. Did Jessica know she was really his own daughter? What entertaining conversations they might have!

Standing protectively beside the youthful Jessica were a younger woman dressed as a Fremen and a dark-haired young man—the perfect image of Paolo, only older. "Why, is this young Paul? Another Paul Atreides?"

A swift slash, a mere nick from the poisoned dagger, and the rival Kwisatz Haderach would be gone. But he shuddered to think how Omnius would react to that. The Baron wanted Paolo to assume his position of power, of course, but he wasn't willing to sacrifice his own life for the boy. Though the Baron had raised and trained Paolo, he was still, after all, an *Atreides*.

"Hello, Grandfather," Paul said. "I remember you as being much older and fatter." The Baron found the demeanor and tone irritating. And even worse, he felt an odd, swooning sensation . . . as if Paul had always been meant to say this, as if he had seen it in a dozen different visions.

Still, the Baron clapped his hands in mock applause. "Isn't ghola technology marvelous? This is like an encore at the end of one of the Emperor's tedious jongleur performances. All back together again for a second run, eh?"

Paul stiffened. "House Atreides crushed the Harkonnens into extinction long ago. I anticipate a similar outcome now."

349

"Oh, ho!" Though amused, the Baron-ghola didn't step any closer. He gestured to his Sardaukar guard. "Have a doctor and a dentist look them over before they get close to me. Pay particular attention to their teeth. Look for poison capsules."

Having fulfilled his purpose, the Baron was about to march out of the no-ship when, among the gathered refugees, he spotted a small girl who stood quietly beside a thin boy of around twelve years, watching everything. Both had an Atreides look about them. He froze, recognizing Alia.

Not only had this bloodthirsty child jabbed him with the poison gom jabbar and haunted his thoughts, now she even stood before him! *Look, Grandfather—now we can torment you inside and out!* Her voice pierced him like ice picks in his head.

The Baron reacted, not caring about consequences. Snatching the ceremonial dagger from his hip, he grabbed the little girl by the collar and raised the blade. "They called you Abomination!"

Alia fought like a rabid animal, but didn't scream. Her tiny feet drove with surprising power into his stomach, knocking the wind out of him. The Baron reeled, and without a second's hesitation, thrust the poisoned tip deep into her side. It went in easily. He yanked the knife back out and stabbed again, this time directly into Alia's heart.

Jessica screamed. Paul rushed forward, but too late. Duncan roared with anger and shock, and threw himself at the nearest Sardaukar guard, killing him with a bone-shattering blow to the throat. He struck a second guard, snapping his neck as well, and charged toward the Baron like a wild creature. The Baron didn't even have time to feel fear before his guards closed ranks around him, and four others held Duncan back. The rest of the faux Sardaukar raised their guns to keep the shocked captives at bay.

Regaining his composure, the Baron sneered down at the little girl dying swiftly in his grip. "That's turnabout for killing me." Laughing at the blood on his hands, he tossed her to the floor like a discarded doll. And inside, not a sound from his tormentor. Was she gone as well?

Murderous desperation showed on the faces of the nearby captives, making the Baron uneasy. With Face Dancer Sardaukar surrounding him protectively, he backed away smiling. The two dead soldiers had reverted to Face Dancers, and none of the captives seemed the least bit surprised. The Atreides rabble gathered around the murdered child while the Sardaukar picked up their comrades.

Sheeana stopped Duncan from lunging forward in another suicidal attack. "One death is enough, Duncan."

"No it's not. It is only a start." He controlled himself with a visible effort. "But it will have to do for now."

The Baron laughed, and the Face Dancers hurried him away. When he looked at his escort, the shape-shifters showed disapproval at what he had done. "What? I don't have to justify my reasons to you. At least that Abomination is gone now."

Gone, you say? A little girl's loud titter like breaking glass inside his skull. *Gone? You can't discard me so easily! I was rooted inside your head before that ghola was ever born.* The voice grew louder. *Now I shall torment you more than ever. You leave me no choice but to serve as your conscience, Grandfather.*

The Baron marched away at a faster pace, trying to shut out her mocking presence.

The stake in a total war is total—to conquer is to save everything, to succumb is to lose everything.

—a warrior of Old Terra

While the thinking machines maintained a tight cordon around the no-ship, Sheeana watched Jessica carry little Alia's body away. How painful it must be for her. With her memories restored, Jessica knew intimately who Alia really was and understood her great potential. How bitterly ironic, too. St. Alia of the Knife—felled by a knife.

Jessica cradled the limp child in her arms, shuddering as she fought to contain sobs. When she looked up at Sheeana, there was a cold deadliness in Jessica's eyes. Duncan stood beside Jessica, his face a mask of grim anger. "We'll have our revenge, my Lady. So many of us despise the Baron, he can't survive for long." Even Yueh sat coiled and dangerous, like a loaded weapon.

Paul and Chani clasped hands, drawing strength from each other. Leto II watched in silence, undoubtedly holding an avalanche of conflicting thoughts in his mind. The boy always seemed to have so much more to him, like a giant iceberg whose bulk was concealed beneath the surface. Sheeana had long suspected that he might be the most powerful of all the gholas she had created.

Jessica held her head high, finding strength within her. "We'll take her to my quarters. Duncan, would you help me?" Dr. Yueh, desperate for forgiveness, hovered close to them.

Filled with anxiety, frustration, and anger, Sheeana watched the tableau. In addition to losing the Bashar, Alia had been murdered, while three key gholas—Paul, Chani, and Leto II—remained unawakened. Stilgar and Liet-Kynes were left on Qelso, and Thufir Hawat had been a Face Dancer. Now that they were facing the Enemy and needed the ghola children to fulfill their destinies, too many of her "weapons" were not available to her! She had only Yueh, and Jessica . . . and Scytale, if she could count on the Tleilaxu.

Exhaustion threatened to overwhelm Sheeana. They had fled for so long, carrying their plans and hopes, but never finding an end. This, though, was not at all what they had hoped for.

The quiet and distant voice of Serena Butler awakened within her again, angered by the revelation about the Enemy. She spoke from firsthand knowledge. *The evil machines have always wanted to exterminate humanity. They do not know how to forget.*

"But they were destroyed," Sheeana said aloud.

Apparently not. Trillions of people died during the Butlerian Jihad, but even that was not enough. In the end, I was not enough.

"I am pleased to meet you finally," said a raspy female voice. A lone old woman strolled down the no-ship's corridor, a broad grin on her wrinkled face. Despite her apparent age, she moved fluidly and had a deadly look to her.

Sheeana immediately guessed that this must be the mysterious old woman who was their relentless hunter. "Duncan has told us about you."

The woman smiled in an unnerving manner, as if she could see through Sheeana to her innermost thoughts and intentions. "You were quite a troublesome quarry. All those years wasted. Have you guessed my true identity yet?"

"You are the Enemy."

Abruptly the crone's face, body, and clothing rippled like molten, flowing metal. At first Sheeana thought this was another Face Dancer, but the head and body took on a sheen of highly polished platinum, and the matronly clothes became a plush robe. The face was smooth, with the same smile set in radically different features. A robot.

Deep in her consciousness, Sheeana felt a tumult in Other Memory. And out of the clamor, Serena Butler's familiar voice rose to cry, *Erasmus! Destroy him!*

With great effort she shunted aside the voices in Other Memory, and said, "You are Erasmus. The one who killed Serena Butler's child, setting off the centuries-long Jihad against thinking machines."

"So I *am* still remembered, even after all this time." The robot sounded pleased.

"Serena remembers you, all right. She is within me, and she hates you."

Pure delight shone on the robot's face. "Serena Butler herself is in there? Ah yes, I know about your Other Memory. Face Dancers have brought many of you Bene Gesserits back to us."

Inside her, the clamor of memories returned. "I am Serena Butler, and she is me. Though thousands of years have passed, the pain is as sharp as ever. We cannot forget what you destroyed, and what you started."

"It was only one life—merely a baby. Logically, can't you see how your race overreacted?" The robot sounded so reasonable.

Sheeana felt a change in the tenor and cadence of her own voice, as if her body were being taken over by a force within. "Only one life? Merely a baby?" Serena was speaking now, thrusting herself to the forefront of the innumerable lives. Sheeana let her talk. After such a great length of time, this was *Serena's* confrontation with her greatest nemesis. "That *one* life led to the military defeat of your entire Synchronized Empire. The Butlerian Jihad was a Kralizec in its own right. The end of that war changed the course of the universe."

Erasmus seemed delighted by the comparison. "Ah, interesting. And perhaps the end of this Kralizec will reverse that result and put thinking machines in charge again. If so, we will be much more efficient this time."

"That is how you foresee the end of Kralizec?"

"That would be my preference. Something fundamental must change. Can I count on you to assist me?"

"Never." Serena's projected voice was cold and implacable.

Looking at the independent robot, Sheeana understood more than

ever before that she was part of something far greater and more important than one life, that she was linked to a vast continuum of female
ancestry stretching into the past and—hopefully—into the future. A
remarkable assemblage, but would it survive?

"There is a familiar fire in your eyes. If any part of you is indeed Serena Butler, then we must catch up on old times." Erasmus's optic threads
gleamed.

"She no longer wishes to converse with you," Sheeana said in her
own voice.

Erasmus ignored the rebuff. "Take me to your private quarters. A
human's den reveals much about the individual personality."

"I will not."

The robot's voice hardened. "Be reasonable. Or should I decapitate
a few of your fellow passengers to encourage your cooperation? Ask
Serena Butler inside you—she knows I will do it."

Sheeana glared at him.

The robot continued in a calm tone, "But a simple conversation
with you in your quarters may slake my appetite for now. Wouldn't you
prefer that to carnage?"

Motioning for the others to remain behind, Sheeana turned her
back on the robot and walked to one of the still-functional lifts. With
gliding footsteps, Erasmus followed.

In her chamber, the robot was intrigued by the preserved Van Gogh
painting. *Cottages at Cordeville* was one of the oldest artifacts of human
civilization. Standing rigidly, Erasmus admired the artwork. "Ah, yes! I
remember this clearly. I painted it myself."

"It is the work of a nineteenth-century Terran artist, Vincent Van
Gogh."

"I have studied the Madman of France with great interest, but I assure
you, this is actually one of the canvases I myself painted thousands of
years ago. I copied the original with the utmost attention to detail."

She wondered if he could possibly be telling the truth.

Erasmus removed the delicate painting from the wall and examined
it closely, passing his metal fingertips over the thin plaz that protected
the rough oil-paint surface. "Yes, well do I remember each stroke, each
whorl, each point of color. Truly, this is a work of genius."

Sheeana caught her breath, knowing how old and priceless it was. Unless it really was a forgery perpetrated long ago. "The *original* was a work of genius. If this is what you say, then all you did was copy someone else's masterpiece. There can be only one original."

His optic threads gleamed like a galaxy of stars. "If it is the same, exactly the same, then both are works of genius. If my copy is perfect down to every single brushstroke, does it not become a second original?"

"Van Gogh was a man of creativity and inspiration. You merely mimicked his work. You might as well call a Face Dancer a work of art."

Erasmus smiled. "Some of them are."

Abruptly, with powerful hands, the robot ripped the painting and its frame into tiny pieces. As if putting a punctuation mark on the grotesque display, Erasmus whirled and stomped on the broken pieces, saying, "Call this artistic temperament." Moving to depart, he added, "Omnius will summon your Kwisatz Haderach soon. We have waited a long time for this."

What is the difference between data and memory? I intend to find out.

—ERASMUS,
Laboratory Notebooks

The independent robot's memories of Serena were as fresh as if the events had occurred only days ago. Serena Butler . . . such a fascinating woman. And just as Erasmus had survived through the millennia as a package of data nearly destroyed and then recovered, so Serena's memories and personality lived on, somehow, in the Other Memories of the Bene Gesserit.

This posed an intriguing question: No Bene Gesserits could be Serena Butler's direct descendants, for Erasmus had killed her only child. Then again, he couldn't be sure what had happened to all of his experimental clones over the years. He had tried many times to bring Serena back, with no success.

Aboard this no-ship, however, the humans had grown gholas from their past, just as his own plan had brought back Baron Harkonnen and a version of Paul Atreides. Erasmus knew that a nullentropy tube hidden in a Tleilaxu Master had contained a wealth of ancient and carefully gathered cells.

He was confident that a real Tleilaxu Master could succeed in bringing Serena back, where his own primitive experiments had failed.

Erasmus and Omnius had both absorbed enough Face Dancers to have instinctive reverence for the abilities of a Master. The independent robot knew exactly where he had to go before leaving the no-ship.

Erasmus found the medical center and the axlotl chambers where the whole library of historical cells had been catalogued and stored. If Serena Butler was among them . . .

He was surprised to find a Tleilaxu already there, harried and frantic. The diminutive man had disconnected the life-support systems of the axlotl tanks. With his olfactory sensors, Erasmus noted the smells of chemicals, melange precursors, and human flesh.

He grinned. "You must be Scytale, the Tleilaxu Master! It's been a long time."

Scytale whirled, looking fearful at the sight of the robot.

Erasmus took a step closer, and studied the Tleilaxu's face. "A child? What are you doing?"

The Tleilaxu drew himself up. "I am destroying the tanks and the melange they produce. I had to surrender that knowledge as a bargaining chip. I won't let thinking machines and traitorous Face Dancers simply take it from me—from *us*."

Erasmus showed no concern for the sabotaged axlotl tanks. "But you appear to be very young."

"I am a ghola. I have my memories back. I am everything that any of my previous incarnations were."

"Of course you are. Such a marvelous process, perpetuating yourself through serial ghola lives. We machines understand such things, although we have much more efficient methods of performing data transfers and backups." He looked intensely at the genetic library that held the potential ghola cells . . . Serena Butler . . .

Noting the robot's keen interest, the Tleilaxu sprang to stand in front of the sealed wall of specimens. "Beware! The witches placed security sensors on these gene samples to prevent anyone from tampering with or stealing them. The library has a built-in self-destruct system." He narrowed his dark, rodentlike eyes. If this Master was bluffing, he was doing a remarkably convincing job. "I need only yank on a drawer, and this entire cabinet will be flooded with gamma radiation, enough to ionize every single sample."

"Why?" The robot was perplexed. "After the Bene Gesserit took those cells from you and used them for their own purposes? Didn't they force you to cooperate? Would you truly stand on their side?" He extended a platinum hand. "Join us instead. I would greatly reward you for your assistance in growing one particular ghola—"

In a threatening motion, Scytale placed his small hand on one of the many cell containers. Though trembling, he seemed entirely determined. "Yes, I would stand with them. I shall always stand *against* the thinking machines."

"Interesting. New enemies make unexpected alliances."

The Tleilaxu didn't move. "In the final assessment, we're all humans—and you are not."

Erasmus chuckled. "And what about Face Dancers? They fall between, don't they? These aren't the shape-shifters you produced long ago, but are instead far superior biological machines that I helped create. And because of them, Omnius and I are, in effect, the greatest of all Face Dancers—among many other things."

Scytale didn't move. "Haven't you noticed the Face Dancers are no longer reliable?"

"Ah, but they are reliable to me."

"Are you sure?"

The robot took a tentative step forward, testing. Scytale tensed his fingers on the handle of the sample cabinet. Erasmus amplified his voice. "Stop!" He eased himself backward, giving the Tleilaxu Master more room. There would be plenty of time to return and test Scytale's loyalties. "I leave you to this facility and your cellular samples."

Erasmus had waited more than fifteen thousand years for Serena, and could continue to do so. For now, the robot had to return to the machine cathedral and prepare for the final show. The evermind was not quite so patient to achieve his ultimate goals as Erasmus was.

*Come, let us eat and sing together. We will share a drink and laugh
at our enemies.*

—from an ancient ballad by

GURNEY HALLECK

The computer evermind sent his troops to bring Paul from the
Ithaca to the machines' cathedral-like nexus. New-model robotic
guards swarmed down the corridors like quicksilver insects. Approaching Paul, one of them said, "Come with us to the primary cathedral."

Chani grabbed his arm and held on, as if she too had sprouted
metal hands. "I will not let you go, Usul."

Looking at the inhuman escorts, he said to her, "We can't keep
them from taking me."

"Then I shall come with you." He tried to argue with her, but she
cut him off. "I am a Fremen woman. Would you try to stop me? You
might just as easily fight these machines."

Concealing a small smile, he faced the sleek machines that clicked
and flittered in front of him. "I will accompany you without resistance,
but only if Chani comes with me."

Emerging from her quarters where Alia's body now lay on the narrow bed, Jessica placed herself between Paul and the robots. Bloodstains
still marked her shipsuit. "He is my son. I have already lost a daughter
today, and cannot bear to lose him as well. I'm going with you."

"We are here to escort Paul Atreides to the primary cathedral," one of the robots said, its freeform face flowing like heavy rain on a Caladan window. "There are no other restrictions."

Paul took that as agreement. For some reason, Omnius wanted *him*, even though he did not have his memories back. All other passengers and crew were apparently extraneous baggage. Had he been the subject of the hunt from the beginning? How could that be? Had the thinking machines somehow known he would be aboard? Paul gripped Chani's hand and said to her, "It will be over soon, in whatever manner fate decides. All along, our destinies have hurtled us toward this point, like levitating trains out of control."

"We will face it together, my love," Chani said. He only wished that he could recall all his years with her . . . and that she could do the same.

"What about Duncan?" he asked. "And Sheeana?"

"We must depart now," the robots said in unison. "Omnius waits."

"Duncan and Sheeana will know soon enough," Jessica said.

Before they left, Paul made a point of taking the crysknife Chani had made for him. Like a Fremen warrior, he wore it proudly at his waist. Although the worm-tooth blade would do nothing against the thinking machines, it made him feel more like the legendary Muad'Dib—the man who defeated powerful empires. But in his mind he again saw the horrible recurring vision, the flicker of memory or prescience in which he lay on the floor in a strange place, mortally wounded—looking up at a younger version of himself who laughed in triumph.

He blinked and sought to focus on reality, not possibilities or destiny. Following the insectile robots down the corridors, he tried to tell himself he was prepared to face whatever lay in store for him.

Before the gholas could emerge from the ship through the ragged hole the machines had made, Wellington Yueh tried to push his way past the ranks of escort robots. "Wait! I want . . . I need to go with you." He fumbled for excuses. "If someone gets hurt, I'm the best Suk doctor available. I can help." He lowered his voice and pleaded, "The Baron will be there, and he'll want to see me."

Still wrestling with her reinjured feelings toward him, Jessica sounded harsh and bitter. "Help? Did you help Alia?" Hearing this, Yueh looked as if she had slapped him.

"Let him come, Mother." Paul felt resigned. "Dr. Yueh was a staunch childhood supporter and mentor to the original Paul. I won't turn down any ally or witness to whatever is about to occur."

Following the robots, they emerged onto flowing roadways that carried them along like floating plates. Batlike fliers streaked high overhead, and mirrored watcheyes flitted about in the air, observing the group's progress from all angles. Behind them, the huge no-ship had been incorporated into the machine metropolis. Sentient metal buildings of freeform architecture had grown around the *Ithaca*'s hull like coral swallowing up an old shipwreck beneath the seas of Caladan. The buildings seemed to alter whenever the evermind had a fleeting thought.

"This whole city is alive and thinking," Paul said. "It's all one changeable, adapting machine."

Under her breath, his mother quoted, "'Thou shalt not create a machine in the likeness of the human mind.'"

Speakers appeared in the solid silver walls of the looming buildings, and a simulated voice mockingly repeated Jessica's words. "'Thou shalt not create a machine in the likeness of the human mind.' What a quaint superstition!" The laughter sounded as if it had been recorded from somewhere else, distorted freakishly, and then played back. "I look forward to our encounter."

The escort robots brought them into an enormous structure with shimmering walls, curved arches, and enclosed parklike spaces. A spectacular lava fountain spouted plumes of hot, scarlet liquid into a tempered basin.

In the middle of the great cathedral hall, an elderly man and woman awaited them, dressed in loose, comfortable garments. Dwarfed by the enclosure, they certainly did not look menacing.

Paul decided not to wait for their captors to play control games. "Why have you brought me here? What do you want?"

"I want to help the universe." The old man stepped down the polished stone stairs. "We are in the endgame of Kralizec, a watershed that will change the universe forever. Everything that came before will end, and everything that comes in the future will be under my guidance."

The old woman explained. "Consider all the chaos that has existed over the millennia of your human civilization. Such messy creatures you are! We thinking machines could have done a much neater, more efficient job. We have learned of your God Emperor Leto II, and the Scattering, and the Famine Times."

"At least he enforced peace for thirty-five hundred years," the old man added. "He had the right idea."

"My grandson," Jessica said. "They called him Tyrant because of the difficult decisions he made. But even he did not do as much damage as your thinking machines did during the Butlerian Jihad."

"You cast blame too loosely. Did *we* cause the damage and destruction, or did humans like Serena Butler? That is a matter for debate." Abruptly the old woman cast off her disguise, like a reptile shedding its dry skin. The robot's flowmetal face—male now—displayed a wide smile. "From the beginning, machines and humans have been at odds, but only we are able to observe the long span of history, and only we can understand what must be done and find a logical way to achieve it. Is that not a valid analysis of your legendary Kralizec?"

"Only an interpretation," Jessica said.

"The correct one, though. Right now we are involved in the necessary business of uprooting weeds in a garden—an apt metaphor. The weeds themselves do not appreciate it, and the dirt may be disturbed for some time, but in the end the garden is vastly improved. Machines and humans are but manifestations of a long-standing conflict that your ancient philosophers recorded, the battle between heart and mind."

Omnius retained his old man form, since he had no other familiar physical manifestation. "Back in the Old Empire, many of your people are trying to make their last stands against us. It is futile, for my Face Dancers have ensured that your weapons will not work. Even your navigation machines are under my control. Already my fleet approaches Chapterhouse."

"Our ship has had no contact with either the Guild or Chapterhouse since before I was born," Paul said in a dismissive tone. He pointed to Chani, Jessica, and Yueh, all of those gholas born on the ship in flight. "None of us has ever been in the Old Empire."

"Then allow me to show you." With a wave of his hand, the old man displayed a complex holo-image of stars, indicating how far his immense fleet had progressed. Paul was stunned by the scope of the conquest and devastation; he didn't think the evermind would exaggerate what the machines had done. Omnius didn't need to. Hundreds of planets had already been destroyed or enslaved.

In a soothing voice, Erasmus said, "Fortunately, the war will soon be over."

The old man approached Paul. "And now that I have you, there is no question of the outcome. The mathematical projection states that the Kwisatz Haderach will change the battle at the end of the universe. Since I control you *and* the other one, we will now finish this conflict."

Erasmus stepped forward to inspect Paul, like a scientist examining a valuable specimen. His optic threads glittered. "We know you have the potential within your genes. The challenge lies in determining *which* Paul Atreides will be the better Kwisatz Haderach."

Optimism may be the greatest weapon humanity possesses. Without it, we would never attempt the impossible, which—against all odds—occasionally succeeds.

—MOTHER COMMANDER MURBELLA,
speech to the gathered Sisterhood

W ithout Obliterators or navigation control, the human warships lay like white-bellied victims on sacrificial altars, all across the last-stand line they had drawn.

Aboard her flagship, Mother Commander Murbella shouted orders, while Guild Administrator Gorus demanded miracles from his underlings. Watching the screens on the navigation bridge, Murbella saw thinking-machine battleships cruise past the Sisterhood's pitiful vessels on their way to destroy Chapterhouse. Similar non-battles must be occurring at the hundred flashpoints across the front lines, key human-inhabited systems now completely vulnerable to the coup de grace. The gamble had failed, utterly.

Weighing heavily on Murbella's mind was her responsibility to humanity, the rest of the Sisterhood . . . and her long-lost Duncan. Was he still alive, and did he even remember her? It had been almost twenty-five years. Murbella had to do this—for him, for herself, or for all those who had survived thus far in the epic war.

Without letting instinctive Honored Matre rage control her actions, Murbella whirled toward Gorus. She grabbed the front of the

Administrator's loose robe and shook him so that his pale braid whipped his face. "What other weapons do your Guildships have?"

"A few projectiles, Mother Commander. Energy weapons. Standard offensive artillery—but that would be suicide! Only the Obliterators could have made it possible for our ships to deal a mortal blow against the Enemy!"

In disgust, she cast him away, so that he stumbled backward and fell to the deck. "This is already a suicide mission! How dare you cringe now, when we have no alternative?"

"But . . . but, Mother Commander—it would waste our fleet, our lives!"

"Obviously, heroism is not your strong suit." She turned to a meek-looking Guildsman and used the power of Bene Gesserit Voice on him for good measure. "Prepare to launch our Obliterators. Blanket space with them. Maybe the saboteurs missed a few."

The Guildsman operated his weapons controls, barely bothering to choose targets. He launched ten more Obliterators, then another ten. None exploded, and the machine ships kept coming.

Her voice low, Murbella said, "Now fire all the standard projectiles we have. And once we deplete our conventional armaments, we'll use our ships as battering rams. Whatever we have."

"But why, Mother Commander?" Gorus said. "We should fall back and regroup. Plan some other way to fight. We must at least survive!"

"If we don't win today, we don't survive anyway. We may be outnumbered, but we can still wipe out part of the thinking-machine fleet. I will not simply abandon Chapterhouse!"

Gorus scrambled back to his feet. "To what purpose, Mother Commander? The machines can just replace themselves."

As they spoke, more Obliterators filled space. So far, all had turned out to be duds.

"The purpose is to show them we can still fight. It is what makes us human, what gives us significance. History shall not record that we abandoned Chapterhouse and tried to hide from the final confrontation between humanity and the thinking machines."

"History? Who will be left to record history?"

Within three minutes of each other, six small foldspace craft raced into the battle zone over Chapterhouse, reporting from the other clusters of ships. They transmitted urgent messages and demanded new orders from the Mother Commander. "Our Obliterators don't function!"

"All navigation systems have shut down."

"How do we fight them now, Mother Commander?"

She answered in a strong, steady tone. "We fight with everything we have."

Just then, a fabulously bright flash blew across at least fifty of the Enemy vessels, vaporizing them in an expanding arc that sent a shudder through the decks of the more distant Guild vessels. Murbella gasped, then laughed. "See! One of the Obliterators still worked! Fire the rest of them."

To her astonishment, space around them suddenly shimmered, cracked, and disgorged hundreds of giant ships. Not human defender vessels.

At first Murbella thought that the Enemy machines had sent yet another devastating fleet, but she quickly identified the cartouche on the curved hulls. Guild Heighliners! They spilled out of foldspace from every direction, surrounding the first massive wave of thinking-machine vessels.

"Administrator, why did you hold out on us?" Murbella's voice was brittle. "There must be a thousand ships here!"

Gorus seemed just as astonished as she was.

A female voice thrummed across the commlines that linked Murbella's defenders. "I am the Oracle of Time, and I bring reinforcements. Mathematical compilers corrupted many Guild vessels, but my Navigators control these Heighliners."

"Navigators?" The white-haired Administrator gasped in consternation. "We thought they were all dead, starved for spice."

The Oracle spoke in a powerful, lilting tone. "And my ships— unlike those made by the traitorous fabricators of Ix—command full armaments. Our Obliterators work as designed. We took them from old Honored Matre ships and hid them away for our own defenses. We intend to use them now."

Murbella's face flushed. She had suspected the rebel Honored Matres had possessed many more Obliterators than were found. So, the Navigators had been hiding them all along!

The Omnius invasion fleet shifted position in response to the Navigator reinforcements, but the machines could not comprehend the magnitude of the astonishing opponent they now faced. They did not react in time as the Oracle's Heighliners spewed out dazzling sunbursts in a flurry of explosions like miniature supernovas. Each incinerating burst of light vaporized entire clusters of the overly complacent Enemy vessels.

Although the machine forces scrambled to defend themselves, their response was ineffective, as if their control functions had been disconnected. The evermind had modeled his plan repeatedly, setting up contingency options for likely turns of events. But Omnius had not foreseen this.

"Thinking machines have long been my sworn enemies," the Oracle said in her ethereal voice.

While Murbella looked on with great satisfaction, precisely targeted Obliterators wiped out countless Enemy ships. If only the Honored Matres had simply turned their stolen weapons against the thinking machines when they'd had the chance, long ago! But those women had never stood together against a common foe. Instead, they hoarded their stolen weapons and used the destructive power against each other, against rival planets. What a waste!

The overlapping detonations, each strong enough to scorch a planet, struck the front line of machine ships. A dozen Heighliners raced deeper into the Chapterhouse system to chase Enemy vessels that had already reached planetary orbit.

"We will do what we can at your other front-line planets," the Oracle said. "Today we hurt the Enemy."

Almost before she could absorb what was happening around her, Murbella saw that the initial wave of thinking-machine forces had been reduced to nothing more than scattered debris. As far as she could tell, the Enemy battleships never got the chance to launch a single shot against the defenders of humanity.

Some of the Heighliners winked out, folding space to go to the other crippled last-stand defenders. There, they would deliver their Obliterators and speed off to further encounters with the Enemy. All across the front lines, at every flashpoint where Murbella had placed her groups of fighters, the Oracle's Navigators struck, and vanished again. . . .

Murbella snapped to Administrator Gorus. "Get me a comchannel! How do we talk to your Oracle of Time?"

Gorus was stunned by the events around him. "One does not request an audience with the Oracle. No living person has ever initiated contact with her."

"She just saved our lives! Let me talk with her."

With a skeptical expression, the Administrator made a gesture toward another Guildsman. "We can try, but I promise nothing."

The gray-robed man fiddled with the commline until Murbella shouldered him aside. "Oracle of Time—whoever you are! Let us join forces to eradicate the thinking machines."

A long silence was Murbella's only response, not even static, and her heart sank. Gorus gave her a superior look, as if he had known to expect this all along. Murbella saw a second wave of thinking-machine ships race in, now that the initial attack had been thwarted. And these would not tauntingly hold their fire. "More machines are coming—"

"For now, I must move on." As the Oracle spoke, Heighliners began to disappear like soap bubbles popping. "My main battle is on Synchrony."

"Wait!" Murbella cried. "We need you!"

"We are needed elsewhere. Kralizec will not be consummated here. At long last, I have found the no-ship that carries Duncan Idaho, and the secret location of Omnius. I must now go there to end this by destroying the evermind. Forever."

Murbella reeled as the unexpected information hit her. The no-ship found? *Duncan was alive!*

Within moments the last of the Heighliners vanished into foldspace, leaving the Mother Commander and her ships alone to face the next wave. The thinking machines kept coming.

*We have our own goals and ambitions, for good or ill. But our true
destiny is decided by forces over which we have no control.*

> — "The Atreides Manifesto,"
> first draft (section deleted by Bene Gesserit committee)

A door in the machines' grand cathedral flowed open like a water-
fall of metal, parting to reveal two figures that stepped forward
in tandem.

It had been hours since Baron Vladimir Harkonnen had murdered
Alia, yet his wide lips still struggled to contain his satisfaction. His
spider-black eyes glinted. Dr. Yueh glared at the Baron, his personal
bête noïre.

Paul did not need ghola memories to recognize the Baron's
companion—a lean young man, barely more than a boy, but whipcord
strong with muscles tuned from constant training. The eyes were
harder, the features sharper, but Paul knew the face that stared back at
him from the mirror.

Beside him Chani gave a strangled cry, but the sound changed to a
growl in her throat. She recognized the younger Paul, and also saw the
terrible difference.

A cold sense of inexorability froze Paul's blood as everything became
clear. His prescient vision in the flesh! So, the thinking machines had
grown another ghola of Paul Atreides to be their pawn, a second poten-

tial Kwisatz Haderach for their private use. Now he understood the recurring dreams of his own face laughing triumphantly, consuming spice, the peculiar image of *himself* stabbed and dying, bleeding out his life's blood on a strange floor. Just like the one on which he stood now, in this vaulted chamber.

It will be one of us. . . .

"It seems we have an abundance of Atreides." The Baron ushered his protégé forward, his hand clamped on the young man's shoulder. Almost apologetically, as if the wary audience cared, he said, "We call this one Paolo."

Paolo pulled away from him. "Before long you will call me Emperor, or Kwisatz Haderach—whichever term grants me the highest respect." Looking on, the old man and Erasmus seemed to find the whole tableau amusing.

Paul wondered how many times he had been trapped by fate, by terrible purpose. How often and in how many circumstances had he seen himself dead from a knife thrust? Now he cursed the fact that he would face this crisis as a shell of his former self, not armed with the memories and skills of his past.

Unto myself, I must be sufficient.

Snickering, the younger boy walked to where his counterpart stood stiffly at attention. Paul looked back at his mirror image without fear. Despite the age difference, they were approximately the same height, and as Paul looked into his doppelganger's eyes, he knew he must not underestimate this "Paolo." The youth was a weapon as sure and deadly as the crysknife at Paul's waist.

Jessica and Chani moved protectively close to Paul, ready to strike. His mother, with her memories restored, was a full Reverend Mother. Chani, though she did not yet have her past life, had shown considerable fighting skills in earlier practice sessions, as if she still felt Fremen blood in her veins.

Paolo's brow furrowed, his expression flickering for just a moment. Then he sneered at Jessica. "Are you supposed to be my mother? The Lady Jessica! Well, you may be older than I am—but that doesn't make you a real mother."

Jessica gave him a brief, shrewd appraisal. "I know my family, regardless of the order in which they were reborn. And you are not one of them."

Paolo crossed the chamber floor toward Chani, leering with exaggerated hauteur. "And you . . . I know you, too. You were supposed to be the great love of my life, a Fremen girl so insignificant that history recorded little of her youth. Daughter of Liet-Kynes, weren't you? A complete nobody until you became the consort of the great Muad'Dib."

Paul could feel her nails digging into his arm as she ignored the boy and talked to him instead. "The Bashar's teachings were right, Usul. A ghola's worth is not intrinsic in its cells. The process can go horribly wrong—as it clearly did with this young monster."

"It's more a matter of parenting," the Baron said. "Imagine how the universe would be changed if the original Muad'Dib had received different instructions in the uses of power—if *I* had raised him, as I tried to do with the lovely boy, Feyd-Rautha."

"Enough of this," Omnius broke in. "My machine battleships are even now clashing with—or should I say annihilating?—the pathetic remnants of human defenses. According to my last reports, the humans were making simultaneous stands across space. That will allow me to destroy them all at once and be done with it."

Erasmus nodded to the humans in the cathedral chamber. "Within a few more centuries your own warring factions would have torn your race apart anyway."

The old man shot the independent robot an annoyed look. "Now that I have the final Kwisatz Haderach here, all the conditions have been fulfilled. It is time to end this. There is no need to bother with grinding every inhabited world to dust." His lips quirked in a strange smile. "Though that would be enjoyable as well."

Musing, Erasmus looked from Paul to Paolo. "Although genetically identical, you two have slightly different ages, memories, and experiences. Our Paolo is technically a clone, grown from blood cells preserved on a dagger. But this other Paul Atreides—what is the origin of your cells? Where did the Tleilaxu find them?"

"I don't know," Paul said. According to Duncan, the elderly man and woman had begun their merciless pursuit well before anyone had suggested the ghola project, before old Scytale revealed his nullentropy capsule. How could the evermind have known that Paul would reappear here? Had the machines rigged a complex game? Had the sentient machines developed an artificial but sophisticated form of *prescience*?

Erasmus made a humming sound. "Even so, I believe you each have the potential to be the Kwisatz Haderach we need. But which of you will prove superior and achieve it?"

"It's me." Paolo strutted around. "We all know that." Obviously the younger boy had been raised with a belief in his role, so that his head was filled with confidence—though it was a confidence born of true skill, not one arising from imagination.

"And how will that be determined?" Jessica asked, looking at both Pauls, weighing them with her eyes.

A side door flowed open near the fountain that sprayed molten metal, and a man in a black one-piece suit emerged carrying an ornate bloodwood box topped with a smaller wrapped package. He was gaunt, with bland features.

"Khrone, there you are! We have been waiting."

"I am here, Lord Omnius." The man glanced at the assemblage and then, either in surrender or a flash of independence, his unremarkable human features faded away to reveal him as a pale and sunken-eyed Face Dancer. Setting the box aside, he carefully unwrapped the translucent fabric of the small package to reveal a brownish-blue paste flecked with gold spangles.

"This is a concentrated and unusually potent form of spice." The Face Dancer rubbed his fingertips and lifted them to his inhuman nose, as if the smell pleased him. "Harvested from a modified worm that grows in the oceans of Buzzell. It will not be long before the witches understand and begin their own operations there to capture the worms and extract the spice. At the moment, though, I hold the only sample of this ultraspice. Its sheer power should be sufficient to plunge the Kwisatz Haderach—one of you—into a perfect prescient trance. You will achieve powers that only prophecy could predict. You will see everything, know everything, and become the key to the culmination of Kralizec."

Erasmus spoke, sounding almost cheery. "After observing how the human race has ruined things without us around to maintain order, the universe definitely needs changing." The robot picked up the blood-wood box and raised the finely etched lid. Inside lay an ornate, gold-hilted dagger, which he picked up with something like reverence. A smear of old blood remained on the blade.

Behind Paul, his mother gasped. "I know that dagger! It's as clear and fresh in my mind as if I just saw it. Emperor Shaddam himself pre-sented it to Duke Leto as a gift, and years later at Shaddam's trial Leto gave it back to him."

"Oh, there is more than that." The Baron's eyes glittered. "I believe the Emperor gave that same dagger to my beloved nephew Feyd-Rautha for his duel with your son. Unfortunately, Feyd didn't quite succeed in that battle."

"I love convoluted stories," Erasmus added. "Later still, Hasimir Fenring stabbed Emperor Muad'Dib with it and nearly killed him. So you see, this dagger has a long and checkered past." He lifted it, letting the light of the cathedral chamber gleam off the blade. "The perfect weapon to help us make our choice, don't you think?"

Paul drew the crysknife Chani had made for him from its sheath at his side. The hilt felt warm in his grip, the curved milky blade perfectly balanced. "I have my own weapon."

Paolo danced back warily, looking at the Baron, Omnius, and Eras-mus, as if expecting them to leap to his aid. He snatched the gold-hilted dagger from the robot's hand and pointed the sharp tip at Paul.

"And what are they to do with these weapons?" Jessica asked, though the answer was obvious to everyone.

The robot looked at her in surprise. "It is only appropriate that we solve this problem in a particularly human way: a duel to the death, of course! Is that not perfect?"

The worm is outside for all to see, and the worm is within me, part of me. Beware, for I am the worm. Beware!

—LETO II,
Dar-es-Balat recordings, in his voice

After Paul and his companions were taken from the no-ship, Sheeana found young Leto II in his quarters. Huddling all alone in the dark, the youth was feverish and trembling. At first she thought he was terrified at having been left behind, but she soon realized he was genuinely sick.

Seeing her, the boy forced himself to his feet. He swayed, and perspiration glistened on his brow. He looked pleadingly at her. "Reverend Mother Sheeana! You're the only one—the only one who knows the worms." His large, dark eyes flicked from side to side. "Can you hear them? I can."

She frowned. "Hear them? I don't—"

"The *sandworms!* The worms in the hold. They're calling me, tunneling through my mind, tearing me up inside."

Raising her hand for silence, she paused, deep in thought. All her life, Shaitan had understood her, but she had never received any actual messages from the creatures, even when she'd tried to become part of them.

But now, by extending her senses she did feel a tumultuous thrumming in her head and through the walls of the damaged no-ship. Since the *Ithaca's* capture, Sheeana had ascribed such feelings to the crushing weight of failure after their long flight. But now she began to understand. Something had been scraping through her subconscious, like dull fingernails raking across the slate of her fear. Subsonic pulses of invitation. *The sandworms.*

"We have to go to the hold," Leto announced. "They are calling. They . . . I know what to do."

Sheeana gripped the boy's shoulders. "What is it? What do we have to do?"

He pointed to himself. "Something of me is *inside* the worms. Shai-Hulud is calling."

With the no-ship safely trapped in living-metal constructions, the thinking machines paid little attention to the vessel. Apparently, they had wanted to own and control the Kwisatz Haderach . . . a goal that was not as simple as it sounded, as the Sisterhood had learned long ago. Now that he had Paul Atreides in his machine cathedral, Omnius seemed to think he possessed everything he needed. The remaining passengers were irrelevant prisoners of war.

The Bene Gesserits had planned the creation of their superman over hundreds of generations, subtly guiding bloodlines and breeding maps to produce the long-anticipated messiah. But after Paul Muad'Dib turned against them and created havoc in their carefully ordered timeline, the Sisters had vowed never to unleash another Kwisatz Haderach. But in the long-ago aftermath, Muad'Dib's twin children had been born before the damage could be fully understood. One of those twins, Leto II, had been a Kwisatz Haderach, like his father.

A key turned in Sheeana's mind, unlocking other thoughts. Perhaps in the solemn twelve-year-old Leto, the thinking machines had a blind spot! Could *he* be the final Kwisatz Haderach they sought? Had Omnius even considered the possibility that the machines might have the wrong one? Her pulse quickened. Prophecies were notorious for misdirection. Maybe Erasmus had missed the obvious! She could hear the inner voice of Serena Butler laughing at the possibility, and she allowed herself to cling to a tiny kernel of hope.

"Let's go to the cargo hold, then." Sheeana took the boy's hand, and they hurried down the corridors and dropchutes to the lower levels.

As they approached the great doors, Sheeana heard explosive thunder from the other side. The frenzied worms charged from one end of the kilometer-long space to the other, smashing into the walls.

By the time they arrived at the access door, young Leto seemed ready to collapse. "We have to go in," he said, his face flushed. "The worms . . . I need to talk with them, calm them."

Sheeana, who had never been afraid of the sandworms before, now hesitated, worried that in their wild state they might not grant safety to her or Leto. But the boy worked the controls, and the sealed door slid aside. Hot, dry air blew onto their faces. Leto waded out and up to his knees in the soft dunes, and Sheeana hurried after him.

When Leto raised his arms and shouted, all seven worms charged toward him like snorting predators, with the largest one—Monarch—at the fore. Sheeana could feel the hot wave of their anger, their need for destruction . . . but something told her that rage was not directed at either of them. The creatures rose up from the sand and towered over the two humans.

"The thinking machines are outside the ship," Sheeana said to Leto. "Will the worms . . . will they fight for us?"

The boy looked forlorn. "They will follow my path if I lay it out for them, but I can't see it yet myself!"

Looking at him, she wondered again if this boy could be the ultimate Kwisatz Haderach, the link in the chain that Omnius had overlooked. What if Paul Atreides was no more than a feint in the final duel between man and machine?

Leto shook himself, visibly bolstering his determination. "But the prior *me*, the God Emperor, had tremendous prescience. Maybe he foresaw this as well and prepared the beasts. I . . . trust them."

At this, the worms dipped in unison, as if bowing. Leto swayed, and they swayed with him. For a moment the walls of the hold seemed to recede, and the sand dunes flowed out to eternity. The ceiling disappeared in a vertiginous haze of dust. Suddenly, everything snapped back into focus.

Leto caught his breath and called out, "The Golden Path is coming to meet *me*! It is time to release the worms—here, and now."

Sheeana sensed the rightness of this and knew what to do. All systems were still programmed to obey her instructions. "The machines deactivated the weapons and engines, but I can still open the great cargo doors."

She and Leto hurried to the controls in the hall, where she input the commands. Machinery hummed and strained. Then, with a loud clank and a bang, a gap appeared in the long-sealed walls. From the corridor, Sheeana and the boy watched the immense lower doors slide open, like clenched teeth being pried apart.

Tons of sand spilled out in a rushing stream and propelled the sand-worms, like living battering rams, into the streets of the machine capital.

Prescience reveals no absolutes, only possibilities. The surest way to know exactly what the future holds is to experience it in real time.

—from "Conversations with Muad'Dib" by the
PRINCESS IRULAN

A duel makes no sense." The Baron frowned as he looked around the cathedral chamber. "It is wasteful. Naturally, I am convinced my dear Paolo will defeat this upstart, but why not keep both Kwisatz Haderachs for yourself, Omnius?"

"I desire only the best one," the evermind said.

"And we could not be certain of controlling *two* of them as they struggled for preeminence with their new powers," Erasmus said.

"Whichever of you wins the duel will receive the ultraspice," Omnius announced. "When the winner consumes it, I will have my true and final Kwisatz Haderach. I can then conclude this wasteful nonsense and begin my real work of remaking the universe."

Chani kept one hand on Paul's arm. "How do you know either of them is your Kwisatz Haderach?"

"You could be delusional," Yueh said, and the boy Paolo shot him a glare.

"And why should I cooperate if I win?" Paul said, but the sickening echoes of recurring visions strangled his protest. He thought he knew what was going to happen, or some piece of it.

"Because we have faith." The Baron, a paragon of unholiness, laughed at his own joke, but no one else did.

Paolo drew designs in the air with the tip of his gold-hilted knife. "I have the Emperor's dagger! You were stabbed with it once."

"That won't happen again. This is my day of triumph." But Paul heard the brittleness in his measured words, the vulnerability behind the bravado. He could see no way to avoid the duel, and wasn't sure he wanted to. In his mind, he drove back the troubling flashes of vision. This perverse version of himself needed to be cut out like a cancer.

The time had come. Paul gathered all of his concentration for the fight. Hardly seeing Chani, he kissed her. The wormtooth dagger she had made felt perfectly balanced in his hand. He had practiced with the crysknife on the no-ship, and he knew how to fight.

I must not fear. Fear is the mind-killer.

Young Paolo pressed his lips together in a tight smile. "I can tell you've had the visions, too! See, we are alike in yet another aspect."

"I've had many visions." *I will face my fear.*

"Not like these." His opponent's knowing smile was maddening, unnerving. . . . Paul stiffened his resolve. He would not give Paolo the satisfaction of showing dread or uncertainty.

Quicksilver robots appeared and removed the human observers to the sidelines of the expansive hall. The Baron stepped back beside Khrone, his gaze flicking back and forth between young Paolo and the tempting dose of ultraspice. He licked his thick lips hungrily, as if wishing he could try some for himself.

On the smooth combat floor of the chamber, Paul stood poised a couple of meters from Paolo. His younger foe tossed the gold-hilted dagger from hand to hand and smiled at him, showing white teeth.

Calming himself, Paul summoned all the important lessons he had learned: Bene Gesserit attitudes and prana-bindu instruction, the precise muscular training and rigorous attack exercises that Duncan and the Bashar had drilled into all of the ghola children.

He spoke to his fear: *I will permit it to pass over me and through me.*

It would all culminate here. Paul felt confident that if he rose to the challenge and won, his Kwisatz Haderach powers would surface, and he would be able to go on to defeat the thinking machines. But if Paolo won . . . He didn't want to consider that possibility.

"Usul, remember your time among the Fremen," Chani called from the side of the hall. "Remember how they taught you to fight!"

"He remembers none of it, bitch!" Paolo slashed the Emperor's knife across the air, as if slitting an invisible throat. "But I am fully trained, a tempered fighting machine."

The Baron applauded, but only a little. "No one likes a braggart, Paolo . . . unless, of course, you succeed and prove to everyone that you were merely stating facts."

Paul refused to be controlled by his visions. *If I am the Kwisatz Haderach, I'll change the visions. I shall fight. I shall be everywhere at once.*

Young Paolo must have been thinking the same thing, for he lunged like a viper. Startled by the abrupt beginning of the duel, Erasmus swept his plush robes aside and stepped quickly out of the way. Apparently he had intended to delineate the rules of the challenge, but Paolo wanted to make it a brawl.

Paul bent backward like a reed and let the Emperor's blade whistle past, within a centimeter of his neck. Young Paolo snickered. "That was just practice!" He held up the dagger, showing the rust-red stains. "I am one step ahead of you, for this knife is already blooded!"

"It's more your blood than mine," Paul said under his breath. He drove forward with the crysknife, weaving, making the blade dance.

The younger ghola responded by mirroring Paul's movements, as if the pair had an unconscious telepathic connection. He stabbed to the side, and Paul flowed in the other direction. Was this a form of pre-science, Paul wondered, subconsciously foreseeing each blow, or did the two of them know and reproduce each other's fighting styles exactly? They had entirely different training, entirely different upbringings. But still . . .

Concentrating on the duel, Paul's hearing became a fuzz of static. At first he heard encouragement, gasps, shouts of concern from his mother and Chani, but he blocked everything out. Did he have the potential to become the ultimate Kwisatz Haderach that Omnius was searching for? Did he want to be? He had read the histories, knew the bloodshed and suffering that Paul Muad'Dib and Leto II had both caused as Kwisatz Haderachs. What would the machines try to accomplish by possessing an even stronger Kwisatz Haderach? Some locked-away part of Paul already had the ability to look where no one else could—into both feminine and masculine pasts. *What other powers lie untapped within me? Do I dare find out? If I win this duel, what will the thinking machines demand of me afterward?*

He felt like a gladiator on ancient Terra having to prove himself in an arena. And he had a fatal weakness: Omnius held Chani, Jessica, Duncan, and so many others as hostages. If Paul got his ghola memories back, his feelings for them would be even stronger.

Obviously, that was how Omnius intended to force Paul to cooperate, if he won this duel. His love for his companions would only intensify, and they would suffer because of him. Since the computer evermind had far more patience than any human, the machines could torture and kill these hostages with impunity, take cell scrapings and grow new gholas. Over and over! Perhaps Erasmus would bring back his sister Alia, his father the Duke, or Gurney, or Thufir. Kill them, resurrect them, and kill them again. Unless Paul Atreides, the Kwisatz Haderach, bowed to their demands, the thinking machines would make his life an unending hell. Or so they intended.

Now he understood the dilemma of his destiny. And again he saw himself dying in a pool of blood. Perhaps some things could not be changed. But if he was a true Kwisatz Haderach, he should be able to defeat such petty tactics.

He fought on with wild passion, driving himself into a sweaty frenzy. Paolo kicked at him with his feet and slashed with the Emperor's dagger. Paul dove, rolled, and the younger ghola pounced on him. The Emperor's blade drove down hard in what would have been a killing thrust, but Paul slipped to the side, barely in time.

The blade slashed his sleeve, cut a thin line of blood on his left shoulder, then clanged against the stone floor. Paolo, his wrist jolted by the sharp impact, barely maintained a grip on the hilt.

On the polished floor, Paul swept his feet sideways, getting them under his rival and kicking upward. He did have the advantage of being physically stronger than a twelve-year-old. Paul grabbed his counterpart's wrist and pulled himself to his feet, but Paolo locked his fingers around Paul's knife arm, preventing the crysknife from stabbing down. Paul pushed, using his leverage to maneuver them both back toward the shimmering lava fountain.

"Not very . . . innovative!" The younger ghola's breath rasped as he struggled, and Paul continued to drive him back. The heat from the fountain gushed in all directions. If he knocked Paolo into the incandescent metal, would he be killing himself—or saving himself?

Paul saw his opponent clearly and could not hate the other ghola. At the core, both of them were *Paul Atreides*. Paolo was not innately evil, but had been corrupted by terrible things that had been done to him, things he had been taught, not things done of his own volition. Paul did not let his sympathy for his rival weaken him. If he did, Paolo would not hesitate to kill him and claim victory. But Paul—because he was *Paul*—would fight with every ounce of his being to save the future of humanity.

Omnius and Erasmus observed without cheering for either fighter. They would accept whichever one proved victorious. Khrone's shadowed, olive-pit eyes held no emotion at all. The Baron was scowling. Paul didn't want to look toward Chani or his mother.

The roaring lava fountain dumped heat into the air. Paul's already sweaty body became slicker. Wiry Paolo used that to his advantage, squirmed, and Paul's grip began to slip. Suddenly, at the very verge of the fountain, the younger man allowed his knees to buckle.

Paul overcompensated, which threw him off balance. He kneed his opponent in the stomach, but young Paolo had untapped reserves. When Paul raised the crysknife in his sweat-slickened grip, Paolo brought his own hand up backward, using the jeweled hilt of his dagger to smash the base of Paul's knife hand. Tendons twitched in reflexive reaction. The crysknife dropped free, clattered on the edge of the fountain, and tumbled into the molten pool.

Gone.

With the force of dominating vision, stronger than just the knowledge of his own death, Paul realized what he should have known from the beginning: *I am* not *the Kwisatz Haderach that Omnius wants. It isn't me!*

Time seemed to slow down and freeze. Was this what Bashar Teg had experienced when he accelerated himself? But Paul Atreides could move no faster than the events around him. They held him captive and squeezed in on him like the steely embrace of Death.

Wearing a venomous grin, young Paolo swung the gold-hilted dagger around in a perfect arc and, with exquisite slowness, drove the point into Paul's side. He slipped the dagger between his opponent's ribs and kept pushing, shoving the deadly point through Paul's lung and up into his heart.

Then Paolo yanked the murderous weapon free, and time resumed its normal speed. From far away, Paul heard Chani screaming.

Blood gushed from his wound, and Paul stumbled against the base of the hot fountain. It was a mortal wound; there could be no denying it. The prescient voice in his head hammered at him to no purpose. It seemed to be mocking him. *I am not the final Kwisatz Haderach!*

He slithered to the floor like a broken doll, barely saw Chani and Jessica running toward him. Jessica had Yueh by the collar and was dragging the Suk doctor over to her bleeding son.

Paul had never known that one body could contain so much blood. With fading vision, he looked up and saw Paolo prancing victoriously, holding the dripping red dagger. "You knew I would kill you! You might as well have driven in the knife with your own hands!"

It was a perfect reproduction of his visions. He lay on the floor, dying as swiftly as his body would allow.

In the background he heard the Baron Harkonnen's boisterous laughter. The sound was intolerable, but Paul could do nothing to stop it.

When they pour in at once, my memories will be like a sandstorm—and just as destructive. Who can control the wind? If I am truly the God Emperor, then I can control it.

—GHOLA OF LETO II,
last preparatory assignment delivered to Bashar Miles Teg

Sand and worms poured out of the entrapped no-ship's hold into the carefully ordered machine metropolis. The writhing creatures plowed into the open streets like maddened Salusan bulls bursting from their pens. Beside Leto, watching the hold empty in a deafening rush, Sheeana opened her mouth, and her eyes went wide with surprise.

Through his strange connection to the worms, Leto II's mind surged outward with them into the sparkling city. Standing high above at the doorway to the immense cargo bay, he felt a wave of relief and freedom. Without a word to Sheeana, he dove into the sliding, flowing sand, following the worms in their wild exodus. He let the grit carry him, like a swimmer caught in an undertow being rapidly whisked out to sea.

"Leto! What are you doing? Stop!"

He could not have stopped to answer even if he had wanted to. The current of flowing powder sucked him downward—exactly where he wanted to be. Leto plunged under the sand, and his lungs somehow adapted to the dust, as did all of his senses. Like a sandworm he saw without eyes, and perceived the creatures ahead of him, as if he were looking at them through clear water. *This* was what he had been born to do, what he had died to do, ever so long ago.

Memories reverberated in him like echoes of the past—not a visceral recollection, but greater than the knowledge he had acquired by reading the *Ithaca*'s archives. Those entries had been about another young man, another Leto II, but still himself. A thought surfaced: *My skin is not my own.* In those days, his body had been covered with interlinked sandtrout, their membranous bodies meshing with his soft flesh and nerves. They had imparted strength to him, enabling him to run like the wind.

Though still in human form, Leto II recalled some of the fantastic power, not from ghola memories but from the pearl of awareness that the original God Emperor had left within each worm descendant. *They* remembered, and Leto remembered with them.

Histories had been written by so many people who loathed him, who misunderstood what he had been forced to do. They decried the Tyrant's purported cruelty and inhumanity, his willingness to sacrifice everything for the extraordinary Golden Path. But none of the histories—not even his own testamentary journals—had recorded the joy and exuberance of a young man experiencing such unexpected and wondrous power. Leto remembered it all now.

He swam through the flow of sand to where the seven giant worms writhed, and then burst upward to break through the surface. Knowing instinctively what he had to do, Leto staggered toward the largest worm, Monarch. He caught the small part of the thrashing tail, leapt onto the hard rings, and scrambled up like a bare-footed Caladanian primitive scaling a rough-barked palm tree.

As soon as Leto touched the greatest of the seven worms, his fingers and feet seemed to acquire an unnatural adhesion. He could climb and hold on, as if he were part of the creature. And in a way, that was true. Fundamentally, he and the sandworms were one.

Sensing that Leto had joined them, all of the worms paused like enormous soldiers coming to attention. Reaching a perch atop Monarch's curved head, Leto surveyed the sprawling complex of living metal structures, and smelled the strong odor of cinnamon.

From his high vantage point, he watched the city of Synchrony as it shifted buildings into formidable barricades, trying to impede the long-confined sandworms. This was Leto's army, his living battering rams—and he would turn them loose against humanity's Enemy.

Dizzy and euphoric in the redolence of spice, Leto held onto the worm's ridges, which parted to expose the soft pink flesh underneath. He found it enticing, and his body longed for the full sensation, direct contact. Leto slid his bare hands between the ring segments, into the soft tissue membrane. There, he felt as if he was touching the nerve center of the beast itself, plunging his fingers into the neural circuitry that joined these primal creatures together. The sensation hit him like a jolt of electricity. This was where he had belonged for eternity.

At his behest, the sandworms reared higher, like angry cobras no longer interested in the soothing music of a snake charmer. Leto controlled them now. All seven of the worms went on a rampage through the machine streets, and Omnius could do nothing to stop them.

When Leto's mind merged with the largest sandworm, he felt a flood of intense sensations and recalled a similar thing that another Leto II had done thousands of years before. Again he experienced the raspy feel of fast-flowing sand beneath a long and sinuous body. He relished the exquisite dryness of old Arrakis, and knew what it had meant to be the God Emperor, the synthesis of man and sandworm. That had been the zenith of his experience. But did something even greater lie in store for him?

As a ghola child raised aboard the no-ship, Leto II was never entirely sure how the Tleilaxu had obtained his original cells. Had they been taken when he and Ghanima underwent routine medical inspections as children? If so, an awakened Leto ghola would have only the memories of a normal child, the son of Muad'Dib. What if, however, the cells in Scytale's nullentropy capsule had been stolen from the actual God Emperor in his prime? Some unlikely scraping of his enormous vermiform corpse? Or a tissue sampling by one of the devout followers who had taken the Tyrant's withered, drowned body from the bank of the Idaho River?

As Leto's mind fused with Monarch, and all of the surrounding worms, he realized that it didn't matter. This incredible joining now unlocked everything that was within his ghola body and within each nugget of awareness buried deep in the sandworms. Leto II finally became his true self again, as well as the conflicted ghola boy he had been—a loner child and an absolute emperor with the blood of trillions on his conscience. He understood in exquisite detail all his centuries of decisions, his terrible grief, and his determination.

They call me Tyrant without comprehending my kindness, the great purpose behind my actions! They don't know that I foresaw the final conflict all along.

In those last years, God Emperor Leto had strayed so far from humanity that he had forgotten innumerable marvels, especially the softening influence of love. But, as he rode Monarch now, young Leto remembered how much he had adored his twin sister Ghanima, the good times they had shared in their father's incredible palace, and how they had been slated to rule the vast empire of Muad'Dib.

Now Leto was everything he had ever been and more, enhanced by the firsthand memories of his own experiences. With his new vision, as fresh precursors of spice from the worm's body pumped through his blood, he beheld the Golden Path extending gloriously before him. But even with this remarkable revelation, he could not quite see around all the corners ahead. There were blind spots.

High atop his worm, young Leto smiled in determination, and with a single thought he sent the serpentine army forward. The leviathans charged between the great buildings, throwing themselves against reinforced barricades and breaking through. Nothing could stop them.

Hands still buried deep between the ring segments, Leto II rode with a shout of joy on his lips. He gazed forward through eyes that had suddenly become blue-within-blue, eyes that saw what others could not.

Now that I have ridden one of the sandworms and touched the immensity of its existence, I understand the awe the ancient Fremen experienced, why they considered the worms to be their god, Shai-Hulud.

—TLEILAXU MASTER WAFF,
letter to the Council of Masters in Bandalong, dispatched
immediately before the destruction of Rakis

The last pair of Waff's sandworm specimens died inside the arid terrarium.

When freeing the first test worms out in the desert, he had kept two with him at the modular laboratory for research, hoping that what he learned would improve their chances of survival. It did not go well.

Waff prayed vigorously each day, meditated on the holy texts he had brought with him, and sought guidance from God on how best to nurture the reborn Prophet. The first eight specimens were now loose, tunneling through the brittle, crusted sand like explorers on a dead world. The Tleilaxu Master hoped they had survived in the blast-zone environment.

In their final days, the last two little worms in his laboratory aquarium became sluggish, unable to process the nutrients he gave them, though the food was chemically balanced to provide the sandworms with what they needed. He wondered if the small creatures could experience despair. When they lifted their round heads above the sandy surface of the holding tank, it seemed as if they had lost their will to live.

And within a week they both perished.

Though he revered these creatures and what they represented, Waff was desperate for vital scientific information with which to better the other worms' chances of survival. Once the specimens were dead, he had little compunction against picking apart their carcasses, spreading their rings, and cutting into the internal organs. God would understand. If he himself lived long enough, Waff would begin the next phase, as soon as Edrik came back for him. *If* the Navigator ever came back, with his Heighliner and the sophisticated laboratory facilities aboard.

His own Guild assistants offered their help—persistently—but Waff preferred to work alone. Now that these men had set up their stand-alone camp, the Tleilaxu Master had no further use for them. As far as he was concerned, the Guildsmen were free to join Guriff and his treasure hunters in seeking lost spice hoards out in the wasteland.

When one of the bland Guildsmen appeared before him, demanding his attention, Waff easily lost the delicate balance of his thoughts. "What? What is it?"

"The Heighliner should have returned by now. Something is wrong. Guild Navigators are never late."

"He did not promise to come back. When is Guriff's next CHOAM ship due to arrive? You are welcome to depart on it." *In fact, I encourage that.*

"The Navigator may not be concerned with you, Tleilaxu, but he made promises to *us.*"

Waff didn't care about the insult. "Then he will return, eventually. If nothing else, he will want to know how my new sandworms are doing."

The Guild assistant frowned at the flayed creature spread out on the analytical table. "Your pets do not appear to be thriving."

"Today I will go out and monitor the specimens I released earlier. I expect to find them healthy, and stronger than ever."

When the flustered Guildsman left, Waff changed into external protective clothing and hopped into the camp's groundcar. The locator signals showed him that the released worms had not ranged far from the ruins of Sietch Tabr. Attempting to be optimistic, he assumed they had found a habitable subterranean band and were establishing their new domain. As more and more worms grew on Rakis, they would become tillers of the soil, restoring the desert to its former glory. Sandworms, sandtrout, sandplankton, melange. The great ecological cycle would be reestablished.

Reciting ritual prayers, Waff drove across the eerie black-glass desert. His muscles trembled and his bones ached. Like the assembly lines in a war-damaged factory, his degenerating organs labored to keep him alive. Waff's flawed body could fall apart any day now, but he was not afraid. He had died already—many times, in fact.

Always before, he'd had the faith and confidence that a new ghola was being grown for him. This time, though convinced he would not return to life, Waff was content with what he had accomplished. His legacy. The evil Honored Matres had tried to exterminate God's Messenger on Rakis, and Waff would bring Him back. What greater accomplishment could a man hope to attain in this life? In any number of lives?

Following the tracker signals, he drove away from the weathered mountains, to the dunes. Ah, the new sandworms must have fled out into open terrain, looking for fresh sand in which to bury themselves and begin their lives anew!

Instead, what he saw horrified him.

He easily located the eight fledgling worms. Much too easily. Waff stopped the groundcar and scrambled out. The hot, thin air made him gasp, and his lungs and throat burned. He could barely see through stinging tears as he hurried forward.

His precious sandworms lay on the hard ground, barely moving. They had cracked the melted crust of the dunes and churned through the soft grainy dirt beneath, only to emerge again. And now they lay dying.

Waff knelt beside one of the weak, failing creatures. It was flaccid, grayish, barely twitching. Another had heaved itself high enough to sprawl across a broken rock, and there it lay deflated and unable to move. Waff touched it, pressed down on the hard rings. The worm hissed and flinched.

"You cannot die! You are the Prophet, and this is Rakis, your home, your holy sanctuary. You must live!" His body was wracked by a spasm of pain, as if his own life was tied to those of the sandworms. "You can't perish, not again!"

But it seemed that the crippling damage to this world was simply too much for the worms. If even the great Prophet Himself could not endure, then these must assuredly be the End Times.

He had heard of it in ancient prophecies: Kralizec, the great battle at the end of the universe. The crux point that would change everything. Without God's Messenger, surely humanity would be lost. The final days were at hand.

Waff pressed his forehead against the dusty, dying creature's yielding surface. He had done everything he could. Maybe Rakis would never again support the behemoth worms. Maybe this was indeed the end.

From what he saw with his own eyes, he could not deny that the Prophet had truly fallen.

People strive to achieve perfection—ostensibly an honorable goal—
but complete perfection is dangerous. To be imperfect, but human,
is far preferable.

—MOTHER SUPERIOR DARWI ODRADE,
defense before Bene Gesserit Council

When the older and inferior Paul Atreides ghola lay dying on the floor, Paolo turned away, pleased with his victory but far more interested in his other priority. He had proved himself to Omnius and Erasmus. The special ultraspice that would unlock all of his prescient abilities was his now. It would elevate him to the next level, to his exalted destiny—as the Baron had taught him for so long. During that time, Paolo had convinced himself that this was what he wanted, brushing aside any nagging qualms or reservations.

Around the cathedral hall, quicksilver robots stood at attention, ready to attack the remaining humans should Omnius give the order. Maybe Paolo himself would decide to issue such a command, once he was in control. He could hear the pleased laughter of the Baron, the sobs of Chani and Lady Jessica. Paolo wasn't sure which sounds he enjoyed more. His greatest thrill was the clear proof of what he had always known: *I am the one!*

He was the one who would change the course of the universe and control the end of Kralizec, guiding the next age of humanity and machines. Did even the evermind know what he was about to face?

Paolo allowed himself a secretive, amused smile; he would never be a mere puppet for thinking machines. Omnius would soon learn what the Bene Gesserit had long ago discovered: A Kwisatz Haderach is not to be manipulated!

Paolo slipped the bloody dagger into his waistband, strode over to the Face Dancer, and held out a hand to collect the spoils of combat. "That spice is mine."

Khrone smiled faintly. "As you wish." He extended the cinnamony paste. Not interested in savoring it, Paolo quickly consumed a whole messy mouthful, far more than he should have. He wanted what it would unlock within him, and he wanted it right away. The taste was bitter, potent, and powerful. Before the Face Dancer could withdraw the offering, Paolo grabbed more and swallowed another mouthful.

"Not so much, boy!" the Baron said. "Don't be a glutton."

"Who are you to talk about gluttony?" Paolo's retort drew a rumbling chuckle in response.

On the floor where he lay dying, Paul Atreides moaned. Chani looked up in despair from beside her beloved, her fingers dripping with his blood. Her face a grief-stricken mask, Jessica held her son's clenching hand. Paolo trembled. Why was it taking Paul so long just to die? He should have killed his rival more cleanly.

Kneeling over him, Dr. Yueh worked feverishly to save Paul, trying to stanch the flow of blood, but the Suk doctor's deeply troubled face told the terrible story. Even his advanced medical training was insufficient. Paolo's knife strike had done all the damage it had needed to.

Those people were all irrelevant now. Mere seconds had passed when Paolo felt the potent melange burst into his bloodstream like a lasgun blast. His thoughts came faster, sharper. It was working! His mind was suffused with a certainty that outsiders might have considered hubris or megalomania. But Paolo knew it only as *Truth*.

He drew himself taller, as if he were growing physically and maturing in all ways, so that he loomed above everyone else in the chamber. His mind expanded into the cosmos. Even Omnius and Erasmus now seemed like insects to him, muddling through their grandiose, but ultimately minuscule, dreams.

As if from a great height, Paolo looked down at the Baron, the self-absorbed snake who had spent so many years dominating him, bossing him around, "teaching" him. Suddenly the once-powerful leader of House Harkonnen seemed laughably insignificant.

The Face Dancer Khrone studied the scene, and then—with seeming uncertainty—turned toward the evermind's manifestation as an old man. Paolo saw through all of them with incredible ease.

"Let me tell you what I will do next." In his own ears, Paolo's booming voice sounded like a god's. Even the great Omnius must tremble before him. Words flowed with the force of a cosmic Coriolis storm, rushing along on a current of ultraspice.

"I will implement my new mandate. The prophecy is true: I *will* change the universe. As the ultimate and final Kwisatz Haderach, I know my destiny—as do all of you, for your actions led to this prophecy." He smiled. "Even yours, Omnius!"

The false old man responded with an annoyed frown. Beside him the robot Erasmus grinned indulgently, waiting to see what the just-hatched superman would do. All of Paolo's visions of domination, conquest, and perfect control were based on prescience. He harbored no doubts in his mind. Every detail unfolded before him. The young man continued to spew pronouncements.

"Now that I have come into my true powers, there is no need for the thinking-machine fleet to obliterate the human-inhabited planets. I can control them all." He waved a hand. "Oh, we may have to annihilate a minor world or two to demonstrate our strength—or maybe just because we *can*—but we will keep alive the vast majority of people, as fodder."

Paolo gasped as even more ideas flooded into his head, building momentum and power. "Once we have swallowed up Chapterhouse, we will open the Sisterhood's breeding records. From there, we will implement my master plan of making brilliant, perfect humans, combining whatever traits I choose. Workers and thinkers, drones, engineers, and—occasionally—leaders." He spun toward the old man. "And *you*, Omnius, will construct a vast infrastructure for me. If we give our perfect humans too much freedom they'll mess everything up. We must eliminate the wild, troublesome genetic lines." He snickered to himself.

"In fact, the Atreides bloodline is the most unmanageable of all, so I shall be the last Atreides. Now that I have arrived, history needs no more of us." He glanced around, but did not see the man who came to mind. "And all those Duncan Idahos. How tedious they've become!"

Paolo was speaking faster and faster, swept along by intoxicating spice visions. The look of confusion on even the Baron's face made the young man wonder if anyone here could comprehend him any longer. They seemed so primitive to him now. What if his own thoughts were so grand that they were beyond the understanding of the most sophisticated thinking machines? That would really be something!

He began to pace around the chamber, ignoring glares and gestures from the Baron. Gradually Paolo's motions became jerky, manic. "Yes! The first step is to sweep away the old, mow down and dispense with the outdated and unnecessary. We must clear a path for the new and the perfect. That's a concept all thinking machines can embrace."

Erasmus stared at him and mockingly reshaped his flowmetal face into a perfect likeness of the old man that represented Omnius. His expression reflected disbelief, as if he considered Paolo's pronouncements a joke, the rantings of a deluded child. A flare of anger rose within Paolo. This robot wasn't taking him seriously!

Paolo saw the whole canvas of the future unrolling before him, broad strokes revealed by the incredible magnifying power of ultra-spice. Some of the upcoming events became razor sharp, and he discerned more specifics, intricate details. The super-potent melange was even stronger than he had imagined, and the future became intensely focused in his mind, fractal minutiae unfolding before him in an infinite, yet completely expected, pattern.

In the midst of this mindstorm, something else was unleashed from within his cells: All the memories buried there from his original life. With a roar that briefly drowned out even the other clamoring knowledge, he suddenly remembered everything about *Paul Atreides*. Though the Baron had raised Paolo and the machines had corrupted him into what they imagined would be their puppet, he was still himself at the core.

He scanned the chamber, viewing everyone from a new perspective: Jessica, dear Chani, and *himself* lying in a pool of blood, still twitching, gasping a last few breaths. Had he done that—a bizarre form of suicide? No, Omnius had forced him. But how could anyone really force a

Kwisatz Haderach to do anything? Details of the fight with Paul clashed in his mind, and he squeezed his eyes shut, trying to drive back the disturbing images. He didn't want to serve Omnius. He hated the Baron Harkonnen. He could not let himself be the cause of such destruction.

He had the power to change everything. Wasn't he the ultimate Kwisatz Haderach? Thanks to the ultraspice and his own Atreides genes, Paolo now possessed a greater prescience than had ever before been possible. Not even the smallest event could slip past him.

In a glorious tableau, he knew he could see everything about the tapestry of the future. Every tiny detail, if he wanted! No unexplored terrain, no wrinkles or nuances in the topography of events to come.

Paolo paused in his restless pacing and gazed ahead, seeing beyond the walls of the grand machine cathedral, feeling overwhelmed by thoughts that no other human could begin to understand. His eyes changed to more than an intense blue-within-blue, to *black* and glassy, rippled and impenetrable like a landscape of seared dunes.

In the background, he heard the Baron's voice. "What's the matter with you, boy? Snap out of it."

But the visions continued to shoot at Paolo like projectiles from a repeater gun. He couldn't dodge them, could only receive them, like an invincible man standing up against ferocious firepower.

Outside in the grand machine city, he heard a tremendous commotion. Alarms rang, and quicksilver robots rushed out of the cathedral chamber to respond. Paolo knew exactly what was happening, could see it from every angle. And he knew how each action would turn out, regardless of how Omnius, the humans, or the Face Dancers tried to change it.

No longer able to move, Paolo stood staring at moments that were yet to come, everything he could influence and all that he could not. Each second sliced into a billion nanoseconds, then expanded and spread out across a billion star systems. The scope of it threatened to overwhelm him.

What is happening? he asked himself.

Only what we brought upon ourselves, whispered the voice of Paul-within.

With new eyes Paolo saw moment by unfolding moment, expanding outward from the machine city, beyond the planet, the whole scope of the Old Empire, the farthest reaches of the Scattering, and the vast thinking-machine empire.

Another nanosecond passed.

The ultraspice had given him absolutely uncontaminated revelation. He saw time folding forward and backward from the focal point of his consciousness.

Perfect prescience.

Caught in the tidal wave of his own power, Paolo began to see much more than he had ever wanted to see. He witnessed every heartbeat a thousand times over, every action of every single person—every *being*—in the entire universe. He knew how each instant would play out from now until the end of history, and in reverse, to the beginning of time.

The knowledge flooded into him, and he drowned in it.

He watched Paul Atreides in his death throes and saw his counterpart go motionless, haloed by the crimson puddle on the floor, eyes staring into blessed oblivion.

Paolo, who had wanted to be the final Kwisatz Haderach so badly he had killed for it, now became petrified by the utter tedium of his own existence. He knew every breath and pulsepoint in the entire history and future of the universe.

Another nanosecond passed.

How could any person endure this? Paolo was trapped in a predetermined path, like a computer's infinite loop. No surprises, choices, or movement. Absolute foreknowledge rendered Paolo entirely irrelevant.

He envisioned himself sinking in slow motion to the floor and lying face up, unable to move or speak, unable even to blink his eyes. Fossilizing. Then Paolo saw the last and most terrible revelation. He was *not* the true and final Kwisatz Haderach, after all. It was not him. He would never accomplish what he had dreamed.

With spice roaring through him, the past went dark, and Paolo could only stare fixedly into the future, which he had already seen a thousand times over.

Another nanosecond passed.

One can always find a battlefield if one looks hard enough.

—BASHAR MILES TEG,
Memoirs of an Old Commander

Remnants of dust and sand from the emptying hold swirled out into the no-ship's corridors, but the worms were gone, and Leto II with them. Bright sunlight from the machine world shone through the gaping holes. Stunned, Sheeana listened to the sounds of the behemoths crashing through Synchrony. She longed to be with them. Those once-captive sandworms were *hers* as well.

But Leto was closer to them, a part of them, and they were part of him.

Duncan Idaho came up behind her. She turned, the smell of grit clinging to her face and clothes. "It's Leto. He's . . . with the sandworms."

He flashed a hard smile. "That's something the machines won't expect. Even Miles would have been surprised." He grasped her arm and hurried her away from the open cargo hold. "Now we've got to do something just as dramatic for ourselves."

"What Leto is doing will be a hard act to follow."

Duncan paused. "We've been running from that old man and woman for years, and I don't intend to sit here in this no-ship prison anymore. Our armory is filled with weapons stockpiled by the Honored Matres. We also have the rest of the mines that the Face Dancers didn't use to sabotage this ship. Let's take the fight outside, to them!"

She felt the steel of his determination and found her own. "I'm ready. And we have more than two hundred people aboard trained in Bene Gesserit combat techniques." Inside her mind, Serena Butler imparted visions of terrible combat, humans against fighting robots, incredible slaughters. But in spite of these horrors, Sheeana felt a strange exhilaration. "It's been programmed into our genes for thousands of years. Like an eagle to a serpent, a bull to a bear, a wasp to a spider, humans and thinking machines are mortal enemies."

AFTER DECADES OF running and many escapes from the tachyon net, this would be their final showdown. Tired of feeling helpless, the *Ithaca* captives crowded forward to the armory. All were eager to fight back, though they knew the odds were heavily against them. Duncan relished it.

The stockpile of armaments was not particularly impressive. Many of the stored weapons fired only flechettes, razor-sharp needles that would not be effective against armored combat robots. But Duncan handed out old-style lasguns, pulse launchers, and explosive projectile rifles. Demolition squads could plant the remaining mines against the foundations of thinking-machine buildings and detonate them.

The Tleilaxu Master Scytale pushed his way through the crowded corridor, trying to reach Sheeana, looking as if he had something important to say. "Remember, we have more enemies out there than just robots. Omnius has an army of Face Dancers to stand against us."

Duncan handed a flechette rifle to Reverend Mother Calissa, who appeared as bloodthirsty as any Honored Matre. "This will cut down plenty of Face Dancers."

The little man announced with a thin smile, "I have another way to help. Even before we were captured, I began to produce the specific toxin that would target Face Dancers. I made sixty canisters of it, in case we had to saturate all the air aboard the ship. Unleash it against the Face Dancers in the city. It may make humans a little nauseated but it is lethal to any Face Dancer."

"Our weapons could do the rest—or our bare hands," Sheeana said, then turned to the other workers. "Get the canisters! There's a battle outside!"

A fierce army of humans streamed out through the gaping hole torn in the *Ithaca*'s hull. Sheeana led her Bene Gesserits. Reverend Mothers Calissa and Elyen guided groups through the shifting streets in search of vulnerable targets. Reverend Mothers, acolytes, male Bene Gesserits, proctors, and workers rushed out carrying weapons, many of which had never been fired before.

With a loud battle cry, a well-armed Duncan charged forward into the bizarre metropolis. In his original lifetime, he had not survived long enough to join Paul Muad'Dib and his Fremen Fedaykin in bloody raids against the Harkonnens. The stakes were more desperate now, and he intended to make a difference.

The streets of Synchrony were in turmoil, the buildings themselves pumping and writhing. Leto's sandworms had already tunneled beneath the foundations of the structures, breaking through the pliable, living metal and knocking down tall towers. Across the galaxy, Omnius's thinking-machine fleet was engaged in numerous climactic battles. Duncan thought of Murbella out there somewhere—if she was still alive—facing them, fighting them.

Combat robots swarmed the streets. They emerged from between buildings, fashioning and firing projectile weapons from their own bodies. The Bene Gesserits scrambled out of the way, finding shelter. Lasbeams cut smoking holes through the fighting machines; explosive projectiles smashed them backward into debris.

Running headlong into the fray, Duncan used his long-dormant Swordmaster skills to attack the nearest robots. He wielded a small projectile launcher as well as a vibrating sonic club that transmitted a deadly blow each time it struck a fighting machine.

From all directions, Face Dancers rallied against the humans, while combat robots turned their attention to the destructive sandworms. The first ranks of shape-shifters advanced with blank and unreadable faces, armed with machine-designed weaponry.

When the first canisters of Scytale's curling, gray-green gas landed among them, the frenzied Face Dancers did not understand what was happening. Soon they began to fall, writhing, their faces melting off their bones. Sensing the danger too late, they scrambled to retreat as Sheeana's fighters launched more poison gas into their midst.

The Bene Gesserits continued to push forward. Their demolition crews planted mines against looming buildings that could not uproot themselves in time. Powerful explosions brought down the shuddering metal towers. Sheeana rushed her teams to shelter until the thunderous collapses were over. Then they surged forward again.

Duncan decided to hang back. In the center of the city, the huge, bright cathedral drew him like a beacon, as if all the intensity of the evermind's thoughts were being channeled through it. He knew Paul Atreides was in that structure, perhaps fighting for his life, perhaps dying. Jessica was inside, as well. Compelling instincts born of memories from his first life told Duncan where he had to go. He needed to be at Paul's side in the den of the Enemy.

"Keep the machines occupied, Sheeana. Even the evermind can't fight on an infinite number of fronts at once." He jerked his head toward the cathedral building. "I'm going *there*."

Before she could say anything, Duncan ran off.

Enduring my own mistakes once was bad enough. Now I am con-
demned to relive my past, over and over.

—DR. WELLINGTON YUEH,
interview notes taken by Sheeana

The Suk doctor, in a teenage body but with the burdens of a very old man, knelt by the dying Paul. Although he had administered every emergency treatment at his disposal, he knew he could not save the young Atreides. With specialized skill, he had halted most of the bleeding, but now he shook his head sadly. "It's a mortal wound. I can only slow his death."

Despite the betrayal in his past life, Yueh had loved the Duke's son. In those bygone days he had been a teacher and mentor to Paul. He had seen to it that the boy and his mother had a chance of surviving in the deserts of Arrakis after the Harkonnen takeover, so long ago. Even with his full Suk knowledge restored, Yueh didn't have the facilities to help this Paul. The knife had penetrated the pericardium, cut into the heart. Through sheer tenacity the young man still clung to a thread of life, but he had already lost far too much blood. His heart was stuttering its last few beats.

Despite the chances offered by a second lifetime, Yueh was unable to escape his previous failures and betrayals. He had been suffering inside, wallowing in the cesspool of his past mistakes. The Sisters on the no-ship had resurrected him for some secret purpose that he had never been able to fathom. Why was he here? Certainly not to save Paul. That was out of his hands now.

On the no-ship he had tried to take action by doing what he thought was necessary and right, but he had only caused more tragedy, more pain. He had killed an unborn Duke Leto rather than another Piter de Vries. Yueh knew he had been manipulated by the Rabbi/Face Dancer, but he could not accept that as an excuse for his actions.

Chani sat on the floor at Paul's side, calling his name in an unfamiliar husky voice. Yueh sensed that something about her had changed; her eyes had a wild steeliness much different from the gaze of the sixteen-year-old girl he knew.

He realized with a start that the horror of holding Paul's bloody, dying body in her arms must have pushed her over the edge. Chani had her original memories back—just in time to experience the full magnitude of her imminent loss. Even Yueh reeled from the cruelty of it.

The Baron made despairing sounds of his own, at first confused, then angry, and now desperate. "Paolo boy, answer me!" He crouched by the glassy-eyed young man, raging. He raised a hand as if to strike the warped copy of Paul Atreides, but Paolo didn't flinch.

From one side the independent robot Erasmus watched the whole scenario with intent curiosity, his optic threads glistening. "Apparently, neither of the Paul Atreides gholas is the Kwisatz Haderach we expected. So much for the accuracy of our predictions."

The moment he saw the Baron's growing confusion, Yueh knew that only one thing remained for him to do. Struggling to regain his composure, he rose from the side of the dying Paul and made his way over to the Baron and Paolo. "I am a Suk doctor." His sleeves and trousers were drenched in Paul's blood. "Perhaps I can help."

"Eh? You?" The Baron sneered at him.

Jessica glared after the doctor, and the restored Chani looked as if she wanted to flog Yueh for leaving Paul's side. But he concentrated only on the Baron. "Do you want me to help, or not?"

The Baron moved out of the way. "Hurry, then, damn you!"

Going through the motions, Yueh bent and passed his hands over

Paolo's face, felt the cold clamminess of the skin and the barely discernible pulse. Young Paolo sat frozen and transfixed, staring into a coma of infinite awareness and paralyzing boredom.

The Baron leaned close. "Make him snap out of it. What is the matter with him? Answer me!"

Grabbing the Emperor's dagger from Paolo's waistband, Yueh spun in a single fluid movement. The Baron staggered back, but Yueh was quicker. He thrust the sharp tip at an angle under the hateful man's chin and rammed it all the way to the back of his skull. "*This* is my answer!"

The answer for being coerced into betraying House Atreides, for all the schemes, the pain, the resultant guilt, and most of all for what the Harkonnens had done to Wanna.

The Baron's eyes opened wide in shock. He flailed his hands and tried to speak, but could only gurgle helplessly as a crimson geyser spouted from his neck.

Spattered in blood, Yueh jerked the Emperor's dagger back out. He considered plunging it into Paolo's midsection, just to be certain he killed both of them. But he couldn't do that. Though the boy had gone wrong, this was still Paul Atreides.

The Baron collapsed onto the hard floor. All the while, the Paolo ghola continued to stare upward without blinking.

Dr. Wellington Yueh allowed himself a relieved smile. At long last he had accomplished something positive and true. Finally, he had done something right. For a long moment he held the dagger, covered with the Baron's blood as well as Paul's. A potent impulse prompted him to turn the point toward himself. Yueh closed his eyes, clutched the handle of the knife, and took another deep breath.

A firm hand clasped his wrists, staying his suicide thrust. He opened his tear-filled eyes to see Jessica standing beside him. "No, Wellington. You don't need to redeem yourself like that. Help me save Paul instead."

"There is nothing I can do for him!"

"Don't underestimate yourself." Her facial muscles tightened. "Or Paul."

No education, training, or prescience can show us the secret abilities we contain within ourselves. We can only pray those special talents are available in our time of greatest need.

—*The Bene Gesserit Acolytes' Handbook*

Death.

Paul skirted the edge of the interior blackness, dipped briefly into infinity, and danced back out. He wavered on the balance point of his own mortality. The knife wound was deep.

Without any awareness of what was going on around him, he felt an intense coldness spreading from the tips of his fingers to the back of his head. Like a distant whisper, he could still hear the lava fountain blazing nearby. Despite the hard stone floor beneath him, Paul felt as if he were floating, his spirit drifting in and out of the universe.

His skin detected a warm, syrupy wetness. Not water. *Blood* . . . his own . . . spreading in a great pool across the floor. It filled his chest, mouth, and lungs. He could hardly breathe. With each feeble heartbeat, more of it spilled out, never to be retrieved. . . .

It seemed as if he could still feel the long blade of the Emperor's knife inside him. Now he remembered. . . . In the last desperate days of Muad'Dib's jihad, the conniving Count Fenring had stabbed him. Or had that occurred at a different time? Yes, he had tasted a knife blade before.

Or maybe he was the old blind Preacher in the dusty streets of Arrakeen, stabbed by yet another knife. So many deaths for one person . . .

He couldn't see. Someone squeezed his hand, though he could barely feel it, and he heard a young woman's voice. "Usul, I am here." *Chani.* He remembered her most of all, and was glad she was here with him. "*I* am here," she said. "All of me, with all my memories, beloved. Please come back."

Now a firmer voice yanked his attention, as if strings were attached to his mind. "Paul, you must listen to me. Remember what I taught you." His mother's voice. *Jessica* . . . "Remember what the real Lady Jessica taught the real Paul Muad'Dib. I know what you are. You have the power within you. That is why you aren't dead yet."

He found words within his throat, and they bubbled up through the blood. He was amazed at the sound of his own voice. "Not possible . . . I'm not . . . *the* Kwisatz Haderach—the ultimate . . ." He was not the superbeing that would change the universe.

Paul's eyes flickered open, and he saw himself lying in the great machine cathedral. That part of the prescient dream had been true. He had seen Paolo laughing with victory and consuming the spice— but now Paolo himself rested on the floor like a fallen statue, frozen and mindless, gazing into infinity. The Baron lay dead, murdered with a look of disbelief and annoyance on his pasty face. So the vision was true, but all the details had not been available to him.

Some kind of commotion came from beside Omnius and Erasmus, and Paul looked there, his gaze bleary. Watcheyes flitted in, displaying images. The old man stood with an impatient expression on his face. The Face Dancer Khrone seemed unsettled. Paul could hear voices shouting. The whole cacophony wove itself in oddly incomprehensible strands through the buzzing tapestry in his head.

"Sandworms attacking like demons . . . destroying buildings."

". . . a rampage . . . armies emerging from the no-ship. A poisonous gas that kills—"

The old man said drily, "I have dispatched combat robots and Face Dancers to fight them, but it may not be sufficient. The sandworms and the humans are causing considerable damage."

Erasmus picked up the conversation. "Rally more Face Dancers, Khrone. You didn't send all of them out."

"That is a waste of my people. If we fight the humans, their poison kills us. If we go out to battle sandworms, we will be crushed."

"Then you will be poisoned, or crushed," Erasmus said lightly. "No need to fret. We can always create more of you."

The Face Dancer's features shifted and blurred, a storm crossing his putty face. He turned and marched out of the vaulted chamber.

Meanwhile Yueh raised Paul's head, ministering to him with Suk medical techniques. But Paul folded his eyes shut again and dropped backward into the pain. Again he danced along the edge of the chasm that opened wider and wider before him.

"Paul." Jessica's voice was insistent. "Remember what I told you of the Sisterhood. Maybe you aren't the ultimate Kwisatz Haderach that the thinking machines want, but you *are* still a Kwisatz Haderach. You know that, and your body knows it as well. Some of your powers are the same as those of a Reverend Mother. A *Reverend Mother*, Paul!"

But he found it too difficult to concentrate on her words, or to remember . . . As he spiraled deeper and deeper into unconsciousness, her voice faded, and he could not hear or feel his heartbeat anymore. What did his mother mean?

If Jessica now remembered her past life, she also remembered the Spice Agony. Any Reverend Mother had the innate ability to shift her biochemistry, to manipulate and alter molecules within her bloodstream. It was how they selected their pregnancies, how they transmuted the poisonous Water of Life. That was why the Honored Matres had searched so furiously to find Chapterhouse—because only Reverend Mothers had the physical ability to fight off the terrible machine plagues.

Why did his mother want him to remember that?

Trapped inside the darkness, Paul felt the emptiness of his body. Completely bled out. Silent.

On Arrakis so long ago, he had undergone his own version of the Agony, the first male ever to do so successfully. For weeks he had lain in a coma, declared dead by the Fremen, while Jessica insisted on keeping him alive. He had seen that stygian place where women could not go, and he had drawn strength from it.

Yes, Paul had that ability within him now. He was a male Bene Gesserit. He could still control his body, every cell, every muscle fiber. At last, he knew what his mother had been trying to tell him.

The pain of dying and the crisis of survival gave him the lever he needed. He stood upon his pain as a fulcrum and used it to pry open his life, his first existence—the memories of Paul Atreides, of Muad'Dib, of himself as Emperor and later as the Preacher. He followed that flood backward to his childhood and his early training with Duncan Idaho on Caladan, including how he had almost been killed as a pawn in the War of Assassins that had ensnared his father.

He remembered his family's arrival on Arrakis, a place Duke Leto knew to be a Harkonnen trap. The memories rushed past Paul: the destruction of Arrakeen, his flight into the desert with his mother, the death of the first Duncan Idaho . . . meeting the Fremen, his knife fight with Jamis, the first man he had ever killed . . . his first worm ride, creating the Fedaykin force, attacking the Harkonnens.

His past accelerated as it flowed through his mind—overthrowing Shaddam and his empire, launching his own jihad, fighting to keep the human race stable without traveling down that dark path. But he had not been able to escape political struggles, assassination attempts, the exiled Emperor Shaddam's bid for power and the pretender daughter of Feyd-Rautha and Lady Fenring . . . then Count Fenring himself had tried to kill Paul—

His body no longer felt empty, but *full* of experiences and great knowledge, full of abilities. He remembered his love for Chani and his sham marriage to Princess Irulan, as well as the first Duncan ghola named Hayt, and Chani dying while giving birth to the twins, Leto II and Ghanima. Even now, the pain of losing Chani seemed far greater than the pain he presently suffered. If he died now, in her arms, he would inflict that same anguish upon her.

He remembered wandering off into the desert, blinded from prescience . . . and surviving. Becoming the Preacher. Dying in a dusty street surrounded by a mob.

He was now everything he had once been: Paul Atreides and all the different guises he had worn, every mask of legend, every power and weakness. Most important of all, he now had the abilities of a Reverend Mother, the infinitesimal physical control. Like a beacon in the darkness, his mother had enabled him to see.

Between his last heartbeats, he searched within himself in the deep and drowning place. He found the knife wound inside his heart, saw the mortal damage, and discovered that his body's defenses were incapable of repairing the grievous injuries on their own. He needed to direct the healing process.

Although in the preceding moments he had seemed to be fading, he now sharpened himself and became part of his own heart, which was no longer beating. He saw where Paolo's blade had slashed open his right ventricle, letting blood spill out of the chamber. His aorta had been nicked, but there was no more blood for it to carry.

Paul brought the cells together and sealed them. Then, droplet by droplet, he began to draw his own blood back from the cavities of his body where it had spilled, and reabsorbed it into his tissues. He literally pulled life back into himself.

PAUL DIDN'T KNOW how long his trance lasted. It seemed as infinite as the death coma caused by touching just a drop of the poisonous Water of Life to his tongue. He became suddenly aware of Chani's grip again. Her hand was warm, and he felt his own flesh, no longer cold and shuddering.

"Usul!" He could hear Chani's faint whisper and detected the disbelief in her tone. "Jessica, something's changed!"

"He is doing what he needs to do."

When he finally summoned the strength to flutter his eyelids, Paul Muad'Dib Atreides rejoined the living, bringing with him both his old life and his new. In addition to those memories and abilities, he returned with a fantastic, even greater revelation. . . .

Just then, a flushed and bloodied Duncan Idaho burst into the great cathedral hall, knocking sentinel robots aside. Erasmus casually gestured to allow the man to enter. Duncan's eyes went wide when he saw the bleeding Paul propped up by his mother and Chani. Dr. Yueh looked astonished at the miracle before him. Duncan ran toward them.

Trying to pull together his thoughts, Paul placed the tableau around him in the context of his internal knowledge. He had learned much by dying the first time, coming back as a ghola, and nearly dying again. He had always had a phenomenal gift for prescience. Now he knew even more.

In spite of his miraculous survival and rebirth, he still was not the perfect Kwisatz Haderach, and clearly Paolo was not, either. As Paul's vision cleared, he focused on a realization that none of them had seen—not Omnius, Erasmus, Sheeana, nor any of the gholas.

"Duncan," he said in a hoarse voice. "Duncan, it's you!"

After hesitating for a moment, his old friend came closer, this loyal Atreides fighter who had been through the ghola process more times than any other individual in history.

"You're the one they've been looking for, Duncan. It's you."

Even prescience has its limits. No one will ever know all the things that might have been.

—REVEREND MOTHER DARWI ODRADE

With her arm around his shoulders, Chani rocked Paul, as she shuddered with joy and relief. Fremen prohibitions were so much a part of her that even after seeing his mortal wound and watching him come within a heartbeat of dying in her arms, she still had not shed a tear.

In the machine cathedral, Duncan wrestled with the revelation that the pale and bloodied Paul had given him. "I . . . am the Kwisatz Haderach?"

Paul nodded weakly. "The final one. The perfect one. The one they were looking for."

The old-man manifestation of Omnius gave the robed form of the independent robot an accusing look. "If this claim is correct, you were in error, Erasmus. You did not allow for the humans to twist fate yet again. You said your predictive calculations were accurate."

The robot remained aloof, even smug. "Only your *interpretation* of my calculations was flawed. The final Kwisatz Haderach was indeed aboard the no-ship, as I said all along. You drew the obvious conclusion that the one we sought must be Paul Atreides. When the Face

Dancer found the bloody knife carrying the cells of Muad'Dib, you falsely reinforced your own conclusion."

Duncan's mind wanted to reject what he was hearing. Even if he truly was the ultimate Kwisatz Haderach, what was he to do with the knowledge?

The old man sneered down at the frozen, useless boy Paolo and the dead Baron. "All that work on our own clone gave us no advantage. Extremely wasteful."

Erasmus shaped his flowmetal face into a sympathetic expression and addressed the recent arrival. "I knew I was drawn to you for a reason, Duncan Idaho. If you really are the Kwisatz Haderach, you stand in a position to alter the course of the universe. You are a living watershed, the harbinger of change. You can choose to stop this conflict that has made enemies of humans and thinking machines for thousands of years."

Duncan realized that Yueh, Jessica, Chani, and Paul had all played their parts, and now the focus had shifted to him.

Erasmus stepped closer to them. "Kralizec means the end of many things, but that end need not be destructive. Just a fundamental change. Henceforth, nothing will be the same."

"Not destructive?" Jessica raised her voice. "You said your thinking-machine ships are attacking worlds in the Old Empire. You've already sterilized and conquered hundreds of planets!"

The robot seemed unperturbed. "I did not say our approach was the only way, or even the best one." The old man glowered at Erasmus as if he had been insulted.

Suddenly the sky above the great machine city was torn by multiple booms of displaced air as a thousand Guild Heighliners appeared like storm clouds. Emerging from foldspace, the fleet of huge vessels easily carried enough weaponry to level the continent.

Omnius's old man guise flickered as his concentration was wrenched by the dramatic shift. Across the city of Synchrony, robots buzzed about, fighting the sandworms that continued to rampage. Now they had to shore up defenses against the new enemy overhead.

Inside the vaulted building, Erasmus altered his form again to the kindly old woman, as if he believed this presentation more convincing and compassionate. "I've run probabilities beyond the limits of my original calculations. I believe you have the power, Duncan Idaho—stop these Guildships from destroying us."

"Oh, please stop prattling," Omnius said.

Duncan looked around, crossed his arms over his chest. "I am not afraid of the Guild and their Navigators. If I have to die to end this, I'm willing to do so."

Yueh added bravely, "Everyone here has died before."

"It doesn't matter. Let them destroy Synchrony." The old man did not seem overly disturbed. "I am dispersed across many locations. Annihilating this entire planet, this node, will never eradicate me. I am the evermind, and I am everywhere."

A crack sounded at the center of the wide cathedral hall. Then, with a blur and a bang of folded space, an image appeared above the bloodstained floor. The shimmering transmission appeared to be solid one moment and a staticky ghost the next. In moments, the shape clarified to a beautiful and statuesque human woman with classically perfect features. Then she shifted to become stunted and dwarfish, with a blunt, unattractive face, short arms and legs, and an overly large head. After another flicker, the image was nothing more than a disembodied face that wavered in the air. It was as if she could not remember exactly what she was supposed to look like.

Duncan immediately knew who—or what—this was. "The Oracle of Time!"

The face swiveled to scan the people and robots in the great hall, before the image hovered closer to him. "Duncan Idaho, I have found you. I searched for years, but your no-ship and your own . . . strangeness protected you."

Duncan no longer questioned the bizarre storm of occurrences around him. "Why did you come now?"

"You emerged from your no-ship only once before on the planet Qelso, but I did not follow you swiftly enough. I sensed you again when your no-ship was damaged and captured. Now, with the thinking machines attacking, I was able to trace the lines of the evermind's tachyon web and follow Omnius to you. I brought my Navigators with me."

"What is this apparition?" the evermind demanded. "I am Omnius. Begone from my world!"

"Once I was called Norma Cenva. Now I am exponentially more than that—far beyond anything a computer network can comprehend. I am the Oracle of Time, and I go where I please."

In the old crone guise, Erasmus reached out like a curious child and touched, but the wrinkled hand passed through her image. "So many of the most interesting humans are women," he mused. The robot experimentally waved fingers through her ghostly likeness, stirring without altering it. She ignored him.

"Duncan Idaho, you have finally come to your realization. Kwisatz Haderach, I tried to protect you. Before you, Paul Muad'Dib and his son Leto the God Emperor were imperfect prophets. Even they realized their flaws. Now through a confluence in the cosmos, the nexus of all nexuses, you have become the singularity in a bold new universe, the vital point from which everything flows outward for the rest of eternity. The hopes of humankind—and much more—are distilled in you."

Still taken aback, Duncan asked, "But how? I don't feel that different."

"The Kwisatz Haderach is a 'shortening of the way,' a figure powerful enough to force a fundamental and necessary change that alters the course of future history, not just for humanity but for thinking machines as well."

"Yes, you have the power, Duncan Idaho." Erasmus sounded just as encouraging as the Oracle. "I rely on you to make the correct choice. You know what will benefit the universe most, and you know that thinking machines can enrich the entirety of civilization."

Duncan marveled at the awareness of his new identity and the unfolding of his thoughts around the astounding truth. Finally, after so many attempts at life in ghola form, he knew his destiny. His mind was fully awakened.

He saw time as a great ocean stretching across the cosmos, and with his awakening powers he envisioned being able to analyze each molecule, each atom and subatomic particle. Perfect prescience would come, but not yet, not too fast or it would induce the same crippling paralysis that had befallen Paolo. Already Duncan's mind could go much faster than a Mentat's, and he sensed he could make his body move at speeds that would have astonished even the Bashar.

I am the ultimate Kwisatz Haderach. There will be no more after me.

The Oracle's image flickered, shifting her shape back to that of the beautiful woman. "After you died the first time, Duncan Idaho—as a soldier fighting to save the Atreides, fighting to save the first Kwisatz Haderach—the powers of the universe compelled your resurrection as a ghola, and many times afterward, over and over. The original God Emperor understood some of your destiny and played an unwitting role in bringing about this moment. The end point of his Golden Path is the beginning of something else."

"I am linked to the Golden Path?"

"You are, but you are destined to go far beyond it."

Paul seemed to be swiftly recovering his strength. Beside him, Jessica said to the otherworldly visitor, "But Duncan was part of no formal breeding program! How did he develop into a Kwisatz Haderach?"

The Oracle continued, "Duncan, with each rebirth, you came closer to completion. Instead of being developed in a breeding program, you went through a process of personal evolution. With every successive incarnation you acquired more knowledge, skills, and experience—as if a sculptor with a tiny chisel was chipping away at a large block of hard stone, slowly, ever so slowly, fashioning a perfect statue. In your one body, you manifested a tachyon evolution, a hyperfast developmental journey that propelled you toward your destiny."

Duncan had lived his life repeatedly for thousands of years. Not only had the Tleilaxu tinkered with his genetics to give him abilities to fight the Honored Matres, they had combined his cells so that he retained *all* of his previous lives, every one of them. With all those memories, he possessed a breadth of experience and wisdom that no one could match. This Duncan Idaho had more knowledge than the most advanced Mentat or the evermind Omnius, and more understanding of human nature than even the great Tyrant Leto II.

Duncan was the same person again and again, perfecting himself, constantly filtering out impurities, like passing through a fine mesh strainer to sift out only the best of qualities, leaving him as the One. He allowed himself a secret smile at the irony. He had succeeded only because of the meddling of the Tleilaxu, though he was certain that the Masters had never intended to create a savior for humanity.

Duncan's Mentat mind burned through the data, confirming his conclusion, knowing that the Oracle of Time must be correct. "Truly, I am the Kwisatz Haderach!" He wished Miles Teg could have been there with him. "And what of the great war—Kralizec?"

"We are in the midst of it now. Kralizec is not merely a war, but a point of *change*." Her image flickered. "And you are the culmination of it."

"But what about the rest of humanity?" *Murbella*. "They need to know. How will they understand what has happened?"

"My Navigators will inform them, perhaps even bring their leaders here. First, however, I need to eliminate a threat that should have been gone millennia ago. An enemy I fought ten thousand years before you were first born."

The Oracle slid through the air toward the indignant-looking old man, Omnius. Facing him, she made her voice boom more loudly than the evermind's speakers ever had. "I must ensure that the thinking machines can no longer harm anyone. That was my mission ages ago, when I was merely a woman, when I invented the concept of the fold-space engine, when I discovered the mind-expanding powers of melange. I shall remove you, Omnius."

The evermind laughed, a remote old man's chuckle. The slightly stooped manifestation suddenly grew larger, looming like a giant over her image. "You cannot remove me, for I am not a corporeal being. I am *information*, so my existence has spread anywhere the tachyon net stretches. I am everywhere."

The female image formed a smile. "And I am more than that. I am the Oracle of Time. Now hear my laughter." In an eerie voice Norma Cenva chuckled long and hard, causing even the oversized Omnius to take a step backward. "I am heard across star systems and eons, across time and space, far beyond the range of your net."

Omnius took another step backward.

"First I crippled your fleet. Now I will rip you out like the weed that you are, and discard you."

"Impossible—" The old man began to dissolve as he retreated into his own network.

"I will extract you—every shred of information from every node." Her misty image became amorphous and seeped around Omnius. He nearly staggered into Erasmus, but the independent robot easily slid out of the way, his old-woman face expressing curiosity and bemusement.

"I will take you to a place where such information is no longer comprehensible, where physical laws do not apply."

Duncan heard the evermind's voice cry out in rage, but it was muffled. In the vaulted hall, the insectile sentinel robots who tried to move forward in the service of Omnius seemed strangely disoriented and sluggish.

"There are many universes, Omnius. Duncan Idaho has visited more than one, and he knows the place of which I speak. I rescued him and his no-ship from it long ago. You, however, will never find your way back."

Duncan considered the incomprehensible struggle before him. Indeed, when he had first stolen the no-ship from Chapterhouse, he had lurched through the fabric of space in a desperate attempt to avoid capture and had taken them to a bizarrely skewed universe. He shuddered to think of it.

"Nothing shall rescue you, Omnius."

"Impossible!" the old man bellowed, losing his physical form and becoming no more than a spangled outline.

"Yes, impossible. Wonderfully so."

The air in the chamber crackled with clouds of electricity that spread thinner and thinner, as the Oracle wrapped herself like a net around the iconic thinking machine. For an instant, Duncan saw Norma's face superimposed over that of the old man. The two countenances merged into one: *Hers*. The beautiful woman smiled, and the air filled with sparkling, hair-fine strands of electricity that she drew around her like an elegant cloak.

Then she uprooted herself from reality and vanished into the incomprehensible void, taking with her all traces of Omnius.

Forever.

Even after the Navigators destroyed the bulk of the Enemy fleet in a flurry of unexpected Obliterators, a second wave of machine ships advanced toward Chapterhouse.

The Oracle, upon locating Duncan Idaho and the lost no-ship, had promptly taken most of her Heighliners to Synchrony, only assigning a small percentage to aid in the defenses of other human-inhabited planets. With the outcome of those missions unknown, some or all of the other planets could still be vulnerable. One thing was certain: At Chapterhouse, Murbella and her defenders faced the remaining machine ships alone. Through it all, the Mother Commander didn't have much time to process her shock at discovering that Duncan was still alive.

Administrator Gorus groaned. "Will they never stop?"

"No." Murbella scowled at him for forcing her to state the obvious. "They are thinking machines."

High over the Bene Gesserit world, her hundred last-stand vessels hung surrounded by the debris from thousands of destroyed machine battleships. This fight had inflicted a substantial toll on the Enemy, but unfortunately it was not enough.

The new wave of Omnius vessels would not thumb their noses at the human defenders, as the first had. Murbella expected no mercy this time and didn't have much hope for the last-stand ships at other strategic points, either. The machines intended to annihilate Chapterhouse and every other world that stood in their way.

She cursed the clumsy, uncooperative Guild vessels that the Junction shipyards had produced and the worthless weapons the Ixians had supplied. She had to think of something on her own. "I won't just let our ships sit here with their throats bared, like lambs waiting for slaughter!"

"The mathematical compilers controlled our foldspace guidance and standard—"

She shouted at Gorus. "Rip out those damned navigation devices—we'll maneuver our vessels by hand!"

"But we will not know where we are going. We could crash!"

"Then we must crash into the Enemy, instead of each other." She wondered if the machines would feel a need for vengeance when they saw the wreckage of the first wave. Honored Matres certainly would.

The Enemy kept coming. Murbella studied the complex tactical projections. Surely they did not need such a vast number of vessels to conquer the minimally inhabited Chapterhouse. It seemed obvious that the evermind had learned the value of intimidation and showmanship, as well as the wisdom of redundancy.

In the Heighliner control center, two Guildsmen argued with Gorus. One claimed that disconnecting the mathematical compiler was impossible, while the other warned that it was unwise. Murbella ended the debate with the compelling power of Bene Gesserit Voice. The Guildsmen shuddered and, unable to resist her, did as she commanded.

Although the machine forces outgunned them by a substantial margin, Murbella did not flinch from what had to be done. Instead, she allowed herself to reawaken her old Honored Matre anger. This was not a time to calculate odds. It was a time to unleash every bit of destruction her people could muster. Their chances were better now than they had been when this last stand began. If they all embraced viciousness and fought like frenzied Honored Matres, they could inflict significant damage. They might still go down in flames, but if they bought sufficient time for the Oracle and her Navigators to defeat Omnius, Murbella would count it a victory. She just wished she could have seen Duncan one more time.

Murbella turned toward the broad projection plate that magnified the oncoming vessels. "Arm all weaponry and stand ready to ram. The moment we deplete conventional armaments, our own ships will become the final weapons. A hundred of us will take out at least as many of their ships."

Up to this point, Gorus had called her battle strategy suicidal. Now, he looked as if he might try something foolish to stop her. "Why not negotiate with them? Would it not be preferable to surrender? We cannot stop them from destroying their targets!"

Murbella fixed her gaze on the Administrator as if he were weak prey. Even the Sisters who had started out as pure Bene Gesserits now reacted with a feral Honored Matre strength. They would never back down.

"And you base this suggestion on the success of your emissaries to the thinking machines? All those emissaries who disappeared?" Murbella's voice sizzled like hot acid. "Administrator, if you'd like to seek another solution, I would be happy to eject you from an airlock and let you fly across the empty vacuum. As the last breath explodes out of your lungs, maybe you can gasp out your personal surrender terms. Be my guest, if you believe the thinking machines will listen to you."

The desperate-looking Guildsman cringed. Around him, the Sisters moved to take control, ready for a final plunge.

Before Murbella could give the command, though, Janess broke in over their tight-linked channel, "Mother Commander! Something's changed with the machine battleships. Look at them!"

Murbella examined the images on the viewing plate. The Enemy vessels no longer moved in a tight, efficient formation. They slowed and began to spread apart, as if they had no goal, like unmanned sailing ships becalmed on a vast cosmic sea.

Left suddenly leaderless.

To her amazement, the thinking-machine fleet floated listlessly in space.

Even when caught up in his own myth, Muad'Dib pointed out that greatness is only a transitory experience. For a true Kwisatz Haderach, there are no warnings against hubris, no rules or requirements to follow. He takes from all things and gives to all things, as he wishes. How could we have deluded ourselves into believing we could control such a one?

—Bene Gesserit analysis

After the Oracle vanished, Erasmus stared at the empty space in the center of the vaulted chamber, his head slightly cocked to one side. "Omnius is gone." His voice sounded hollow to Duncan Idaho's ears. "No vestige of the evermind remains in the network of thinking machines."

Duncan felt his own mind racing, expanding, absorbing new information. The terrible Enemy he had sensed for so long—the threat that the Honored Matres had provoked—was no more. By removing the evermind, uprooting it from this universe and taking it elsewhere, the Oracle had disabled the vast thinking-machine fleet, leaving it without its controlling force.

And we still remain.

Duncan didn't know exactly what had changed inside him. Was it simply the *knowledge* of his raison d'etre? Had he always had access to this potential without realizing it? Assuming Paul was correct, something had lain dormant inside Duncan for all those years, through all of the lives—original and ghola—a latent power that had grown with each iteration of his existence. Now, like a massive genetic program, he had to figure out how to activate it.

Paul and his son Leto II had the blessing and curse of prescience. With their memories restored, each could claim to be a Kwisatz Haderach. Miles Teg had possessed his phenomenal capacity to move at a speed beyond comprehension and might conceivably have become a Kwisatz Haderach himself. The Navigators in the clustered Heighliners overhead could use their minds to see through folds of space and find safe paths for the great ships to travel. The Bene Gesserits could control their bodies, down to their very cells. All had expanded on traditional human abilities, expressing humankind's potential to exceed expectations.

As the ultimate and final Kwisatz Haderach, Duncan believed he might have the capability to do all of those things and much more, reaching the highest pinnacle of humanity. Thinking machines had never understood human potential, even though their "mathematical projection" credited the Kwisatz Haderach with the power to end Kralizec and change the universe.

Confidence infused him, and he thought he might discover a way to make grand, epic changes . . . but not under the control of the thinking machines. Instead, Duncan would find his own way. He would be a real Kwisatz Haderach, independent as well as all-powerful.

Dispassionately, he gazed upon the old woman in her frumpy floral-print dress and gardening apron, complete with scuffs of dirt. Her face appeared careworn, as if from nurturing people her entire life. "Something of Omnius has vanished from me, but not all."

Finally forsaking the old-woman disguise, Erasmus resumed the liquid-metal form of the independent robot attired in an elegant crimson and gold robe. "I can learn much from you, Duncan Idaho. As the new god-messiah of humankind, you are the optimal specimen for me to study."

"I am not another specimen for your laboratory analysis." Too many others had treated him that way, in too many of his past lives.

"A mere slip of my tongue." The robot smiled cheerily, as if attempting to veil his looming violence. "I have long desired a perfect understanding of what it means to be human. Now it seems *you* have all the answers I so assiduously sought."

"I recognize the myth in which I live." Duncan recalled Paul Atreides making similar pronouncements. Paul had felt trapped by his own mythos, which had become a force beyond his control. Duncan, however, had no fear of the forces that would emerge, either for or against him.

With penetrating vision he saw through, and around, Erasmus and his minions. Across the hall he watched Paul Atreides standing unsteadily, aided by Chani and Jessica after his terrible ordeal. Paul drank from a water flagon, which he had taken from a table near the Baron's body.

Outside, the crashing of sandworms against robotic defenders had begun to subside. Though the huge creatures had not destroyed the machine cathedral, they had caused extensive damage to the city of Synchrony.

At the perimeter of the great chamber, quicksilver robots stood attentively, the charges in their integral weapons glowing in a display of readiness. Even without the evermind, Erasmus could direct these machines to fire a deadly barrage against the humans in the vaulted room. The independent robot could attempt to kill every mortal here in a show of petulant revenge. And perhaps he would make the effort. . . .

"Neither you nor your robots can make any difference here," Duncan warned. "All of you are far too slow."

"Either you are overconfident, or you are fully aware of what you can do." The flowmetal smile tightened, just a little, and the bright optic threads glistened a bit more. "Perhaps it is the latter, and perhaps not." Somehow, Duncan knew with absolute certainty that Erasmus meant to unleash all the destructive power under his control, wreaking whatever havoc he could.

Before the robot made half a turn, Duncan was upon him with all the speed Miles Teg had shown, knocking him backward. Erasmus crashed to the floor, his weapons disabled. Was it just a test? Another experiment?

Duncan's heart pounded and his body radiated heat as he stood over the robot, but he felt exhilarated, not exhausted. He could keep fighting like this against any machines Erasmus chose to send against him. At that thought, he left the independent robot where he had fallen, dashed at hyperspeed around the circle, and battered the silvery sentinel robots with quick kicks and punches until they shattered into debris. It was so easy for him now. Before the metal pieces had finished falling to the floor, he was back, looming over Erasmus.

"I sensed your doubts as well as your intentions," Duncan said. "Admit it. Even as a thinking machine, you wanted more proof, didn't you?"

Lying on his back and looking upward through the hole in the dome at the thousands of huge Guild Heighliners in the sky, Erasmus said, "Assuming you are the long-awaited superman, why don't you simply destroy me? With Omnius gone, removing me would assure the victory of humanity."

"If the solution were that simple, a Kwisatz Haderach would not be needed to implement it." Duncan surprised Erasmus, and himself, by reaching down and helping the robot to his feet. "To end Kralizec and truly change the future requires more than just the annihilation of one side or the other."

Erasmus examined his body core and his robes to ensure his appearance, then looked up with a broad smile. "I think we just might have a meeting of the minds—something I never really achieved with Omnius."

Now that the Oracle was gone, several of the Navigators' giant Heighliners overhead folded space and disappeared from Synchrony without explanations or farewells.

Throughout the city, sandworms continued to destroy the living metal buildings. Because Omnius had never allowed them autonomy, the robotic defenders were unable to function effectively without connecting to the evermind. The vaulted hall filled with resounding silence.

Then with a loud crash, the high doors swung open. Dressed in black and followed by a throng of Face Dancers, Khrone marched in from the bright machine streets. Identical, blank-faced drones swarmed into the room. Scytale's poison gas had killed some of the shape-shifters, but many had avoided the battle entirely.

Out in the sprawling machine city, countless Face Dancers had pretended to stand against the rampaging sandworms, but secretly melted away from the barricades the robotic soldiers had set up. Khrone had taken pleasure in watching the worms destroy the great flowmetal buildings, smashing thousands of thinking machines. *Clearing the way. Making our job easier.*

Khrone offered a skeletal smile as he swept forward. "I never cease to be entertained by the erroneous deductions of those who *think* they control us." In his mind, a Face Dancer victory was now assured.

"Explain yourself, Khrone." Erasmus seemed only mildly curious.

Ignoring the humans and their dead, Khrone faced the independent robot, who stood by Duncan Idaho. "This war has been in process for five thousand years. It was never Omnius's idea, anyway."

"Oh, our war has been building for far longer than that," Erasmus pointed out. "We escaped after the Battle of Corrin fifteen thousand years ago."

"I'm referring to a completely different war, Erasmus—one you never realized was taking place. From the moment the first advanced Face Dancers were dispatched by our creator, Hidar Fen Ajidica, we began our manipulations. When we encountered your thinking-machine empire, we allowed you to create more and more of us. Yet the moment Omnius let us in, the Face Dancers became his true masters! We shared with you all the lives we had gathered, letting you believe you were becoming increasingly superior to us and to humans. But we Face Dancers were in control all along."

"There is a diagnosis for your mental condition," Dr. Yueh said boldly. "You have delusions of grandeur."

Khrone's lips peeled back from blunt, perfect teeth. "My statements, based as they are on accurate information, can hardly be called delusions."

The amused expression on Erasmus's face did not change. Khrone found it maddening, so he raised his voice, "You thinking machines helped us implement our Face Dancer plans, all the while believing that we served *you*. But it was exactly the opposite. You were, in fact, *our* tools."

"All machines began as tools," Duncan pointed out, looking from Erasmus to the Face Dancer leader.

Khrone was not impressed. So this was the man who had revealed himself as the final Kwisatz Haderach? Nor could he understand why the independent robot was not more upset, since he prided himself on employing his artificial emotions.

Khrone continued. "Under your guidance, Erasmus, biological

facilities run by thinking machines manufactured millions of enhanced Face Dancers. At first, we ventured into human society as scouts, swiftly infiltrating the fringes of the Scattering, and then the Old Empire. We easily duped the Lost Tleilaxu into believing we were their allies. Wherever humans remained, Face Dancers quietly intruded. We lived long, and accomplished much."

"Exactly as we instructed you to do," Erasmus said, sounding bored with the lecture.

"Exactly as we wished to do!" Khrone snapped back. "Face Dancers are everywhere, a hive mind more advanced than any extrasensory human linkages, more powerful than the network of Omnius. So swiftly and easily we accomplished our aims."

"And our aims, as well," Erasmus said.

Galled by the robot's stubborn refusal to recognize defeat, Khrone felt rage building within him. "Over the centuries, we prepared for the day when we would implement our plan and eliminate Omnius. We never guessed that the Oracle of Time would do it for us." He chuckled softly. "Your empire has fallen. We have superceded all thinking machines. And now that Omnius's fleet and plagues have brought humanity to its knees, we can activate our hidden Face Dancer cells—everywhere, simultaneously. We will take control." He planted his fists on his hips. "It is already over for machines, and for humans."

Behind him, all the identical Face Dancers wore blank expressions. Khrone's featureless face had been duplicated many times over.

"An interesting and insidious plan," Erasmus said. "Under other circumstances, I might applaud you for your ingenuity and duplicity."

"Even if you could rally your robots to kill those of us on Synchrony, it would be of no use. I am reproduced everywhere." The Face Dancer scoffed. "Omnius thought he was seeding the universe for his own conquest, but the true seeds of his downfall were right under his mechanical nose."

Erasmus began to laugh. It started as a chuckle that he imitated from an ages-old dataset, and he added components sifted from other recordings. The resultant sounds were quite enjoyable to himself, and he was sure they were convincing to the others.

Over his long, long lifetime, the unusual robot had expended a great deal of effort in studying humans and their emotions. Laughter particularly intrigued him. An early step, which had required centuries of deep thought, had been to understand the *concept* of humor, to learn what circumstances might elicit this strange, noisy response from a human. In the process, he had compiled a library of his favorite laughter samples. A delightful repertoire.

He played them all now through his mouth speakers, much to the bewilderment of the Face Dancer Khrone. But Erasmus realized that not even these favorite chuckles, snickers, and guffaws were adequate to express the true hilarity that he currently felt.

"What is so funny?" Khrone demanded. "Why are you laughing?"

"I am laughing because even you don't understand the trick that was played on you." Erasmus chuckled again, and this time he created a unique sound that contained flavors and undertones of his best borrowed recordings. This was truly *his* individual sense of humor, something genuinely original. After such long and difficult study, Erasmus was pleased with the new comprehension he had achieved. Surely this was worth all the tribulations of Kralizec!

The independent robot turned to Duncan Idaho, who—after listening to the betrayals upon betrayals—had the faraway look of a man trying to join mismatched puzzle pieces. Erasmus knew that Duncan hadn't the faintest idea of how to achieve his full potential. Just like so many other humans! The robot would have to guide this one.

Ignoring Khrone, he spoke to Duncan. "I am laughing because the inherent differences between humans and Face Dancers are painfully hilarious. I hold great fondness for your species—as more than specimens, more than pets. You have never ceased to astonish me. In defiance of my most careful predictions, you still manage to do the unexpected! Even when those actions work to the detriment of thinking machines, I can appreciate them for their uniqueness."

Khrone and his contingent of Face Dancers closed in, as if expecting to mop up these few robots and humans easily. "Your words and laughter are meaningless."

Jessica supported a still-weak Paul, while Chani picked up the bloodied dagger that Paolo and Dr. Yueh had both used. Now that she had her past memories, Chani held the weapon in the manner of a true Fremen woman, ready to defend her man.

Erasmus smiled to himself. His own confrontation with Duncan had shown only the tip of the iceberg of the Kwisatz Haderach's powers. The robot had found it terribly exciting for a few moments, placing himself at the brink of death, or at least its equivalent for a machine.

The Face Dancers would be in for quite a surprise if they thought Duncan Idaho and these other humans would be an easy conquest. But Erasmus had an even greater surprise to spring.

"What I *mean*, my dear Khrone, is that while humans can astonish me, Face Dancers are woefully predictable. It's a shame. I had hoped for something more original in your case."

When Khrone scowled, every one of the Face Dancers in the chamber mimicked his expression, like reflections in a hall of mirrors. "We've already won, Erasmus. Face Dancers control every foothold, and you have no place to hide from us. We will rise up across the human planets and on all machine worlds. We will look back upon the path of destruction, and only we will remain."

"Not if I choose to stop it." Erasmus's flowmetal face shifted into a placid, disappointed expression. "Omnius might have been convinced that you all were our meek puppets, but I never believed as much. Who can ever trust a Face Dancer? Among humans, that saying has become a cliché. You and your counterparts did exactly what I predicted you would do. How could you not? You are what you are. It was practically programmed into you." The robot gave a sad shake of his head.

"While you Face Dancers were laying down your schemes, sending out spies, and establishing your presence, I watched patiently. Though you thought you were hidden from Omnius, you weren't clever enough. I saw everything you did and *allowed* it to happen because I found your petty power plays amusing."

Khrone adopted a fighting stance, as if ready to attack the robot with bare hands. "You know nothing of our activities!"

"Now who is drawing conclusions from insufficient data? Ever since the end of the Butlerian Jihad, when Omnius and I were sent out here on our long exile to start the machine empire all over again, *I* was the one in control. I allowed Omnius to continue believing he ruled every-thing and made all the decisions, but even in his first incarnation he was a self-aggrandizing annoyance, overconfident and unconscionably stubborn. More so than most humans!" The robot swirled his plush robes. "The evermind never learned to adapt and never bothered to face his mistakes, so I refused to let him ruin our chances again. Thus, I took control of the Face Dancer program from the moment the first of you arrived on our fringe planets."

Khrone remained defiant, though his voice carried a slightly uncer-tain undertone. "Yes, you manufactured us—and made us stronger than ever."

"I manufactured you, and I wisely planted a fail-safe routine in each and every Face Dancer. You are biological machines, evolved and manip-ulated over thousands of years, according to my own exacting specifica-tions." Erasmus moved closer. "A tool should never confuse itself with the hand that wields it."

The gathered Face Dancers seemed to hold the balance of power, and Khrone did not back down. His features shifted into a monstrous, demonic mask of fury. "Your lies cannot control us any longer. There is no fail-safe."

Erasmus emitted a poignant sigh. "Wrong again. This is my proof." With a precise nod of his burnished head, he triggered the implanted shutdown virus that was genetically buried within each of the cus-tomized, "enhanced" Face Dancers.

Like a toy discarded by a petulant child, the Face Dancer standing immediately behind Khrone crumpled lifeless to the floor, arms and legs akimbo, an expression of momentary shock animating his face before it reverted to its blank state.

Khrone stared, unable to comprehend. "What are—"

"And this." Erasmus nodded again. With a swift sighing thump, the throng of Face Dancers in the cathedral chamber also dropped, an army scattered in death as if mowed down by projectile fire, leaving Khrone alive to accept his utter defeat.

Then, after stretching out the moment for effect, the independent robot said, "And *this*. Your services are no longer required."

With his face twisted in rage and desperation, Khrone threw himself toward Erasmus—only to fall to the stone floor, as dead as the rest of his brethren.

Erasmus turned to Duncan Idaho. "So, Kwisatz Haderach—as you see, I control fundamental parts of our intriguing game. I would not suggest my powers are as great as your own, but in this particular case, they are quite useful."

Duncan did not show any awe. "How far will your shutdown virus spread?"

"As far as I wish. Even though the Oracle of Time extracted Omnius from the tachyon net, the strands of that vast interconnected mesh still exist in the fabric of the universe." Erasmus twitched his head again and sent out a signal. "There, I just dispatched my trigger to every modified Face Dancer throughout human civilization. They are dead now. All of them. They numbered in the tens of millions, you know."

"So many!" Jessica exclaimed.

Letting out a whistle, Paul said "Like a silent jihad."

"You would never have known most of them. With memory imprints, some even believed they were human. All across what remains of your former empire, a great many people are probably quite surprised as comrades, leaders, friends, and spouses drop dead where they stand and transform into Face Dancers." Erasmus laughed again. "With a single thought I've eliminated our enemies. Our *common* enemy. You see, Duncan Idaho, we need not be at odds."

Duncan shook his head, feeling oddly sickened. "Once again, the thinking machine sees total genocide as a simple solution to a problem."

Now Erasmus was surprised. "Don't underestimate the Face Dancers. They were . . . evil. Yes, that is the correct word. And since each one was fundamentally part of a hive mind, they were all evil. They would have destroyed you, and they would have destroyed us."

"We've heard that kind of propaganda before," Jessica said. "In fact, I've heard it cited as the primary reason why all *machines* need to be destroyed."

Duncan looked at all the dead Face Dancers, realizing how much damage the shape-shifters had done for centuries, whether they were guided by the evermind or by their own schemes. Face Dancers had killed Garimi, sabotaged the no-ship, and caused the death of Miles Teg . . .

Looking at the robot, Duncan narrowed his eyes. "I can't say I'm terribly sorry, but there was no honor in what you—or the Face Dancers—did here. I cannot agree with it. Don't think we are indebted to you."

"On the contrary, it is I who owe so much to you!" Erasmus could barely contain his pleasure. "That is exactly the way I'd hoped you would react. After thousands of years of study, I believe I finally understand honor and loyalty—especially in you, Duncan Idaho, the very embodiment of the concept. Even after an event that obviously helps your race, you still object to my tactics on a moral basis. Oh, how wonderful."

He looked down at all the Face Dancers, the astonished and confused expression on Khrone's face. "These creatures are the exact opposite. And my fellow machines are not loyal or honorable, either. They merely follow instructions because they are programmed to. You have shown me what I needed to know, Kwisatz Haderach. I am very much in your debt."

Duncan stepped closer, searching for some way to access the new abilities he knew lay dormant inside him. Just knowing he was the much-anticipated Kwisatz Haderach was not enough. "Good. Because now I want something from you."

A single decision, a single moment, can make the difference between victory and defeat.

— BASHAR MILES TEG,
Memoirs of an Old Commander

It's a trap—it must be." Murbella stared at the vast yet motionless Enemy fleet. The human ships were still outnumbered hundreds to one, but the thinking machines made no move. The Mother Commander froze, holding her breath. She had expected to be annihilated.

But the Enemy did nothing. "This is deeply unnerving," she whispered.

"All backup systems ready, as you ordered, Mother Commander," one of the pale young Sisters announced. "It may be our only chance to cause some damage."

"We should open fire!" Administrator Gorus cried. "Destroy them while they are helpless."

"No," said another Sister. "The machines are trying to lure us from our defensive positions. It's a trick."

Everyone on the navigation bridge stared at their dark and quiet foe, afraid to breathe. The robot vessels just drifted out there in the cold void.

"They have no need to trick or trap us," Murbella finally said. "Look at them! They could destroy us any time they like. It was foolish, impulsive Honored Matre violence that triggered this very war in the first place." The Mother Commander narrowed her gaze, studying the overwhelming force of warships. Utter stillness. "This time, I will take a moment to understand before we just open fire."

Murbella's eyes blazed as she struggled to comprehend. She remembered when her eyes had been a hypnotic green—an alluring feature that had helped her ensnare Duncan. *Strange, the thoughts that haunt you when death waits at your door . . .*

At the time of Duncan's escape from Chapterhouse, no one had known the identity of the outside Enemy. Now, the Oracle had said Duncan was on Synchrony at the heart of the thinking-machine empire. Had he managed to get away? If Duncan was still alive, she could forgive him anything. How she longed to see him again, and hold him!

The painful silence stretched out. Another excruciating minute, followed by another. Murbella had seen the thinking-machine forces on the move from planet to planet, and the aftermath of their strikes. She had seen the plagues they disseminated and had buried her own daughter Gianne with so many others in an unmarked grave out in the Chapterhouse desert. "No matter what the reason," she said, "the machines have never been so vulnerable."

From her nearby ship, Janess gruffly acknowledged. "If we are going to die in battle, why not take out as many of the Enemy as we can?"

Murbella had already prepared for this moment. She issued her orders, each word carrying a sharp edge. "All right, I don't know why, but we've got an unexpected reprieve. We may be few, but we'll be like D-wolves with sharp fangs. We'll rely on our own eyes and skills."

One of the Guildsmen who had rushed aboard the ship at the last minute reacted with alarm. He was a bald and pasty-faced man with tattoos on his scalp. "Aiming our weapons will require precision maneuvering, Mother Commander! We can't do it without assistance."

Murbella shot him a wilting glare. "I'd rather rely on my eyes than on Ixian systems. I've already been deceived once today. Target the largest ships. Destroy their weapons, disable their engines, and move on to others."

Janess transmitted to the clustered defenders, "The wreckage of all those Enemy ships can provide cover if the machines fire back at us."

The bald Guildsman objected again. "Every piece of debris is a navigational hazard. No human can react fast enough. We need the Ixian devices back online, at least in a limited fashion."

Even Gorus looked at him strangely. Suddenly, the bald Guildsman shouted, turned from his technical station, and collapsed. Near him, without a sound, another of the new crewmen dropped dead in his tracks. A third slumped over on the upper navigation deck.

Suspecting that their ships were under some kind of invisible attack from a silent, deadly weapon, the Sisters reacted quickly, trying to determine what was happening. Murbella hurried to the tattooed Guildsman, rolled him over, and watched his puttylike face shift to the blank visage of a Face Dancer.

Gorus looked around as if he finally realized how he had been betrayed. The other two fallen bodies also shifted. All Face Dancers! Murbella glared at the Administrator. "You guaranteed me that everyone had been tested!"

"I spoke the truth! But in the rush to lauch your whole fleet, someone might have been missed. And what if one or more of the testers happened to be a Face Dancer?"

She turned from him in disgust. A flurry of transmissions arrived from the other defender vessels, all reporting dead Face Dancers onboard. Amidst the jumble of comm activity, Janess's voice came in sharp and clear. "Five Face Dancers were on my vessel, Mother Commander. All are now dead."

Meanwhile, the listless Enemy ships continued to drift apart, though they could easily have pressed their attack on Chapterhouse and achieved victory. Murbella's thoughts spun, wrestling with yet another mystery. *Face Dancers among us, working for Omnius. But why did they drop dead?*

Not long ago, the Oracle of Time had whisked her numerous Heighliners away from this battlefield to Synchrony . . . to Duncan. Had the Oracle and her Navigators struck a blow that sent ripples through the entire Enemy fleet? Had *Duncan?* Something seemed to have shut down the thinking-machine battle fleet and all their shapeshifter spies.

Murbella indicated the dead Face Dancers sprawled near her. "Get those monstrosities out of here." Not bothering to hide their revulsion, several Sisters dragged the scarecrowish bodies away.

Murbella focused on the screen with such intensity that her eyes burned. The Honored Matre part of her wanted to strike and kill in a frenzy, but all of her Bene Gesserit training screamed for her to *understand* first. Something essential had changed here. Even the voices of Other Memory couldn't counsel her. Thus far, they had been mute.

Representatives of the remaining populations on Chapterhouse transmitted urgent messages, demanding reports from the front, wondering how long they might expect to survive. With no answers for them, Murbella didn't respond.

Janess transmitted a brash suggestion. "Mother Commander . . . should we board one of the Enemy ships? It could be our best chance to discover what's happened."

Before she could answer, space distorted again around them. Four huge Heighliners reappeared, emerging in the debris-strewn battle zone so close to the human defenders that Murbella shouted for evasive action. The Guild pilot on one of the nearby ships reacted with an exaggerated maneuver, pulling his heavy cruiser out of the way and nearly colliding with Janess's vessel. Another careened into a debris field of destroyed first-wave machine ships.

A third defender acted impulsively and opened fire on the silent thinking-machine fleet, launching a volley of explosive projectiles into the conical nose of the nearest machine battleship. Fiery eruptions burst out in a repeating pattern along the Enemy vessel's hull.

Alarms rang out, and Murbella demanded reports, wondering if the machines would respond with a massive display of force. No more caution. "Prepare to fire! All ships, prepare to fire! Hold nothing back!"

But even thus provoked, the darkened Omnius fleet remained motionless. The Enemy vessel damaged in the impulsive barrage careened in a slow drift, still burning. Very slowly it crashed into an adjacent machine ship and caromed off, sending them both spinning.

The Enemy ships did not fire a single return shot. Murbella couldn't believe it.

In the midst of the surprise and mayhem, a Navigator's voice sounded calm and otherworldly. "The Oracle of Time has sent us here to locate the commander of the human forces."

Murbella pushed her way to a commline station. "I am Mother Commander Murbella of the New Sisterhood . . . of all humanity."

"I have orders to escort you to Synchrony. I will now take command of your foldspace engines."

Before her Guildsmen could scramble to their stations, the Holtz-man engines hummed at a higher pitch. Murbella felt a familiar shift-ing sensation.

It is too simplistic to state that humans are the enemies of all think-
ing machines. I strive to understand these creatures, but they
remain incomprehensible to me. Even so, I greatly admire them.

—ERASMUS,

private files, secure database

Y ou want something from me?" Erasmus seemed to find Duncan's
demand amusing. "And how will you force me to obey?"

The man's lips quirked in a faint smile. "If you truly understand honor,
robot, I won't need to. You will do what's right and pay your debt."

Erasmus was genuinely delighted. "What else do you wish from me?
Isn't it enough that I eliminated all Face Dancers?"

"You and Omnius were responsible for far more mischief than those
shape-shifters."

"Mischief? It was rather more than mischief, wasn't it?"

"And to atone for it, there's something you need to do." Duncan's
attention was entirely focused on the robot, not on the dead Face
Dancers, not on the destructive sounds of sandworms outside in the
city. Paul, Chani, Jessica, and Yueh all remained quiet in the chamber,
watching him.

"I am the final Kwisatz Haderach," Duncan said, feeling the nascent abilities embedded within him all the way down to his DNA, "yet
I need to comprehend so much more. I already understand humans—
maybe better than anyone else—but not thinking machines. Give me

a good reason why I shouldn't just eliminate you all, now that the thinking machines are weakened. It's what the evermind would have done to us."

"Yes, it is. And you are the final Kwisatz Haderach. The decision is yours." Erasmus seemed to be waiting for something, his optic threads gleaming like a cluster of stars.

"And is there a way that doesn't require the annihilation of one or the other? A fundamental change in the universe—Kralizec." Duncan stroked his chin, thinking. "Omnius's fleet contains millions of thinking machines. They're not destroyed, but simply without guidance, correct? And I believe your empire contains hundreds of planets, many of which would never be habitable to humans."

With his robes flowing around him, the platinum robot began to stroll through the great vaulted hall, stepping over Face Dancer corpses that lay strewn everywhere like marionettes with their strings cut. "That is an accurate assessment. Do you want to find them all, destroy them all, hoping you never miss one? Now that they are without the evermind, it's even possible that some of the more sophisticated machines could develop independent personalities during a time of long deprivation, as I did. How confident are you in your abilities?"

Duncan followed him closely. Several times, Erasmus glanced back at him, and made an odd series of expressions, from inquisitive scowls to tentative smiles. Did he see a bit of fear there, or was it feigned? "You're asking me if I want victory . . . or peace." It was not a question.

"You are the superhuman. I say it again—decide for yourself."

"Through more lifetimes than I can count, I've learned patience." Duncan took a long, deep breath, using an old Swordmaster technique to center his thoughts. "I'm in a unique position to draw both sides together. Humans and machines are both battered and weakened. Do I choose extermination for one side as the solution?"

"Or recovery for both?" Erasmus stopped, and with a blank expression faced the man. "Tell me, what precisely is that dilemma? Omnius has been ripped from the universe, and the rest of the thinking machines have no leadership. In one swift blow I have expunged the entire Face Dancer threat. I fail to see anything left to solve. Hasn't the prophecy come true?"

Duncan smiled. "As is the case with so many prophecies, the details are vague enough to convince any gullible mind that everything was 'foretold.' The Bene Gesserit and their Missionaria Protectiva were masters at that." He looked closely at the robot. "And so, I think, are you."

Erasmus seemed both surprised and impressed. "What are you suggesting?"

"Since you were in charge of the 'mathematical projections' and the 'prophecies' based on them, you were in a position to write predictions however you wished. Omnius believed everything."

"Are you saying I *made up* the prophecies?" Erasmus asked. "Perhaps as a way to guide an evermind stubbornly intent on a narrow-minded course of action? Perhaps to bring us precisely to this juncture? A very interesting hypothesis. One worthy of a true Kwisatz Haderach." The grin on his face seemed more genuine than ever.

Smiling coolly, Duncan said, "As the Kwisatz Haderach, I know there are—and always will be, even as I evolve—limitations on my knowledge and my abilities." He tapped the robot in the center of his chest. "Answer me. Did you manipulate the prophecies?"

"Humans created countless projections and legends long before I existed. I simply adapted the ones I liked best, generated the complex calculations that would produce the desired projections, and fed them to the evermind. Omnius, with his usual myopia, saw only what he wanted to see. He convinced himself that in the 'end' a 'great change in the universe' required a 'victory' for him. And for that he needed the Kwisatz Haderach. Omnius learned many things, but he learned arrogance too well." Erasmus swirled his robes. "No matter what the evermind or the Face Dancers thought—*I* have always been in control."

Raising his hands, the robot gestured to the sentient metal cathedral around them, indicating the whole city of Synchrony and the rest of the thinking-machine empire. "Our forces are not entirely leaderless. With the evermind gone, I now control the thinking machines. I have all the codes, the intricate, interlinked programming."

Duncan had an idea that was part prescience, part intuition, and part gamble. "Or the final Kwisatz Haderach can take control."

"That seems a much neater solution." An odd expression moved across the robot's flowmetal face. "You interest me, Duncan Idaho."

"Give me the codes and the access I need."

"I can give you more than that—and, yes, it will require much more. A whole machine empire, millions of components. I would have to share an . . . *entirety* with you, just as my Face Dancers shared all those marvelous lives. But for a Kwisatz Haderach, that would be just the thing."

Before the robot could laugh again, Duncan reached forward and grabbed the platinum hand that extended from the plush sleeve. "Then do it, Erasmus." He pressed closer, reached out his other hand and pressed it against the robot's face in a curiously intimate gesture. Prescience seemed to be guiding him.

"Duncan, this is dangerous," Paul said. "You know it."

"I'm the one who's dangerous, Paul. Not the one in danger." Duncan pulled himself to within inches of Erasmus, feeling all the possibilities roil within him. Though there were troublesome blind spots in the future, pitfalls and traps he might not be able to foresee, he felt confident.

The robot paused, as if calculating, then gripped Duncan's hand and—in a like gesture—reached out with the other to touch his face. Duncan's dark brows knitted as he experienced strange sensations. The cool metal felt alarmingly soft, and he almost had the sensation of falling into it. He extended himself, stretching his mind toward the uncharted territory of the independent robot's thoughts, just as Erasmus did the same to him. The robot's fingers elongated, spreading out over Duncan's hand like a glove. As flowmetal covered Duncan's wrist and ran up his forearm, it felt bitingly cold as Erasmus began to talk. "I sense a growing trust between us, Duncan Idaho."

As moments passed, Duncan couldn't tell if he was taking from the robot, or if Erasmus was surrendering what the nascent Kwisatz Haderach needed, *everything* he needed. And, though the two of them were fused, Duncan had to go further. A viscous, metallic substance covered his arm like the sandtrout that had engulfed young Leto II's body, so long ago.

I hear the clarion call of Eternity beckoning me.

—LETO ATREIDES II,
records from Dar-es-Balat

With the machine city heavily damaged and the evermind Omnius gone, the major components of Synchrony stopped moving. The buildings no longer pumped and shifted like interlocking puzzle pieces, no longer morphed into strange shapes. Like an immense broken engine, the city had ground to a complete halt, leaving many streets blocked, structures half buried or partially formed, and tramcars suspended in the air, dangling on invisible electronic wires. Grotesque Face Dancer bodies and smashed combat robots littered the streets. Columns of fire and smoke rose into the sky.

Exhausted even in victory, Sheeana stared around the city, her face filled with awe and pleasure. As she walked alone down a devastated street, she saw a young boy standing there by himself between the towering, exotic buildings. Looking wrung out but far more powerful than she had ever seen him, was the transformed boy Leto II. He had left the sandworms, having directed them off into the city, but even though he stood here in front of her, he was still part of them.

As Leto craned his neck to look up at one of the dangling tramcars, Sheeana noticed an oddness about him, a looming presence that hadn't been there before. She understood. "You have your memories back."

"In perfect detail. I've been reviewing them." Leto's eyes were full of centuries, now completely blue-within-blue due to incredible spice saturation from the bodies of the sandworms he had controlled. "I am the Tyrant. I am the God Emperor." His voice sounded louder, yet carried a deep and abiding weariness.

"You are also Leto Atreides, brother to Ghanima, son of Muad'Dib and Chani."

In response, he smiled as if she had lifted some of his burden. "Yes, that too. I'm everything my predecessor was—and everything the worms are. The pearl of dreaming inside them has been broken open. He sleeps no more."

Sheeana recalled the quiet boy aboard the no-ship. His past had been worse than anyone else's, and now that innocent boy was truly gone.

"I remember every death I caused. Every one. I remember all of my Duncans, and the reasons each died." He looked up, then grasped her arm and pulled her back toward a twisted building that was stuck halfway out of the ground.

Seconds later, the invisible suspensor line high above snapped, and the tramcar hurtled down to smash on the street exactly where the two had been standing. Dead Face Dancers lay sprawled in the wreckage.

"I *knew* it would fall," Leto said.

She smiled gently. "We each have our special talents."

The two of them climbed the high rubble of a collapsed building to get a better view of the city's wreckage. Confused and disoriented robots milled around the smoldering piles of wreckage and broken structures, as if waiting for instructions.

"I am a Kwisatz Haderach," Leto II said, his voice distant. "And so was my father. But it is much different now. Did I plan for all this long ago, as part of my Golden Path?"

As if he had summoned them, four sandworms rose noisily from the churned and smashed ground and loomed over the wreckage. She heard loud grinding noises, and the remaining three worms came from other directions, knocking buildings aside, tunneling through the wreckage. Slightly larger than before, they circled Leto and Sheeana.

The largest worm, the one she had named Monarch, turned its head toward the two of them. Unafraid, Leto climbed down the remains of the building to approach the creature.

"My memories are back," Leto said to Sheeana, stepping forward, "but not the dreaming existence I had as the God Emperor, back when man and worm were one." Monarch laid its head on the base of the rubble pile, as did the companion worms, like suppliants before a king. The cinnamon odor of melange filled the air from the exhalations of the beasts.

Reaching out, Leto stroked the rounded edge of Monarch's mouth. "Shall we dream together again? Or should I let you go back to a peaceful sleep?"

Without fear, Sheeana also touched the worm, feeling the hard skin of the rings.

With a sigh, the boy added, "I miss the people I used to know, especially Ghanima. Your ghola program didn't bring her back with me."

"We didn't consider personal costs or consequences," Sheeana said. "I'm sorry."

Tears welled in Leto's dark blue eyes. "There are so many painful memories from before I took the sandtrout as part of me. My father refused to make the choice I did—refused to pay the price in blood for the Golden Path, but I thought I knew better. Ah, how arrogant we can be in our youth!"

In front of Leto, the largest worm lifted. Its open mouth looked like a cave full of rich spice.

"Fortunately I know how to go back into the dreaming essence of the Tyrant, the God Emperor. To the real son of Muad'Dib." With a glance at her, he said, "I take my last few sips of humanity." Then he entered the towering mouth and climbed over the maw-fence of crystalline teeth.

Sheeana understood what he was doing. She had tried the same thing herself, though ineffectively. The worm engulfed Leto II, closed its mouth, and reared back. The boy was gone.

Sheeana struggled to keep her knees from buckling. She knew she would never see Leto again, though he would be with the worms eternally, merged into Monarch's flesh from the inside, becoming a pearl of awareness once more. "Goodbye, my friend."

But the spectacle was not finished. The other worms rose beside Monarch, and all towered over her. Sheeana stood motionless, at once horrified and fascinated. Would they devour her, too? She steeled herself for her own fate, but had no fear of it. As a young girl, after a worm had destroyed her village on Rakis, Sheeana had run wildly out into the desert and screamed at the huge creature, calling it names, insisting that it eat her. "Well, Shaitan—do you have an appetite for me, now?"

But they did not want her. Instead, the seven worms gathered together, tumbling one upon the other, writhing like a mass of snakes. With Leto inside them now, the worms were transforming. Six worms wound themselves around the largest beast that had swallowed the boy. They twisted and twined, wrapping their sinuous bodies like vines around a tree, and then moved together.

Sheeana scrambled back up the rubble pile to keep herself safe from falling debris. The fleshy rings of the separate sandworms began to merge and metamorphose into a much larger form. The differentiation among the creatures became less distinct; the rings united, joining into one incredible sandworm: a behemoth greater even than the largest monsters from legendary Dune.

Sheeana stumbled, falling backward on the rubble but unable to tear her gaze away from the immense sandworm that towered in front of her, rippling and twining, its body stretching back hundreds of meters.

"Shai-Hulud," she murmured, intentionally refusing to use the term *Shaitan*, just as she had always done. Truly, this was the godlike Old Man of the Desert. The dizzying odor of melange was stronger than ever.

At first she thought the leviathan would consume her after all, but the giant worm turned away and smashed down into the ground with a great thunder of noise, tunneling downward beneath the machine city.

Its new home.

A shudder of supreme pleasure ran through her. She knew the great worm would divide beneath the surface. This union between Leto II and the creatures would have a greater resistance to moisture, enabling them to survive until they could remake parts of this former machine planet into a domain of their own. One day, new sandworms would grow and thrive on this world, always lurking beneath the surface, always watching.

To defeat the humans, one option is to become like them, granting no quarter, chasing and destroying them to the last man, woman, and child. Just as they tried to do to us.

—ERASMUS,
databank on human violence

With my curiosity, ages of existence, and understanding of both humans and machines," Erasmus mused as he and Duncan remained joined, fused together mentally and physically, "am I not the machine equivalent of a Kwisatz Haderach? The Shortening of the Way for thinking machines? I can be in many places at once and see a myriad of things that even Omnius never imagined."

"You are not a Kwisatz Haderach," Duncan said. He became aware of his comrades rushing toward him. But the liquid metal now flowed across Duncan's shoulders and face, and he felt no desire to tear himself away.

Duncan let the physical reaction between him and the robot continue. He didn't want to escape. As the new standard bearer of humankind, he needed to advance. So he opened his mind and let the data rush in.

A voice rang out in his head, louder than all the whirlwind memories and streams of data. *I can impress all of the key codes you seek, Kwisatz Haderach. Your neurons, your very DNA, form the structure of a new networked database.*

Duncan knew this was the point of no return. *Do it.*

The mental floodgates opened, filling his mind to bursting with the robot's experiences and coldly factual, regimented information. And he began to see things from that entirely alien viewpoint.

In thousands upon thousands of years of experimentation, Erasmus had struggled to understand humans. How could they remain so mysterious? The robot's incredible range of experiences made even Duncan's numerous lives seem insignificant. Visions and memories roared around the Kwisatz Haderach, and he knew it would take him much more than another lifetime just to sift through it all.

He saw Serena Butler in the flesh, along with her baby, and the startling reaction of the multitudes to what Erasmus had thought was a simple, meaningless death . . . howling humans rising up in a fight they had no chance to win. They were irrational, desperate, and in the end, victorious. Incomprehensible. Illogical. And yet, they had achieved the impossible.

For fifteen thousand years, Erasmus had longed to understand, but had lacked the fundamental revelation. Duncan could feel the robot digging around inside him, looking for the secret, not out of any need for domination and conquest, but simply *to know.*

Duncan had difficulty focusing amidst so much information. Presently he withdrew, and felt the flowmetal move the other direction, away from him—though not completely, for his internal cellular structure was forever changed.

In an epiphany, he realized that he was a new evermind, but of an entirely different sort from the original. Erasmus had not deceived him. With eyes that extended to centillions of sensors, Duncan could see all of the Enemy ships, the fighting drones and worker robots, every cog in the awe-inspiring reborn empire.

And he could stop everything in its tracks. If he wanted to.

When Duncan returned to himself, in his relatively human body again, he looked through his own eyes around the great chamber. Erasmus stood before him, separate now and smiling with what seemed to be genuine satisfaction.

"What happened, Duncan?" Paul asked.

Duncan let out a long breath of stale air. "Nothing I didn't initiate, Paul, but I'm here, I'm back."

Yueh rushed up. "Are you hurt? We thought you might be trapped in a coma like . . . like him." He gestured toward the still-frozen Paolo.

"I'm unharmed . . . but not unchanged." Duncan looked around the vaulted chamber, and gazed out into the vast city with a new sense of wonder. "Erasmus shared *everything* with me . . . even the best parts of himself."

"An adequate summation," the robot said, undeniably pleased. "When you merged into me and kept going deeper and deeper, you made yourself vulnerable. Had I wished to win the game, I could have tried to take over your mind and program you to do exactly what benefits me and thinking machines. Just as I did with the Face Dancers."

"But I knew you wouldn't," Duncan said.

"From prescience, or faith?" A crafty smile crept across the robot's face. "You now have control of the thinking machines. They are yours, Kwisatz Haderach—all, including me. Now you have everything you need. With the power in your hands, you will change the universe. It is Kralizec. See? We have made the prophecy come true after all."

Seemingly alone in the remnants of a vast empire, Erasmus walked casually around the chamber again. "You can shut them all down permanently, if that is your preference, and eliminate thinking machines forever. Or, if you have the courage, you can do something more useful with them."

Jessica said, "Shut them down, Duncan. Finish it now! Think of all the trillions they've killed, all the planets they've destroyed."

Duncan looked at his hands in wonder. "And is that the honorable thing to do?"

Erasmus kept his voice carefully neutral, not pleading. "For millennia I studied humans and tried to understand them . . . I even emulated them. But when was the last time humans bothered to consider what thinking machines could do? You only despise us. Your Great Convention with its terrible stricture, 'Thou shalt not make a machine in the likeness of a human mind.' Is that really what you want, Duncan? To win this ultimate war by exterminating every vestige of us . . . the way Omnius wanted to win the war by eliminating you? Didn't you hate the evermind for that fixed attitude? Do you have the same attitude yourself?"

"You have an abundance of questions," Duncan observed.

"And it is up to you to choose the single answer. I gave you what you need." Erasmus stood back and waited.

Duncan felt a new sense of urgency, perhaps imparted to him by Erasmus. Possibilities roiled through his head, accompanied by a rip-tide of consequences. With his growing awareness he saw that in order to end Kralizec, he needed to stop the eons-old schism that separated man and machine. Thinking machines had originally been created by man, but though intertwined, each side had tried repeatedly to destroy the other. He had to find a common ground between them, rather than let one dominate the other.

Duncan saw the great historical arc, a social evolution of epic proportions. Thousands of years ago, Leto II had joined himself with a great sandworm, thereby acquiring vastly greater powers for himself. Centuries later, under the guidance of Murbella, two opposing groups of women had joined forces, fusing their individual cultures into a stronger synthesized unit. Even Erasmus and Omnius had been two aspects of the same identity, creativity and logic, curiosity and rigid facts.

Duncan saw that balance was required. Human heart and machine mind. What he had received from Erasmus could become a weapon, or a tool. He had to use it properly.

I must serve as a synthesis of man and machine.

He locked gazes with Erasmus, and this time he and the robot connected without making physical contact. Somehow the Kwisatz Haderach retained a ghost image of Erasmus within himself, just as Reverend Mothers carried Other Memories inside.

Drawing a deep breath, Duncan faced the overwhelming question. "When you and Omnius manifested yourselves as an old couple, you demonstrated the differences between you. Erasmus, while maintaining your own independence, you acquired the evermind's vast storehouse of data, the intellect, while Omnius in turn learned about *heart* from you, what it means to have human feelings—curiosity, inspiration, mystery. But even you never fully achieved all the aspects of humanity you sought."

"But now I can. With your consent, of course."

Duncan turned to face Paul and the others. "After the Butlerian Jihad, human civilization went too far by completely banning artificial intelligence. But in forbidding any sort of computers, we humans denied ourselves valuable tools. That overreaction created an unstable situation. History has shown that such absolute, draconian prohibitions cannot be sustained."

Jessica said skeptically, "Yet eradicating computers for so many generations forced us to grow stronger and become independent. For thousands of years, humanity advanced without artificial constructions to think and decide for us."

"As the Fremen learned to live on Arrakis," Chani said with clear pride. "It is a good thing."

"Yes, but that backlash also tied our hands and prevented us from reaching other potentials. Just because a man's legs will grow stronger by walking, should we deny him a vehicle? Our memory improves through steady practice; should we therefore deny ourselves the means to write or record our thoughts?"

"No need to throw the baby out with the bathwater, to use one of your ancient clichés," Erasmus said. "I threw a baby off a balcony once. The consequences were extreme."

"We didn't do without machines," Duncan said, crystallizing his thoughts. "We just redefined them. Mentats are humans whose minds are trained to function like those of machines. Tleilaxu Masters used female bodies as axlotl tanks—flesh machines that manufactured gholas or spice."

When Paul looked back at him, Duncan thought that the young man's face seemed deeply old. Recovering from his past life had drained him even more than his mortal wound had. As a Kwisatz Haderach himself, as Muad'Dib, Emperor, and blind Preacher, Paul understood Duncan's dilemma better than any human present. He nodded slightly. "No one can choose for you, Duncan."

Duncan let his eyes take on a far-off glaze. "We can do much, much more. I see it now. Humans and machines cooperating fully, with neither side enslaving the other. I shall stand between them, as a bridge."

The robot responded with genuine excitement. "Now you see, Kwisatz Haderach! You have helped me to achieve understanding along with you. You have shortened my way, too." Erasmus's flowmetal body shifted like a mechanical version of a Face Dancer, becoming again the wrinkled body of the kindly old woman. "My long quest is complete. At last, after thousands of years, I understand so much." He smiled. "In fact, there is very little that interests me anymore."

The old woman walked over to where the still-transfixed Paolo lay, staring blankly upward. "This failed, ruined Kwisatz Haderach is an object lesson for me. The boy paid the price of too much knowledge." Paolo's unblinking eyes seemed to be drying out. He would probably wither away and starve to death, lost in the infinite maze of absolute prescience. "I don't want to be bored. So I ask you, Kwisatz Haderach, help me understand something I could never truly experience, the last fascinating aspect of humanity."

"A demand?" Duncan asked. "Or a favor?"

"A debt of honor." The old woman patted his sleeve with a gnarled hand. "You now epitomize the finest qualities of man and machine. Allow me to do what only living beings can do. Guide me to my own *death*."

Duncan had not foreseen this. "You want to die? How can I help you do that?"

The old woman shrugged her bony shoulders. "All your lives and deaths have made you an expert on the matter. Look inside yourself, and you'll know."

Over the millennia since the Butlerian Jihad, Erasmus had considered distributing backup copies of himself as Omnius had done, but he had decided not to. That would have made his existence far less stimulating, and less meaningful. After all, he was an independent robot, and needed to be unique.

Duncan saw that along with all the codes and commands that controlled the host of thinking machines, he had received the life-function commands that regulated Erasmus. He could shut down the independent robot as easily as Erasmus had shut down all of the Face Dancers.

"I am curious to see what lies on the other side of the great divide between life and death." The robot looked at Khrone and the identical shape-shifter bodies strewn on the floor of the cathedral chamber.

But it wasn't as simple as flipping a switch or sending a code. Duncan had lived and died over and over, and learned more about life and death than anyone. Did Erasmus want him to understand whether or not a robot could have a soul, now that the two of them had been inside each other's mind?

"You want me to serve as a guide," Duncan said, "not just an executioner."

"A fine way to put it, my friend. I think you understand." The old woman looked at him, and now her smile held a hint of nervousness. "After all, Duncan Idaho, you have done this over and over again. But this is my first time."

Duncan touched her forehead. The skin was warm and dry. "Whenever you're ready."

The old woman sat on the stone steps. Folding her hands in her lap, she closed her eyes. "Do you suppose I will ever see Serena again?"

"I can't answer that." With a mental command, Duncan activated one of the new codes he possessed. From inside his own mind, reaching down to touch his own numerous death experiences, he showed Erasmus what he knew, even if he didn't entirely comprehend it himself. He wasn't certain the ancient independent robot could follow. Erasmus would have to make his own way. He and Duncan parted, both of them traveling on utterly separate journeys.

The aged body slumped quietly on the steps, and a long sigh flowed from the old woman's lips. Her expression became utterly serene . . . and then went completely motionless, with the eyes staring straight ahead.

In death, the robot's human shape held.

*Where there is life, there is hope . . . or so the old sayings tell us.
But for the truly faithful there is always hope, and it is not determined by either death or life.*

—TLEILAXU MASTER SCYTALE,
My Personal Interpretations of the Shariat

Out under the burned sky of Rakis, Waff's despair took him to a
place as bleak and dry as the devastated landscape around him.
On a vitrified dune nearby, only one of his precious armored sandworms stirred with the last flickerings of life, while the others were
already dead. He had failed his Prophet.

The cellular modifications he had made were insufficient, and he
had neither sandtrout specimens, nor the proper facilities to create
additional test worms. He felt the last grains of sand slipping through
the hourglass of his life. His body wouldn't last long enough for him to
try again with a new line of the hybrid worms, even if he'd had the
chance. Only the hope of restoring these sandworms to Rakis had kept
him from surrendering to the damage in his accelerated ghola body, but
now he was falling apart.

Raising his fist to the sky and shouting into the dry, caustic air, he
demanded answers from God, though no mortal had the right to do so.
He hammered his hands on the hard, cracked ground and wept. His
clothes were dirty, his face smeared with sooty residue. Sprawled atop

what had once been magnificent dunes lay the dead worm specimens. Truly, they symbolized the end of all hope.

Rakis was forever cursed, if even the Prophet no longer wished to live there.

Then, as he huddled on the ground, Waff felt a shudder from deep beneath the surface. The resonant vibration grew stronger, and he looked up in wonder, blinking his stinging eyes. The last dying worm twitched, as if it, too, could sense something important happening.

With a thunderous crack in the thin, whistling air, a fissure raced across the glassy ground. Waff stumbled to his feet and stared at the zigzag progress of the widening split, hardly able to comprehend what he was seeing.

Widening, jagged lines appeared like fine fractures in reinforced plaz struck by a hard blow. The dunes bucked and heaved as something emerged from below.

Waff staggered backward. At his feet the last slumped sandworm stirred, as if to warn the Tleilaxu Master that it was about to end its days—and that the man, too, was about to die.

A sequence of explosions erupted like sand geysers from deep beneath the dunes. The crevices gaped wider, revealing forms stirring underground. As if in a waking dream, he saw enormous ridges crusted with stones and dust, huge behemoths rising in a cascade of sand.

Sandworms. Real sandworms—monsters of the size that used to roam the desert in the days when this world was known as Dune. A legend and a mystery reborn!

Waff stood transfixed, unable to believe, yet filled with awe and hope rather than fear. Were these survivors of the original worms? How could they still be alive after the holocaust?

"Prophet, you have returned!" At first he saw five of the gigantic sandworms, then a dozen emerging at once. All around him the broken ground spawned more and more. Hundreds of them! The whole dead world was like an immense egg, cracking open and giving birth.

Breaking free of their underground nest, the sandworms rampaged toward the distant encampment in the rubble of Keen. Waff supposed they would swallow up Guriff and his prospectors, devouring all of the Guildsmen.

The sandworms would make Rakis their own again.

He reeled forward in ecstasy, his hands raised in joyous worship. "My glorious Prophet, I am here!" God's Messenger was so great that Waff felt like a minuscule speck, hardly worth noticing.

His faith swelled again, and he saw that his insignificant efforts on Rakis had never mattered. Regardless of how hard he had worked with the sandtrout, trying to seed these dead dunes with enhanced worms, God had His own plans—always His own plans. He showed the way by producing a flood of life, like the wordless revelation of *s'tori*.

And Waff realized what he should have known all along, something every Tleilaxu should have understood: If each of the sandworms spawned from God Emperor Leto II's great body actually contained a pearl of the Prophet inside them—how could the *worms themselves* not have been prescient? How could they not have foreseen the coming of the Honored Matres and the impending destruction of Rakis?

He clapped his hands in glee. Of course! The great worms must have envisioned the terrible Obliterator weapons. Forewarned that the surface of Rakis would become a charred ball, some sandworms had been guided by Leto II's prescience to tunnel deep and encyst themselves protectively far beneath the sands, perhaps kilometers down. Away from the worst destruction.

This world can take care of itself, Waff thought.

Arrogant humans had always caused trouble here. When it was a pristine desert planet, Rakis was what it should have been before human pride and ambition terraformed it. The efforts of outsiders to "improve" Dune had resulted in the apparent extinction of the great worms, until the death of Leto II brought them back. After which humans—the Honored Matres—had wiped out the ecosystem again.

Rakis had been beaten, stepped on, raped . . . but in the end, the magnificent world had saved itself. The Prophet had remained there all along and contributed mightily to the survival of Dune. Now all was as it should be, and Waff was immensely pleased.

Two giant sandworms churned toward the Tleilaxu man, who stood transfixed. Plowing through the crusted ground, the worms scooped up the flaccid carcasses of the weak test worms, devouring them as if they were mere crumbs.

Overcome by joy, Waff fell to his knees and prayed. At the last moment, he looked up into the giant mouth, with its deep, simmering flames and crystalline teeth. He smelled the spicy exhalations.

Smiling beatifically, the Tleilaxu Master lifted his face to heaven and exclaimed, "God, my God, I am yours at last!" With the speed and fury of a crashing Guild Heighliner, the worm descended. Waff inhaled a deep, satisfying breath of spice and closed his eyes in rapture as the monster's cavernous mouth engulfed him.

Waff became one with his Prophet.

Life is about determining what to do next, from moment to moment. I've never been afraid of making decisions.

—DUNCAN IDAHO,
A Thousand Lives

Through the broken cathedral's high dome, a preoccupied Duncan saw the sky flicker like a pattern changing in a kaleidoscope. A wealth of vessels appeared side by side, pulled along by the returning Navigator-controlled Heighliners.

Even before the signal came to him, Duncan sensed that someone very special was aboard one of the newly arrived ships. His expanded mind showed him her face, very little changed after all these years. *Murbella!* Some past part of him was terrified at the prospect of being near her again, but he was so much more than that now. He was eager to see her.

A thousand Navigator-faction Heighliners hovered over Synchrony, uncertain of their role, now that the Oracle was gone. Using his newly acquired abilities, Duncan communed with them all in a common-denominator language. The Navigators would understand him in their own way, as would the thinking machines and the humans. Duncan barely touched on his enhanced knowledge to do so.

Important changes. Necessary changes.

The human ships sent lighters down. Looking up through the dome's skylights Duncan saw the glints trailing through the sky and knew that Murbella would be with them. She would come down first, and he would see her again. Almost twenty-five years . . . a mere tick on the eternal clock, yet it had seemed an eternity all its own. He waited for her.

But the woman who entered the vaulted hall was *Sheeana*, worn and weary from her fighting out in the machine city. Her eyes were full of questions as she took in the blood on the floor, the smashed sentinel robots, the supine bodies of the Baron and glassy-eyed Paolo. Just by looking at the four young gholas Sheeana could tell that Paul and Chani had their memories back.

She noticed the motionless body of the old woman slumped on the stairs and recognized her. Speaking through Sheeana's mouth, the inner voice of Serena Butler lashed out. "Erasmus killed my innocent—*the innocent baby. He was the one responsible for—*"

Duncan cut her off. "I didn't hate him in the end. I think I pitied him more. It reminded me of when the God Emperor died. Erasmus was flawed, arrogant, and yet oddly innocent, guided only by insatiable curiosity . . . but he didn't know how to process what he already understood."

Sheeana stared down, as if expecting the old woman's eyes to snap open and a clawlike hand to grab her. "Erasmus is really dead, then?"

"Completely."

"And Omnius?"

"Gone forever. And the thinking machines are no longer our enemies."

"Do you control them, then? Have they been defeated?" Wonder shone on her face.

"They are allies . . . tools . . . independent partners more than slaves, and so different. We have a whole new paradigm to grapple with, and a lot of new definitions to make."

WHEN MURBELLA AND a party of Guildsmen and Sisters were ushered into the chamber by courier drones, Duncan set all questions aside and just stared at her.

She stopped in mid-step. "Duncan . . . you've hardly changed in more than two decades."

He laughed at that. "I've changed more than any instrument could measure." All the machines in the hall, in the whole city, turned toward Duncan at the comment.

He and Murbella embraced automatically, uncertain of whether this contact would rekindle their past feelings. But each sensed the difference in the other. The river of time had carved a deep canyon between them.

As he touched Murbella, Duncan felt a bittersweet sadness to know how much damage her addictive love had done to him. Things could never be the same between them again, especially now that he was the Kwisatz Haderach. He also guided the thinking machines, but he was not their new evermind, not their new puppet master. He didn't even know how they could exist without a controlling force. They had to adapt or die, something humans had done well for millennia.

From across the room, Duncan recognized the spark in Sheeana's eyes—of genuine concern rather than jealousy; no Bene Gesserit would allow herself the weakness of jealousy. In fact, Sheeana was such a staunch Bene Gesserit that she had stolen the no-ship from Chapterhouse and fled with her refugees, rather than abide by the changes Murbella had forced on the Sisterhood.

He spoke to both women. "We have freed ourselves from the traps we set for each other. I need you, Murbella—and you, Sheeana. And the future needs all of us more than I can express." An infinite number of machine thoughts coursed through his mind, giving him the sudden awareness that countless human planets needed help that only he could provide.

With a thought, he dispatched the guardian robots out of the hall, marching them away as if in a military exercise. Then he stretched his mind through the empty pathways of the tachyon net, and across the universe. With his instantaneous connection to all of the human defender ships once controlled by corrupted Ixian machines, as well as the machine battleships linked to Omnius's command—*Duncan's* command, now—he summoned the vessels to the former machine planet, dragging them all simultaneously through foldspace. They would all come here, to Synchrony.

"You, Murbella, were born free, trained as an Honored Matre, and finally made into a Bene Gesserit so that you could gather the loose ends. As you were a synthesis between Honored Matre and Bene Gesserit, so I am now a fusion between free mankind and thinking machines. I stand in both domains, understanding both, creating a future where both can thrive."

"And . . . what are you, Duncan?" Sheeana asked.

"I am both the ultimate Kwisatz Haderach and a new form of the evermind—and I am neither. I am something else."

Alarmed, Murbella glanced at Sheeana, then back at him. "Duncan! Thinking machines have been our mortal enemies since before the Butlerian Jihad—more than fifteen thousand years."

"I plan to untie that Gordian knot of misunderstandings."

"Misunderstandings! Thinking machines slaughtered trillions of human beings. The plague on Chapterhouse alone wiped out—"

"Such is the cost of inflexibility and closed-minded fanaticism. Casualties are so often unnecessary. Honored Matres and Bene Gesserits, humans and thinking machines, heart and mind. Don't our differences strengthen us rather than destroy us?" The reality-expanding wealth of information Erasmus had given him was tempered by the wisdom he had earned through numerous lifetimes. "Our struggle has reached an end and a watershed." He flexed his hand, and he could feel innumerable thinking machines out there listening, waiting. "We have the power to do so much now."

Utilizing perfect prescient and calculational knowledge, Duncan knew how to bring about an everlasting peace. With humanity and thinking machines balanced in the palm of his hand, he could control them all and seize their powers, preventing them from making further war. He could force cooperation among the Navigator-faction Heighliners, the Ixian-modified ships, and the thinking-machine fleet.

With his developing prescience, he foresaw the joint future of humankind and thinking machines—and how to implement it every step of the way. Such breathtaking power, greater than the God Emperor or Omnius combined. But power had eventually corrupted Leto II. How, then, could Duncan handle this even greater burden?

Even if Duncan Idaho acted for the most altruistic of reasons, there were bound to be dissenters. Would he eventually be corrupted, regardless of his good intentions? Would history remember him as an even worse despot than the God Emperor?

Facing an avalanche of questions and responsibilities, Duncan vowed to use the lessons of his numerous lifetimes for the benefit and survival of the human race and thinking machines. Kralizec. Yes, the universe had indeed changed.

How terrible for a mother to bury her own daughter. There is no greater pain, not even the Bene Gesserit Agony. Now I have had to bury my daughter twice.

—LADY JESSICA,
Lament for Alia

J ust one casualty among uncounted trillions.

Later, as Jessica gazed sadly at the cold form of her daughter, she knew that one little girl did matter as much as all the others. Each life had value, whether a ghola child or a natural-born person. The titanic struggle that changed the future of the universe, the defeat of the thinking machines, and the survival of the human race seemed as nothing to her. She was completely preoccupied with preparing Alia's body for burial.

As she touched the small pale face, stroking the forehead and wispy dark hair, she remembered her daughter. An Abomination, Alia had been called: a child born with the full intelligence and genetic memories of a Reverend Mother. It had come full circle now. In her original lifetime, the little girl had killed Baron Harkonnen with the poison gom jabbar; later, as an adult and haunted by the evil presence of the Baron, Alia had taken her own life, throwing herself through a temple window high above the streets of Arrakeen. Now the reborn Baron had killed the reborn Alia, before she'd ever had the opportunity to reach the potential she deserved. It was as if the two of them were forever locked in mortal combat, on a mythical scale.

A tear rolled down Jessica's cheek with the grace of a falling rain-drop. She closed her eyes and realized that she had been frozen in the same position for a long moment, caught up in memories. She hadn't even heard the visitor approach her quarters.

"Is there any way I might help you, my Lady?"

"Leave me. I want to be alone." But when she saw that it was the somber Dr. Yueh, her demeanor softened. "I'm sorry, Wellington. Yes, come in. You can help me."

"I don't wish to intrude."

With a wan smile she said, "You've earned the right to be here."

For long moments the unlikely pair stood together without speaking. Grateful just to have him there, Jessica finally said, "Long ago when you were with us at Castle Caladan, I cared for you. You always kept your life private, and when you betrayed us, I hated you more than I thought possible."

He hung his head. "I would throw myself upon a knife ten thousand times if I could take back the deeds I've done and erase the pain I've caused, my Lady."

"History can only move forward, Wellington, not backward."

"Oh? *We've* been dredged out of the dustbins of history, haven't we?"

On old Arrakis, the Fremen had made a solemn ritual of recovering a body's water in a deathstill and sharing it among the tribe. On Caladan, the tradition had been a funeral pyre or an ocean burial. While the *Ithaca* wandered through space, their dead had been ceremoniously ejected into the void.

Using stain-free fabric from the no-ship's sheets, they wrapped Alia's small, frail body. Here in the post-Omnius machine city, however, Jessica wasn't sure how best to honor her daughter. "We don't really have a funeral tradition anymore, so I don't know what to do."

"We'll do what we must. The symbols don't matter, but the thought does."

LONG AFTER THE last echoes of the battle on Synchrony had died away and survivors from the no-ship ventured out to discover the new face of the universe, Jessica and Yueh joined Paul, Chani, and Duncan in their own private funeral procession. Paul and Jessica carried the tiny wrapped body out into the streets where the sandworms had caused so much damage, where explosions in the battle against the Face Dancers had destroyed countless structures.

"Such a tiny body . . . and so much lost potential," Paul said. "I miss my sister terribly, even though I didn't get to know her this time as well as I would have liked."

Duncan led the group, shunting aside his other responsibilities for the time being. "I don't remember the original little girl, but I remember the woman. She hurt me and loved me, and I loved her passionately."

They didn't have far to walk. Jessica had selected a particular broken tower, a slumped, thin pyramid that would serve as an appropriate grave marker. Jessica and Paul said their goodbyes during the procession, so that when they reached the collapsed structure they carried the girl inside through a lopsided trapezoidal opening, pushed debris aside to clear a space for her, and laid Alia Atreides on the smooth metal floor. Then Jessica stood over the wrapped child, saying another quiet farewell. Paul grasped his mother's hand, and she squeezed back.

After a lingering, painful silence, she turned and spoke to Duncan. "We've done all we need to do."

"I'll take care of the rest," Duncan said. When they had withdrawn from the fallen pyramid, Duncan raised his hands, fingers splayed, and his face took on a distant expression. The metalform buildings around them began to tremble and sway, growing and curving. The remnants of the pyramid folded around Alia's body and reinforced the walls, drawing polished alloys from other structures. Like a magnificent crystal and quicksilver monument, the ruined spire then rose heavenward. The rapidly growing tower crackled and clanged like mechanical thunder as flowmetal streamed upward. Its curves and angles were streamlined, its polished surfaces perfectly reflective.

Duncan guided the semisentient structures with greater care and focus than the evermind ever had. When he was finished, he had created a tomb, a memorial, a work of art that would amaze anyone who looked upon it.

It left a mark on Synchrony that could never compare with the mark her daughter's loss left on Jessica's heart.

Some problems are best solved with an optimistic approach. Optimism shines a light on alternatives that are otherwise not visible.

—SHEEANA,
Reflections on the New Order

In the aftermath, the humans in Synchrony gradually began to believe that their race would survive.

When Sheeana looked at Duncan, he seemed strangely distant, though that was to be expected. Often his gaze flicked from side to side as if he were in a thousand places at once.

While Mother Commander Murbella called down lighters from her newly arrived battleships, and the Guild provided shuttles full of workers and administrators to help consolidate the strange city, Sheeana watched self-guided robots clean up remnants of the bloody duels in the cathedral chamber.

The *Ithaca's* refugees had taken shelter inside the torn-open ship. The vessel would never fly in space again, even if Duncan forced the living-metal docking cradle to release the no-ship.

Courier drones and buzzing watcheyes, now personally directed by Duncan, led crowds of people through the broken streets, summoning them to a meeting where they would discuss the changed universe. Sheeana's renegade Bene Gesserits from the no-ship were uneasy about facing the former Honored Matre Murbella.

But the Mother Commander had grown much wiser in the inter-
vening quarter century since the schism. Years ago, had she known of
Sheeana's plan to steal the no-ship, Murbella would have killed her
rival outright. Sheeana wondered what the former Honored Matre
would think of all those years Duncan had pined for her. Did Murbella
still love him? For that matter, had she ever?

Reverend Mothers Elyen and Calissa led a weary and uneasy crowd
into the enormous cathedral hall. Guild crewmen from the ships
above also entered the chamber, Administrator Gorus among them.
He appeared drained, no longer in control of anything, and remained
silent, following rather than leading his fellow Guildsmen.

When they had settled into a low hum of conversation approaching silence, Duncan took his place in the center of the chamber where
Omnius and Erasmus had once presided over their thinking machines.
He used no amplification system, yet his words resounded through the
hall.

"This fate, this grand culmination of Kralizec, is what we sought for
so many years." He swept his gaze over Sheeana and the refugee Bene
Gesserits. "Your long journey is at an end, for this is the new heartland
you dreamed of finding. The planet is yours now. Use the remnants of
Synchrony to form an entirely new Bene Gesserit order, your base far
from Chapterhouse."

The gathered Sisters were confused and astounded. Even Sheeana
had not known Duncan would propose this. "But this is the heart of the
thinking-machine empire!" cried Calissa. "The homeworld of Omnius."

"It's your homeworld now. Stake your claim and build your future."

Sheeana understood. "Duncan is exactly right. Challenges strengthen
the Sisterhood. The universe has changed, and we belong here, regardless
of the difficulties we may face. Even the sandworms have come to Synchrony, burrowing deep underground." She smiled. "They may reemerge
when we least expect them. Someone has to keep an eye on the restored
Tyrant."

Beneath the hall, Sheeana thought she felt the ground trembling,
as from a great behemoth moving under the foundations. Many robots
had been destroyed or damaged during the sandworm attack, but thousands more of the machines remained perfectly functional. Sheeana

knew that the Bene Gesserits here would have all the labor pool they could possibly desire, if the machines would work with them.

Murbella spoke up. "I shall return to Chapterhouse. It will take some effort to spread news of the new reality." She gazed at Sheeana. "Don't worry. My combined Sisterhood doesn't need to be at odds with your orthodox Bene Gesserit base here. There have always been many schools, many trains of thought. In proper balance, rivalry promotes strength and innovation—so long as we can avoid the acrimony of conflict and mutual destruction."

Sheeana knew that Duncan would go back to Chapterhouse with Murbella, at least for a time. With his guidance, Murbella would shepherd the reintroduction and integration of superior technology into a thriving society. If handled properly, Sheeana saw no reason for humans to fear cooperation with thinking machines any more than they needed to fear religion itself, or competition among Bene Gesserit elements. Any group could be dangerous if managed improperly.

Sheeana, though, would remain here. She saw no point in going back. Addressing Murbella, she said, "Even before Honored Matres destroyed Rakis, the Bene Gesserit order made me the centerpiece of a manufactured religion. For decades I had to hide while the Missionaria spread myths about me. I let the legend continue without me. What would I achieve if I stopped it now? So I say, leave it, if the thought comforts people. My place is on this planet."

She saw that Scytale was also in the audience. The last of the Tleilaxu Masters had, in the end, proved greatly helpful, fighting for instead of against them. "Scytale, will you remain with us? Will you join my new order here? We can use your knowledge and genetic expertise. We are, after all, founding a colony, and we have only a few hundred people."

"I expect others from the outside will eventually join you," Murbella said.

The little Tleilaxu was surprised by the invitation. "Of course I will stay. Thank you. My people have no other place now, not even sacred Bandalong." He smiled at Sheeana. "Perhaps at your side I can accomplish something worthwhile."

Duncan walked among the Bene Gesserit refugees. "You are gardeners laying down flagstones on our path of destiny. Many of us will return to worlds we once called home, but you will remain here."

With a warm feeling toward him, Sheeana touched Duncan's arm. Though still flesh and bone, and human, she knew he was far more than that. And his words rang true. "Thanks to you Duncan, my Sisters and I are finally home."

The worst part of going back is that the past is never exactly the way you remember it.

—PAUL ATREIDES,
Notebooks of a Ghola

Back in the Old Empire, the last Chapterhouse defenders waited, tense and alert, but nothing changed for days. The machine warships had not moved, and Bashar Janess Idaho had received no further word from the Navigator ships that had whisked the Mother Commander away. Fast scouts flitted back and forth from the hundred last-stand groupings, and the situation was the same along the entire front.

Waiting. No one knew what was happening.

Janess reacted with alarm and dismay when a large swarm of ships burst out of foldspace in all sizes and configurations. Shouting into the commline, the bashar rallied all of her functional defensive craft that remained in orbit. At first she did not recognize the configurations, but then she saw that the newly arrived cluster included smaller human and thinking-machine vessels that had been towed along by the Holtzman engines of great Guildships.

"Identify yourselves!" Janess said to the unexpected armada.

On the bridge of her large battleship, returning home, Murbella smiled at Duncan. "That is your—*our* daughter."

He raised his eyebrows and performed quick mental calculations. "One of the twins?"

"Janess." Murbella frowned slightly. "The other one, Rinya, didn't survive the Agony. I forgot you didn't know. Tanidia, the middle one, is alive and well, assigned with the Missionaria among the refugees. But we lost Gianne, our youngest—born just before I became a Reverend Mother. She died during the Chapterhouse plague."

Duncan steadied himself. How odd to feel a blow of genuine grief to learn of the death of two children he had never met. He hadn't even known their names until now. He tried to imagine what the young women might have been like. As Kwisatz Haderach and evermind, he could do many things . . . almost anything. But he couldn't bring back his daughters.

Duncan studied Janess's features on the screen: dark hair and round face from his own genes, a petite figure, intense eyes, and a hard expression showing she would never run from a challenge. A synthesis of himself and Murbella. He activated the commline himself. "Bashar Janess Idaho, this is Duncan Idaho, your father. I am with the Mother Commander."

Murbella leaned into the field of view. "Stand down, Janess. The war is over. You have nothing to fear from us."

Janess seemed suspicious. "There are thinking-machine ships with you."

"They are *my* ships now," Duncan said.

The female bashar did not flinch. "How do I know you're not Face Dancers?"

Murbella answered, "Janess, when we stood against the thinking machines and discovered that Ixians and Face Dancers had deceived us, you and I were ready to throw away our lives in a final burst of glory. Don't be so eager to die now that we finally have hope."

The image of Janess stared at them from the viewing plate. Duncan was proud of his daughter's caution. He said, "We will all meet in the great hall of the Keep. A good place for us to discuss the future." He smiled wistfully. "I never actually saw the inside of the Keep when I was here. . . . I had to remain aboard the no-ship at all times."

Janess hesitated just a moment longer, then nodded curtly. "We will have guards."

Duncan already missed his no-ship comrades, but they had their own places to go now, important niches to fill. Paul and Chani would return to Arrakis, where they had always known they belonged. Jessica had chosen Caladan, and she surprised many by asking Yueh to go with her. And on Synchrony, Scytale's nullentropy capsule still contained a wealth of cells, a treasure chest of prizes.

Duncan had already decided on the first request he would make of the Tleilaxu Master. The turmoil and changes, the repercussions and adaptations would last for decades, even centuries. He would value the assistance and advice of a great man. He needed Miles Teg at his side again. . . .

As the ship descended toward the main city on Chapterhouse, Duncan knew he could never think of this world as home, despite the time he'd spent there. In his genetic incarnations he had experienced many places and known innumerable people. Duncan's developing prescience, and his mental connection to decillions of eyes spread across the cosmos and linked through the evermind's tachyon net, made the entire universe his home now.

Now you begin to understand the fascinating obligation I helped you to assume, said a familiar-sounding voice in his mind. Erasmus! *I could have made it much harder on you, Kwisatz Haderach. Instead, I cooperated. This is only an echo of me, an observer. You can access me as you like. Use my knowledge like a databank. A tool. I am curious to see what you will do.*

"Are you haunting me now, like a demon?"

Consider me an advisor, but my research continues. I will always be here to guide you, and I am confident you will not let me down.

"Like the witches' Other Memory, but far bigger, and more easily accessible."

You are here to serve both humans and thinking machines—and the future. It is all under your command.

Duncan laughed softly to himself at the friendly bantering between the two of them. Though Erasmus was in a subservient position, he still had a bit of humanlike pride, even if he was only an echo, and an advisor.

Entering the Keep, Duncan and Murbella marched into the echoing great hall, side by side. Watcheyes followed them, along with a pair of sentinel robots. The robots greatly disturbed the people who waited there, but in the future humans must learn to set aside their fears and preconceptions.

Without Omnius, the thinking-machine empire continued to function but without a unified mind or mission. Duncan would direct them, but he refused to simply continue the endless cycle of enslavement. They had potential to be more than tools or puppets, more than just a destructive force. Some of the machines were merely that, but more sophisticated robots and advisory mechanisms could grow and develop into something far superior. Erasmus himself had become independent, developing a unique personality when he was isolated from the homogenizing influence of the evermind. With so many thinking machines spread across so many planets, other prominent figures would arise if given the opportunity. If guided. If Duncan allowed them.

He had to achieve a balance.

The Mother Commander's imposing chair stood high and empty in front of a segmented window that looked out on the arid, dying landscape. Janess stood to one side, welcoming Murbella to the empty seat, with nearly a hundred of the New Sisterhood's guards standing at high alert in the chamber. Though all of the insidious Face Dancers had been exposed and killed, Janess was not letting down her guard, and Duncan felt proud of his daughter.

She bowed formally. "Mother Commander, we are glad to have you back. Please, take your place."

"It is no longer only my place. Duncan, your daughter has been raised in the Bene Gesserit ways, but she also made a point of learning about you. She trained herself to become the equivalent of a Ginaz Swordmaster."

Thinking bittersweet thoughts about all he had missed, Duncan formally shook his daughter's hand and found her grip pleasingly strong. Until this moment they had been strangers who shared a bond of blood and patriotic allegiance. Their real relationship was just beginning.

Murbella had fought a long and bloody battle to combine the opposing forces of the Honored Matres and the Bene Gesserits, after which she had wrestled with the disparate groups of humanity to forge them into one whole. On an even larger scale, Duncan, through his new-found abilities, was shaping an even greater, farther reaching union.

Everything was woven together in a tighter tapestry than history had ever known, and at last Duncan grasped the extent of his new-found strength. He was not the first human in history to possess great power, and he vowed not to forget what he had learned as a pawn of the God Emperor, Leto II.

The human race would never forget the thousands of years under that terrible reign, and Duncan's comprehensive racial memory held a roadmap that showed him where the pitfalls were, thus enabling him to avoid them. The great Tyrant had suffered from a flaw he hadn't rec-ognized. Weighed down by his sense of terrible purpose, Leto II had isolated himself from his humanity.

In contrast, Duncan clung to the knowledge that Murbella would be with him, and Sheeana, too. He could talk with his daughter Janess as well, and perhaps even his other surviving daughter, Tanidia. In addition, he had all the memories of great and loyal friends, of dozens of loves, and a succession of comrades, wives, families, joys, and beliefs.

Though he was the ultimate Kwisatz Haderach with immeasurable power, Duncan had known the best parts of being human. Life after life. He didn't need to feel alienated and worried, when he could be filled with love instead.

But his would not be a conventional kind of love. His love needed to extend much farther, to every living person, and to thinking machines. One form of sentient life was not superior to the other. And Duncan Idaho was greater than the flesh that encompassed his body.

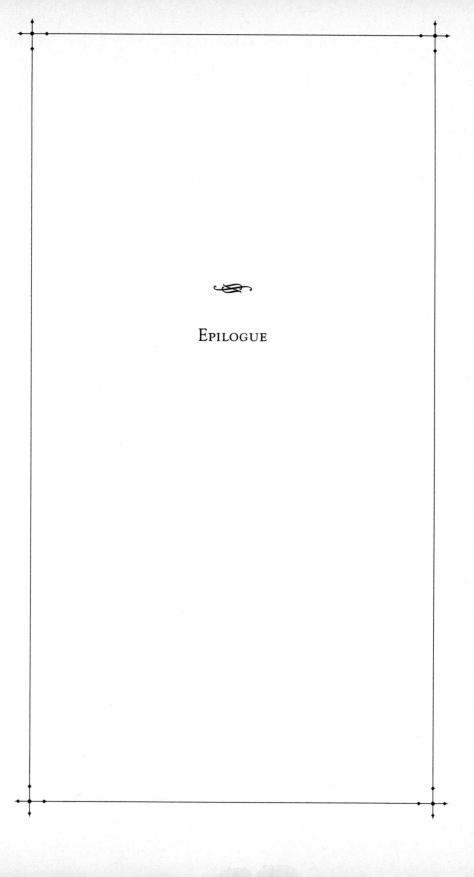

Epilogue

In a war, be watchful for unexpected enemies and unlikely allies.

—BASHAR MILES TEG,
final log entries

More than a year had passed on Qelso. The unnatural desert continued to spread as sandtrout reproduced and commandeered more and more of the planet's water. Though their fight seemed hopeless, Var's commandos stood against the forces that were killing their environment.

Stilgar and Liet-Kynes did their best to assist in the struggle. Both desert-bred gholas felt that their more important work was to show the natives how they could live in cooperation with the encroaching desert, rather than fight it.

During the many months since the pair had departed from the no-ship, the dry sands had extended much farther into the continental forests and plains. Var's camp had moved time after time, retreating from the oncoming dunes, and the desert kept following them. Though they had killed dozens of sandworms using water cannons and moisture bombs, Shai-Hulud was not so easily thwarted. The worms grew larger, despite all the efforts of the Qelso commandos.

With the first faint light of dawn, Liet stepped out of his rock-walled sleeping chambers and stretched. Although he and Stilgar were still teenagers, they remembered being adults once and having wives. Among the commando women on Qelso, many would accept either of them as a husband, but Liet had not yet decided when he could justify getting married and fathering children. Maybe he would have another daughter, and name her Chani. . . .

No matter how much Liet-Kynes worked to remake Qelso, it would never be Dune. The fertile landscape was giving way to dry waves of sand, but it would not be the same. Eons ago, had Arrakis been fertile? Had some forgotten superior civilization transplanted sandtrout and sandworms there, much as Mother Superior Odrade had when she sent her Bene Gesserit to Qelso? Perhaps it had been the Muadru, who left mysterious symbols on rocks and cliffs, and in caves across the galaxy. Liet didn't know. His father might have been intrigued by the mystery, but Liet considered himself more practical.

Preparing for the day's work, he looked over at Stilgar, whose eyes had begun to turn blue-within-blue. For years the people here had stubbornly denied themselves the use of melange, but Stilgar called it a sacred reward from the desert, a gift from Shai-Hulud. He had small groups harvesting spice for their own uses, and Liet knew that spice was like a velvet chain—pleasant enough, until one tried to break free of it.

Two chattering and flirtatious teenage girls brought the men break-fast on a tray, knowing what Stilgar and Liet preferred for their morning meal. The girls were lovely, but so *young*. Liet knew they saw only his youthful body, not knowing how many years he carried in his mind. At times like these, he truly missed his wife Faroula, Chani's mother. But that had been so long ago. . . .

Stilgar, however, remained the same. After they finished their coffee and sweet cakes, Liet stood and clapped his friend on the shoulder. "Today we will go out into the deep dunes and plant weather devices. We need better resolution to track the desiccation patterns."

"Why do you obsess over details? The desert is the desert. It will always be hot and dry, and here on Qelso it will keep growing." The former naib did not see anything particularly tragic or wrong with the dying ecosystem. To Stilgar, it was the natural order of things. "Shai-Hulud continues to build his domain no matter what you do."

"The scientist pursues knowledge," Liet said, and his companion had no answer for that.

Taking one of the small flyers the *Ithaca* had left behind, he had gone to the northern and as yet undamaged latitudes where the forests stood tall, the rivers flowed, and snowcaps crowned the mountains. Cities and towns still flourished in the valleys and on the hillsides, though the people knew they would all be gone before long. Var's commandos were poignantly reminded every day of how much they were missing, how much they had lost. Stilgar did not see it.

The two friends, along with a group of rugged volunteers, donned newly manufactured stillsuits and adjusted the fittings. When the commandos marched into the open desert, they walked in single file on the dunes. Liet had them practice the random stutter-step that would not attract a worm. The yellow sun grew swiftly hotter, reflecting off the granular sands, but they plodded onward, practicing their lives here. Far in the distance Liet saw the rusty-brown smear of powdery smoke that indicated a spice blow, and he thought he saw the rippling tracks of a worm moving out there.

Stilgar shouted and pointed up at the sky. The desert men instinctively clustered together in a defensive formation.

Hundreds of huge metallic ships suddenly descended, made of angular plates bristling with weapons and powered by enormous engines. The vessels looked like nothing Liet had ever seen before. Enemy ships?

For a moment he hoped the *Ithaca* had returned with them, but these were unlike the no-ship and unusual in their formation, moving in a coordinated fashion. They dropped indiscriminately onto the open desert, scattering sand and flattening dunes. Their pilots seemed oblivious to the fact that the dull vibrations would attract sandworms. As Liet stood gaping at the ships' sheer size, he had no doubt that their weapons could brush aside a worm attack as if it were no more than a nuisance.

The dusty commandos looked to the two gholas for answers. Liet had none, though, and despite the impossible odds, Stilgar appeared ready to attack, if need be.

With an ominous humming and clanking, the ships extended support struts and raised themselves on thick, powerful anchors. Then numerous doors began to open, turning loose an army of metal-skinned machines: heavy lifters, ground crushers, and excavators. Moving on treads, the lumbering self-guided behemoths crawled across the dunes. Behind them marched ranks of heavyset metal robots that smashed forward like deadly warriors . . . or were they workers? Helpers?

The commandos had only small weapons. Some of the eager ones drew their projectile launchers, dropped to their knees on the soft sand, and took aim. "Wait!" Liet cried.

A hatch at the top of the largest landed ship opened and a pale form emerged, stepping out onto an observation platform. A human form. When the man called down to them, his voice echoed in an eerie chorus transmitted from thousands of speakerpatches on the lines of machine forces. "Stilgar and Liet-Kynes! Don't be so quick to declare yourselves our enemies."

"Who are you?" Stilgar shouted defiantly. "Come down here so that we may speak to you face to face."

"I thought you would recognize me."

Liet did. "It's Duncan—Duncan Idaho!"

Flanked by an honor guard of robots and accompanied by a troop of human workers wearing outfits that Liet did not recognize, Duncan came down to stand with them on the dunes. "Liet and Stilgar, we left you here to face the onslaught of the desert. You said this was your calling."

"It *is*," Stilgar said.

"And the Jews? Are they here with you?"

"They formed a sietch of their own. They are thriving and happy."

Duncan's honor guard stepped forward, women in black singlesuits and similarly garbed men who walked beside the females as equals. One of the women wore insignia and carried an air of command. He introduced her as his daughter Janess. "I confronted the Enemy, the thinking machines, and ended the war." He extended his hands, and all of the robot workers turned to face him. The awesome ships themselves seemed to be alive and aware of every move Duncan made. "I have found a way to bring us all together."

"You surrendered to thinking machines," Stilgar said, his tone acidic.

"Not at all. I decided to show my humanity by not annihilating them. In many solar systems, they are building great things, achieving impressive works on planets inhospitable to humans. We work for the same purpose now, and I have brought them here to assist you."

"Assist us?" one of the commandos said. "How can they help? They're just machines."

"They are allies. You face an insurmountable task. With as many robot crews as you require, I can help you accomplish what you need." Duncan's dark eyes glittered, as he watched from a million eyes all at once. "We can build a barrier against the desert, stop the sandtrout from spreading, and keep the water on a portion of the continent. Shai-Hulud will have his domain, while the rest of Qelso remains relatively unscathed. Humans can have their lives and slowly learn to adapt to the desert, but only if they choose to."

"Impossible," Liet said. "How can a force of worker robots stand against the tide of the desert?"

Duncan flashed a confident smile. "Don't underestimate them—or me. I fill the roles of both Kwisatz Haderach and Omnius. I guide all the factions of humanity and control the entire Synchronized Empire." He shrugged, and smiled. "Saving one planet is well within the scope of my capabilities."

Liet couldn't believe what he was hearing. "You can stop the desert and turn back the worms?"

"Qelso will be both desert and forest, as I am both human and machine." At a gesture and a thought from Duncan, the massive excavating equipment rumbled out into the sand, heading toward the boundary where the dunes met the still-living landscape.

Liet and Stilgar followed Duncan, who walked ahead of the heavy convoy. As a planetologist, a ghola, and a human being, Liet had innumerable questions. But for now, watching the machines begin their work, he decided to wait and see what the future held.

When Leto II envisioned his Golden Path, he foresaw the direction that humankind should take, but he had blind spots. He failed to see that he was not the ultimate Kwisatz Haderach.

—Bene Gesserit fact-finding commission

In the eleven years Jessica had been back home, she had realized more and more that some things did not add up. This planet might indeed be Caladan, or Dan, but this was not the same home she and her Duke had loved so long ago.

On a stormy evening, as she walked through the restored castle, the incongruous details finally became more than she could bear. Pausing in an upper hallway, she opened a finely carved elaccawood cabinet, an antique that some decorator had placed there. This time, she stood staring at the ornate interior, and on impulse pressed a wooden extrusion in one corner. To her surprise, a panel opened, and inside she found a small blue statuette of a griffin. Perhaps placed there by the Baron ghola, the griffin was the ancient symbol of House Harkonnen. He must have hidden it there as a clever reminder of the falseness of the castle.

As she stared at the statuette, feeling the wrongness of the object, she considered all of her hard work since returning to Caladan. She had directed crews of local laborers to dismantle the Baron's torture devices and the Face Dancer Khrone's offensive laboratories from the underground chambers. Through it all she had worked side by side with the cleaning teams, sweating and angry as she scrubbed away every stain, every odor, every hint of the unwanted presence. But Castle Caladan still reeked with reminders. How could she make a fresh start when so much of the past—at least this awkward, out-of-focus echo of the past—hung all around her?

Behind her, moving silently, Dr. Yueh said, "Are you all right, my Lady?"

She looked at the Suk doctor. He wore an expression of deep concern on his buttery face; his dark lips turned downward as he waited for an answer.

"Everywhere I turn, I am reminded of the Baron." She frowned at the griffin figurine in her hand. "Some of the articles in this castle are authentic, such as that dropleaf desk with the hawk crest, but most are bad copies."

Making up her mind, Jessica stepped to a segmented window at the end of the hall and swung it open to let in the stormy night air. In a dramatic gesture, she hurled the griffin figurine out to the crashing sea. The waves would soon erode it and break it into unrecognizable pieces. A suitable fate for the Harkonnen icon.

A cold, wet wind whispered into the hall, bringing spatters of rain. Outside, scudding clouds parted to reveal a crescent moon on the horizon, casting cold yellow light on the water.

Moments later she tore down a wall tapestry that she had never liked, and was about to throw that out the window, too, but—not wanting to spoil this beautiful planet—she instead tossed the tapestry on the floor, promising herself to cast it on the trash heap the following morning. "Maybe I should just tear this whole place down, Wellington. Can we ever remove the taint?"

Yueh was shocked at the suggestion. "My Lady, this is the ancestral home of House Atreides. What would Duke Leto—"

"This is a mere reconstruction, fraught with errors." A gusting breeze blew her bronze hair away from her face.

"Maybe we waste too much time trying to recreate what we see in our old memories, my Lady. Why not build and decorate your home as you choose?"

She blinked as cold rain blew into her face, drenching her jade green dress and wetting the rug. "I thought this place would help my Leto, give him comfort, but maybe it was more for me than for him."

A ten-year-old boy with coal-black hair came running down the hall, his smoke gray eyes widening with excitement and alarm when he saw the open window. He was even more surprised when neither Jessica nor Yueh reacted to the blowing rain that drenched the rugs and tapestries. "What's happening?"

"I was considering moving somewhere else, Leto. Would you like me to find us a normal home in the village? Maybe we'd be happier down there, away from this pampered life."

"But I like this castle! It's a Duke's castle." Jessica could not think of her Leto as a child. He wore fishing dungarees and a striped shirt, just like the ones he had worn when Jessica had first come to Caladan as a concubine purchased from the Bene Gesserit. The young nobleman had put a knife to her throat that day, a bluff . . .

Yueh smiled. "A Duke . . . Such titles no longer mean anything with the Imperium long gone. Do the people of Caladan even need a Duke anymore?"

Jessica's reaction was automatic, making her realize she had not thought through her notion. "The people still need leaders, no matter what title we use. And we can be good leaders, as House Atreides has always been in the past. My Leto will be a good Duke."

The boy's eyes glittered as he listened with rapt attention. Beyond his youthful features, Jessica could see the seeds of the man she loved. This young Atreides was among the first of a new generation of gholas produced by Scytale. The baby had been shipped to Caladan and christened there—just as the original Paul had been.

Since leaving Synchrony, Jessica and Yueh had struggled to recover here, endeavoring in the process to bring back a degree of glory to the quiet water world. The tangled threads of their initial and ghola lives made them ironic allies, two people with shared tragedies and shared pasts. Finally, though he could never have his beloved Wanna back, Yueh had found some measure of peace.

Jessica, though, knew that her true Duke waited for her. Eventually he would grow to manhood. When he got his memories back, his physical age would not matter.

Jessica's partnership with Leto would be unusual, but no stranger than the relationships of all the mismatched gholas that had grown up on the no-ship. As a Bene Gesserit, she could slow her own aging process, and with melange readily available from the operations on Chapterhouse, Buzzell, and Qelso, they could both enjoy extended lives. She would prepare Leto, and when the time was right, she would help trigger his true awakening. Miraculously, he would once again be the man she loved, with all his thoughts and memories.

She only had to wait a decade or two. As a Bene Gesserit, she could be patient.

Jessica grasped his small hand. This time there would be no political reason to prevent them from getting married, if that was what he wanted, and she wanted. It only mattered to her that they would be together again.

"Everything will be the same when you finally remember, Leto. And everything will be different."

The future is around all of us, and it looks very much like the past.
— MOTHER SUPERIOR SHEEANA,
at the founding of the Orthodox School on Synchrony

The mangled and permanently grounded *Ithaca* had become the new headquarters building for Sheeana's splinter group. Innovative human architects in conjunction with construction robots had remodeled the large vessel into a unique and imposing headquarters. The navigation bridge, the highest deck on the no-ship, had been opened up and converted into an observation tower.

Mother Superior Sheeana stared across the breathtaking, rebuilt city of Synchrony. Dipping into her deep reservoir of memories, she drew parallels to one of the original Bene Gesserit schools on Wallach IX, which had also been founded in an urban setting. Here many of the machine spires remained, and some even moved as they had before, processing materials in automated industries.

Years ago, Duncan and the willing machines had helped her reconstruct the unusual metropolis, though he balanced his "miraculous" work with the necessity of letting the humans achieve their own successes. He and Sheeana knew the dangers of letting people grow too soft, and he had no intention of allowing them to rely on him for things they could do for themselves. Humankind needed to solve its own problems as much as possible.

At the same time, clusters of thinking machines had begun to grow apart, given manageable goals, inhabiting niches unbearable to humans: blasted planets, frozen asteroids, empty moons. The galaxy was a vast place, and so little of it was suitable for biological life. There would be more lebensraum than any empire could possibly need.

Some of the robots had started showing traits of personalities, unique characters of their own. Duncan suggested that, in time, these could eventually become some of the greatest thinkers and philosophers history had ever known. Sheeana remained unconvinced of this, and vowed that her special trainees here would prove him wrong with their own superior achievements.

Every month fresh candidates came to join the orthodox Bene Gesserit center on Synchrony, while others joined Murbella's New Sisterhood on Chapterhouse. Surmounting early difficulties, the two orders now worked in harmony with one another. Sheeana and her stricter ways attracted a different sort of acolyte, which she knew would have pleased Garimi. Sheeana tested the applicants harshly and rejected all but the most acceptable. Far away, Murbella's order had its own attractions. In this new universe, there was plenty of room for both views.

Sheeana's conventional Bene Gesserit breeding program was in full swing now, and it warmed her heart to see so many pregnant women each day. She counted seven of them outside among the people leaving and entering the headquarters. The sight gave her confidence that her order would expand and continue into humanity's future.

Later that day, the Tleilaxu Master Scytale contacted Sheeana on the navigation bridge that had become her center of operations. Transmitting from one of his Synchrony laboratories, he actually sounded cheerful now instead of harried. "I finished cataloguing the remaining cells and sifted out all traces of Face Dancer contamination. We must introduce some of those traits into the Bene Gesserit again."

"After Duncan, we will breed no further Kwisatz Haderachs. It's not even a matter for discussion." As far as she was concerned, many things did not need to occur again. . . .

"I merely mean to preserve our knowledge. It's like finding the seeds of long-forgotten but beautiful plants. We shouldn't just discard them."

"Perhaps not, but we must set up strict fail-safe mechanisms."

Scytale did not seem bothered by the restrictions Sheeana was placing on him. "I honestly feel that the Tleilaxu race will recover their lost knowledge." Quickly he added, "With changes for the better, of course."

"For the advancement of humankind," Sheeana said.

She had never known him to work so hard. Scytale had used the cells in his nullentropy capsule to regrow gholas of the last Tleilaxu Council, and now the little ones followed him everywhere, reminding her of a mother duck trailed by ducklings.

Scytale raised the group in a manner different than was traditional for Tleilaxu males. In separate quarters, he was also raising Tleilaxu females—from newly discovered cells—though they would never be relegated to the horrific, degrading conditions their predecessors had endured. Never again would Tleilaxu females be forced to become axlotl tanks, so there would be no chance of creating another set of ferocious, vengeful enemies like the Honored Matres. In particular, Sheeana and her Sisters would monitor the council members closely, keeping watch to ensure that they did not corrupt the Tleilaxu people as they had before.

There were still axlotl tanks, of course—some women volunteered for personal reasons, while others left instructions for their bodies to be converted in the event of serious accidents. As always, the Bene Gesserits met their own needs.

After she ended the conference with Scytale, the Mother Superior gazed through the broad windows of the navigation bridge. Far away on the horizon, beyond the redefined boundaries of the gleaming city, the ground was churned and torn up, and many of the geometric structures built by Omnius lay toppled and crushed into rubble.

She adjusted one of the windows, increasing its magnification. From this vantage point she could see the new desert and one of the sandworms rising up from the debris, its eyeless head questing about. Then the creature smashed down hard, breaking part of a wall. Like huge, determined earthworms churning the soil, they had begun the process of converting the abandoned buildings into the desert they preferred.

Soon, Sheeana thought, she would go and speak to them again.

She looked down at the little girl at her side and grasped her small hand. Perhaps one day she would even take her protégée with her, the young ghola of Serena Butler.

It was never too early to start preparing Serena for her role.

The desert has a beauty I could not forget in a thousand lifetimes.
— PAUL MUAD'DIB ATREIDES

B athed in the golden rays of sunset, two figures made their way along the crest of a dune, their steps irregular so that they did not attract the huge sandworms. The pair walked side by side, inseparable.

It was warm on Dune, but not like old times. Because of the severe damage to the environment, the weather had cooled and the atmosphere had thinned. But with the return of the worms, along with sand-plankton and sandtrout bursting through the cracked shell of glassy dunes, the old planet had begun to come back. As Chani's father Liet-Kynes used to say, everything on Dune was tied together, an entire ecosystem that included the land, the available water, and the air.

And, thanks to Duncan Idaho, an extensive work force of hardened machines continued the excavation process in latitudes where the sandworms had not yet returned. Methodically, the mechanical army prepared the old sand section by section, opening the way for worms to expand their territory. Massive planting and fertilization work performed by powerful thinking-machine tractors and excavators had stabilized the seared ground, establishing a new biomatrix, while Paul's hardy settlers monitored the growth and did their own work alongside. Through his wide-reaching thoughts, Duncan made sure the thinking machines understood what Dune had once been, before outsiders meddled with its ecosystem. Misused technology had devastated the desert planet, and now technology would help bring it back.

Paul stopped a hundred meters from the nearest rock formation, where a work crew had found the ruins of an abandoned sietch. With a small group of determined settlers, he and Chani had been salvaging the Fremen habitat with their own hands. Reclaiming the old ways.

In bygone days, he had been the legendary Muad'Dib, leading a Fremen army. Now he was content to be a modern-day Fremen, a leader of 753 people who had established austere homes in the rocks, which were on the way to becoming thriving sietches.

Paul and Chani flew out regularly with survey crews. Instilled with fresh optimism, he saw the magnificent potential for Dune. Near the excavated sietch, he had discovered an underground grotto that he and his followers planned to irrigate and artificially illuminate, to support a planting project for grasses, tubers, flowers, and shrubs. Enough to support a small population of new Fremen, but not enough to shift the desert ecosystem that the new worms were recreating, year after year.

One day, he might even ride the great worms again.

Paul turned to see the pale yellow sunrise appearing over the ocean of sand. "Dune is reawakening. Just as we are."

Chani smiled, seeing both her beloved Usul of memory and the ghola she had grown up with. She loved each Paul for himself. Her abdomen protruded just a little, where their growing baby was beginning to show its presence. In five months, it would be the first child born on the recently resettled planet. In her second lifetime Chani did not need to worry about Imperial schemes, hidden contraceptives, or poisoned food. Her pregnancy would be normal, and the child—or children, if they were again blessed with twins—would have great potential, without the curse of terrible purpose.

Chani, even more in touch with the weather than he was, turned her face into a cool breeze. The sunrise began to show a new richness of coppery colors from dust stirred into the air. "We'd better get back to the sietch, Usul. A storm is brewing."

He watched her glide forward gracefully, her red hair blowing behind her. Chani sang the walking song of lovers on the sand, her words lilting beautifully and in a stutter rhythm, like the cadence of her feet:

> "Tell me of thine eyes
> And I will tell thee of thy heart.
> Tell me of thy feet
> And I will tell thee of thy hands.
> Tell me of thy sleeping
> And I will tell thee of thy waking.
> Tell me of thy desires
> And I will tell thee of thy need."

When they were halfway back to the rocks, the wind picked up. Blowing sand stung their faces. Paul held onto Chani, doing his best to shelter her with his own body against the abrasive wind.

"Yes, a fine storm is brewing," she said, as they finally reached the sietch entrance and hurried inside. "A cleansing one." In the low light of a glowglobe, exhilaration flushed her features.

Catching her by the arm, Paul spun her around and wiped sand from around her eyes and mouth. Then he drew her close and kissed her. Chani seemed to melt into his arms, laughing. "So you have finally learned how to treat your wife!"

"My Sihaya," he said as he held her, "I have loved you for five thousand years."